Still Not Dead Enough

Book 2 of *The Dead Among Us*

When the dead refuse to rest in peace, perhaps they just need a helping hand.

by

J. L. Doty

TELEMACHUS PRESS

Cover designed by Telemachus Press, LLC

Cover art:
Copyright © iStockPhoto/000002520985/sweetandsour
Copyright © iStockPhoto/000012285942/maridav
Copyright © iStockPhoto/000022927708/juanmonino

Published by Telemachus Press, LLC
http://www.telemachuspress.com

Visit the author website:
http://www.jldoty.com

Follow the author on Twitter:
http://www.twitter.com/@JL_Doty

ISBN: 978–1–938701–33–7 (eBook)
ISBN: 978–1–953757–06–7 (paperback)
ISBN: 978–1–953757–17–3 (hardcover)

Version 2022.11.16

KEpuz!po!KJNEFTLUPQ:
Formatted using eTools for Writers 3.8.8, Nov 29 2022, 16:53:38
Copyright © 2013-2016 by J. L. Doty

Printed in the United States of America

10 9 8 7 6 5 4 3 2 1

Still Not Dead Enough

Book 2 of *The Dead Among Us*

Prologue:

Salt, Silver, Iron

"FOCUS," MCGOWAN GROWLED angrily. "Try to remember that feeling you got when your wife's spirit came to you."

Seated at the table in McGowan's kitchen, with the older man seated opposite him, Paul only made a half-hearted attempt to comply. The feeling he'd gotten when Suzanna had come to him—relief that she'd come back, and fear that he was bug-fuck nuts—the old man didn't understand.

"For me it's like an itch," McGowan said. "Kind of in the back of my thoughts."

They wanted him to learn some simple spells—in this case a fire spell—so he could develop control. If he could turn simple spells on and off at will, then he'd have a conscious understanding of what he'd been doing spontaneously, and, hopefully, he'd get rid of the spontaneous part. At least that was the theory, a theory that didn't seem too valid at the moment. After three such lessons Paul had failed miserably.

"For you it'll probably be different. It's different for everyone. You have to find your connection to power, and focus it."

Paul clung to a belief—or perhaps more a hope—that these wizards and witches were all a bunch of nut cases. Even after his experience with Cassius, the Secundus demon, he wanted desperately to find a rational explanation for all the irrational crap he'd gone through. He'd rather just walk away from it all, start rebuilding his life, a normal life where wizards and witches and demons and pointy-eared elves were nothing more than great fun in some book. But they wouldn't let him. If he didn't apprentice to someone, they were afraid he'd start doing crazy stuff again. And then they'd all want him dead, including the Mad Queen and her fairy friends. Certainly, McGowan was better than that asshole Russian.

"The spirit of your wife didn't just come to you," McGowan continued. "You brought it with an act of will."

He did remember how Suzanna and Cloe had come to him. His desire to see them again had combined with the pain of losing them, and that had coalesced into something real and solid deep inside him, a hot spark of need.

"Yes," McGowan said, "I can feel it. Your power is coalescing nicely. Now focus on the paper, feed the power into the paper. And don't think of it as heat. Remember, fire is an elemental. Think of it as pure fire, a primitive form of life that can consume almost anything."

McGowan had placed a cast-iron frying pan in the middle of the table with a crumpled piece of paper in it. Somehow, Paul was supposed to light that paper on fire with this magic stuff. *Play along,* Paul thought. *Play along and keep them happy.*

Paul focused that hot spark of need on the paper in the pan. He felt some sort of energy swirling about him, a quiet maelstrom that didn't manifest in a physical sense, and he fed some of that into the spark, though still nothing happened. But the spark responded almost as if it were alive, as if it was a conscious being rather than some form of elemental energy. And he sensed it hungering for more. He reluctantly gave it a little, and it responded like a small kitten purring happily.

"That's it," McGowan said. "You're headed in the right direction. I know this is difficult for a beginner, but you're not strong enough to cause any harm. So focus and give it everything you've got."

I want your all, the spark said to him, a silent whisper buried somewhere deep in his soul.

"Don't hold back," McGowan said. "Push yourself."

All right, Paul thought. He wanted to say, *Just shut up and give me a fucking chance.*

He took hold of the maelstrom forcibly, let it have a little more of whatever it was he was letting it have. But like a petulant child who'd been given a piece of candy, it demanded more. It pulled at him, and he sensed its hunger, a ravenous need that Paul feared might overpower him.

"You're holding back," McGowan shouted. "Give it all you've got."

Paul reluctantly fed the beast a little more of this thing they called *power*, and the elemental gobbled it up greedily, pleading with him, its need a palpable force. Then the scales of whatever balance he had tipped precariously in favor of the beast, and as the sense of falling from a great height washed through him, his control over the primitive life he'd called forth vanished.

A massive ball of fire roared to life in the middle of the table, and a blast of hot air forced Paul to stand up and step back, singing hairs on his face and arms. On the other side of the table McGowan shouted, "Holy shit!" He jumped up from his chair and backed away from the raging inferno licking at the ceiling of the kitchen.

The life Paul had sensed in the spark had come fully awake, though it was nascent, almost embryonic, and it wanted more from him. McGowan said something and waved his arms, somehow manipulated that maelstrom of energy and the spark receded. As the flames died, Paul had the oddest feeling that the life he'd sensed hadn't really left him, though sooty black smoke continued to rise from the ruin of the kitchen table as a reminder that something had come from somewhere and joined them in the kitchen, no matter how briefly.

Sarah, McGowan's personal assistant, appeared in the kitchen entrance, feet spread, fists knuckled on her hips, an angry scowl on her face. "I warned you this kind of training should be done in your workshop."

McGowan said something to her but Paul had stopped listening, had turned inward and focused on that spark of power within him. It was there, and he had nearly burned down McGowan's house with it. He, Paul Conklin, necromancer-at-large, had done some magic stuff, some very dangerous magic stuff. That, he couldn't deny.

····

"Salt," Katherine said, "silver and iron." Paul and she were seated across from each other at the new kitchen table in McGowan's home. Katherine lifted a mug of coffee to her lips, blew on it and took a sip. Paul sipped his own coffee as she continued. "Three substances that are unique when it comes to the Three Realms."

It had taken three weeks to repair the ruin of the kitchen. Paul had melted the cast-iron frying pan into a blob of slag, and it had burned a hole right through the table, would have burned its way through the floor to the rooms below had McGowan not quenched it with his own powers. The ceiling and cabinets had been scorched, the appliances scored and blackened, an amazing amount of damage for such a simple little spell. For anyone else it would have taken a couple of months to gut the kitchen and repair it properly. But money talked, and apparently, McGowan had plenty of that kind of talk.

In the middle of the kitchen table sat a simple arrangement of salt and pepper shakers, a small basket of paper napkins, and a vase of colorful flowers. Katherine reached out, took the saltshaker, twisted off its cap and poured a thumbnail-size pile on the table in front of her. Then she pinched a bit of salt between her thumb and forefinger, and rubbing the two fingers together in a circular motion, she sprinkled a fine dusting of white crystals in front of her on the table. She did it slowly, almost absentmindedly.

She'd been like that since that night Paul had destroyed the Secundus demon and they'd learned he was a necromancer, distant, absent. Whenever Paul was around it was as if she wasn't there, her thoughts focused elsewhere. Either that or she was in a hurry to be away from him.

"Salt is quite unique," she said, drawing a line with her finger through the dusting of powder on the table. To a cursory glance one might think she was looking at her finger tracing the line through the salt, but her eyes remained unfocused in a thousand-yard-stare. "It makes an excellent protective circle, though you can use almost any substance for that, and each has certain advantages. But lay down a ring of salt, push power into it and invoke the proper spells, and you can form an impenetrable circle, a circle no being can cross—mortal, demon or fey—a circle through which no magic can pass, through which no physical substance can pass."

One side benefit of apprenticing to McGowan was that Paul had more opportunity to run into Katherine, purely by chance, of course, as had happened today.

She looked up from the salt on the table and her eyes settled on Paul, though it took them a long second to focus. "Salt can also break a spell, or mute it badly. You saw that happen when we were doused with seawater at the Secundus's mansion. It's good to carry a little salt on you. If you're ever spelled, mix it with water and rub yourself down."

Paul had come to McGowan's place for one of his lessons. He'd run into Katherine, and as soon as she'd seen him she'd tried to leave, and he had to insist she sit down and talk to him, had to be almost rude about it. And then she'd managed to avoid really talking to him by turning it into an impromptu lesson.

"Now silver," she said, "is quite interesting. Soft and compliant here on the Mortal Plane, you'd never think to make a knife or sword out of it. But take that same piece of silver into Faerie, and it's harder than the hardest steel. Sidhe warriors carry thin rapiers made of pure silver, and they can easily cut a man in two with such a blade—at least in Faerie. Their silver swords are absolutely useless here on The Mortal Plane."

She picked up her mug of coffee, held it just below the edge of the table and brushed the salt into it. Then she stood and crossed the room to the sink. Now that her bruises had healed, she'd returned to wearing expensive looking business suits, the skirt cut just above the knees, high-heels clacking on the kitchen floor. The suit would fit in any corporate boardroom, but it was cut to emphasize her figure, and somehow, on her, a business suit was something quite sexy. She dumped the salted remains of her coffee into the kitchen sink, rinsed the cup out with a little tap water and left it there. She said she looked good in high-heels, and she did, but Paul wasn't looking at her shoes.

A voice whispered in Paul's ear, "You're staring at my daughter's ass."

Paul jumped and turned to find that McGowan had snuck up on him, was standing over him frowning unhappily. All he could think to say was, "Uh!"

Katherine said, "Was he now?"

Paul spun back to her. She was still standing with her back turned toward him, but had twisted about to look down at her own butt. "A girl likes to know her best . . . assets . . . are appreciated." Her eyes lifted to look at Paul, and it was the Katherine he knew, no blushing, no shyness. She batted her eyelashes at him. "I'm flattered, Conklin."

McGowan snarled at her, "Don't act slutty."

She turned toward him and marched across the room, saying, "Don't act like such a father. I'm a grown woman so I get to be as slutty as I want."

McGowan rolled his eyes as she turned to Paul. "We can finish talking about salt, silver and iron—and my ass—later. I've gotta go."

She turned and headed toward the front door. Paul got up to follow her, but McGowan stepped in his way. "You can't leave. We've got a lesson."

Paul said, "I'll be right back," then stepped around McGowan and into the hall just in time to see the front door closing. By the time he got out to the street Katherine was thirty feet up the sidewalk.

"Katherine, wait," he called.

She hesitated, turned and waited for him, and as he approached her he realized the other, more reserved and distant, Katherine had returned. "Why are you avoiding me?" he asked.

She eyed him warily, suspiciously, thought about that for a moment, then said, "You're a necromancer. None of us really understands what that means, and I think that's probably a very dangerous thing to be. And I've thought about that a lot, and I really don't need a dangerous man in my life. Been there, done that."

She turned away from him, but he caught her arm. "What does that mean?"

She shook her head. "I don't want to talk about it." She turned and marched away, marched like a soldier going to battle, making it clear she didn't want Paul to follow her.

••••

With the Summer Queen standing beside him High Chancellor Cadilus watched Katherine's image in the scrying bowl as she marched up the street. When Paul turned and returned to the Old Wizard's house, she said, "I am pleased. You have . . . unusually adept talent on the Mortal Plane."

Cadilus nodded respectfully. "I've spent centuries developing the conduits needed to function there. I've set the spells myself, and I'm using some of our mages to maintain them."

She smiled, and he knew by the absence of flames in her eyes that she was pleased. "I see you're driving a nice wedge between the two young people."

Again, Cadilus nodded. "As you requested, Your Majesty, though I must move cautiously and subtly to be certain the Old Wizard doesn't detect my interference. Interestingly enough, his fatherly protectiveness of the young lady is actually helping."

She turned away from him, saying, "What spells are you using?"

A set of tall French doors appeared in the wall in front of her, and she stepped through them. Cadilus followed her out onto a balcony overlooking the countryside of Faerie. "Just a simple spell to make her doubt him, and to question her own feelings. Those short-lived mortals don't truly understand the nature of a necromancer, so it's not difficult to introduce doubt into the equation, leavened by a bit of suspicion and paranoia. The effect of my spells wanes when she's protected within the wards of the Old Wizard's home, or if, for any other reason we can't reach her. But when she emerges and one of my assistants regains access to her, the spells are quickly reinforced."

She turned toward him and smiled, her emerald green eyes bathing Cadilus in the glory of the Summer Queen. "You have done well. Separated and untrusting, those two young mortals are weaker. We'll need that weakness when the time comes. Have the Realms calmed?"

"On the surface, yes, Your Majesty."

Her eyes narrowed unhappily. "That doesn't sound . . . comforting."

Cadilus shook his head. "The young man is a necromancer, which explains some of his unusual abilities. The mortals all now accept that he's not a demon, though I wonder if a necromancer can really exist without some demon blood in his veins."

"Surely, you don't believe that. Demons cannot mate with mortals."

He shrugged. "Who knows what the last necromancer was capable of?"

The shadows of undeveloped, primordial Sidhe spirits coalesced about the Summer Queen's flame-red hair.

Cadilus spoke carefully. "The Netherworld is quiet, Your Majesty, with no overt unrest. But when I look closely there is a certain watchfulness there; I suspect some high-caste nether beings are quite interested in this necromancer, and I find their anticipation discomforting."

The flames had returned to her eyes, and the spirits fluttering about her had become unsettled. "And let's not forget the Morrigan," she said.

Cadilus nodded. "Yes. The triple goddess is . . . aroused, though quiescent. But the mere fact that she is focused on the matter, that she finds it of such keen interest . . . I know not what to make of that."

"Perhaps you should have a word with the *black*."

Cadilus grimaced, and Magreth frowned sympathetically. "Yes, my dear Cadilus, an unpleasant task, and difficult, and so a task I can only trust to you."

Cadilus sighed. "I'll have to think carefully how to approach them. And who among them to approach. And what inducement I can offer such unstable creatures."

"I'm sure you'll come up with something," she said. "The *black* are, after all, most effective when focused on the right target."

••••

Anogh waited impatiently in the old fortress. He sensed that Taal'mara was near, and the prospect of seeing her again sent his heart racing. He stood on a high balcony looking out upon the territories of the non-aligned fey, ruled by neither Court, beholden to none, the home of the wild fey: leprechauns, brownies, sprites, pixies, banshees—and most dangerous of all—the *black fey*.

"My darling," Taal'mara whispered behind him as her arms encircled his waist.

He turned slowly to face her, still held within her arms, wrapped his own arms about her and reveled in her beauty. Her almond shaped eyes had dark, vertically slit pupils framed by amber irises, offset by the pale white skin of true Sidhe royalty. Her dark hair cascaded past her shoulders in a wealth of ringlets and curls. And she'd chosen a diaphanous gown that thrilled and excited him with delightful hints of the pleasures that awaited them both. Their lips met, a long, delicate kiss. It had been months since their last assignation, and Anogh just wanted to hold her for a moment, to glory in the scent of her, the nearness of her.

When their lips parted she whispered, "I've missed you so."

"And I you," he said.

"If only we could be wed, then we'd no longer need to meet in secret, to steal hidden moments, concealed trysts, veiled glances at some event we must both attend."

Anogh sighed wearily. "We've talked of this a thousand times. Ag would never allow the Summer Knight to wed the Winter Princess. If he knew his daughter had given her heart to me . . . it could mean war."

She laid her head on his shoulder. "Yes. We must content ourselves with our little stolen moments." She stepped out of his arms, took his hand, turned and led him into the bedroom . . .

. . . Anogh stared at the portrait of Taal'mara. It was the only pleasure not denied him in more than six hundred years. She had stolen his heart then, long ago, and Ag had stolen her from him.

"And so my brother knight weeps for his lost love. How touching!"

Anogh turned slowly toward the sound of Simuth's voice. The Winter Knight strode toward him across the Hall of Memories, a broad grin splitting his face. As always, his rapier hung at his side, and also, as always, he wore a cloak of arrogance and cruelty. "Does her image make your heart beat fondly, even after all these centuries, my brother?"

"You know nothing of my heart," Anogh said coldly. "Nor of any heart, for that matter . . ." He spit sarcasm in Simuth's face, ". . . my brother knight."

Simuth's grin disappeared. "Do not mock me, oh tenderly devoted knight, he who still foolishly loves a princess dead now for more than six centuries. Bring forth my ire, and you'll regret it dearly."

It was Anogh's turn to grin. He called forth his own rapier to hang at his side, took a menacing step toward the Winter Knight with his hand resting casually on its hilt. "My oaths bind me only so much, my brother knight. They will not prevent me from spoiling your lovely smile, should you choose to be the aggressor."

Simuth stepped back, successfully hiding his fear, though Anogh saw it plainly. "You have only begun to pay the price of your folly with Taal'mara," Simuth snarled. "Six hundred years is nothing, Anogh. I have all eternity to watch you squirm."

Anogh smiled coldly. "Perhaps you do, Simuth. Then again, perhaps not."

••••

When Paul returned to McGowan's kitchen, Colleen was waiting for him, seated at the table with a steaming cup of tea in front of her. As he sat down opposite her she swept her hair back from her face, but it refused to obey and fluttered forward, almost as if it were elemental with a mind of its own. It draped about her shoulders, bright red locks intertwined with small silver charms. If he looked away from her, looked slightly to one side so she was only visible in the periphery of his vision, he got the distinct impression her hair drifted on a light wind. But when he looked directly her way there was no such breeze, and her curly red locks lay static and immobile, though even looking directly at them he still had the impression of motion.

"Walter sends his apologies," she said. "He's been called elsewhere, so I'll work with you today." She lifted the cup of tea to her lips and blew softly at the steam. "He said Katherine was teaching you about salt, silver and iron. Tell me what you learned."

Paul repeated the points Katherine had made about salt and silver. "I don't think she was finished with silver, and she really didn't talk about iron."

Colleen fingered one of the silver trinkets in her hair. "For we mortals, silver has two primary uses. It's an excellent focus to contain spells, or to hold power for later use, though that's a bit advanced for you at this stage. More importantly, silver will burn the flesh of a nether being, and spelled silver can annihilate a netherlife that's crossed to the Mortal Plane."

"That's why my bullets had an effect on that Tertius in Katherine's home, right? But why the iron? Why does Devoe mix iron in the bullets too? He said something about the fey."

Colleen spoke thoughtfully. "I don't know Mr. Devoe at all well, but apparently he can be a very dangerous man. And Walter swears by him. And you say he mixes iron in his ammunition?"

"He told me so himself. Iron and silver."

"That means he wants to be prepared to kill fey as well as demons. Iron doesn't exist in Faerie in any form, and cold iron burns the flesh of the fey the way silver burns that of a demon. The royal Sidhe are immortal. They don't age and die, but that doesn't mean they can't be killed, though we only have rumors as to how. It must involve iron in some way, but just shooting one with an iron bullet, or stabbing one with an iron or steel knife; that alone won't do it, though it will give them considerable pain and grief until the bullet or knife is removed. It's rumored beheading is involved, but again that alone won't do it. And again that's only unconfirmed rumor."

"They can survive being beheaded?"

Colleen looked into her tea thoughtfully, and Paul wondered if she would now teach him how to read tea leaves. "The royal Sidhe are reputed to be able to heal any wound, given time and power. But then I've never killed one, or beheaded one, nor has any mortal I know of, so it's all speculation."

She changed the subject abruptly. "I don't sense your arcane abilities as I did a few weeks ago. You've been practicing, eh?"

Paul had become quite adept at the fire spell. He could turn it on and off at will, could control its intensity and the size of the blaze, could even hold fire cupped in the palm of his hand without the need for something like paper to burn, and could do it without burning himself.

"Ya," he said. "You want me to demonstrate?"

Colleen glanced at the ceiling, the table and the floor, and her eyes widened. "No fire spells."

Paul shook his head. "I'm never going to live that down, am I?"

She grinned. "Not for some time yet, young man. Let's go out on the patio. Things are less flammable there."

••••

She was such a lovely child, blonde hair, blue eyes. The first time he'd seen her she'd worn a gray pinafore over a pale-blue dress, with white knee-high stockings and shiny black shoes—very *Alice in Wonderland*. He loved *Alice in Wonderland*, not the story but the girl. He wished Alice was real so he could love her, truly love her.

"Alice," he said to her, as she sat shivering in the passenger seat next to him. He reached out and ran a finger along her jawline.

"My name's not Alice," she said, her voice barely more than a squeak. "Y'all got the wrong girl. Let me go. Please, let me go."

It had been trivial to spell her, though the spell itself was not trivial. He had to control her, make her walk willingly into his car, make her cooperate; do as he said without screaming or crying out, or making any kind of scene that might attract attention. He'd woven the spell into a simple piece of paper, then chose a day when she was waiting at the bus stop at her school. He'd walked past her, pretending to be absorbed in a magazine article, and let the piece of paper slip out and flutter to the ground behind him. She had made it easy, because she was a polite and obedient young girl.

"Sir," she'd called out. "Sir, you dropped this."

He'd turned, pretending surprise as she waved the piece of paper and ran up to him. She held it out to him, he reached out and accepted it, and in that instant, with them both touching it, he triggered the spell in the paper.

"Thank you," he'd said, then turned and walked away. At that point all he had to do was wait a week, so that no one would connect such a chance encounter with later events.

The spell was complex because, while it forced her to cooperate, her perception of the situation must not be masked. She mustn't be absolved of the fear. The fear was too important, the terror too much a part of his need. He wished he could spare her that, but his soul would never allow that.

He caressed her cheek again and she shivered, tears streaming down her face.

She pleaded, "I ain't who you think I am."

She had a deep, south Texas accent, and the *am's* came out more like *ayum*, a good syllable and a half. *I ain't who you think I ayum.*

Someday she'd be a pretty little cheerleader in high school.

No, the voice said. It crawled across his soul like sandpaper on old wood. *She's not going to high school.*

He turned down a street not far from her home, pulled off to the side of the road and killed the engine. It was early evening, dark, just after dinner, a residential street. This wouldn't take long.

"No," she said. "No . . . no . . . no."

"Alice," he said, though now his words carried the timbre of the *voice* within him, a harsh growl. "This is how it must be."

He reached out, his actions no longer his to control, gently caressed the girl he loved and released the *voice* within his soul.

She screamed, she cried and she struggled. She fought, but he was careful not to harm her in any way, not in any physical way, not in any visible way. There mustn't be any outward signs of trauma or harm.

As she struggled he leaned across the seat of the car, cupped the back of her head in one hand and tilted her head back. She opened her mouth to scream, but in the same instant he opened his mouth and covered hers with his. Then he exhaled, and as he leaned away from her a black shadowy stain extended from his mouth to hers, flowing from him to her, entering her soul. For just an instant she looked at him with blood-red, goat-slitted eyes. Then a spasm shook her, and she thrashed about, shaking and coughing and gagging. She struggled for what seemed an eternity, but really only the blink of an eye for mortal men. And then she died, and her death washed over him, filled him with sorrow. It would have been wonderful if he could have loved Alice a little longer, just for a time, the two of them.

He dropped the body off near her home. There'd be less suspicion that way.

1

No Safe Harbor

KATHERINE MCGOWAN MET her father in the reception room outside her office. "Hi, father," she said, and gave him a big hug. He just grinned, followed her back into her office, sat down on the couch against one wall.

She asked, "So what's so urgent it can't wait until we have dinner this weekend?"

Walter McGowan took a deep breath and she knew she wouldn't like what he had to say. "I need your help with Paul. I need you to take a more active role in his training. And next week Salisteen wants me to bring him down to Dallas. She suspects some sort of netherlife crossed over some time ago and is feeding in the Dallas area, and she'd like to see if Paul's special abilities might prove advantageous."

The old man had clearly omitted something. Katherine said, "Paul's not ready for a hunt. It was pure luck that the fiasco with the Secundus didn't end in a terrible tragedy."

Her father was a horrible liar, and at that moment he looked exceedingly uncomfortable. "I don't think it was luck," he said. "I've read up on necromancers—had to brush up on my Latin. I've got a grimoire written by a ninth century Saxon monk. I trust his written word more than most because his spells and incantations actually work. And he believed chance conforms subtly to the needs of a necromancer, and the people he needs to help him do whatever he's supposed to do, are drawn to him."

He shut up and let her chew on that for a moment. She didn't like the idea she might be drawn into some arcane, mysterious sequence of events, regardless of her own desires. But if practitioners were drawn to Paul, that meant . . . "Wait! You mean you and Colleen and me?"

McGowan nodded slowly, thoughtfully. "Colleen and I have discussed this, and yes, that's probably what's happened. And, oddly enough, that probably means he needs those asshole Russians in some way."

She couldn't hold back her anger, stood and leaned forward on her desk. "No! Absolutely not! Before he came along I was just a simple, little witch. I'd never met a demon, never been to the Netherworld, never met leprechauns and Sidhe, never been kidnapped to Faerie—never even been to Faerie for that matter, never had a bunch of crazy Russians shooting at me . . ." She ran out of steam, sat down in her chair and closed her eyes.

"You know how strong he is?" the old man asked calmly. "When I was trying to locate him he repeatedly snapped my locator spell with nothing more than a shrug."

Now that was intriguing. There weren't more than a couple practitioners in the world who could snap one of Walter McGowan's spells, let alone do so with so little effort.

The old man continued. "I thought you liked him."

She opened her eyes. "I do. I did. But . . . there's something wrong about him. It just doesn't feel right. You know, he told me himself he thought he was nuts, and he's probably right."

"I thought shrinks didn't use words like nuts."

"Okay," she said. "Then let's use the proper technical terms. He's probably all fucked up. You know, bongo, wacko. I don't need to be around someone like that."

"But he's not. He's quite sane. He thought he was bug-fuck nuts—those are his words, by the way. I would never use such derogatory terms—"

She groaned, "Ah jeeze! Get to the point. Please."

The old man hesitated, and for the first time in her life he seemed uncertain. She suddenly felt a chill, and fear gripped her. "My dear," he said calmly, carefully, pointedly, "the point is, he is sane. And the point is . . . I don't understand much of the magic he's using."

"Oh my God," she whispered, and closed her eyes again.

••••

Anogh had been summoned, and when he entered Ag's private audience chamber he was surprised to find the unpleasant Russians there as well. Ag and Karpov were seated in large, comfortable chairs near the back of the room, speaking in hushed tones, while Karpov's two thugs gawked about like bumpkins, and Simuth looked upon them with obvious distaste.

Anogh approached Ag but stopped at a polite distance and waited. Ag and Karpov conversed for several more minutes; then Ag looked up and took notice of the Summer Knight. Ag stood and Karpov stood with him. As they walked toward the center of the room, Anogh, Simuth and the two thugs joined them there.

"Sir Knights," Karpov said, acknowledging Anogh and Simuth. "It appears we have a common cause."

"Yes," Ag said, looking pointedly at Anogh. "This necromancer is a problem for us all. And I find it disquieting he's bound himself to the Old Wizard. It would be better if he were bound to the Winter Court, or, to our good friend Vasily here. And you'll help him, won't you, my Summer Knight?"

Anogh bowed slightly. "If that is Your Majesty's desire, then, of course."

Karpov looked at his two thugs and said, "And His Majesty tells me he believes a necromancer must have some demon blood in his veins."

The big bearish fellow grumbled, "I knew he was a fucking demon."

Karpov's hand lashed out and struck the fellow across the cheek, a slap that resounded loudly in the small room. The strike had been fast, inhumanly so, like that of a pit viper. "You will not use such crude language in the presence of His Majesty. Apologize."

"I am sorry, Your Majesty," the big bear grumbled in his thick accent, lowering his eyes. "Please forgive me."

Ag waved a hand impatiently and spoke to Karpov. "These young fools all have so much to learn." He looked Anogh's way. "But I think you'll find Sir Anogh to be quite resourceful on the Mortal Plane."

••••

Leftover pizza, the breakfast of champions. Paul finished the last cold, congealed slice, gulped down the last of a cup of coffee, stuffed both Sigs and his holsters into a cloth shopping bag, pulled on his coat and shot out the door.

He couldn't find it in his heart to return to his old place. He and Suzanna had lived there since before they were married, and Cloe had spent her entire life there. And after the "home invasion" by the Russians, it had been easy to break the lease. Paul had found a new apartment, a nice apartment as apartments went, just a little lonely. He missed Suzanna and Cloe, but he'd sworn a silent oath he wouldn't fall into that trap again. They were gone, and he'd accepted that, whether he liked it or not.

The new place was South of Market, an area of San Francisco devoid of the quaint charm of nineteenth-century, wood-frame houses with three or four stories of bay windows. A few years ago Paul read an article predicting South of Market was destined to become a new, upscale, yuppie enclave. Paul hoped no one took stock market tips from the guy who wrote the article. Some people wanted to call South of Market *SoMa*, hoping to give it a fashionable flair like SoHo in New York. But tall, modern office buildings dominated the north side of the district, while the south was filled with cheap hotels, a few rundown buildings, and some apartment buildings four or five stories high, boxy structures with little charm. In any case, Paul had signed a lease on a three-and-a-half room bachelor flat: living room, bedroom, small bathroom, half a kitchen.

When he arrived at McGowan's the old man met him at the door and hustled him into a car with the cryptic explanation of, "We're going to see Clark, introduce you properly."

As McGowan pulled out onto Van Ness, he shifted into his lecture voice and said, "On the way let's talk about the Three Realms: the Mortal Plane, the Netherworld, and Faerie. They're also sometimes referred to as the three lives. First—"

"Wait," Paul said. "First let's talk about why you're doing this for me."

McGowan frowned as Paul continued. "I'm nothing to you. Nobody. But it must be costing you a great deal of money to take care of me, and certainly a great deal of effort. And most importantly, I am, apparently, a dangerous unknown. And now you're willing to put that aside. Why?"

McGowan frowned in thought for a moment. "A lot of reasons, kid. First, if you had continued the way you were going, someone, probably me, would have had to kill you to prevent you from harming others. Think about Cassius. Two, three, four hundred years ago some sorcerer let that Secundus loose on the Mortal Plane. And a demon like that needs to consume two or three lives a month. Do the math. It doesn't matter if that ancient sorcerer let him loose through evil intent, or merely sloppiness or inexperience. If there was the possibility you might do the same, we'd stop you, even if that meant killing you. But while I will admit I can be ruthless, I'd rather not commit murder until I know I can't fix you properly."

"So if I don't cooperate, you, or someone else, will kill me?"

McGowan shrugged. "I honestly don't know. You're not what we thought—a simple rogue—so I'd probably hold off. But I can't vouch for those Russians.

"Another reason I'm working with you is that you're an unknown, to us all. There hasn't been a necromancer around for twelve hundred years, not that we know of. So I need to understand why you're here, now, at this time and place."

"There has to be a reason?"

"Ya, I think so." McGowan looked away from the road, looked at Paul carefully for a moment, studying him, evaluating him. His eyes returned to the road and he said, "Our history books are written by historians who don't believe in magic or sorcery, so they make events fit into their mundane framework. But I've spent years translating and studying ancient grimoires—basically cookbooks for magic and sorcery with little bits of history thrown in—written by men and women hundreds of years ago with a vastly different perspective. And believe me it's a bitch trying to understand them. They're vague, and superstitious, so a lot of interpretation is needed. But an alternate interpretation that emerges is that a couple thousand years ago a Primus caste demon, one of the nine princes of hell, crossed over to the Mortal Plane. That led to the fall of the Roman Empire and the beginning of the dark ages. And it wasn't until about eight or nine hundred years later that a necromancer came along to banish the Primus back to the Netherworld."

"Jesus!" Paul said, his thoughts racing. Maybe he could just run away and hide. Play along with McGowan for a day or two, yank all his savings out of the bank, take only cash, move to some south Pacific island, grow a beard, become a beach-bum and just hide.

"Paul!" McGowan said. "Calm down. It's just all speculation, and conjecture. I told you it's all subject to wide ranging interpretation. And you should see some of the crap those superstitious idiots wrote ten, twelve hundred years ago. Remember, these are the same morons who came up with the test for a witch: drown her, and if she lives she's a witch so kill her, but if she dies she's innocent, so pray for her when you bury her."

Paul forced himself into an artificial calm. "Well, at least now that everyone knows I'm a necromancer they're not out to kill me anymore."

McGowan sucked air through his teeth. "About that . . ."

"Ah shit! Please tell me I'm not a target again."

"Welllllll!" McGowan grimaced unhappily. "It's not that simple. You see, the Sidhe don't have souls, so they're kind of . . . not really considered among the living, so . . . you may have some extra special powers over them, and they don't like that."

Paul turned on him and demanded, "What kind of powers?"

McGowan's grimace remained. "We don't know. Maybe none. But the Sidhe Courts, as a rule, don't take any chances in such matters, so don't assume anything."

"Well, at least the fucking Russians aren't trying to kill me anymore."

McGowan added a frown to his grimace. "About that too. It's really hard to bring a Primus caste over, even for me, but maybe not for a necromancer. So your very exist-ence might make it possible."

Paul managed to get his voice down to a growl. "So everyone thinks I'm going to cause the destruction of civilization?"

McGowan glanced at him apologetically. "I just wouldn't assume there is anyone who isn't out to kill you. Well . . . you can count on me and Colleen and Katherine and Clark. We're on your side. That's why we're going to see Clark."

"Clark?"

"Ya. Clark Devoe."

"Who?"

"Gun shop owner. You met him when you came to his store. And then again the night you took out that Secundus. That was a nice piece of work, I might add. Earned you a few brownie points among my colleagues. That's why some of them won't . . . well . . . *might* not try to kill you."

McGowan pulled the car into a parking spot in front of *South-Bay Guns and Ammo*. Paul remembered the place from his one and only visit. It was still rather seedy, a sim-ple, unassuming storefront with a neon sign. And it needed a coat of paint.

McGowan pulled a briefcase out of the back seat, nodded toward Paul's shopping bag containing his Sigs and said, "Grab your stuff, kid."

Paul followed him into the shop. It had only been a few months since he'd first wandered into the place and it hadn't changed, a long row of glass display cases running down the right side with handguns displayed under glass, racks of rifles on the wall behind the cases. Along the left wall were racks of ammunition, clothing, holsters, cleaning kits, all sorts of paraphernalia.

The plump female with frizzy, unkempt hair sat behind the counter toward the back. She wore another moo-moo, or maybe the same one, and was eating something out of a plastic refrigerator tub. "How ya doin', Mr. McGowan," she said around a mouth full of food. "Clark's expecting you. Go on back."

Clark Devoe was waiting for them in the back room. He looked to be in his mid-sixties with shoulder length gray-blonde hair pulled back into a ponytail, and three or four days of stubbly beard growth. Paul thought he might be wearing the same old army fatigue jacket and NRA cap he'd had on the first time Paul met him.

"Mr. McGowan," Devoe said, shaking McGowan's hand.

He turned to Paul, shook Paul's hand in a hard grip and said, "Nice job you did on the vamp." He looked down at Paul's shopping bag. "Let's see what you bought."

Paul upended the bag on a nearby workbench. Both Sigs were in their hinged, blue, plastic, factory cases. Devoe opened one, lifted the weapon, ratcheted the slide back, then quickly field stripped it, removing the slide and the barrel. He sighted carefully down the barrel. "This is good hardware, little expensive, but a good choice. And it looks like you're cleaning it and oiling it properly."

Devoe went through the same process with the other Sig. Paul apparently passed muster on that one as well. The man questioned him a bit on his background as a child hunting with his father, was happy to hear he'd gone through a couple thousand rounds at a gun range to get the feel of the two weapons. Devoe wasn't so pleased with the holster. "This is okay, but it could jam you up a little, slow you down in a pinch. Leave it with me for a few days and I'll make some mods."

McGowan opened his briefcase, handed Paul a small card and an envelope full of paperwork. "That's a CCW permit—to carry a concealed weapon—for the state of California. You don't know it but you applied for it and received it several months ago."

Devoe nodded toward the card. "Those're hard as hell to get in this state. Mr. McGowan has connections."

Devoe gave Paul a pump-action sawed-off twelve-gauge and a couple hundred rounds of his "special double-ought."

Paul looked at McGowan and Devoe and said, "Where's the Uzi, and maybe a fifty-caliber machine gun? I could mount it on the floor of my living room to cover the front door."

Devoe frowned and looked at McGowan. "Kid ain't gonna live long if he don't start taking this seriously."

••••

He watched her walk to the bus stop, the beautiful little Mexican girl. Watched her carefully and couldn't take his eyes off her.

Her parents had dressed her in a blue pinafore over a pale red dress, and matching blue knee-high stockings ending in shiny black shoes—very *Alice in Wonderland*. He loved *Alice in Wonderland*, not the story but the girl.

The little Mexican girl's parents must be very proud of her, must love her very much. She had incredible raven-black hair that hung past her shoulders, flawless olive skin and almond shaped eyes. He thought she might even be more beautiful than the little blonde, and that brought a pang of guilt. It felt like cheating to desire the little Mexican girl more than the little blonde, a horrible act of infidelity.

No, the voice said, a faint hiss somewhere deep within his soul. *She is the one.*

Yes. He'd loved the little blonde so much, but now she was gone and he so desperately needed someone to hold, someone to share his affection. But this one would be different. This time he would just watch from afar, admire her, love her even, but never touch her. He didn't want to hurt her. She was too beautiful to be hurt. He just wanted to hold her closely, tell her how much he loved her, how much he needed her.

Own her. We must have her, all of her, nothing held back.

"No," he pleaded, closing his eyes, grimacing as he tried to shut the voice out of his soul. "Not this time. Please not this time."

Yes, always. Look at her.

He opened his eyes. The young girl had stopped to talk to a boy her own age, Mexican like her, though his features were a little darker than hers.

Imagine touching her, caressing her carefully, running your fingers along such delicate, flawless skin.

"Yes," he said. "Yes . . . yes."

Once she knows how much you love her, how deeply you care for her, she'll love you back, love you with all her heart.

He could see that she must have a loving heart, a kind heart. "Yes . . . yes, she will."

2

The Black

KATHERINE WATCHED FROM the sidelines as Paul tried a small fire spell. He and Colleen were seated opposite one another at a table they'd dragged into her father's workshop, while Katherine and her father, standing to one side, looked on. She'd come here with considerable trepidation, but now, after about an hour with the four of them working together in her father's workshop, she couldn't understand why she'd been so fearful of working with Paul, fearful of just being in the same room with him. It didn't make sense.

Paul held both hands out, cupped together as if trying to hold water or beg for alms. He concentrated and a faint glow appeared just above his hands. It wavered for a moment then steadied and became a small, hot spark illuminating the room like an uncovered light bulb.

Her father was right. She didn't recognize the arcane power Paul used. If it was earth magic, or he was tapping a ley line, she'd sense his manipulation of such forces. But she got nothing. She looked at her father and he nodded, as if to say, *See what I mean.*

Colleen spoke softly to Paul and he extinguished the bright spark. Then she said, "Close your eyes and focus on me, try to sense what I'm doing."

Colleen extended one palm and, with a thought, she tapped a nearby ley line and fire appeared just above her hand. But unlike Paul's hot, bright spark, this was a flickering, dancing flame a few inches tall. Katherine easily sensed her use of the arcane forces.

Colleen asked, "Were you able to sense what I did?"

Paul kept his eyes closed as he said, "I felt . . . feel something."

Colleen nodded. "Good. I'm going to hold this flame, and I want you to extend your hand again, and try to repeat what I did."

Paul extended a hand and his brow wrinkled with concentration. The hot spark appeared, but he said, "No," and it just as quickly disappeared. And again Katherine had felt nothing. Then a small flame fluttered to life in his palm, and Katherine felt him pulling normal power, pulling on the same ley line. It was interesting that he could pull on a ley line so instinctively. Katherine had expected him to naturally gravitate to earth magic, and from the expression on her father's face, so had he.

The flame suddenly flared and grew to about a foot in height, then it shrank back and steadied, though it flickered wildly. Normal magic, with a beginner's lack of control, but still normal.

"Release the spell," Colleen said, as her flame disappeared.

Paul did so, and his too disappeared.

Katherine had a sudden inspiration. There were some techniques she'd used with troubled children that might help here. She walked up to the table and said to Colleen, "I have an idea. Let me try something."

Colleen stood and walked over to McGowan. Katherine didn't take her place, but paced back and forth in front of the table as she said to Paul, "I want you to show me something. Not repeat something we've taught you. Just something on your own."

He looked at her skeptically. "Show you what?"

"I don't know. There must be something you can do that no one else can do. Maybe something unique, something you're really good at. Think about it."

He lifted an eyebrow and said, "I'm assuming you don't mean belching the national anthem at a beer drinking frat party."

She stopped pacing. "Can you actually do that?"

"No, but I knew a guy who could."

"Come on," she said. "There must be something you can do that's unique, and doesn't involve disgusting bodily functions."

He pondered that for a moment, then a little sparkle appeared in his eyes.

She prompted him, "There is something, isn't there?"

"Well, ya," he said reluctantly. "But it's just a party trick. I used to do it in college." He grinned. "It was great for meeting girls."

She looked over to her father and said, "See, he's slutty too."

She turned back to Paul. "What is it?"

He was clearly embarrassed at having to make the admission. "I can throw knives. Well, anything that's metal and sharp: nails, whatever. I can stick it every time, and I can hit a half-inch target from across the room."

"Did you practice this a lot?"

"No. I can just do it."

"So you could do it now?"

He shrugged, still clearly embarrassed. "I suppose, though I haven't tried since I was in college."

She stopped pacing and faced him squarely. "Let's give it a try."

She turned to her father. "Any knives down here?"

He shook his head. "Not that aren't heavily spelled."

She looked around the workshop. There were three old wooden cabinets against one wall, all about six feet high, scratched and scarred old things. She pointed at one, looked at her father. "Mind if we use that as a target?"

McGowan shrugged. "Sure, go ahead."

Katherine turned to Colleen. "Would you go up to the kitchen and grab a random selection of knives?"

Katherine walked over to her father's workbench, scrounged in a drawer and found a black ink marker, walked over to the cabinet and quickly painted several small circles on the face of it, each about the size of a thumbnail. By the time she'd finished, Colleen had returned and dumped an assortment of knives on the table in front of Paul. He stood and examined them carefully.

Pointing at the cabinet, Katherine said, "Okay, Conklin, let's see what you got." Then she stepped several feet to the side, well out of the way.

"Thanks for the show of confidence," he said, as he picked up a small paring knife and flipped it in the air a few times, catching it each time by the handle. "Okay. Now in the movies, the knife thrower always holds the knife by the blade when he throws it." He flipped the knife a few more times, was clearly warming up to the show. "But that's not necessary when you're as good as I am." He flipped the knife a few more times as he spoke. "You know, I met Suzanna doing this." He stopped abruptly, and with a flick of the wrist tossed the knife across the room, stuck the point in one of the targets she'd drawn.

She walked over to the target, noted that the knife was perfectly centered in the small bull's-eye. She'd felt a flow of power as he'd thrown the knife, just the tiniest bit, probably just enough to nudge the direction of the knife. But he wasn't drawing on a ley line, or earth power, and she didn't think he'd used his own life force.

She turned back to him. "Not bad, Conklin. Let's see it again."

"Okay, sweetheart," he said in a bad Bogart imitation, now juggling three knives easily. A flick of the wrist, another flick, another flick, and all three knives were stuck perfectly in three targets.

She shouted, "Wooooooo!" and slapped her hands together, applauding loudly. "I'm impressed, Conklin." She pulled the knives out of the cabinet. It wasn't difficult since they'd hardly penetrated the wood. She laid the knives back on the table in front of him. "Can you throw them harder?"

"I don't know. I suppose. Why?"

She wanted to get him to use more power than just the hint she'd sensed. "Oh, I don't know. I'd think if you're throwing a knife as a weapon, like they do in the movies, you'd have to throw it a lot harder than that. Otherwise, you'd just give someone a nasty cut. And in the movies they always drop the bad guy with one throw."

Paul picked up one of the larger knives. "I'll give it a try." He flipped the knife in the air a couple of times, then drew back his arm and threw it hard. It thudded into the cabinet with considerable force, again centered in the target. But his throw had disappointed her. He'd still only used a hint of power to direct the knife, while the extra force had come from his arm.

"Come on, Conklin. You can do better than that. Harder."

He picked up another knife, followed the formula of flipping it a few times, then threw it so hard he grunted with the effort. Again the knife landed home, but again all its force had come from his arm.

"Come on, Conklin. Harder."

He picked up another, followed his usual formula and threw it with all his strength. But again no real use of power, though she saw his frustration growing as she taunted him. And that was exactly what she wanted.

She pulled a bit of power, formed a small spell to increase his frustration, fed the power into it and tossed it at him as she shouted, "That's not it. I want to see you throw it really hard, much harder than that. Harder, damn it."

He picked up another knife, flipped it in the air several times, concentrating on it. He had become clearly, visibly frustrated. But this time, with each flip she kept shouting "Harder," and she sensed him drawing power from somewhere and concentrating it in the knife, most likely doing it unconsciously, instinctively. And each time he drew power she felt a chill wash over her. Then he suddenly drew back his arm and threw the knife with a tremendous release of power.

Katherine heard a loud crash and her knees went weak. She dropped into a chair gasping for air, had trouble catching her breath as if she'd just run a mile, wrapped her arms around herself and shivered uncontrollably. Amazingly enough, her breath formed a cloud of steam in the chill air.

"Jesus!" she heard Paul say. The knife was buried to the hilt in the face of the cabinet. He put one hand against the cabinet, tried to pull the knife out with the other, grunted a couple of times and finally gave up.

Katherine's shivering grew uncontrollably violent as Colleen sat down next to her and her father approached Paul. Colleen wore a sweater which she quickly pulled off and wrapped around Katherine. "You're bordering on hypothermia."

Katherine noticed that everyone's breath was visible in the air. Her father looked at Paul but spoke for the benefit of them all. "He pulled the energy out of the air, pulled it out of Brownian motion—heat energy—dropped the temperature around the two of you by about thirty degrees."

Colleen put a hand on Katherine's forehead and said, "He also pulled it out of her, dropped her core temperature by a couple of degrees."

Katherine's father nodded. "That adds up. The body is mostly water, which has a considerable heat capacity. Air temperature would drop much more than body temperature."

Katherine felt warmth flowing into her from Colleen's touch. The shivering slowly subsided, but she was still weak in the knees. Colleen helped her to her feet and they started across the workshop.

Paul looked badly shaken, stunned, and his gaze kept switching between the knife and Katherine. Colleen hesitated at the workshop door, looked at him angrily and said, "You could have killed her. You really need to control that."

••••

Paul looked at the knife buried in the cabinet. The cabinet was made of heavy oak. The knife, with a blade about six inches long and a handle made of some sort of hard, black material, had plunged a good inch past the end of the blade, splitting and cracking the handle. It was impossible, utterly fantastic, and yet he remembered how he'd done it, that feeling of control over the environment around him. There had been a vast well of . . . something. He couldn't put a name to it. Maybe it was energy, as the old man had said. But for Paul it had just been there, something he could tap into without consciously thinking about it. He had pulled on it effortlessly, drawn it to him, into him. And as Katherine had shouted at him, he'd drawn more and more of it, filling him with a sense of strength and confidence.

The two women had left, leaving him alone with the old man, who was still staring intently at the knife handle protruding from the cabinet. "Physical magic," McGowan said. "There's no other word for it, and nobody does that." He looked at Paul. "At least not until you came along."

Paul asked, "I almost killed her, huh?"

"No, not really. You scared the shit out of Colleen and she overreacted a bit. You'd have to pull a lot more heat out of Katherine than that to kill her."

McGowan continued to stare at the knife handle. "You told me that when Alexei tried to shove your hand in that food processor and you pulled energy out of him, you didn't feel anything. Right?"

"Ya."

"No sensation of increased strength or power flowing into you or anything like that?"

"Ya, that's what I said." Paul had told McGowan he'd gained almost superhuman strength when he'd pulled power out of the demon, but he'd gotten nothing from the Russian. And they'd agreed it would be wise to keep that information to themselves.

"I'm guessing what you just did here was similar to what you did to Alexei. Doesn't sound like you pulled heat out of him, but maybe it was some sort of physical energy."

McGowan looked away from the knife, looked at Paul and shook his head. "I just don't know."

••••

Katherine felt a lot better, still a little weak in the knees, but only slightly. Colleen insisted on walking her to her car.

As Katherine fumbled for her keys the sensation of being watched came back to her. But before she could react, Colleen hissed, almost growled, and marched over to a car parked about twenty feet away. She put both hands on her hips and spoke to a shadow in the lee of the car. "Show yourself, little man."

The shadow shimmered for a second, then Jim'Jiminie appeared, a little man about knee-high. He wore green leggings, a brown doublet, purple shirt, with a floppy red hat perched jauntily on his head. He leaned casually against the car's tire. "Now sure, sweet darlin'," he said. "I'm just a simple fellow standin' on the street, mindin' me own business."

Colleen's accent grew quite thick. "And I'm a pink unicorn, you little madman. Do you really want to be playing your games with me, little man?"

The little man shrugged. "I can smell him all over her." He nodded toward Katherine. "And if such as me can sense it, do you really believe the Sidhe of the royal blood will be fooled?"

"Why are you telling me this?"

Again he shrugged. "Not all fey are enamored of the Summer and Winter Courts, mortal. It would not be in our best interest to see him bound to either Seelie or Unseelie. For try to bind him they will, even if they have to use her to do so. And with that, I bid you adieu, fair lady." He doffed his hat, bowed from the waist, and disappeared in a sparkle of fairy dust.

••••

Cadilus rarely suffered from apprehension or doubt. Given any situation he could invariably determine the correct course of action. And yet now, standing on a pristine, gravel-strewn path in the Garden of Sorrows, the ramparts of the seat of the Seelie Court rising high above him, he felt like the lowliest of peasants.

"You have chosen an ally?" Magreth asked.

"Yes, Your Majesty . . . an . . . ally."

"You hesitate. How unlike you. Do you doubt him?"

"She, Your Majesty. The ally is of the fairer sex."

Magreth turned to face him. "Do you mock me?"

Cadilus lowered his eyes. "No, Your Majesty. Never. I have asked Sabreatha to join us."

Magreth hissed, a sharp intake of breath. The shadows of the ancient Sidhe spirits appeared, dancing about her head and shoulders. "An ally of dubious distinction. And you believe that's wise?"

"There is no wise course of action, Your Majesty, not with a necromancer active on the Mortal Plane. But I do believe I have taken an expedient course of action. Though, I must admit, a dangerous one."

She stood still and lifeless for an eternity, staring at him, judging him. Her eyes didn't blink, her breast didn't rise and fall with the breath of the living. And then slowly she nodded once, an almost imperceptible tilt of her head. "Very well. Summon her forth."

Cadilus did so with a thought. Nothing happened for a moment, or two, or three. Then a shadow flitted above the ramparts high above, and an angry shriek echoed across the garden, something akin to the sharp cry of a hunting hawk. The shadow flittered in and out of existence at different places among the embrasures and merlons of the parapets, like a wary predator sniffing carefully at prey, fearful that a larger and more dangerous predator might be lying in wait. Another shriek echoed through the garden, the shadow disappeared, then, an instant later, reappeared among the shadows of a large oak in the far corner of the garden.

The figure hesitated in the shadows there for several seconds, clearly surveying her surroundings. Then she stepped carefully out into the light of Faerie, and even Cadilus, one of the most powerful mages of the Seelie Court, and here on his home ground, even he had difficulty penetrating the magic of this most-wild of *black fey*. He had the impression of a tall humanoid shape walking toward them, but obscured by untamed shadows that fluttered like a flame struggling in a harsh breeze.

The tall shape stopped before Magreth at a warily safe distance and faced her squarely. The flames appeared in Magreth's eyes and danced there angrily as she stared at the wild magic before her. After several seconds she said, "You come before me, an invited guest, granted my parole and protection while here . . . and you show not the least modicum of common courtesy?"

Sabreatha, with her shadows that never stilled, remained motionless for several seconds. Then again the shriek of some wild predator echoed through the garden, and slowly she lowered herself to one knee. She bowed her head, and the shadows fluttering about her dissipated. It was a slow process, as if it took a strong effort of will to banish the darkness that enveloped her. One by one her features became more defined and distinct, though the shadows didn't disappear completely, for there was always a hint of them fluttering about her. But now, before Magreth, knelt a woman dressed in tight gray leathers, a long-sword strapped to her side, an unstrung longbow in her left hand. She had pale, golden hair, twisted into dreadlocks that, with her head bowed, hung past her face and obscured it.

"That's better," Magreth said. "You may rise."

In the blink of an eye Sabreatha had risen and stood proudly, stood over them both for she was easily a hand-span taller than Cadilus, and he was not a small man. Her eyes shifted color continuously, blue, brown, hazel, amber, black, every color imaginable, and her dreadlocks fluttered slightly as if touched by a light breeze, though Cadilus noted the air was still. She opened her mouth, hesitated as if she found it difficult to speak an ordinary tongue. And when her lips moved, her voice was no more than a haunted whisper on the wind. "You asked, and I have come."

It was an overt reminder that she was here at their request, and too, that it was up to them to state the purpose of this meeting.

Cadilus said, "We have a commission for you."

The whisper of her words brushed across his senses. "And what kind of commission would that be?"

Magreth said haughtily, "For what kind of commission do you think we would summon one such as you."

Sabreatha's lips parted in something akin to a smile, but not a smile. She was quite beautiful in a strangely haunted way. "One such as me. An interesting turn of phrase."

Magreth clearly did not like the tone of this meeting. "You are what you are, and we may desire your services."

"I am what I am . . . and I am all that I am not."

"You know what we need. This necromancer, he is dangerous if not controlled properly."

Sabreatha stared at them for a long moment before speaking. "And what would you have me do?"

Magreth swept a hand out dismissively. "I leave that up to you."

Again, a long pause filled with silence. "Perhaps *les flèche du coeur.*"

Cadilus flinched, and Magreth said, "An extreme solution. But, nevertheless, a solution."

Sabreatha nodded her ascent. "I will deliver *les flèche du coeur.* And payment?"

"What do you desire?"

Now Sabreatha did smile. "Parole to walk the domains of the Seelie Court."

Magreth shook her head. "Never."

Cadilus intervened. "Perhaps, Your Majesty, if we placed the proper restrictions on such parole . . . you might find it acceptable."

Magreth considered that for a moment. "Yes," she said. "Yes, we may be able to come to an accommodation here."

••••

He pulled his car into the parking lot of the strip mall across the street from the bus stop. He had crafted a spell to hide the car from any watchful eye, a difficult spell he'd reinforced over a period of several months. It turned the eye subtly, made the watcher want to look elsewhere, and drew their interest away from the vehicle and its driver. But it was always wise to be cautious, so he found a parking place near other cars, but with empty slots next to it. It wouldn't do to park way at the edge of the lot where all the stalls were empty. A lone car would stand out, and someone might take notice, if they could resist the pull of the spell.

He killed the engine, rolled down a window, opened a newspaper and pretended to read, as if waiting for someone. He'd carefully chosen the position of the car so he could look past the edge of the paper at the bus stop.

It was late afternoon and the little Mexican girl's bus should be along shortly. He actually read a bit of the newspaper while he waited. But when the school bus appeared up the street it had his full attention.

The bus stopped at the corner, flared out a stop sign on its side and traffic going both ways came to a halt. A half-dozen kids scampered off the bus, some met by their parents, some not. No one met the little Mexican girl, but as she walked up the sidewalk the little Mexican boy accompanied her, the same boy she'd spoken with the other day. Today she wore a colorful dress that flared out at the waist and ended at knee height, and her hair was in ponytails. Lovely!

She looked at the boy coyly and giggled. It was too far to be certain, but he probably blushed a little as he smiled at her. As they walked she swung a knapsack back and forth carelessly, and danced around him a bit while he marched slowly forward. She never took her eyes off him, clearly wanted his approval, wanted his attention.

She's paying too much attention to this boy, the voice said. *Way too much attention.*

"Yes, she is. He can't have her. She's ours."

We may have to do something about him.

"Yes, we may have to."

3

An Old Story

PAUL HAD NEVER been inside Katherine's practice. He'd briefly stalked her outside her offices, trying to make contact after his first misadventures with the Russians and the big hoodoo demon in the Netherworld.

Katherine had furnished her reception area with comfortable chairs and a couch, side tables with stacks of magazines neatly arranged, like almost any doctor's office anywhere. Behind a large desk sat a middle-aged woman, attractive, well dressed, light brown hair cut just above her shoulders.

Paul said, "I'm Paul Conklin."

She smiled. "Nice to meet you, Mr. Conklin. Dr. McGowan's expecting you, so go on in."

Old man McGowan had arranged for Katherine to give Paul his first lesson in protective circles, said she was quite good at it. Paul opened the door to Katherine's office and stepped in. Seated behind her desk she looked up at him and frowned slightly, not a terribly welcome expression. "Give me a moment, Conklin."

She scribbled a signature on something, flipped the page aside, scribbled something on another page, put down her pen and looked at him. "Thanks for being patient, the rest can wait. I'm to teach you about circles, huh?"

Paul shrugged. "Teach away. I'm a willing pupil."

Today she wore a gray business suit, coat and slacks, with a pale blue blouse, one of those blouses ever so slightly translucent so that one could just barely make out the silhouette of the black bra and something else lacy beneath it. She did an awfully good job of making something sexy out of the most conservative business attire.

She stood, came around from behind the desk, headed for a door in the side of her office. "Let's go to my workshop."

He followed her, tried not to admire the way the slacks gave a nice view of her shape. She led him into a room with a hardwood floor, a small, wooden workbench against one wall with a couple of stools, and next to it a locked storage cabinet. Against another wall were a comfortable couch and a couple of chairs, with the center of the room clear and open. Katherine approached the storage cabinet, pulled some keys out of her pocket, fumbled at the lock for a moment, then opened the doors wide. In it, Paul saw shelves filled with bottles, jars, packages, all sorts of things that meant nothing to him. She pulled out a blue, cylindrical canister.

"Salt?" Paul asked.

"Yes," she said, kicking off her high-heels. She walked to the center of the room, opened the tap on the canister of salt, poured a line of it in a circle about three feet in diameter. "As I told you it makes for a great circle. Now, step over the line of salt and into the circle."

He did as told. She sat down on the floor just outside the circle, crossed her legs, closed her eyes, and he saw them squint as she concentrated. He also felt the unmistakable sensation of someone drawing power, a perception he'd only recently come to understand. She sat that way for about a minute, then suddenly opened her eyes and blurted out, "Motherfucker."

"Motherfucker?" Paul asked her.

She blushed. "Long story," she said. But when he raised a sardonic eyebrow she added, "But I can see you're not going to let me get away without telling it."

He didn't say anything, just grinned and nodded.

"Okay," she said. "You see, it's easiest to initiate certain kinds of spells if you associate a specific and unique word with the moment of setting the spell. It can be any word you choose, but after you've done it enough times, a trigger word makes it easier to focus your power."

"Motherfucker?" he asked her again.

Again she blushed. "I was at a rebellious stage, early teens, purposefully doing things to piss-off my father. I thought it was cool to smoke cigarettes and swear a lot, turned a bit Goth, all of which met with lots of disapproval from him, which was exactly what I wanted. Teenage girls can be such nasty little bitches."

"Really pushed his buttons, huh?"

"Every chance I could. Even had my navel pierced, but it got infected, for which I'm actually grateful because it was quite painful, and that made me leery of piercings and tattoos. Thank god I never got any I couldn't easily hide, but I've still got that small scar on my navel. Anyway, that was about the time he taught me circles. My first attempt was a miserable failure, and the power I drew slammed into my hand like a hammer. I ran around the room shaking my hand shouting, 'Motherfucker, motherfucker, motherfucker.' I've tried to associate other words with setting a circle, and they sort of work, but for me that one word works better than anything else."

Paul nodded, grinned, raised that eyebrow again and said knowingly, "Motherfucker."

She blushed again and said, "Stop that."

"Stop what?" he teased.

"If you don't stop that I'll leave you in that circle all day." She grinned evilly. "Don't bump your nose, smart ass, but just try to step out of that circle."

Paul reached forward carefully and his hand pressed against an invisible wall above the line of salt. He put both hands against it, tried to push through it, put some serious weight behind it and failed utterly. There was no visual sense that anything occupied the space there, no shimmer in the air, no bending of the light passing through it, as there would be with a pane of glass.

"Bend down and try to break the circle of salt."

He tried, couldn't touch it.

"You can set a circle around yourself to protect yourself, keeping everything else out. Or, you can set a circle from without to lock something evil and disgusting in, like I've done here."

Paul sat down on the floor in the circle facing her. "I'm evil and disgusting?"

She smiled. "Maybe not evil and disgusting, but definitely low moral standards."

He laughed. "My moral standards aren't low." He carefully looked into her eyes. "I'm just attracted to beautiful women." Again she blushed.

"What about the shape of the circle?" he asked. "Does it have to be perfect?"

She shook her head. "No, though the farther you deviate from a perfect circle, the weaker it becomes. But you have to deviate quite a bit before you seriously weaken it. One variation, and this only works for demons, is to put the circle inside a pentagram, with the circle touching all interior sides of the pentagram. You'll create a much stronger circle, but again, only for demons.

"The interesting thing about circles is that even someone relatively weak can hold a circle against someone quite powerful like my father. That's because a circle is a natural shape. Nature wants to see a circle maintained, so once it's in place it's virtually impossible to break from the other side."

She reached forward, passed a finger through the salt. "I just broke the circle."

Paul asked, "How powerful is your father?" Paul had learned there were three kinds of practitioners. There were hedge witches and minor practitioners who knew instinctively when they were in the presence of another practitioner, but nothing more. Then those like Paul and Katherine who could spot another practitioner, but could also read their level of capability in comparison to their own. McGowan and Colleen fell into the third category. They were so powerful they could hide their level of capability from everyone else, though they couldn't hide the fact that they were practitioners from another practitioner.

She shrugged. "I don't really know, though all my life I've noticed many practitioners look upon him with a kind of reverent awe. So I think he's pretty serious stuff."

She sighed. "Back to circle school. Keep in mind that if I hadn't kept feeding that circle power it would weaken, and with some effort you would have eventually been able to reach the salt and break it. An alternative is to push a lot of power into a circle after initially setting it, then leave and forget it. It's like putting gas in a car, the more you put in the tank, the farther it'll go, or in the case of a circle, the longer it'll last after you've left it. But it'll eventually weaken, and can then be broken."

Abruptly she stood, offered him a hand. "Here, you make a circle around me." She helped him to his feet.

She got a broom and a dustpan, swept up the circle she'd made. "Why can't we just use that circle. Seems a waste of salt."

"That's another thing," she said. "It can be salt, chalk, precious metal, silver, a bunch of stones, almost anything will do. A precious metal is best, depending upon what you're trying to contain, salt is second best, and you can reuse the salt, but *you* must construct the circle if you're going to set it." She finished sweeping up the salt, then sat down where the circle had been.

He took the canister of salt, poured a reasonably accurate circle around her and sat down on the floor facing her.

"Now I want you to think of the circle as an impregnable wall, all the while concentrating on the salt as the foundation of the wall."

He focused, recalled the invisible wall she had created around him.

"Now start drawing power," she said. "It doesn't take much, and don't feed it into the salt. That'll just blow the salt around. Instead, start feeding it into the imaginary wall. The salt is only the foundation. There'll come a moment when the wall is complete, and you'll know it on an instinctive level, then pick a word, and seal the circle."

As she spoke he saw the wall forming, not in any visible sense, but with his newly formed arcane senses. And when the moment came, as she'd told him, he knew it in his bones. He said, "Okay," and the salt scattered as if blown about by a breeze.

She helped him sweep up the salt and he laid down another circle, and again she sat within it. "This time use a trigger word, something stronger than *okay*."

He again fed power into the imaginary wall, and when it was ready he tried, "Abracadabra." Again, the salt scattered. He tried again, set the circle with, "Fiddle-de-de," and nothing worked. Each time he set the circle, and each time the salt scattered.

They set the salt one more time, and again she sat within it. He concentrated and fed power into the barrier, tried to put his frustration aside and keep his attention centered on the exercise.

She said, "You need to focus better."

She said it just as he was ready to set the circle, just as he shouted, "Bullshit!"

"What do you mean?" she asked angrily. "I'm not bullshitting you. Everything I said is true. I—"

"No, no, no," he said. "I didn't mean bullshit on you. Bullshit's my word. If you get to have *motherfucker*, I get to have *bullshit*."

She laughed, shook her head. "You're incorrigible." They both looked at the salt circle and it hadn't scattered. She reached out carefully, and he saw the palm of her hand flatten as it pressed against the inside of the circle he'd set. "Very good! I guess the lesson is complete. Go ahead and break the circle. I have to get back to work."

He leaned back, grinned evilly and said, "I tell you what. You show me one of those tattoos, and I'll break the circle."

Her eyes narrowed angrily. "I said I didn't get any tattoos."

"That's not what you said. You said you didn't get any that you, and I quote, 'couldn't easily hide.' "

He leaned a little to the side and leered at her ass. "Any tattoos that you can hide?" She blushed and he knew he was right. "Show me one and I'll let you out."

She jumped to her feet, put her hands on her hips. "You listen to me, Conklin. This is extortion. I won't stand for it." She pushed irrationally at the circle, muttering a few well-chosen curses at him.

Still sitting on the floor with her standing over him, he realized he wasn't getting the reaction he'd hoped for, so he reached out and broke the circle. But at that moment she was pushing on it, and with her weight against it she toppled forward. Sitting there he looked up, realized what he'd done, leapt back to try to catch her, and she landed right on top of him. He let out a loud, "oomph," as she knocked the wind out of him.

Laying on top of him as he gasped for air she laughed. "Well, well, funny man. You got exactly what you deserved. That's poetic justice if I've ever—"

He shut her up by putting his hand gently behind her head, pressing his lips against hers and kissing her deeply. He didn't have to force her, would never have done so. She groaned, closed her eyes, responding with an almost desperate need, their tongues dancing hungrily back and forth. It was a long, eager kiss during which her entire body responded and melted against him comfortably, warmly, passionately. But then she tensed, her eyes widened, she put a hand on his chest and pushed away from him. She scrambled off him, climbed quickly to her feet and backed across the room. "I'm not going to cross that line."

She turned and almost ran from the room.

Paul picked himself up off the floor. "God damn it," he said softly and headed for the door, hoping to catch her and apologize.

••••

Anogh traced the line of Taal'mara's hip as she lay naked beside him, sleeping peacefully, lying on her side with her back to him. They were taking a chance meeting on the eve of the festivities of the equinox. But his hunger for the taste of her skin grew with each clandestine rendezvous, with each kiss, each session of their lovemaking. She was, after all, Unseelie, and the courtiers of the Winter Court were legend for their sexual proclivities, even more so than the Seelie Court, which had a reputation of its own. He was deeply ensnared in their love, though no more ensnared than she. They both knew they were taking too many chances, and had repeatedly sworn they would be more careful, see each other less frequently. But she had confessed that, like he, each moment they were apart was an eternity, and each day they shared together seemed but a blink in time.

She sighed deeply, stretched sensuously and rolled over. "My love," she whispered, then wrapped her arms around him and kissed him. And as his passion blossomed, he wondered again how they had come to be so foolish, wondered at how it might end, though deep inside a piece of him knew there was little chance it would end well . . .

"Sir Anogh," Ag called, bringing him out of his reverie. "You must join us . . . here in the present. Don't you find the past a bit dated?" The room full of Unseelie courtiers twittered at Ag's humor.

Anogh nodded his head respectfully. "Forgive me, Your Majesty."

Ag had that look of cruel anticipation that always precluded unpleasantness. "She was a lovely creature. I should have bedded her myself a few times." A father, speaking so casually of bedding his own daughter, did not raise eyebrows here as it would in the Seelie Court.

Anogh knew he was a fool to succumb to temptation as he said, "Certainly you would have enjoyed it far more than she."

The beating that ensued was vicious, cruel and brutal.

••••

Standing at the right hand of Ag's throne, Simuth watched Sabreatha stride across the floor of Ag's formal audience chamber. She was a fearful sight, a tall specter of untamed shadows and wild magic with a broadsword strapped to her back and an unstrung longbow in her left hand. She stopped at the base of the steps beneath the throne, stood straight and tall with her shadowed head canted at a slight angle, as if regarding Ag with disdain, a clearly intentional violation of protocol.

Simuth bent close to Ag's ear and whispered, "We don't need this *black fey*. Let me kill him myself. I'll—"

Ag raised his right hand, silencing Simuth, though his gaze remained on Sabreatha. He and she stared at each other for several seconds, then Ag finally broke the silence. "Thank you for coming, child of dark magics."

Sabreatha's head merely nodded once. When she spoke her voice crawled through Simuth's heart like the hiss of water spattering on a hot brand. "You summoned, I came. State your business."

Ag shrugged, tried to be nonchalant as he said, "The Unseelie Court may have common cause with the *black fey*."

"I doubt it," Sabreatha hissed. "State your business."

"There is the matter of this necromancer—"

"State your business."

"He is a danger to us all, and something must be done about him—"

"State your business."

Ag flinched, agitated that she showed so little deference. "This necromancer is . . . how shall I say—"

"State your business."

Ag snarled, "I'm trying to, but you—"

"State your business."

Ag stood and screamed, "I want him dead. I don't care how it's done. I want him dead."

The ever-changing shadows dancing about Sabreatha's face slowly dissipated, and she looked upon the king with her multi-colored eyes. She turned her gaze upon Simuth, and he realized she really didn't look upon him, but rather through him, an unnerving glance filled with contempt. He shuddered, and was relieved when she looked back at Ag and said, "Perhaps *les flèche du coeur.*"

"Yes," Ag said, stepping forward to the edge of the dais greedily. "Yes, deliver the arrow of the heart and I'll grant you anything." He hesitated, thought better of such a bargain. "Well, almost anything. What would you have?"

The shadows returned to obscure her face and eyes. "Free access to the domains of the Unseelie Court."

"Yes," Ag agreed. "We have a bargain."

Sabreatha reached above her head, gripped the hilt of the broadsword protruding there and drew the blade. A steel blade, it reminded him that Sabreatha could touch cold iron, the only fey that could do so.

She swung the blade down, and it rang out as it tore a chip of stone from the first step of the dais in a shower of sparks. "My signature," she said, "for a bargain signed and sealed."

She slid the sword into its sheath and, without waiting for leave, turned and strode from the hall.

When Ag and Simuth were once again alone, the king sat down and breathed a long sigh of relief. Simuth couldn't take his eyes from the chipped first step of the dais, Sabreatha's *signature*. He said, "Anogh will be furious when he hears of this."

Ag growled, "Don't be a fool. The Summer Knight must not know of this."

••••

As Paul stepped onto the street outside of Katherine's office, a strange otherworldly screech sent a shiver down his spine. It was not unlike the high-pitched cry of a hunting hawk. He paused on the sidewalk, looked up toward the sky and caught a hint of movement out of the corner of his eye. Something flittered high above, just at the roof-line of the buildings around him. Perhaps a hawk of some kind, but so obscured in shadow, try as he might he couldn't focus on it, couldn't discern its true nature.

Twice more, on his walk back to his apartment, he heard the strange shriek and looked up, but never saw anything that might utter such a cry. It must have been a hawk or a falcon that had drifted into the city and become confused by the cacophony of sights and sounds. Easily explained, though he couldn't as easily put the encounter out of his mind, and it continued to bother him late into the night. He slept poorly, and when his alarm rang the next morning he climbed out of bed feeling rather groggy.

He packed his bags, walked to the BART station and caught some sleep on the train down to the airport. McGowan, Coleen and Katherine were waiting for him.

••••

As the airplane banked, far below the cluster of skyscrapers that was Dallas came into view. Colleen had spent the entire flight drilling Paul in various exercises that would help him control what other practitioners sensed in him. "No spells on the plane," she said. "We'll just work on control. It wouldn't do to light the plane on fire."

Colleen, McGowan and Katherine were all obviously a bit uneasy about him meeting this Salisteen. It had become clear that Colleen, McGowan, Karpov, Salisteen and a few others were in a league all their own when it came to throwing around this magic stuff, and there was more to this than just making a good impression on Salisteen. But Paul didn't know how much more, and though Katherine had joined them on this trip, she'd remained distant. Paul could no longer count on her to fill him in on what he didn't know.

"That's much better," Colleen said. "If I didn't know to look, I wouldn't know you were a practitioner."

Paul had worked hard to camouflage his abilities. Colleen had told him that only a few months ago he'd stood out like ". . . a petulant child throwing a temper tantrum at a sedate gathering of older people." It had helped considerably that he'd learned to *see* the maelstrom that hovered about other practitioners.

"By the way," Colleen said, "you're less subject to an arcane attack when you shield yourself that way. That maelstrom, as you call it, is linked to your aura, and when you suppress its perceptibility to others, you prevent them from manipulating you or attacking you through it."

Paul had spent weeks trying to accomplish this level of control.

"Tell me about Suzanna," Colleen said without warning.

"Suzanna!" Paul said, a bit startled by the sudden change of subject. "What brought that on?"

"If you can talk about her, and still maintain your shields, then I'll know you're getting the hang of it." She hesitated for a moment, as if trying to decide if she'd tell him more. "And I'm curious. I suspect there was a reason you two were attracted to one another, so I'd like to know more."

Paul recalled the evening he'd met Suzanna. "There's not much to tell. We met in college, in our senior year. Met at a party thrown by a mutual friend. Hit it off right away, started dating, fell in love. Couldn't afford to get married right away, so we worked for a couple of years before tying the knot. Couldn't afford to have children right away, so we worked for a couple more years before having Cloe. Nothing really unusual or special about us. Quite ordinary, in fact."

"And the friend who introduced you?"

"He didn't really introduce us. He just threw a party and we both showed up, happened to run into each other. Pure chance."

She raised an eyebrow skeptically. "There may not be a lot of chance where you're concerned. How did Suzanna die?"

Paul really didn't want to look into that dark hole in his soul. "She just disappeared one day, gone without reason or a word. I spent a week just crazy-nuts trying to find her. Then the cops identified her body in a car accident, totaled it, head-on with a big truck. I'm pretty certain they figured it was suicide, though around me they only dropped a few hints about that. More in the questions they asked. You know: was she depressed? That kind of stuff."

"And you didn't believe it was suicide?"

"No," he said, and he couldn't hide the anger in his voice. "I checked into it, studied up on it. She didn't show any of the symptoms. Not a one."

"And Cloe, what about her?"

That hole was even deeper and darker, and he had trouble getting the words out. "Couple months later, hit-and-run, right outside her school."

Colleen reached out and put a comforting hand on Paul's shoulder. "What about Suzanna's parents?"

"She was an orphan, didn't really have any. She'd spent a lot of years in foster homes, but never more than a few years in any one place, not long enough so anyone really thought of her as their daughter. She grew up surprisingly normal, for all that."

They both sat there in silence. The pilot announced their final approach into DFW. The attendants picked up the trash, the plane maneuvered around a bit, then settled into the long, straight path to the runway. The plane jerked and the wheels screeched, and the plane coasted to a stop at the end of the runway. The engine pitch rose again and the pilot taxied toward their gate.

"Paul," Colleen said. "There's something I've suspected about Suzanna for some time now. And I think you just confirmed my suspicions."

Paul felt anger swelling up within him as he looked sharply at Colleen and said, "I don't want to hear anything bad about her. She's gone, so leave it at that."

Colleen shook her head. "No, Paul. It's not bad. I just think she was a Sidhe foundling."

"What's a foundling?"

Colleen hesitated. "Your apartment had the scent of long-term Unseelie habitation. Not the kind of scent you'd detect with your nose, but rather an arcane residue. It's considerably diminished, which would be consistent with the fact that Suzanna has been gone for more than a year, but it's unmistakable."

Paul's patience had shredded. He tried not to sound angry as he again demanded, "What's a foundling?"

"I'm guessing a Sidhe woman of the Unseelie Court took a mortal lover, bore a child, was pressured in some way to give up the child or wanted to hide the birth, left her here as an orphan in the Mortal Plane. Possibly never had contact with her again."

"But Suzanna never had any Sidhe powers."

"All Sidhe have extraordinary powers in Faerie, but one must be a mage, a wizard or a witch, to have powers here in the Mortal Plane. If Suzanna was merely half-Sidhe, but not a mage, then however powerful she might or might not have been in Faerie, she would have been quite normal here."

Paul stared at the back of the seat in front of him as the plane pulled up to the gate, the chime sounded, the passengers stood and began gathering up their possessions. Colleen stood, then leaned down close to Paul's ear, "I know it's a lot to take in."

Paul stood, and as he did so Colleen smiled at him and said, "By the way, you held your shields nicely while talking about Suzanna and Cloe."

••••

It would be rather easy to learn where they lived, the little Mexican boy and the pretty Mexican girl. He'd just follow them home, but he'd do so carefully. He couldn't follow behind them in his car as they walked, barely moving along at two or three miles an hour. That would be pushing the limits of the spell that hid the car. And it would be far too dangerous to walk behind them; they were just ambling along and he'd have to walk too slowly. No, much too obvious. But he'd done this before, and it was easy.

He'd parked his car in a different spot in the strip mall, one that gave him a good view of the bus stop, and the street they'd take when they walked away from it. When the bus dropped them off he fired up the engine of his car and watched them carefully. Again the little boy walked slowly, and the girl skipped around him, seeking his attention. As they approached the corner he backed out of his parking place and drove slowly across the mall parking lot. He pulled out on the road just as they turned the corner and walked out of sight. He drove slowly down the street, and by the time he turned the same corner, they were just reaching the next corner, and by the time he passed them they had walked straight without turning. He continued on and didn't look back. Patience. It required patience to do this right.

The next day he approached them from the opposite direction, saw them continue to walk straight for another block. The next two days he stayed away, and the following day he confirmed the next turn in their walk home. Now it was time to stay away from the entire neighborhood for a while. He'd come back in a few days, a long enough absence to ensure that some observant parent didn't spot a pattern and take notice of his car.

He now knew the routine of their day, knew the school they attended, the route the bus took to bring them home and the bus stop. Eventually, he'd watch each of them walk right up to their front door as he drove past.

Soon, the voice said. *Soon.*

4

The Hunt

SALISTEEN SENT A chauffeured limo for them. The passenger compartment—*back seat* really didn't do it justice—had two seats facing each other, with plenty of leg-room for all. Paul and McGowan sat in a seat facing Colleen and Katherine. The limo also had a wet bar, TV, the works.

As the limo drove out of the airport Colleen and Katherine were quietly discussing something, so Paul asked McGowan, "I take it she's loaded."

"More than me, kid."

"Are all top practitioners loaded?"

"Pretty much."

"Why?"

"Better to have money than not."

Paul tried a different approach. "I guess I really mean how? Do you predict the future or something and invest in the stock market? Something like that?"

McGowan frowned and considered Paul's question carefully. "It's pretty hard to predict the future. Only some of us can do it, and then only to a limited extent. I can teach you a couple of incantations, the same ones good old Nostradamus used, but the results are always vague and subject to wide interpretation. That was his big problem, eventually drove him nuts trying to figure out what the results meant."

McGowan looked at Paul carefully. "But that's not what you're really asking. Is it?"

"No. I'm just wondering if you game the system in some way."

McGowan shrugged. "Most of us don't need to. We tend to live rather long lives, and because we are practitioners, opportunities do come our way. But if you wanted to game the system and make some money, you'd have to be careful what you did. You might spell some dice and win big at the casinos, and they'll let you win once or twice then cut you off. And a couple of them—though they don't realize it—employ practitioners as heads of security. Practitioners are good at spotting anyone trying to beat the system. And they consider it cheating, so you might end up with your legs broken."

McGowan looked at him pointedly and frowned. "You want to get rich?"

Paul shook his head adamantly. "No, not that, I'm just trying to understand the rules."

McGowan pursed his lips and thought carefully. "There aren't many. I suppose the big one is: don't bring mundane attention to your abilities, or those of others. There was a time when strong practitioners were respected, and often employed as royal advisors and counselors. But then we went through that nasty time when they burned witches at the stake, and that left us all a little shy about notoriety. You want to murder someone, you want to use your power to do it, that's between you and the law, as long as they don't find out about your abilities, though I personally don't like criminals and might just choose to see justice done. On the other hand, you start leaving a string of bizarre, unanswered killings behind you, and there'll be no *maybe's* about it. There are several of us who will definitely step in and stop you, permanently.

"Say you figure out an alchemical spell for turning lead or iron into gold. Go ahead, make yourself rich. But don't make so much gold that you start affecting world financial markets. That might prompt someone to start asking the kind of questions we don't want asked. We'll step in.

"And you already know about setting a demon loose in this life, either purposefully or by accident, we'll step in. We'll get rid of the demon, then sit down and have a talk about how we can be certain you won't do it again. And if the talk doesn't reassure us sufficiently, you probably won't survive it."

McGowan kept referring to *we*, as if there was some organization. "Who's *we*? Is there some group, or council or something?"

McGowan shook his head. "There's about a dozen of us worldwide that are in a league all our own. There's me, Karpov and Colleen. You're about to meet Salisteen. Then there's Charlie Stowicz in New York, three or four in Europe, three or four more in Asia, couple in South America, one in Australia. We're a pretty stubborn, contrary bunch that, by and large, don't usually get along well. But there are certain things that'll make us band together."

McGowan chuckled, laughing at some private joke. "That Russian wants us to get organized, write down rules, have an executive council. We'd have rank based on power; the more powerful you are, the higher your rank. All that kind of stuff."

Paul grimaced. "And I suppose Karpov wants to be the head of this executive council?"

"Exactly," McGowan said, shaking his head sadly. "Though the rank-power relationship thing already exists in a de facto fashion. It's only natural."

"Where would that put you?"

"I'd be up there, kid. I've been at the top of the feeding chain for a long time."

"And me?"

McGowan looked at Paul as if appraising him carefully. "Too soon to say, kid. Clearly you'll be well above the middle ranks. But how much above, only time, practice and experience will tell. And you are unique."

"The necromancer thing?"

"Ya, the necromancer thing?"

"Sounds like there's a bunch of factions. What faction are you part of?"

McGowan shrugged and grinned. "You might say I'm one of the leaders of the anarchist faction: no organization, no committees, and we already have enough rules."

Paul thought it through carefully. "So you help me out, you teach me, I'm the sorcerer's apprentice and all that, and I'll naturally feel indebted. So you'll probably gain a supporter, and who knows how much rank I'll be able to put behind that support."

McGowan threw his head back and laughed loudly. "Well, you ain't stupid, kid."

"What about the Sidhe? How do they play into this?"

"Good question. The Sidhe are enormously powerful in Faerie, but weaker here in the Mortal Plane. With a few exceptions, here they're more like mid-level practitioners. If they can control one or more of us, then that gives them strength here."

"And how would they control me?"

McGowan's focus drifted away for a moment, and he smiled as if at a fond memory. "The Sidhe of the royal blood can be quite beguiling, and that is probably the only capability they have that isn't weakened here on the Mortal Plane. When they want to be, the men and women both are the most beautiful beings you have ever seen. They can turn it on and off like a light switch. I've seen mortal men without the slightest homosexual tendency, become so obsessed with a Sidhe male they destroy themselves with the compulsion. But more than that, if you're not prepared, they can make you want them, desire to please them, willing to do anything to make them happy. You become a virtual slave without even knowing it, obsessively, compulsively needing their constant approval."

The limo pulled into a large U-shaped driveway in front of an enormous McMansion, easily twenty thousand square feet. Paul gawked like a country bumpkin when McGowan said, "This is Highland Park. Lot of money in this neighborhood."

••••

Anogh waited well down the street from the mansion of the powerful witch. Hidden within a simple glamour in the shadows of a large tree, he watched the limousine pause at a wrought-iron gate. After a brief delay the gate swung open and the large car pulled forward onto the grounds of the estate. The druid, the Old Wizard, his daughter and the necromancer emerged from the limo and disappeared into the mansion.

He also watched Cadilus's two young mages stalking the periphery of the mansion's grounds. Both had shape-shifted into small falcons and flitted back and forth on drafts of warm air, careful to remain beyond the mansion's wards. Shape-shifting was difficult magic for a Sidhe mage on the Mortal Plane, so both were clearly powerful and dangerous.

A sharp cry broke the quiet of the afternoon, and a large red-tailed hawk swooped down out of the sky. Much bigger than the falcons, its attack was unexpected, and it nearly impaled one on its talons, but the smaller bird dodged at the last moment and escaped without damage. The falcons counterattacked, harrying the larger bird and trying to benefit from their two-on-one advantage, but this particular hawk was not so easily defeated and knew how to use its girth and longer talons to good effect. Outmatched by the larger bird, the two falcons fled into the distance, both missing a few feathers. The hawk landed on the wall surrounding the compound of a neighbor.

A mortal might think the little drama quite ordinary, predators contesting their hunting territory. But the cry of the hawk had an arcane quality to it Anogh recognized.

How had the black fey *come into this?* he wondered. *But more importantly, why this particular being, this most dangerous of beings?*

••••

Salisteen met them just inside the front door of the McMansion in a foyer larger than Paul's apartment. It had two curved staircases winding left and right around a massive crystalline chandelier, both leading up to a second floor landing.

She was a tall, elegant black woman, African-American, looked like a retired model a bit past her prime, but still quite good looking. She wore a knee length dress, long legs ending in tall, spike heels, curly, brown hair cut in a very short afro. When McGowan introduced them Paul extended his hand. Salisteen beamed at him gorgeously and smiled, gripped his right hand in hers, but reached out with her left hand and took hold of his elbow, then pulled him toward her to within a distance that bordered on intimate. "Paul," she said sensuously, their faces only inches apart. "It's a pleasure to meet you." She had an accent that could only be described as Texas elegant, every vowel articulated carefully. The word *pleasure* came out like a promise, and Paul grew uncomfortably aware of some very attractive cleavage not far below his chin, though he was careful not to look down and stare at it.

She stepped back from him and released his hand, but she paused and looked him up and down carefully, as if examining her next meal. Her smile broadened, and in a slow drawl she said, "This should be very interesting."

Katherine said, "My dear, Paul is not an appetizer for dinner."

Salisteen turned and looked at her. "Of course not, darling." She glanced back at Paul. "I think he'd be an entire meal all by himself, including desert. And I am in the mood for desert."

She turned and walked toward the interior of the house, spoke as she walked, "Come with me. The servants will take care of your luggage. I have rooms prepared for you."

Paul noticed there was a preponderance of rather good-looking young men among Salisteen's servants, some of them runway-model caliber, all rather weak practitioners. They wore simple white coats that ended just below their waistline. There were also a few individuals dressed in business suits, male and female, all good looking but nothing like the runway-model servants. The *suits* were further distinguished from the *servants* in that each had a little curly, flesh-colored wire running from an ear into the collar of their coat, and also each was a much stronger practitioner. No one needed to tell Paul the *suits* were security.

Salisteen led them to a large office with floor-to-ceiling windows that looked out onto a patio and an enormous lawn. Waiting in the office was a fellow that looked like a dockworker, short, stocky, a little overweight, heavily muscled. He had the kind of dark, black hair that left a five-o'clock shadow ten minutes after shaving.

"Charlie!" McGowan said, obviously surprised to see the man there. "What are you doing here?"

"Walter," the man said. To all outward appearances they were two old friends, but there seemed an element of tension between them. "Salisteen asked me to come and help too." He spoke with a thick New York accent.

McGowan made introductions, and Paul learned the fellow was Charlie Stowicz. That meant they had four of the five most powerful wizards in North America present in the room. McGowan's uneasiness put Paul on edge. Whereas Salisteen wanted to eat Paul for desert, Stowicz looked at him like he wanted to hang him from the nearest tree. Colleen confirmed Paul's suspicions when she leaned close to his ear and whispered, "The only reason Charlie would be here is to see you. And I'm not sure if that's good."

••••

Dinner was a casual affair, a simple help-yourself buffet. Katherine would have enjoyed it more, but when that cougar Salisteen heard Paul had never tasted Texas barbecue, she personally introduced him to every dish on the table. The slut never lost physical contact with him: a hand on his elbow, her hip brushing against his. She was probably spelling him, and Katherine considered checking his aura.

What am I doing? she asked herself. *First I avoid him like the plague, then I turn into a seething bag of jealous hormones?* She had no claims on Paul, and if he wanted that over-sexed, middle-aged trollop, he could damn well have her.

They sat at picnic tables on one of the many patios. Katherine sat opposite Paul while Salisteen carefully chose a seat next to him, her hip brushing up against his. The conversation immediately turned to the demon kills. "It seems to have progressed to about one or two victims a month," Salisteen said. "And it's careful, never strikes in the same municipality twice, at least not without waiting several months between victims. Only strikes in larger communities that deal regularly with unusual deaths. The victims are all young girls about eight or nine years old. But other than that, no set pattern to victim type: white, black, Hispanic, blonde, brunette, rich, poor."

Paul asked, "But wouldn't someone connect the dots on a string of murders like that?"

Stowicz lifted his napkin to his face and wiped a bit of sauce from his chin. "No sign of trauma, right?" He looked to Salisteen for confirmation and she nodded.

He turned to Paul. "No sign of trauma, no drugs in the system, no needle marks, nothing that'll show up on an autopsy. Medical examiner just chalks it up to natural causes, sometimes of unknown origin, sometimes they take a guess."

Salisteen added, "And the greater Dallas/Fort Worth area has a population of well over six million. They deal with thousands of deaths from all causes every day." She stared at her food for a moment, used her fork to push it around the plate without tasting it. "This one's careful. But I don't think it's ventured outside the Dallas/Fort Worth area."

Colleen asked, "And what brought it to your attention?"

Salisteen frowned and continued to stare at her food as if recalling a bad memory. "A friend of mine, Mike Ramirez, Sergeant in the Rangers, good cop, smart cop."

She looked pointedly at Paul. "As you say, he connected the dots."

She took a pull on a bottle of beer. "He's also a practitioner of middling talent, checked out one of the bodies and spotted the demon stink, knows when to ask for my help. In these kinds of cases Mike'll bring me on board as a consultant, pays me a small fee—a very small fee—to make it look right. That allows me and my associates limited, but official, access to view a body or something like that. He's identified four confirmed victims and four or five other possibilities.

"I called in a number of local practitioners, and with phone calls from Mike paving the way, we canvassed the morgues in the greater Dallas area, looking closely at any death that didn't have an obvious cause. But we'd have to get court orders and exhume the bodies to be sure. It looks like it's gone on for about six months."

The conversation moved on and they talked about some sort of police procedure, but Paul looked deeply troubled, had stopped eating and just toyed with his food.

"Little girls eight or nine," he said, his voice barely a whisper. "Cloe would be eight now."

Katherine's heart lurched as she realized what this meant to him.

Salisteen turned to him and asked sharply. "Who's Cloe?" The conversation at the table abruptly halted.

"The little girls," Paul said. "Any pattern there?"

Salisteen frowned at the obvious evasion and she shook her head. "Mostly white and Hispanic, though we suspect one black girl was a victim, but we won't know for sure without exhumation. They were all different hair color, different economic status. No pattern."

Paul nodded, stared at his food with blank, vacant eyes. "There has to be a pattern," he said.

Salisteen dismissed him rather casually. "None we've been able to spot so far. The most recent victim hasn't been buried yet, so we're going to see her tomorrow."

••••

He'd timed it perfectly; as he turned onto the street two blocks away the little Mexican boy and the pretty Mexican girl parted, each walking down a different street. He had no interest in the little Mexican boy; *he* wasn't Alice. He could never be Alice. But he could be a problem, might get in the way at the wrong moment, so he decided to follow the boy instead of pretty little Alice.

He drove slowly, but not too slowly. There was an art to remaining unnoticed, a skill he'd acquired slowly with much practice and patience. And the power of the voice within him helped too, and his own skills as a practitioner helped immeasurably.

He watched the little Mexican boy walk up to the front door to his house, an above-average house that meant his parents had above-average money. He drove past and continued on without looking back.

5

The Bearer

PLANO, TEXAS WAS about twenty miles north of the center of Dallas, a rather well-off community of about 300 thousand people, with a lot of high-tech industry. For the most part the population was well educated with a higher-than-average income. But none of that had helped poor Monica Clarkson. Her little body lay quietly in a refrigeration unit in the Collins County Medical Examiner's Office in McKinney, a few miles north of Plano.

Paul expected to be escorted to a large room with stainless-steel, coffin-shaped, refrigeration drawers, and like on TV, a bored, uncaring morgue technician would slide open one of the drawers and they'd all stand there looking at the body. It was nothing like that.

And he expected Mike Ramirez, Texas Ranger, to be a big man wearing a big western Stetson, a large, silver belt buckle the size of his fist, and cowboy boots. Ramirez was a big man, stood a couple inches over six feet, only an inch or two taller than Paul, outweighed Paul by a good thirty pounds, most of it in his shoulders with only a touch of middle-age gut peaking over his belt line. And he looked more like a Harvard MBA than a cowboy, wearing a neat business suit, faintly Hispanic features, dark brown hair, handsome, with a pleasant smile. Paul thought Salisteen should be all over him.

She made the introductions. When Paul shook Ramirez's hand he said, "I really appreciate y'all helpin'." He spoke with a strong Texas accent.

He pulled out his cell phone, dialed a number, waited a moment with it pressed to his ear, then said, "Ramirez here. We'll be there in about five."

Ramirez got them badged up, then escorted them past a security barrier and led them toward the back of the building. After a few minutes of walking he stopped, opened a door and held it for them. They filed into a room with a large glass window in the back wall that looked into another room with four, stainless steel gurneys lined up in a row. It was a cold, sterile room, with a ceramic tile floor pockmarked by steel drains. A young black fellow finished adjusting a green sheet over a small body on one of the gurneys.

The place had a faintly antiseptic smell that masked a hint of something like sewage, or rotting meat. The underlying scent of decay was so faint Paul couldn't really place it, but it bothered him.

Ramirez turned to face them. "Anyone here going to puke?"

Paul recalled the day he'd identified Cloe's body in a somewhat similar setting. He might break down crying, but he wasn't going to puke.

"I warn you," Ramirez added, looking specifically at Paul and Katherine. "This ain't like looking at your old dead grandma who passed away in her sleep."

Paul said, "I'll be okay."

Katherine nodded. "Me too."

Ramirez led them into the room with the gurneys. When Paul stepped through the door the smell hit him like a bucket of sewage in his face. He gagged, choked and coughed, struggling desperately to hold his breakfast down, leaned against the wall and almost did puke.

"What's wrong?" Katherine asked.

Paul's mouth watered profusely and he swallowed hard several times. Colleen put a hand on his shoulder. She glanced toward the morgue technician before whispering, "Demon stink."

They had all paused and looked at Paul oddly. The young technician smirked knowingly. Ramirez looked at him and hooked a thumb over his shoulder. "I'll call you when I need you."

The kid's smirk disappeared. He slipped out of the room quickly and closed the door.

"It stinks in here," Paul said. "Really strong smell, like we're in a sewer."

"It's not a smell," Colleen said. "We call it demon stink, but it's really not a smell. Your arcane senses are apparently opening up, and you don't know how to interpret them so your mind thinks it's picking up a smell, a particularly bad smell."

She looked at the rest of them. "And I think he's probably more sensitive than the rest of us."

Ramirez and Stowicz frowned, while the rest of them nodded. To reassure them Paul said, "Don't worry; I'm not going lose my breakfast."

They gathered around Monica's body and Paul was thankful her foot wasn't sticking out of the green sheet with some sort of identification tag wired to one of her toes. The tag was probably there, but at least he didn't have to look at it. Ramirez folded back the sheet just enough to expose her face. She had blonde, shoulder-length hair that needed washing, and since her eyelids were closed he didn't have to look into her pretty blue eyes. He said a silent prayer of thanks that she didn't look like Cloe. She was about the same age and size, and like Cloe she had a skinny-little-girl kind of body, but any resemblance ended there, though Cloe had also been a blonde, but a darker shade of blonde than Monica. As Paul looked at poor Monica lying there his thoughts returned to the last time he'd seen Cloe, lying on a similar gurney in a similar morgue, and he realized then that any little girl he saw lying on a stainless steel gurney would look just like Cloe, no matter how different her features or skin color or race might be.

He turned to Katherine and whispered, "I keep seeing Cloe. I can't do this."

He turned away from the gurney, spotted a flat bench seat against one wall, walked over to it and sat down. He leaned back and closed his eyes, trying to put the image of Monica-Cloe out of his mind.

Mr. Paul, a tiny voice said to him, and something tugged on his sleeve. Paul opened his eyes and looked down on Monica seated next to him. She wore a gray pinafore over a pale-blue dress, with white knee-high stockings and shiny black shoes, her hair in pigtails. She looked quite dead; there was no life in her open blue eyes, and she looked up at him with a worried frown on her face. She really only looked a little bit like Cloe.

Mr. Paul, she pleaded. Her lips moved, though no real sound emerged. *Y'all gotta help the little Mexican girl. He wants her, and y'all gotta help her.* She had a strong Texas accent.

Paul reached out and took her hand in his, patted it gently and said, "I don't know what to do."

Y'all gotta help Alice, she pleaded. *Please. And y'all gotta help the little Mexican boy too.*

••••

Katherine's heart lurched when Paul turned to her and whispered, "She looks just like Cloe. I can't do this."

As he turned and walked away Stowicz gave him an angry look. Katherine didn't know what Cloe had looked like, but this must be really hard for Paul. Her father, Colleen, Stowicz and Salisteen were having a rather animated conversation over the little girl's body, while Ramirez stood patiently in the background. Katherine couldn't focus on their words, could only stare at the little girl's lifeless face.

"Katherine," a deep baritone voice said, and she looked up to see a tall man with coal-black skin standing behind her father and Stowicz. She knew a three-thousand dollar Armani suit when she saw one.

It occurred to her she hadn't seen him enter the room. There was only one door, and she stood facing it, couldn't have missed seeing him come through it and cross the room toward them.

"Come," he said, nodding to one side. "Let's talk."

Katherine couldn't have resisted him if she'd wanted to, while the others stood frozen like statues made of stone. He stepped away from the group surrounding the gurney, carrying something long and thin wrapped in some sort of canvas. She joined him and stood facing him.

"I am Dayandalous," he said, carefully unwrapping the bundle. "And you are the bearer. Remember that."

He finished unwrapping the bundle and handed her a sheathed sword. The sheath was over four feet long, and the hilt protruding from it could easily support a two-handed grip, with a simple cross-guard. She accepted the sword, and felt an overwhelming desire to look upon the blade, so she held the sheath in one hand and wrapped the fingers of the other about the hilt. But Dayandalous reached out and rested a hand on hers, stopping her.

"You are not the wielder," he said. "You are the bearer. You are his strength, his resolve, and with you at his side he will remain steadfast."

"Sure, and we're going be having some fun now," a small voice said in a thick accent.

She looked down to see the leprechaun Boo'Diddle standing beside her. Then she looked carefully at the sheathed sword in her hands, wondering how she'd come across a sword, and why she now stood off to one side with the leprechaun. Then she sensed something evil enter the room, and instinctively she turned toward Paul.

••••

You have to help her, Mr. Paul. Please help her.

"Who is she?" Paul pleaded, holding the little girl close, his arms wrapped tightly about her. "Help me find her and I'll try to help her."

She looked up at him, pleading with her eyes.

"Don't be looking in her eyes, you daft fool," Jim'Jiminie said.

Paul started, looked away from Monica to find the leprechaun standing in front of him, wearing his signature green leggings, a brown doublet over a purple shirt, with bright orange-red hair spilling out from a floppy, red, felt hat perched jauntily on his head.

Mr. Paul.

Paul looked back at Monica, looked into her eyes, and deep within he saw pain and sorrow and fear. And then her eyes flared blood-red, and in their goat-slitted pupils he saw evil and hatred. He drowned in her eyes, felt his soul plunge deep into hers, knew it was up to him to purge the malevolence he sensed there, knew she'd have no peace in the afterlife if he didn't help her now.

"I told you not to look in her eyes."

The evil within her had wrapped itself tightly about her soul. He pulled on it, knew he must be hurting the little girl terribly, but better that than leave her soul imprisoned for eternity. She leaned back, arched her spine painfully, opened her mouth and cried out, and from her lips a black stain emerged, coalescing in the room like smoke from the fires of hell. It took on a vague undefined form that left the impression of taloned claws and serpent scales, a mouth filled with razor sharp teeth drooling maggots. The only thing he saw clearly and solidly were its blood-red, goat-slitted eyes as it reached down, gripped him by the throat, lifted him off his feet and tossed him across the room. He landed on the tile floor tumbling, smashing his elbows and knees and head painfully.

"Paul," Katherine screamed, and the monster turned on her and one of the leprechauns. It flowed slowly toward them like smoke drifting on a gentle breeze.

The leprechaun standing next to her shouted, "He needs the sword, girl."

Katherine and the little man back stepped as Paul scrambled to his feet. The monster had them cornered, and as it closed on them Paul charged at it, limping on a painfully twisted ankle. He reached it a second before it reached her, felt the emotionless hatred of death, a cold so deep he shivered as he passed through it and slammed into her. They tumbled into the leprechaun and the three of them hit the floor in a sprawl of tangled arms and legs.

Boo'Diddle grunted. "Clumsy idiot!"

Paul tried to stand, wobbled precariously as he staggered up onto his feet. Katherine moved faster than him, hooked a forearm under his armpit and pulled him away from the monster. The leprechaun scrambled to one side on his hands and knees. As the apparition drifted almost casually toward them, Katherine stopped, turned to Paul and held out, of all things, a sheathed sword. "Here," she screamed, offering him the hilt. "Do something with this."

"A sword?" he demanded. "A fucking sword? What the fuck am I going to do with a fucking sword?"

Eyes wide with fear, Katherine shouted back, "I don't know what you're supposed to do with it. Just fucking use the fucking thing."

At that moment the apparition enveloped them, wrapped itself about them like a death shroud, wrapped them in a cold so intense Paul saw Katherine's breath. It squeezed them together almost in a lover's embrace, the sword pressed between them, its hilt rising just above her shoulder. It lifted them both off the floor as Katherine swooned and her eyes rolled back. Just beyond her shoulder Paul saw the blood-red, goat-slitted eyes smiling at him, and he screamed, "Nooooo!"

He gripped the hilt of the sword with both hands, slid it clear of the sheath and lifted it high over his head. Then he shouted, "Fuck you, asshole," and plunged the point into the blood-red eyes.

••••

By the look on Salisteen's face, Colleen and she both sensed it at the same moment.

"What the hell!" Walter snarled, clearly sensing it as well, while Stowicz erupted with a string of profanity.

Colleen turned and scanned the room quickly. "Paul, Katherine, where are they? They're gone." Paul and Katherine had completely disappeared.

All five of them were looking toward the bench where Paul had retreated when something in the room popped. Paul materialized seated on the bench; Katherine and two leprechauns materialized standing in front of him. Paul and Katherine were both bloodied, their clothing torn. Katherine stumbled on a broken high-heel and collapsed.

••••

Katherine struggled to her hands and knees, shivering uncontrollably in the intense cold. Paul sat on a flat bench against the wall, blood flowing freely from his nose, a nasty gash on his cheek adding more blood. He'd turned slightly to one side, had his arms wrapped about something she couldn't see. She opened her arcane senses fully and her *sight* blossomed. He had the indigo and violet aura of a strong practitioner, but intertwined with his primary colors were the black threads of a necromancer. His aura had blossomed outward and engulfed something seated next to him on the bench. Katherine could make out a faintly human shape but saw no details, just a hazy shimmer within Paul's extended aura. There was no sign of the monster they'd just fought.

Katherine got back to her feet and stumbled on a broken high-heel, so she kicked her shoes off. She approached Paul slowly, moving carefully, the two leprechauns at her side. She looked down at Jim'Jiminie. "How do I help him?"

The little fellow shook his head. "You don't, girl. This is what he does."

She saw Paul speaking softly to the human-like shape wrapped in his aura, a tiny shape no larger than a child, and she realized who it must be.

He put his arms around the shape, pulled her close to him and patted her on the head as he rocked back and forth. "It's all right, Monica," he said. "It's all right."

A breathless hush settled over the room, and Katherine heard the footsteps of the others as they gathered behind her. She heard Colleen hiss, "Leave them alone. The two of them can handle this."

Katherine squatted down in front of Paul. He continued to rock back and forth. His eyes were open and she saw anger smoldering there. The pain and fear and sorrow emanating from the presence in his arms slowly dissolved, and Katherine felt a calm lethargy settle over the spirit, like the relief one feels when pain medication finally takes hold. And then the presence dissipated and was gone.

Paul leaned back wearily and sighed. "She said we have to help a little Mexican girl and boy. The bastard that killed Monica wants the little girl now; I think her name is Alice."

Paul's aura churned, and Katherine felt anger radiating from him like heat from a raging fire. "But I'm going to find the son-of-a-bitch first and kill him myself."

••••

"No," he pleaded. "No. Alice isn't ready yet."

But I am diminished and I hunger, I need.

"But she's not ready. And the little boy is in the way."

Then someone else. Now! Tonight!

"But there's no one else ready. It's too dangerous. If we're caught they'll banish you and it will all end."

But I need, I hunger.

"I know. But you'll have to be patient. I'll accelerate preparations for the little Mexican girl."

Hurry.

"Yes, I'll hurry. Just be patient."

6

The Secret Uncovered

SIMUTH STALKED WARILY up the stairs of the old fortress in the non-aligned territories. His suspicions had grown for years, and it had taken careful planning on his part to trace the movements of the Winter Princess. One moved cautiously in such matters.

The fortress was ancient, had been abandoned long ago and had decayed little by little as the centuries passed. He'd searched the lower floors methodically, but nothing had been out of place. He'd gone through dozens of chambers and rooms, all strewn liberally with the detritus of past ages. On the upper level he found more rooms filled with the debris of neglect and decay. He was beginning to doubt his own suspicions as he turned toward the north wing, the only portion of the fortress he had yet to search.

How could he have been so wrong? he wondered. He'd found nothing in the rest of the fortress, and with growing certainty he knew he'd find nothing here. He was about to turn back and abandon the search when he recognized the subtle influence of the spell; doubt, uncertainty and misgivings induced by the delicate application of understated magics. It was well done, extremely well done, crafted by a powerful mage, but with restraint and control.

He stepped back out of the north wing, spent some minutes crafting a counter-spell, then returned and released it. The debris in the hallway disappeared in the blink of an eye. Dust still carpeted the floor, and the signs of age and decay remained, but someone had gone to some trouble to clean this portion of the fortress. And the farther he penetrated into the north wing the more confident he grew that his suspicions were correct.

Instinct led him to a large, oaken door at the far end of the hall. It appeared to be ancient like the rest of the fortress, but it swung open easily on beautifully maintained hinges. And beyond it he found a suite of rooms arrayed with the most elegant of furniture and tapestries. There was a small, intimate dining chamber, a grand sitting room, and most importantly, a bed chamber that reeked of the scent of his prey.

The sheets on the large bed were tousled and tumbled in disarray, but among them he found a beautiful, silk scarf he recognized. He lifted it to his nose, and was not surprised to find the arcane scent of Taal'mara. And most damning of all, mixed in with her scent was that of Anogh. He threw his head back and laughed . . .

Simuth watched Anogh report to Ag and recalled that day more than six centuries ago. He enjoyed evoking those memories and the events that followed, for it had been a great personal triumph over his most hated enemy.

••••

"Conklin," Katherine shouted, standing in the middle of Salisteen's kitchen, holding a broken high-heel in one hand and pointing an angry finger at Paul. "You are absolute hell on a girl's wardrobe." She turned and stormed across the kitchen, hair in wild disarray, her expensive suit torn in several places, walking unevenly because she refused to abandon the one high-heel that wasn't broken.

Paul leaned over the sink while Salisteen administered to his bloody nose and the cut on his cheek.

Stowicz demanded, "What the hell happened back there?"

Ramirez had quickly hustled them out of the morgue before anyone started asking questions they didn't want to answer.

Paul said, "How the hell should I know. One minute I'm sitting there comforting poor little Monica, and the next she pukes up some monster, and it's trying to kill me. If Katherine hadn't given me that sword, I don't know what we would have done."

They all turned to look at Katherine with a mixture of distrust and anger. In a more subdued tone McGowan asked, "You gave him a sword?"

Katherine stopped her angry pacing and frowned thoughtfully. "Ya," she said, shaking her head as if trying to recall some lost memory.

"Where did you come up with a sword?"

She continued to shake her head, her frown deepening. "I don't know."

"And where is it now?"

"I don't know."

Stowicz gave Paul a look of intense distrust and growled, "I don't like this. What are you pulling here? How do I know you didn't bring a demon over?"

Colleen said, "Charlie, you saw the little people."

"Ya, so?"

"You know full well they wouldn't help Paul if he trucked with demons."

Holding a wet towel to his nose Paul sat down in a chair at the kitchen table. He couldn't get the poor little girl out of his mind, kept seeing her lifeless body lying on the stainless steel gurney. And every time he thought of her he saw Cloe lying there, and he couldn't get her out of his mind, and his hands shook with anger. But he just didn't know who to be angry at.

Ramirez towered over him. "Buck up man," he growled. "Show some cojones. We're depending on you."

Katherine stormed up behind Ramirez, grabbed his arm and spun him to face her. "Back off, asshole."

She stepped around Ramirez and spoke softly. "It's Cloe, isn't it?"

Ramirez demanded, "Who the hell's Cloe?"

Katherine spun back to him. "His daughter, you jerk. Killed about a year ago. About the same age as Monica."

Ramirez's shoulders slumped and he deflated like a balloon with a bad leak. "Ah shit!" He shook his head. "Why didn't someone tell me?"

Katherine didn't let up, "I just did, asshole."

Colleen stepped between them. "Everyone calm down. Let's try to reconstruct what happened. And let's do so without all the shouting."

Ramirez turned and stormed out of the kitchen. Katherine sat down opposite Paul, reached out and took hold of his hands. She spoke carefully. "Tell me what you saw."

Her hands were warm and soft, and his stopped shaking as he carefully put all thought of Cloe out of his mind. "I saw Monica. Dead Monica."

Ramirez marched back into the kitchen carrying a bottle of bourbon just as one of the male-model servants put a cup of coffee in front of Paul. "Sorry, man," Ramirez said as he pulled the cork on the bottle. "I didn't know."

He poured a healthy splash of bourbon into Paul's coffee. "This'll help a little. This's got to be hard for you."

Colleen sat down next to Katherine and held her coffee out toward Ramirez. "I could use a wee dram of that too, darlin'."

They passed the bourbon around as Paul took a sip of his coffee and Katherine said, "You were telling us about Monica."

"There isn't much to tell," Paul said. "She looked pretty normal, except her eyes were dead, no life in them at all."

"What did she say?"

"She tugged on my sleeve and said I had to help the little Mexican girl and boy. She said he wanted her and I had to help her. She called her Alice. Then she opened her mouth and something like black smoke came out. But it was a lot nastier than just smoke."

McGowan made Paul and Katherine describe in considerable detail what they remembered. "I don't know where I got that sword," Katherine finished. "But when I saw that monster it was just there, and I knew Paul needed to use it to stop that thing."

Throughout the retelling of the events Stowicz had stood silently at the far end of the kitchen. He stepped forward, coffee cup in hand. "You said she said *he* wanted her. She didn't say *it* wanted her."

Paul thought about it for a moment, tried to reconstruct the few brief words she'd uttered. "No, not *it*. She definitely said *he*."

Salisteen, McGowan and Stowicz exchanged a rapid sequence of surprised looks, while Colleen just stared into her coffee cup and nodded.

"What is it?" Katherine demanded.

"My dear," she said. "Information you get from a spirit can be quite obtuse. But in some respects they're very precise. If Monica had been killed by a demon, and if it was a demon loose on the Mortal Plane stalking this little Mexican girl, Monica's spirit would have referred to it as *it*, not *he*."

Paul asked, "So what's that mean?"

Colleen swirled the coffee in her cup, continued to stare at it as she said, "We're not merely looking for an emergent loose on the Mortal Plane. We're looking for some sort of human killer that somehow feeds like a demon, or is maybe working in concert with a demon."

She looked up and her eyes bored into Paul's. "And it makes me wonder if that means we're looking for another necromancer?"

••••

Anogh spurred his steed into a gallop as they approached the seat of the Unseelie Court. For a diplomatic mission of this nature, he wore the full regalia of the Summer Knight—the hereditary armor, the masked helm—and he was accompanied by a retinue of twelve twelves of Seelie warriors, all arrayed similarly.

The invitation from Ag had been vague, which was not unusual, but it nevertheless required the appropriate response. It might be some trivial issue Ag wished to discuss, possibly some slight he had imagined. They would discuss and dispute the matter for several days, eventually come to a resolution, then Anogh and his retinue would return to the Seelie Court to debrief Magreth. If nothing more it would be an excuse to see Taal'mara, though only from afar. They dare not meet in secret under such close scrutiny.

The gates of the great Unseelie castle stood open for them. Simuth sat astride his own steed waiting just outside the castle's moat, backed by a similar troupe of Unseelie warriors. At a discreet distance Anogh raised his hand and brought his troupe to a halt. Then, as required by the ancient formulas, he and Simuth both rode forward at an easy canter and met half way between the two forces.

"Brother Knight," Simuth said. "By what warrant do you traverse the Unseelie territories?"

Anogh bowed his head lightly. "I come in peace, Brother Knight, by invitation of your sovereign."

"And you bear the proper warrant?"

It was an ancient formula established in a far distant past. Anogh reached into his tunic, saying, "I do, signed personally by your king, and it bears his seal."

He retrieved a parchment and handed it to Simuth, who pretended to read it, for of course he had known of this visit and the invitation well in advance. Simuth nodded, "Then do accompany me, Brother Knight, as my guest."

With the formalities complete, Simuth turned and nudged his mount toward the castle. Anogh and his retinue followed.

In the castle yard their horses were taken in hand by grooms. Anogh must first present himself to the king, so Simuth led him through the halls of the Winter Court, though having followed this formula many times through the centuries Anogh well knew the way.

When he stepped through the massive entrance of the great throne room he paused, and waited while the chamberlain announced him to the waiting throng and the king. It took some seconds to speak his many titles and his full name, but when the chamberlain finished Anogh marched forward, his pace carefully dictated by protocol. Taal'mara stood beside her father on his left side, dressed in a gown of pale green brocade, her hair piled high atop her head and decorated with gems of all colors. But as Anogh walked the length of the great room, while his thoughts could not turn away from his heart's desire, he was careful to keep his eyes on Ag seated upon his throne, to give no hint of his love for the Winter Princess.

Simuth climbed the dais and took a position at Ag's right hand. Anogh stopped at a discrete distance from the bottom of the dais. He bowed from the waist. "Your Majesty, as you requested I have come, and I bring the felicitations of my queen."

"Rise," Ag said. "Face me, Summer Knight."

Anogh stood straight and tall and looked up to the Winter King. Ag regarded him carefully as he lifted a glass of wine to his lips. His eyes locked on Anogh over the rim of the goblet as he sipped delicately. When he lowered the glass he raised a silken scarf and lightly dabbed at his lips.

Taal'mara's eyes darted to the scarf, and with a look of surprise and horror all color drained from her face.

Simuth smirked openly.

The scarf was not the kind of thing one would ordinarily use as a simple napkin, more an elegant thing of beauty to be worn by a courtier. But Anogh couldn't understand why the sight of it brought such fear to Taal'mara's features. It was just a scarf, one that seemed slightly familiar, but still just a scarf.

Slightly familiar! Anogh had seen it before and he dredged through his memories to recall where: draped delicately over Taal'mara's shoulders as she joined him in their hidden love nest. They had chatted briefly and tried to restrain themselves, but it had been many months since he'd last experienced the taste of her skin, and once his restraint had faltered, it had vanished quickly. He'd personally removed the scarf from her shoulders, dropped it to the floor of the bed chamber, the first of many articles of clothing he removed from her.

"Yes," Ag said, smiling unpleasantly. "I can see by the look on your face, Summer Knight, that you have now gleaned the purpose of this meeting."

Taal'mara dropped to her knees and bowed her head. "Your Majesty. Please, we have done nothing."

"Now, now, my child," Ag said, reaching out and patting her gently on the top of her head. He put a finger beneath her chin and tilted her head up to meet his eyes. "You have done quite a bit, haven't you, daughter?"

Anogh stepped forward and said, "But, Your Majesty—"

Ag looked to Anogh and screamed, "Silence!"

He turned back to Taal'mara, and again he spoke gently. "You have allowed the Summer Knight to seduce you. You have allowed him to pluck the most delicate flower in the Winter Court. You've sullied yourself with base lust and desire."

"I'm sorry, father, but we're in love, a beautiful thing between us."

"A beautiful thing, is it?"

Again Anogh stepped forward. "Yes, Your Majesty. I would gladly wed her." He struggled to find some reason for Ag to forbear his wrath. "It would be a powerful union, joining both Sidhe Courts as never before. I would do anything to prove the honor of my intentions."

Ag grinned. "You would do anything, eh?"

Anogh dropped to one knee and bowed his head. "Anything, Your Majesty."

"An interesting thought, my Summer Knight. Perhaps it would be of some benefit to join the two Courts in this way."

Ag paused, clearly considering the matter. "Very well, I will grant you my daughter's hand in marriage. But only on the condition you take solemn oath to protect her, to see that no harm ever comes to her, and that should you fail in that oath, you will be bound to the Winter Court for all eternity."

Anogh looked up at Ag. "I cannot take such an oath, Your Majesty. My oaths to the Summer Court prohibit such an open-ended binding."

Ag smiled. "Very well, then. Should you fail to protect the Winter Princess, you will be bound to the Winter Court until the death of the Winter Knight. And you may not take his life, nor arrange for another to do so. Now that's not so open-ended, is it?"

"But he's immortal."

Ag's smile widened and he nodded. "Yes, he is. Granted, it's a subtle and fine distinction, but that is enough of a limitation that it will not violate your oaths to the Summer Court. Eh, Summer Knight?"

Anogh lowered his head again. "Yes, Your Majesty. I can take such an oath."

. . . Anogh had been such a fool, all those many centuries ago. He knew that now, had even, deep down, known it then. But he'd been blinded by his love for Taal'mara, and his need to have her by his side. And in any case, no one would be foolish enough to harm Taal'mara and face the wrath of the Summer Knight and the Winter King.

Yes, he'd been such a fool.

••••

It was McGowan's idea to try to raise the spirits of the other victims. "It can't hurt," he'd said, "and maybe we'll learn something."

If they wanted to go to graveyards and raise the spirits of the dead, that was fine with Paul, as long as he didn't have anything to do with it. Raising the dead; the whole idea was just too creepy. And then, listening to them talk, Paul realized it wasn't *they* who were going to raise the dead. They expected him to do it.

"Me? Raise the dead?" he asked, pacing back and forth in Salisteen's kitchen. "I don't know anything about raising the dead."

Paul turned to Stowicz, who nursed a cup of coffee at the kitchen table. "You're this super, wizard magic guy. Why don't you do it?"

Stowicz grimaced. "I could, but that's extremely difficult sorcery, and quite dangerous. It takes days of preparation for anyone but a necromancer. And you're the necromancer du jour. It's supposed to be easy for you."

"But I don't know anything about necromancy."

McGowan walked into the kitchen carrying a notebook. "The kid's got a point, Charlie. None of us really know anything about necromancy."

McGowan sat down next to Stowicz and opened the notebook. "Take a look at this. I got this grimoire a while back, gotta be thirteen, fourteen hundred years old. Pretty authentic too. Fellow who wrote it was a nut-case monk, but, based on the spells he documented, he was a pretty good sorcerer, claimed to have assisted the Merlin, documented some of his necromantic spells, though he was smart enough not to try them himself."

McGowan flipped through the pages of the notebook, opened it to a particular page and spread it flat in front of Stowicz, then stabbed a finger at the page. "I think this one. What do you think?"

Stowicz's head began tracking side-to-side as he read the writing on the page in front of him. Colleen and Salisteen crossed the room to stand behind him and look over his shoulder. Paul pointed at the notebook. "That doesn't look fourteen hundred years old."

"Nah," McGowan said. "That's just my notes, and some translation. Original's too delicate to carry around."

Stowicz nodded. "Ya, this just might do it."

Standing behind the two men Colleen and Salisteen both nodded their agreement. Colleen added, "But it'll have to be done at midnight, in the cemetery. And it'll require a death."

7

An Ancient Invocation

GREENWOOD CEMETERY WAS on the northwest side of Fort Worth. They arrived about an hour before midnight. Apparently, when a sergeant of the Texas Rangers wanted access to a cemetery at midnight, there were no questions asked. Or maybe Ramirez was experienced at fielding questions about unusual requests.

The caretaker let them in through the main gate. Like the surrounding countryside the cemetery was flat and sprawling. Wide lanes bisected plots of graves situated among large, old oak trees. The whole place seemed peaceful and well maintained. As they spilled from two cars Colleen said to Katherine, "Do you sense it?"

Katherine nodded, "Yes. It's strong."

"What?" Paul demanded.

Katherine took Paul's arm and held back as the rest of the retinue followed Ramirez's flashlight. "There's a strong ley line running right through the cemetery. Not unusual really."

"Ley line. What's that?"

"You tapped one when you torched my father's kitchen." She tripped as one of her high-heels caught on something. Paul caught her in his arms, held her there for a moment, and the old Katherine emerged. "Conklin, you have a one track mind."

"Hey, buddy," McGowan shouted. "Get your hands off my daughter. And let's have some focus here."

Katherine pulled herself out of Paul's arms with a laugh, turned and followed the others. Paul followed her. "Ley lines," she said. "They're alignments of natural—or even man-made—features of significance, and they facilitate the flow of power between the Realms. Could be an old path people have followed for centuries, especially if it connects to an old monument or place where people gathered, or, for that matter, died or were buried."

She stopped and turned around to face him. "Let's try something. Close your eyes and try to clear your thoughts."

He did, though he was nervous about performing the necromantic spell and it was difficult to get that out of his thoughts.

"Now try to sense the ley line," she said. "It's like using the *sight*. This one is strong enough it should be easy for you to sense it."

Paul certainly felt something he couldn't define, a sense of personal power, as if the cemetery itself lent him strength. He focused on that feeling that didn't seem to be a normal part of him, had an impression of something flowing like a river about the edges of the cemetery.

He described it and Katherine said, "Yes, that's it. We'll have to practice more ley line techniques later."

Paul had spent the afternoon memorizing a string of Latin. He knew nothing of Latin, but even the translation McGowan read to him was meaningless gibberish, stuff about "transcending the boundaries of the living," and "fomenting the corporal life of the hereafter."

Paul said, "It's a bunch of nonsense."

McGowan shrugged. "I told you he was a nut-case monk, probably locked himself away on some mountaintop and smoked the evil weed all day."

Tandy Simpson's grave was a flat, marble marker laid flush with the lawn. Tandy Simpson, beloved daughter of Andrew and Laura, had died of unknown causes at the age of nine. They gathered around Tandy's grave and Ramirez said, "This one I got to before they buried her. Demon stink all over her."

McGowan had brought along a number of items, including a small cage with a sedated chicken in it. On the ground near Tandy's grave he placed a crucifix, an iron knife and a flint axe—Paul didn't even want to ask how he got his hands on a flint axe. By prior agreement Katherine and Paul would work the spell, so the rest of them walked back to the cars and waited there.

Even though he'd memorized the Latin, Paul had a flashlight and a cheat-sheet. He and Katherine stood on opposite sides of Tandy's grave, though Katherine wobbled a little, trying to stand in the grass on high-heels. Paul glanced down at her feet and did a poor job of hiding the look on his face.

"Listen to me, Conklin," she said angrily. "This is dangerous stuff. So if something happens to me, I'm not about to die, or go to the hospital, in flats, or, god forbid, sneakers."

Paul smiled and said, "My mom always told me to wear nice underwear in case I ended up in the hospital." He leered openly at her ass. "What kind of nice underwear did you wear, McGowan . . . just in case you end up in the hospital?"

She leaned toward him, the beam of the flashlight adding emphasis to the angry glare on her face. "Just the kind you, or any healthy man, would really like to see, Conklin. And if you don't wipe that leer off your face, it's the kind you're never going to see."

Off in the distance old man McGowan shouted, "Focus, children."

Paul bent down, and as he'd been instructed he removed the chicken from its cage. McGowan had sedated it with some sort of spell, and when Paul placed it carefully on Tandy's grave it sat on the grass quietly, its head lulling lazily from side to side. Paul used the flashlight to scan the cheat-sheet one last time, then bent down, took the iron knife and plucked the tip of his thumb with its point. A little squeamish about drawing his own blood he didn't press hard enough the first time, then pressed too hard the second time. "Damn," he said as blood flowed down his thumb and into the palm of his hand.

Katherine hissed, "Be careful! Just seven drops."

Paul had a small puddle in the palm of his hand. "Can I dump the excess over in the bushes?"

"No. You might raise some other spirit. Here." She handed him a terrycloth towel and he wiped up the puddle of blood. Then he stood over Tandy's grave and carefully squeezed the cut on his thumb while Katherine counted the drops and they fell to the ground in the beam of the flashlight: seven drops. He wrapped the towel around his hand to make sure he didn't spill anymore.

He and Katherine both squatted down over Tandy's grave with the chicken between them. Paul took up the flint axe in his right hand, held the chicken's head pressed against the ground in his left hand. Katherine checked her watch, and they waited for a few minutes until she said, "Okay, you can start."

She held the cheat-sheet in front of his nose, lighting it with the beam of the flashlight. And Paul began the chant.

Thirteen times he repeated it. He started out carefully, reciting the Latin in what was undoubtedly poor pronunciation, but McGowan had told him that wouldn't make any difference. He didn't feel anything unusual until he began the seventh repetition, and then a shiver crawled up his spine, though he chalked it up to nerves. But by the end of the seventh repetition he sensed something in the graveyard, as if some undefined essence observed and watched and waited.

The feeling grew with each repetition, and by the end of the tenth he grew exceedingly nervous. By the end of the twelfth Katherine, looking closely at her watch, held out her hand signaling him to slow down. He needed to finish the thirteenth repetition at precisely midnight, so he paced his words carefully. And it had to be solar midnight for the spot of earth on which they stood.

The sense of watchfulness had grown palpable, and in Katherine's eyes he saw that she too sensed it. And as he approached the end of the thirteenth repetition she twirled her finger in the air to get him to speed up while he raised the flint axe a few feet above the ground. By that time he no longer needed to look at the cheat-sheet, and oddly enough the Latin had begun to make an odd sort of sense. He timed it carefully, following the cadence of her finger like a violinist following the baton of the conductor, and with the last word of the thirteenth repetition he brought the axe down and chopped it hard into the chicken's neck.

Something in the graveyard snapped with an almost audible twang. Paul's heart lurched at the same moment, and as the ground pitched crazily beneath him he fell forward onto his hands and knees on Tandy's grave.

Shouts of fear and anger broke the quiet of the night. The ground beneath his hands churned unnaturally, then a small hand erupted from the dirt and gripped his wrist with vice-like strength.

He looked at Katherine; she too had fallen to her hands and knees opposite him, and another small hand had erupted from the ground to grip her wrist. Behind her a zombie from some cheap monster film erupted from a nearby grave and climbed stiffly to its feet, its rotted face falling away in chunks of corrupted flesh. It lunged toward Katherine, but Colleen stepped in its way, and with her hand glowing with some sort of weird fire she slapped it down. More ghoulish creatures erupted from the ground all around them, tipping over gravestones as their emergence churned the earth of the graveyard.

Jim'Jiminie and Boo'Diddle appeared next to them. One gripped Katherine's wrist and the other Paul's, and both tried to pull their wrists free of the grip of the small hands protruding from the ground.

Paul looked into Katherine's eyes, saw his own fear starkly reflected there. A stream of maggots poured up out of the earth between them, followed by the decayed and corrupted head of a small child. In its blood-red, goat-slitted eyes Paul saw the same evil he'd seen in Monica.

Tandy rose up out of the ground, a specter wearing a colorless pinafore over a white dress, knee-high socks and shiny black shoes, her hair in pigtails. She opened her mouth to scream, and a dark, oily cloud of smoke poured forth, enveloping Paul before he could react. It wrapped his heart in a wave of bitter cold, and a malign presence clutched at his soul, dug into it with talons and claws not visible to mortal eyes.

••••

Katherine saw it all this time, the tiny, childish hands that erupted from the ground to clutch at her wrist and Paul's. She saw the maggots boil forth, saw the decayed head of the dead child emerge between them, then watched as the ghostly child rose up and vomited a cloud of evil. She saw the cloud envelop Paul, watched him collapse to the ground and roll away from the grave.

Jim'Jiminie screamed, "Help him, girl."

All around them every monster from every horror movie ever made erupted from the ground: zombies and shades and ghosts and spirits. Her father and the older practitioners waded in, fighting them off.

Katherine struggled to her feet, found that again she clutched the sheathed sword in her hand, wondered only for an instant how it had come to her. She staggered across the quaking ground to Paul, who lay lifeless on the ground, the monstrous cloud of corruption slowly entering him through his eyes and ears and nose and mouth. A tendril of it swirled around behind him, beneath him, seeking any point of entry it could find. "The sword," she screamed at him and held it out, but his eyes saw nothing but pain and terror and fear. Then the dark, smoky substance swirled about her and wrapped itself around her ankles. Her legs went numb to the knees, and she fell forward, landing on Paul heavily.

The corruption enveloped her completely. She felt it probing at her legs sensed that it was trying to give her pleasure, a sensation so revolting her dinner threatened to boil up out of her stomach. The sword! Her right hand still clutched the sheath pressed between her and Paul's chests, the hilt nestled close to their cheeks. But she was not the wielder, and Paul's face had contorted in a rictus of agony.

She reached down with her left hand, found his right elbow, then his forearm, and wrist and hand. She grabbed his wrist, tried to pull it up to the hilt of the sword, but his muscles were locked in the spasm of a powerful seizure. Little by little she bent his elbow, brought his hand higher, closer and closer to the hilt—and then the monster slid between her legs and entered her, and a powerful orgasm washed through her, a foul, disgusting agony of pleasure that sickened her. It wanted her to yield, and it would reward her with infinite pleasure, and she could not resist, and it knew it had her, even as, with her last effort, she pressed the palm of Paul's hand against the hilt of the sword.

••••

Paul hurt everywhere with a strange combination of joyful pain and disgusting pleasure. He had an erection so demanding it almost hurt, and his memories were clouded by thoughts of a sword, and thoughts of Katherine, and thinking of her he relaxed, realizing then it was her lying on top of him. He took comfort knowing his hand rested on the hilt of a great sword. But the sword was soft, and yielding, and fleshy, and it had a nipple, an erect nipple.

"Con'lin," Katherine mumbled muzzily. "Get your hand off my hilt."

One of the leprechauns said, "This ain't the time for that, boy-oh."

In his own defense, Paul said something like, "Guff um sward nabba."

Katherine struggled groggily to her hands and knees, one hand nearly dislocating his jaw as she leaned on his face like it was a rock on the ground, and only then did he realize his hand was tangled up in her torn blouse, caught between her breast and her bra.

"Oua track mind," she said, and at point-blank range vomited in his face.

••••

Aaahhhh! the voice cried deep in his soul. The pain and agony it radiated startled him so much he fell to his knees in his living room. *Again, I am diminished. It hurts, it hurts so much.*

Tears streamed down his cheeks as he covered his face with his hands.

I need sustenance. I must feed. It hurts to be so weak.

He sensed the diminished capacity of the voice, and for the first time it felt fragile and brittle, and that made him feel weak. Since the voice had come to him he had known control over anything and anyone he chose, and he now hated feeling weak and helpless. Control, and the sense of power that came with it, had become a blessed addiction.

I must feed.

"Yes," he said aloud. "But not Alice. She's not ready yet. The little Mexican boy. We need to get him out of the way anyway."

••••

"What, pray tell, was that?" Magreth demanded, her eyes aflame with white-hot sparks of anger. "What just happened on the Mortal Plane?"

Cadilus lowered his eyes. It was never wise to look directly upon such fury. "The necromancer was active . . . in a rather impressive way."

"Impressive," she screamed, and the ancient Sidhe spirits fluttered fearfully away into the far corners of the audience chamber. "Impressive is not the word. Try spectacular, or stupendous."

Cadilus stared at the toes of his shoes. "Yes, Your Majesty. As you wish, Your Majesty."

Magreth suddenly calmed, and everyone in the Seelie Court sensed it, but it was a hard and cold calm. "Forgive me, dear Cadilus. It is wrong of me to vent my anger on you. Where is Sabreatha in this? Why hasn't she acted?"

"Sabreatha moves in her own time, at her own pace. But I have no doubt she will move soon."

••••

Anogh leapt to the top of a large monument in the graveyard not far from the parked cars of the mortals, then lifted a hind paw and scratched behind his ear. He actually liked wearing the shape of a cat, a lithe and agile animal.

He watched the mortal wizards and witches help the young man and woman to their cars. The Old Wizard's daughter could barely stand, needed the help of the Druid to walk, and even then could do little more than stagger and stumble. The young man was in even worse shape: barely conscious, held up by his armpits by two of the wizards. He tried to walk, did a poor job of putting one foot in front of the other. His feet left a trail in the dirt as they half carried, half dragged him to the cars.

The cemetery remained calm and still, with no sign of the destruction that had occurred, at least none visible to mundane, mortal eyes. Ag would have sensed this event; anyone with any arcane capability would have sensed it. And Ag would want a report.

Anogh jumped off the monument and headed for the boundary of the graveyard.

8

The Cloe Card

"I THINK IT was the translation into the plural that did it," McGowan said, just as Paul reached the bottom of the stairs. He heard Stowicz and McGowan in the kitchen arguing over what had gone wrong with the spell. He'd only been half conscious of returning to the mansion last night. They'd cleaned him up a bit and then he'd slept like the dead, woke that morning feeling like he had the worst hangover of his life. A hot shower had improved his outlook a bit, though it didn't wash away the ache of so many strained muscles.

"Ya," Stowicz said. "This old Latin is tricky. We'll have to try an alternate wording next time."

That's it, Paul decided. Everything hurt as he walked like an old man into the kitchen. "There isn't going to be another fucking *next time*," he shouted. "I'm done with this shit."

The tableau in the kitchen froze at his entrance: McGowan and Stowicz seated at the table pouring over his notebook; Salisteen and Colleen standing behind them looking over their shoulders; Katherine standing at the window with her back to them all, oddly enough dressed in jeans, a T-shirt and running shoes; one of the male-model servants rinsing some dishes in the sink and loading a dishwasher. They all looked at Paul and froze.

Salisteen's eyes narrowed angrily. "Watch your tongue, young man."

"Watch my tongue?" he shouted angrily. His voice rose with each word, and he knew he shouldn't let it, but he was beyond controlling it. "A year and a half ago I was a normal, happily married guy with a wonderful wife and kid. Even a few months ago, while I may have been nuts, at least I was normal nuts. Now I've barely escaped a demon in the Netherworld, been kidnapped by a mad fairy queen, nearly been killed by a demon more than once. It's demons and faeries and leprechauns and dragons, and I've got scars to prove it. When do I get to meet Frodo and Gandalf?"

They all just stared at him silently. He could see sympathy, and pity, but no understanding. "No. Wait a minute here," he shouted. "I haven't met Frodo yet, but I think

I've sure as hell met Gandalf." He nodded at McGowan, and Colleen started giggling. He pointed at Colleen. "And none of that from you, Goldberry. Where's Tom Bombadil?"

Katherine turned away from the window and spoke in a voice barely above a whisper. "He's got a point. Or two, or three. Twice now, in as many days, Paul and I have nearly been possessed by something very horrible. If he weren't afraid and angry and upset like me, I'd doubt his sanity."

With Katherine on his side Paul felt a little calmer. He lowered his voice and said to Salisteen, "Sorry about the profanity."

Salisteen smiled. "Apology accepted. Now, let's get some breakfast into you. You'll feel better with a full stomach."

Salisteen turned to the servant and asked him to scramble some eggs, toast some bread and fry up some ham. Paul sat down at the table and someone shoved a cup of coffee in front of him. He'd definitely feel better with a full stomach, but that wouldn't make him willing to raise any more dead, though he didn't voice that thought.

He asked, "What the heck happened last night?"

Stowicz said, "You raised half the dead in that cemetery."

"How'd I do that?"

McGowan grimaced. "Translating old Latin is a bit problematic. We think we used the plural when we should have used the singular, so it turned into an open ended incantation. With one of us, it wouldn't have been as spectacular. But with you . . ."

Paul wanted to forget the previous evening. "It doesn't matter anyway, because I'm not doing anything like that again."

The four older practitioners traded glances, and McGowan said, "I hate to play the Cloe card, Paul, but I have to."

Colleen sat down opposite him. "From what you and Katherine describe, it appears something is haunting the dead girl's souls. We think it's a powerful demon, quite possibly a primus caste. It must gain some power from them, or some strength here in the Mortal Realm, and those young girls can't pass on unless we free them. And with your help we can end this sooner rather than later."

Stowicz said, "We can do it without you, but it'll take a lot longer. And that's time during which he'll take the lives and souls of more little girls." He hesitated for a moment, then added, "And every one of their deaths will be because you failed to act."

Colleen turned on Stowicz angrily. "That's not fair, Charlie."

"No," he said, "it's not. But it's true. And it had to be said."

They had Katherine and Paul relate in detail exactly what they'd experienced in the graveyard. Paul told them what he could, though he didn't tell them of the disgusting sexual nature that permeated the experience. When Katherine told her story she was subdued. He noticed she also edited out a few embarrassing details, and he suspected there were other bits he didn't know about, things she didn't want to discuss with any-one.

When she finished no one spoke for the longest moment, then Stowicz growled. "You're holding something back. Both of you. What is it?"

Katherine got up and stormed out of the room. Paul hurt too much to do any storm-ing, so he looked Stowicz in the eyes and lied his ass off. "I've told you everything."

Stowicz glared at him angrily while Colleen got up and followed Katherine.

••••

Katherine went out through some French doors onto one of the mansion's patios, stood in the shade and tried to focus her thoughts. The experience in the cemetery was a confusing mess of disjointed memories. Most disgusting of all there had been pleas-ure, even if purely physical and only briefly. She wondered what kind of deviant person she must be that a part of her had enjoyed that.

One of the French doors opened and Colleen stepped out onto the patio. She stood there for a moment saying nothing.

"It kind of . . ." Katherine said. She couldn't overcome her embarrassment at what had happened. "Last night was . . . unsettling."

Colleen let the silence hang for a moment, then said, "You felt some pleasure, didn't you? Though it would have been purely physical."

Katherine couldn't meet Colleen's eyes. "You know what happened?"

"Not really, my dear. But powerful demons always try to seduce with pleasure. They don't truly understand we mortals, don't understand the emotional connection that comes with love. They can give intense physical pleasure on a whim, but not the emo-tional attachment that makes it a truly joyful experience. Normal, healthy mortals like you and Paul are disgusted by it, whereas a thrall is seduced by it, and only wants more."

Katherine couldn't hold it in any longer and unwanted tears streamed down her cheeks. Colleen wrapped her arms around her, and the tears turned to open sobs.

"Don't tell the others," Katherine pleaded.

"No, my dear. Of course not. And Salisteen and I'll make sure those two foolish old men know to let it be."

••••

Just as Colleen left the kitchen one of Salisteen's security *suits* walked in, leaned close to her and whispered something in her ear. Her eyebrows lifted with a look of surprise, and she asked, "You didn't invite him in, did you?"

He frowned at her and said with a touch of irritation in his voice, "Of course not."

She ignored his irritation and said, "If he's willing to give us his complete parole, plainly spoken, then admit him. You know the formula. Bring him to the library, and ask Colleen and Katherine to join us. I believe they're out back."

The suit nodded, turned and left the room. Salisteen turned to McGowan and Stowicz. "Cadilus is here."

Both reacted with a frown. Paul asked, "Who's Cadilus?"

Salisteen said, "High Chancellor to the Seelie Court. An extremely powerful Sidhe mage and warrior. He's Magreth's right-hand man."

Stowicz growled, "I don't like this one bit."

McGowan stood. "None of us do. Let's go see what he wants."

The library was a large room with a large fireplace centered in one wall and a lot of books lining the rest. Subdued lighting gave the room an air of quiet and calm. There were several wingback chairs with small end-tables distributed among them, each with a reading lamp on it. Salisteen took a seat in one of the wingback chairs, much like a queen on her throne, while McGowan and Stowicz stood to one side. Paul picked out a chair farther back in the room and sat down. When Colleen and Katherine entered, Colleen chose a chair next to Salisteen, and Katherine walked over to stand by Paul.

Paul recognized Cadilus immediately as *Pointy-Ears*, the Sidhe who'd abducted him and Katherine off the streets of San Francisco. To Paul, Cadilus looked like a British diplomat. He wore an expensive, conservatively cut, dark, pinstripe suit, white shirt, dark tie. He didn't have a Bowler hat, but he did carry a silver-tipped walking stick. His nose, cheeks and jaw line could only be described as aristocratic, with dark hair that had just the right hint of gray at the temples. A few months ago when Paul had last seen him his ears had been pointed and his eyes slitted vertically like those of a cat. But now both ears and eyes appeared normal, probably due to some glamour he had affected.

When the *suit* escorted him into the library he turned immediately to Colleen and Salisteen. He bowed deeply and said in a refined accent, "Lady Armaugh. Lady Salisteen."

"Lord Cadilus," Salisteen said. "It's always a pleasure to see you. What brings you among us mortals?"

Since Paul was located behind and to one side of Colleen and Salisteen, Cadilus didn't have to turn to look at him. He merely lifted his eyes slightly, pale green eyes that looked at Paul with the intensity of spot lights. Cadilus said to Salisteen, "Why, with four such powerful practitioners gathered in one place . . ." He pointedly turned his head slightly toward McGowan and Stowicz to acknowledge their presence, but his eyes never left Paul. ". . . such a gathering would naturally draw the interest of the Seelie Court."

Salisteen laughed like a schoolgirl flirting with a handsome young man. "I think the interest of the Seelie Court goes far beyond us four."

He smiled and spoke with feigned innocence. "I can't imagine what would eclipse the four of you."

He looked pointedly at Katherine. "Miss McGowan," he said. "It's always a pleasure to set eyes on such a beautiful young woman. And your companion"—he pointedly looked at Paul—"the young wizard."

Cadilus turned his head slightly, as if moving his gaze to Salisteen, but his eyes remained locked on Paul. "Would the young man be responsible for that rather dramatic incident last night?"

McGowan stepped forward. "I am responsible because he is my apprentice, and he was acting under my tutelage."

Stowicz said, "And mine."

Colleen said, "And mine."

Salisteen said, "And mine."

Cadilus continued to stare at Paul as his eyes narrowed. "All of Faerie wonders what danger his presence on the Mortal Plane brings upon us."

McGowan laughed. "That is the conundrum, isn't it? Is he a danger to us all? Or is he here to protect us from a danger to us all? Are we in more danger with him, or without him?"

Cadilus's gaze remained locked on Paul. "Until he learns the proper use of his necromantic abilities, he is a danger to us all."

On impulse Paul stood and walked the few paces necessary to stand beside Colleen and Salisteen. He didn't want to appear to be hiding behind them, as if he needed their protection, though he probably did. "And who will teach me the proper use of my necromantic abilities? You?"

Cadilus's face stiffened with anger, "There has never been a necromancer among the fey."

Paul nodded and grinned unpleasantly. He kept his eyes locked on Cadilus, and for some reason he now saw through the fellow's glamour, saw the pointed ears and the amber irises of his vertically slit pupils. "Exactly. And there hasn't been a necromancer on the Mortal Plane for twelve hundred years. So I guess we're bound to stumble about a bit here. And I wouldn't be surprised if there were a few more dramatic incidents like last night."

Cadilus's eyes narrowed and he stared at Paul for a long moment, then turned to McGowan. "While we do not practice necromancy, we may be able to offer some guidance, perhaps through old texts in our possession."

He waited, but McGowan didn't respond. When it became clear McGowan wasn't going to, Cadilus added, "But there will be a price."

McGowan's lips curled upward ever so faintly, almost a smile, but not quite. But again the old man gave no response.

After a moment of silence, Cadilus turned back to Salisteen, switched the charm of the British diplomat back on and smiled. "By your leave, I must report to my queen. May I go there directly?"

She nodded. "As long as you remain true to your parole."

He bowed deeply, like a courtier of the eighteenth century. "Of course, dear lady."

As he straightened Paul sensed a shift in reality, an odd twist down a spiral track that left him with a slight sense of vertigo. And by the time Cadilus had straightened fully, he was no longer in the room.

Paul asked, "Why do I feel like he and I were just a couple of stray cats hissing at each other?"

Stowicz laughed heartily. "Well put. Yes, he was here to gauge you. And you played that nicely."

"Ya, kid," McGowan added. "You did good."

Salisteen's purse erupted with a chorus of classical music. She opened it, pulled out a cell phone, touched the screen and said, "This is Salisteen."

She listened for a moment, then said, "But I—" Clearly the person at the other end interrupted her.

She listened further, then killed the call and carefully put the cell phone back in her purse. She looked up at McGowan and Stowicz and said, "Those nasty Russians are in town. They just landed at DFW and they're on their way here. And Karpov is livid about last night."

••••

He'd left his car parked in a busy strip mall about a half mile from the school. He had the advantage of a rather ordinary appearance, so as long as he didn't do something to stand out, people didn't really notice him. But he was too gringo to go unnoticed in this neighborhood, so he'd carefully prepared a spell of illusion, a glamour to give him the appearance of an elderly Latino man, old enough that no one would consider him a threat, but not so old as to appear decrepit. This time of year dusk came early, and a comfortably gray evening settled in as he walked down the sidewalk toward the school.

The voice inside him had gone quiescent in anticipation of the kill. He sensed its hunger, though he couldn't share that hunger, not for the little Mexican boy. Only Alice could satisfy his need, so he would take little pleasure from this. The little boy was really just food, sustenance for the voice within him, a means to strengthen it, to sate its needs, to return it to a state of power so it could help him satisfy his one desire: little Alice.

The little Mexican boy took remedial English lessons after school on Tuesday and Thursday afternoons. His parents had high hopes for him, wanted him to go to college, to speak English without an accent, and had the means to pay for a tutor. He considered them to be quite progressive in that respect. But it meant the little boy couldn't take the bus home and must wait for his father to get off work and pick him up. And at this time of year that meant he waited on the sidewalk in front of the school, in the gray dusk of early evening. Sometimes he waited alone. Perfect!

He'd tried this two nights ago Tuesday evening, but the boy hadn't been alone. There'd been a couple of classmates standing on the sidewalk with the young fellow. So he'd merely strolled on past the boy, though the boy had nodded politely and said, "Good evening, sir." Indeed, very polite.

Tonight, as he turned the corner a block away from the school, he saw clearly that the boy waited alone. As he strolled slowly toward the young fellow he reached into his pocket and retrieved the small charm he'd prepared. A complex charm, it had taken hours to concoct, and when activated would release a compulsion spell. He wouldn't have to take any overt action, wouldn't have to drag the boy kicking and screaming to his car. The child would merely feel curious about the old gentleman that passed him in the night, would think about it for a few moments, and when the old fellow was about a half block away, would decide to satisfy that curiosity and follow the old man, but at a discrete distance. And later, if someone chose to inquire about the boy's last minutes alive, and if anyone happened to have noticed, they'd tell how the boy had walked away from the school alone.

He was only a dozen paces from him when the boy looked his way and smiled. He smiled back, and as he approached him he lifted his hand to his mouth, concealing the charm within it. When he reached the boy he coughed into his hand as an excuse to spit on the charm, then he faked a stumble and lunged feebly at the boy. Instinctively, and politely, the boy reached out to help the old man, and at that moment he pressed the activated charm against the skin of the boy's hand.

The charm exploded with an excruciating flash, knocking him to the ground, his hand and arm throbbing painfully. The little boy staggered but didn't fall, put a hand to his forehead and swayed slightly as if stunned. Standing over the older man he looked down and said, "What happened? Are you hurt?"

"Yes," the voice within him said. "I'm hurt. Help me."

No, he wanted to scream, but the voice had complete control of him now. As the boy leaned down toward him he opened his mouth. *No, there's something wrong, don't.*

I must feed, the voice said within him, and the oily black cloud emerged from his mouth, rose up and enveloped the boy.

The boy screamed, staggered, fell and convulsed spasmodically on the sidewalk.

The voice, screaming in pain, wanted the little boy, wanted to try again, but it was weakened and he regained control of his body. He staggered to his feet, staggered up the street away from the scene. Surely someone had heard the boy's scream and would take notice. He needed to get away, but it was imperative he not draw further attention to himself, not run, not rush. His arm hurt terribly, and the voice within him groaned in pain.

He made it to the end of the block, turned and walked out of sight of the school. By the time he reached his car in the strip-mall parking lot, he heard the scream of a siren in the distance. His right arm was useless, so he dug his keys out of his right pocket with his left hand. He sat down behind the wheel, reached across with his left hand to turn the key and start the engine. He backed out of the parking place slowly, drove across the parking lot and out onto the street, careful not to rush, not to speed. He'd only driven a short distance when the flashing lights of an ambulance passed him going the other way.

••••

"Valter," Karpov snarled as he stormed into Salisteen's library. "Vhat in hell are you doing?"

They had agreed to meet Karpov as they'd met Cadilus, though Paul remained standing this time. Karpov ignored the rest of them as he marched up to McGowan. The old man grinned at him and said, "Why, Vasily, just helping Paul practice a little necromancy."

"But what happened? Everyone on the continent must have felt it."

McGowan shook his head dismissively. "Just a little learning experience, Vasily."

Boris and Joe Stalin walked into the room warily. Behind them walked a fellow with blonde hair and Nordic good looks, about Paul's height. With senses Paul had only recently begun to develop, the fellow was clearly a practitioner, a strong one. And he didn't have the thuggish appearance of Karpov's usual bootlickers.

Katherine, standing beside Paul, tensed at the sight of the fellow. He glanced her way and watched her eyes narrow angrily, so he leaned close to her and whispered, "Who's the Nordic god?"

She turned to Paul and hissed angrily, "My ex. Eric Reichart. And he's not that good looking, not when you get to know him."

Mr. Nordic god hesitated when he spotted Katherine, then turned and crossed the room toward her, stopped only when he stood so close to her it was down-right intimate. "Katherine," he said, his voice sensual, his eyes looking her up and down, pausing briefly on her breasts as he obviously stripped her naked in his mind and look-fucked her. "As always, you look beautiful."

She lifted a hand casually, placed a fingertip on his chest and pushed him back a step. It was clear he would have resisted had the two of them been alone, but he dare not in the presence of them all. "And as always," she said scornfully, glancing at Karpov and his thugs, "you've found some friends that share your principles."

Paul didn't say anything, but it gave him a little satisfaction to see her open dislike of the fellow.

Reichart smiled, and managed to dismiss her completely with nothing more than that. "My colleagues offer certain advantages."

"Like money," Katherine said. "You were always in need of that."

His eyes narrowed angrily. "I never lived beyond my means."

She smiled at him unpleasantly. "Wrong, you never lived beyond *my* means, but always well beyond your own." She looked again at Karpov. "I suppose that's what's driving your ethical standards now."

He ignored her, gave Paul a nasty look, then turned away from them and walked over to join Boris and Joe.

Karpov and McGowan had been arguing the whole time, clearly hadn't noticed the little confrontation between Katherine and Reichart. Karpov's voice was strained, elevated and angry. "Ve have to have rules, Valter."

McGowan stood a head taller than Karpov, and grinning, looking down on the Russian, he responded calmly. "We have enough rules, Vasily."

McGowan's calm, almost humorous, response irritated Karpov even further. "Ve make a committee. Ve plan a schedule for his training. Ve monitor it carefully."

"And who would be on this committee?"

Karpov rubbed his chin, pretended to think on the matter carefully, when all there knew he'd thought this through long ago. "Why . . . I suppose three or four senior practitioners. Ve should have no trouble finding willing tutors."

McGowan nodded, and slowly turned his head to look at Salisteen, drawing everyone's eyes with him, including Karpov's. Then he pointedly shifted his gaze to Colleen, paused for a moment, then moved to Stowicz. He kept his eyes on Stowicz as he said, "I guess we already have such a committee. A de-facto one, but nevertheless one comprised of four of the most senior practitioners alive today."

Karpov started and stepped back a pace, glancing angrily about the room, only then realizing the corner into which he'd boxed himself.

McGowan glanced over Karpov's shoulder, and for the first time spotted Reichart. "What's he doing here?" Clearly, the old man didn't like Katherine's ex.

Reichart stiffened, stood erect like a military cadet standing at attention and looked at McGowan warily. Karpov retreated from his earlier argument, crossed the room and put a kindly hand on Reichart's shoulder. "Eric is my friend. He's kindly offered to assist me in certain matters."

He spun back to McGowan. "Ve need to know what you are planning next."

Apparently, raising the dead was serious enough, and dangerous enough, that McGowan couldn't refuse to provide at least some explanation, though he did a masterful job of keeping it to a minimum. He briefed them on the demon kills and what they'd discovered so far and what they hoped to do.

When he finished Karpov looked at Paul, his eyes narrow and pinched. "You sure he's not responsible for this demon?"

"Ya," Joe Stalin growled. "Fucker's half demon anyway."

Salisteen stood angrily and pointed a finger at Joe. "You don't use that kind of language in my house."

Karpov swung out with a wide, roundhouse swing and slapped Joe in the face. "Apologize, you idiot."

Joe, his eyes downcast, mumbled a few polite words.

Stowicz said, "To answer your question, Vasily, yes, we're sure. All four of us."

Colleen and McGowan nodded their agreement. Salisteen stood and said pointedly, "Exactly. Now, if you'll excuse us, my chief of security can probably recommend a good hotel where you and your colleagues can find accommodations."

9

The Alice Connection

PAUL CLIMBED OUT of the car: another cemetery, another gravesite, another suspected demon kill. At least it was daylight, no spilling his own blood, no beheading a chicken, no midnight ritual. He didn't even know the name of the cemetery or its location; just somewhere in the greater Dallas/Fort Worth area. At least he didn't have to put up with the Russians breathing down his neck at all hours of the day.

Somewhere overhead a hawk cried, and the sound of its scream sent a shiver up Paul's spine. *Just a hawk*, he thought. He'd grown jumpy after recent events, now saw spooks and ghosties behind every bush. "Just a hawk," he said aloud, inwardly scolding himself for being so jumpy.

As he helped Katherine out of the car, she asked, "What did you say?"

"Nothing," he said. "Just jumpy."

"Me too," she said as she straightened her skirt. She'd gone back to wearing an expensive business suit, skirt cut just above the knees, and high heels. The suit was dark gray, with pin stripes, and the skirt just a bit tight, which Paul rather liked. She added, "I'm getting downright paranoid."

"Paranoid?" Paul asked, pulling his eyes away from her. "What did you say?"

McGowan growled, "He didn't hear a word you said. He was too busy staring at your ass again."

Colleen snapped, "Shut up, old man."

Katherine leaned in close to Paul and whispered just loud enough for her father to hear, "You have my permission to stare all you want."

It was just the four of them, plus one of Salisteen's chauffeurs. Ramirez had a list of suspected demon kills, and they all agreed having Paul raise all of them, only to find that some had died of more mundane causes, would be an exhausting and time consuming waste of his arcane energies. It was Colleen who came up with an alternative, a spell far less complicated and much easier to perform, and one unlikely to resurrect some shadowy monster if the child had been killed by a demon. McGowan and Stowicz added a variation on Colleen's idea that allowed any one of them to perform the ritual, though with a little practice Paul could perform it rather easily, while the rest of them needed to put some effort into it. And that clearly fueled Stowicz's suspicious attitude toward Paul.

They'd split up into three groups and were canvassing Ramirez's possible demon kills one-by-one. So far the four of them had confirmed that two were victims of this demon, and three not. As yet, they hadn't heard anything from Salisteen, Stowicz, Ramirez and the Russians about their results. Paul would have to go back to the real kills later and purge the demon from the children's souls. Oddly enough, when he thought of Cloe and how it could have been her soul haunted by such a monster, he rather enjoyed the idea of kicking some demon ass, as long as the demon didn't do any kicking of Paul's ass.

After traipsing through a field of gravestones they found their suspected victim. It was McGowan and Colleen's turn to cast the spell while Katherine and Paul looked on. McGowan, with Colleen standing over him, crouched down beside the young girl's grave and began tracing a complex rune. Paul was only just beginning to understand the difference between rune-based spells, ley line power, earth power, elementals, and his unique physical magic—he had a lot to learn. The spell McGowan cast would tell him if the young girl's soul had departed cleanly, or if it remained behind in some sort of torment, and if so, he'd get a strong sense of the demon's presence if that was the cause.

The hawk screeched again, and again it sent a shiver up Paul's spine. It sounded sorrowful, as if it mourned something. Paul shook his head to clear it, knew he was letting his imagination get away from him.

McGowan straightened and shook his head. "This one's clean. That's the last on our list. Let's head back to Salisteen's."

McGowan and Colleen led the way, ambling between gravestones toward the car, with Katherine following and Paul last in line. The hawk cried again and he looked up, spotted it circling high overhead, descending slowly toward them. Perhaps it had spotted some prey among the gravestones. Paul watched it descend with growing curiosity, for it did seem to be descending toward them, and he would have thought a wild animal should be more fearful of humans.

It cried out again, an eerie sound, then pulled in its wings and plummeted toward him in a dive. He hesitated while the others continued on; they were apparently oblivious to the animal plunging toward him. He tensed, ready to dive to one side to avoid the hawk's talons. But at the last instant the hawk flared its wings, pulled up a few feet off the ground, killed its speed, and transformed into a tall humanoid shape obscured by shadows that fluttered about her maddeningly. Clearly female, she faced Paul squarely from about ten paces with a strung bow in her left hand and a shadowy broadsword in her right. Then slowly the darkness that enveloped her dissipated, and one-by-one her features cleared.

                                    J. L. Doty

Before him stood a woman easily seven feet tall, with pale golden hair twisted into dreadlocks that fluttered slightly as if touched by a light breeze, though the air remained still. She walked toward Paul, one cautious, careful step at a time, stopped close enough that he saw the color of her eyes shifting continuously. Those eyes seemed to devour him, to hold him helplessly chained to the spot, and he could not have moved to defend himself if she chose to behead him then and there with that sword.

She opened her mouth, clearly found it difficult to speak, and when her lips moved, her voice was no more than a haunted whisper on the wind. "They want your death, mortal."

Deep inside her eyes he saw pain and torment. But it was divided and isolated into several hot sparks dancing within her spirit, as if she were haunted by a multitude of souls.

"There are many of you," Paul said, "aren't there? Many souls in one body."

She flinched, and the shadows dancing about her suddenly stilled. "Ah, mortal, your vision is a fearful thing. Beware, lest it betray you."

Paul recalled her first words and asked, "Who wants my death?"

She smiled and cocked her head slightly to one side, and as a wind that didn't exist fluttered her dreadlocks he noticed she had pointed ears. "Those who rightly fear you . . . but wrongly fear your destiny, your purpose. They think they have bargained for your death. And a bargain is a bargain, though they know not the true nature of their contracts."

She turned away from him, turned her back on him with insulting indifference, as if to say she had nothing to fear from him. She took two steps then paused and looked back. "Remember this, mortal. No one who is truly mortal can survive *les flèche du coeur*—no one truly mortal."

Then she turned away from him again, took two more steps, broke into a run, leapt into the air and spread her arms, transformed into the hawk, and rose into the sky on the beat of powerful wings.

Somehow Paul now walked only a few feet behind Katherine, walking toward the car as if he'd never stopped, as if the strange hawk had not come out of the sky and transformed into an even stranger woman.

••••

As the limo rolled out of the cemetery Paul kept replaying in his mind the strange scene with the strange dreadlocked woman.

"You seem preoccupied," Katherine said.

Paul looked at her and asked, "Did that hawk's cry sound strange to you?"

There must have been something in the tone of Paul's voice, for McGowan and Colleen, who'd been engaged in a conversation of their own, suddenly went silent and looked at Paul carefully. Katherine frowned and said, "I don't recall hearing a hawk cry out."

Colleen said, "Nor I," and McGowan shook his head silently.

There was no question in Paul's mind that he should tell them what had happened. "I think I just hallucinated something really bizarre." He told them about the hawkwoman, carefully tried to describe the incident in detail. When he began Katherine, Colleen and McGowan had looked at him with open curiosity, but by the time he'd finished all three frowned deeply.

Colleen looked at McGowan and asked, "*Black fey?*"

He shrugged uncertainly. "Could be, but I can't really say for sure. I've never met one."

Paul asked, "What's *black fey?*"

Colleen shook her head and her frown deepened as she spoke. "We don't know much about them. They're part of the non-aligned fey, but they're quite elusive." She looked pointedly at Paul. "And you say you sensed several souls in this one?"

Colleen and McGowan seemed almost frightened by his story. "I really don't know what I sensed."

"Fey don't have souls," Colleen said. "But then again, we know so little about the *black*, anything is possible."

McGowan's cell phone interrupted them, chiming softly. He looked at the phone's display and said, "It's Salisteen."

He touched the screen, put it to his ear and said, "Yes."

He listened intently for several seconds, then said, "Good. We'll see you there."

He put the cell phone in his pocket. "There's been another demon attack. But this time a little boy—and he survived. Apparently his grandmother's a witch, and she had him warded with some decent protective spells, though he's in pretty bad shape. Salisteen's already told our driver to head for the hospital. We'll meet her there."

••••

Children's Medical Center was a sprawling affair, part of a large complex of hospitals that occupied several city blocks on the northwest side of Dallas. Ramirez met them in the lobby at the main entrance and escorted them into an elevator. As the lift started up Ramirez said, "He's in the ICU, in a coma. No question it was a demon attack. I just don't understand why a boy this time. I hope to God we're not dealing with two demons."

As the elevator doors opened in the ICU they spotted Salisteen and Stowicz huddled with a tall fellow in a white lab coat with a stethoscope around his neck. Salisteen saw them and waved them over. She introduced the fellow in the lab coat as Dr. Sanders, then she led them down the hall away from the nurse's station, and in a soft voice said, "Dr. Sanders is a practitioner so you can speak openly with him."

She introduced each of them, and when she introduced Paul, Sander's eyes narrowed, and with a strong Texas accent he said, "You're the necromancer. I hope you know what you're doing."

Paul didn't like the challenge in his voice. "As a matter of fact, I don't."

Salisteen grimaced and said to Sanders, "He's got a point, Frank. None of us can really tell him how to be a proper necromancer. Why don't you bring everyone up to speed?"

Sanders said, "The boy's mother died some years ago so his father and grandmother are raising him. The father's not a practitioner, though he's aware we exist. And he's really skittish about this."

Salisteen said, "From what I can tell the wards are still protecting the boy. But there's some primitive piece of the demon that's trying to break them down, while the grandmother keeps reinforcing them. She's a local *curandera*, a healer and shaman. And she's apparently pretty good, but she's out of her depth here, and she knows it."

With the father so jumpy, Sanders wanted everyone but Paul, Salisteen and Ramirez to wait out in the hall, but Katherine insisted, "I'm in on this too."

Sanders started to object, but Salisteen put a hand on his arm and said softly, "Frank, for some reason none of us understand, Katherine and Paul are a team in these matters. It's one of those things where they're stronger together than the sum of the parts."

Sanders led them down the hall to a large room filled with a lot of computers and other equipment. At one end of the room a nurse sat behind some sort of central monitoring station. Had it not been for all the equipment, the room was large enough to hold a dozen beds. As it was there were two occupied beds present, with empty spaces for only another four.

The nurse at the monitoring station was an attractive, middle-aged woman with light-brown hair cut in a short bob. Sanders stopped to speak with her. "Slow day, eh Pam?"

She shrugged and rolled her eyes. "Just wait till rush hour."

"Ya. How's the Garza boy?"

"Unchanged. Stable, no need for life support. Weird, though."

"How so?"

She sat up a little straighter to look over the top of the computer monitors. "No reason for that coma. None at all."

"Ya, that's a stumper." Sanders nodded to Paul and Katherine. "I brought a couple of colleagues of mine in to consult. They're from out of state, just lucky they happened to be here."

Pam looked at Paul and Katherine, clearly appraising them. Paul felt self-consciously that he didn't look much like a doctor, whatever a doctor was supposed to look like in her eyes. She nodded and looked back at Sanders. "If he remains stable, Admin will want him moved out of the ICU pretty soon."

Sanders shook his head. "I can't really argue with them on that. Say hi to the husband for me."

"Sure nuf."

As Sanders led them away from Pam he lowered his voice and said, "She's not a practitioner, so we have to be careful here."

He led them to one of the beds in the far corner, beside which stood a tall, distinguished fellow in an expensive business suit. Sanders introduced him. "This is Mr. Garza." Sanders turned to Paul and Katherine. "These are some colleagues of mine."

Garza asked, "More doctors?" He had a slight Latino accent.

Sanders simply said, "No."

Garza's eyes narrowed, he looked at Paul angrily and growled a question. "Brujo?"

A tiny, little, old woman stepped around Garza; his bulk had concealed her. She stood only a little over four feet tall, was thin as a rail, dressed in slacks and a sports coat that, like Garza's suit, appeared expensive. "Raphael," she said calmly, putting a hand on his arm. She said something in Spanish Paul couldn't follow.

Garza turned to her respectfully, but angrily, and they argued in Spanish, him cold and angry, her calm and reassuring. Paul heard the word *brujo* again, but always accompanied by another word: *brujo blanca* or *brujo negra.*

Ramirez leaned close to Paul's ear and said, "They're arguing about whether you're a white or a black witch. She says you have characteristics in your aura that are black, but she's confident you're a white witch. But he's not to worry because she's watching you closely."

Garza finally capitulated. Then they both stepped aside and turned to face the occupant of the bed. It was the first time Paul had looked at the boy, and while bedsheets covered most of him, a swirling, oily, black cloud obscured his features.

Paul stepped forward to stand beside the boy. Katherine stepped to the other side of the bed and stood facing Paul. "What do you see?" he asked.

"Just a boy," she said, looking at Paul with a question in her eyes.

Paul remembered that, unlike him, she was trained enough to turn her *sight* on and off at will. "Use your *sight.*"

She nodded, looked down at the boy and her nose wrinkled as she concentrated. Then her eyes widened with terror, and she turned away, gagging and choking, gulping to hold down her lunch. The old woman walked up to her, put an arm around her shoulders and said, "Si. Si."

Katherine got her gag response under control, turned back to Paul. "Conklin, you got to warn me about these things."

The old woman spoke English with a thick accent. "It ees terrible, yes?"

Paul said, "Yes."

Movement in the corner of his eye drew his attention. He saw through large, glass panes that a small group had gathered in the hall, among them a pretty, young girl with dark Latino features dressed in a pink pinafore over a light-blue dress, her hair in pigtails. A shiver crawled up Paul's spine as he asked, "Who's that?"

Garza answered him, "A neighborhood friend of David's. They go to school together, ride the bus together."

"Is her name Alice?"

"No. Maria."

Katherine asked, "What is it, Conklin?"

Paul reached across the bed and grabbed Katherine by the arm, desperately trying to recall the events in the graveyard. "In the graveyard, you saw Tandy, yes?"

"Yes, I did."

"What was she wearing?"

She frowned and looked at him doubtfully. "Um. Let me think." She put a hand to her forehead, clearly struggling with the memory. "A pinafore . . . I think it was grayish . . . over a white dress . . . and knee-high socks."

Paul demanded, "And her hair?"

"In pigtails."

Ramirez looked at Maria standing in the hall, then back at Paul. "What are you saying, Conklin?"

Paul closed his eyes, trying to remember the scene in the morgue. "Monica, when she came to me in the morgue; she wore a gray pinafore over a pale-blue dress, with white knee-high stockings and shiny black shoes. And her hair was in pigtails."

Standing around the bed, it was almost comic watching all of them turn their heads to look at Maria, than back to Paul, then back to Maria. Katherine said, "But none of them are named Alice."

"Shit," Ramirez growled. "Shit. That's it. Alice in fucking Wonderland."

Salisteen said, "Watch your tongue, young man."

••••

Anogh had formally requested a private audience with his queen, and because of that formality he wore the ceremonial armor of the Summer Knight. She received him in one of her private, though by no means small, audience chambers. The Seelie Court would be abuzz with gossip and speculation about Anogh's purpose, but they'd know the truth of it soon enough.

Cadilus admitted him to the chamber. Anogh approached Magreth carefully, the winged helm of his armor clutched beneath his left arm. At the prescribed seven paces he dropped to one knee and bowed his head. "My queen."

She answered him with silence, and looking at the carpet on the floor he heard Cadilus withdraw, heard the door close, and heard Magreth breathing.

"You may rise, Sir Knight."

He rose slowly, lifted his chin at the same time and looked her in the eyes. The ancient Sidhe spirits fluttered erratically about her head, perhaps a sign of her own apprehension at such a meeting.

"We have not seen you at court of late, Sir Knight," she said, extending her hand.

He stepped forward slowly, bent deeply at the waist, took her hand in his and kissed the large ruby ring that signified the power of the Summer Court.

"Do the duties of your office weigh so heavily upon you that you cannot grace us with your presence more often?"

"Please forgive me, Your Majesty. I have been preoccupied of late."

She frowned, tilted her head slightly and said, "What dire circumstance occupies your thoughts so?"

"Not dire, Your Majesty, but a circumstance of joy and happiness."

Her eyebrows lifted in mock surprise. "Joy and happiness?"

"Yes, Your Majesty. I have found love. True love."

She smiled and the spirits hovering about her head calmed a bit. "Love? It is rare that we Sidhe find the strings of our hearts pulled by love, and so it is a thing to cherish, truly a thing of joy and happiness. Now that I know what to look for I see it in your eyes. But am I to guess at the nature of this audience?"

"I will be wed, Your Majesty, and I seek your blessing."

"You seek my blessing, but not my permission?"

He purposefully avoided a direct answer to that question. "I will be wed, Your Majesty, and I do seek your blessing."

The spirits had become agitated again. "And to whom will you be wed?"

"Taal'mara, the Winter Princess."

Magreth didn't move, didn't flinch or react in any way. She could have been made of stone for all the life she displayed. But Anogh caught a glint deep in her eyes, a glint that sharpened and grew, until bright red flames flared in their depths. "And Ag has sanctioned this?"

"Yes, Your Majesty."

She stood silent for several heartbeats, then said, "Very well, you have my blessing. But you are a fool."

. . . *Yes*, Anogh thought, staring at the portrait of the long dead Taal'mara, he had been a fool those many centuries ago. A complete and utter fool.

••••

Since little David Garza was stable, with no need for life support, his grandmother insisted they bring him home, even though he remained comatose. She argued that since the hospital could do nothing for him, they could take better care of him there. Ramirez said her hidden agenda was to get him to a more private place so the *brujo* could help him without mundane eyes looking on.

The Garza's had a nice, large house in a middle-class Latino neighborhood on the outskirts of Dallas. Paul was a bit embarrassed when they descended on the place en masse: the four older practitioners, Ramirez, Karpov and his thugs, and him and Katherine. Everyone wanted to be in on it, and a heated argument erupted between the older practitioners and Raphael.

Paul stayed out of it, walked to the far end of the room and leaned against a wall. Katherine saw him there and joined him.

"This is ridiculous," she said.

"Ya. I've a mind to tell them all to go to hell."

Ramirez, standing near the group of older practitioners, his shoulders slumped in frustration, looked toward Paul and Katherine. Paul caught his eye, and nodded. Ramirez got the hint and walked over to them. Paul nodded toward Mrs. Garza, who stood in the entrance to a hallway, arms folded resolutely as if to make it clear no one would get past her unless she allowed them.

"The kid's grandmother," Paul said. "Seems like a pretty strong lady. Like maybe she won't take any shit."

Ramirez eyed Paul, evaluating him as if it were the first time he'd really considered him. But all he said was, "And."

"Can you translate for me?"

The rest of them didn't notice Paul, Katherine and Ramirez approach Mrs. Garza.

Ramirez spoke with her briefly in hushed tones, then asked Paul, "What did you want to say to her?"

"Tell her I'm new at this, but Katherine and I will do everything we can to help her grandson."

As Ramirez spoke to her in Spanish, she eyed Paul carefully, though there appeared to be no hostility in the look. Paul continued, "Tell her we need the help of the tall older man with gray hair and the older hippy woman, but no one else."

Katherine said, "That won't fly, Conklin. Karpov will raise holy hell."

Paul grimaced. "There's no way I'm taking Karpov or any of his thugs with us."

Katherine looked back toward the group of older practitioners still arguing, and her eyes narrowed thoughtfully. "Let's bring Eric as Karpov's representative. That should satisfy Karpov, and I can handle Eric."

"You're sure?"

She nodded, grinned unpleasantly and said, "Quite."

Ramirez and the old woman spoke back and forth in Spanish several times. Then Ramirez turned to Paul and said, "She has one question. She wants to know if you're scared."

Paul looked the old woman in the eyes and said, "Scared shitless."

Apparently that didn't need any translation. She smiled, lifted an arm and politely brushed the three of them aside so she had a clear line to the group arguing in the middle of her living room. "Silenciar," she barked loudly, using the *voice*, and that one word clawed its way up Paul's spine.

In Spanish she spoke to Raphael like a general issuing commands to a subordinate. She finished by pointing at Paul and saying something that included the word *brujo*.

Raphael pointed at Colleen, McGowan and Reichart and said, "You, you and you will join the young lady and the brujo. And the brujo is in complete charge. He says you do something—you do it. There'll be no more discussion."

That started an uproar. Mrs. Garza gave it a few seconds, then repeated her earlier performance with the *voice*. "Silenciar."

In the silence that followed she looked at Paul expectantly, so he spoke calmly. "Since I'm the one who has to do this, and since none of you can really help me, we're doing this my way."

Ramirez looked at Paul, his lips slowly curled upward into a smile, and he said, with a Texas accent about three shades thicker than Paul had heard before, "Ya know, Conklin, I think I like working with you."

10

Immortality Truncated

KATHERINE WAS RATHER pleased Mrs. Garza took forceful control of the situation. The tiny little woman intimidated even Karpov. He groused a bit about not being included, but she slashed a hand through the air like a knife. He got the message and shut up.

Raphael remained at the entrance to the hall to the back of the house. He stood there like a sentinel as the old woman led the five of them to the boy's bedroom. Little David lay on his bed with his arms at his sides, a blanket up to his chin. Katherine had to look closely to see his chest rise and fall with each shallow breath.

Her father and Colleen were there more as advisors, ready to step in and help if they could. Katherine and Paul stood on one side of the little boy's bed, Eric and Mrs. Garza on the other, McGowan and Colleen behind them.

Katherine carefully opened her *sight*. This time she was prepared for the oily, smoky cloud that enveloped the little boy, though beneath it she saw the boy's aura, protected and, as yet, untainted by the monster. "His aura is still clean," she said. "It hasn't gotten past her wards."

Mrs. Garza said, "Si."

Paul said, "I'm not sure what to do."

Eric sneered. "It's just a demon. I've banished plenty of them before. If you don't have the guts to do it, I will."

He leaned down to the boy's still form, but Paul reached out and put a hand between him and the boy. "Stand down, Reichart. You're just an observer here."

Mrs. Garza looked back and forth between Paul and Eric, then said in struggling English. "Not amigos."

Eric looked down on her and growled, "No, we're not amigos."

Mrs. Garza's eyes narrowed, she reached out with her arm in a slow, sweeping gesture, and made Eric take a step back from the bed. "You stay," she said.

That clearly angered Eric. "Listen, old woman, I'm the best chance you've—"

McGowan stepped forward and said, "Reichart, shut up."

Eric stood there seething. He'd always bulled ahead arrogantly, unprepared and shooting from the hip, confident he could handle any situation. More often than not he got in trouble and needed someone to bail him out. More often than not, it had been Katherine.

Paul said, "Let's try that spell we prepared."

Katherine had worked out a variation on a spell used to exorcise spirits that possessed a soul. It was meant to work on a spirit haunting a soul, not a demon, so Katherine, with help from her father and Colleen, had modified it. "Remember," she said, "it's untried, untested."

Paul retrieved a small pair of scissors from his pocket. They all agreed he was the only one among them who could touch the oily darkness surrounding young David and have a chance of coming away from it unscathed. He bent carefully over the boy and lifted a lock of his hair. The unclean darkness climbed up his wrist, but stopped as if something prevented it from going further. Paul gagged, and Katherine thought he might blow lunch all over the floor. But he managed to control his reflexes as he held the scissors out and looked to Mrs. Garza for permission. She understood such spells and nodded.

Paul snipped a small lock of the boy's hair and it came away without any of the corruption attached to it. He reached into his pocket and retrieved the charm they'd prepared, a small, silver trinket in the shape of a pentagram. Demons didn't like silver, and the pentagram was a powerful symbol. Katherine and he had spent an hour weaving runes about it, symbols of purity and joy.

Paul tied the lock of hair about the trinket in the shape of a figure eight lying on its side, the symbol for infinity. Then he looked at Katherine, a question, almost a plea, in his eyes.

She shrugged and said, "Are you as scared as me?"

"What do you think?" he said. He lifted the charm to his lips and spit on it, then carefully laid it on David's chest.

Katherine wasn't prepared for what happened, which was nothing. Just plain nothing. No arcane power filled the room. The demon essence surrounding the little boy didn't cry out in agony, or disappear or react in any way. Nothing.

"Gramma! Gramma!"

Katherine heard the words only in her soul. They were not words spoken by a mortal mouth, but they did sound like the voice of a young boy.

Mrs. Garza looked down at her side, and Katherine sensed something there, something invisible to her eyes and other senses. "David," the old woman said, and she knelt, wrapping her arms around something.

Paul gasped. "Do you see him? It's young David, or at least his spirit."

Katherine said, "I don't see it, but I sense something."

Paul walked around the bed to stand beside Mrs. Garza. Katherine followed him, watched him look in awe at something beside the old woman.

"Oh, for Christ's sake!" Eric snarled.

Katherine spun back toward him, saw him standing over the bed. He lifted a hand to his mouth, spit into it, reached out, and as Katherine shouted, "No," he dropped a charm into the oily corruption on David's chest. With her *sight* still active Katherine saw a line of arcane energies connecting his hand to the charm like a tether. Unaware of it, he turned his head toward her. "Someone had to do this right."

He wasn't yet conscious of the line connecting him to the charm, but Katherine watched the dark essence of the demon crawl slowly up that line toward his hand. When it had tried to climb up Paul's arm something had stopped it, but that didn't happen now with Eric. When it reached his hand, only then did he sense it, and by the time he lifted his hand to his face and opened his *sight*, it had crawled up his arm to his elbow.

"Get it off me," he shouted. "No! No! Get it off me."

One of the leprechauns popped into existence next to Mrs. Garza, and the other appeared at David's bedside. Katherine felt a sudden weight in her left hand, looked down to find it holding the sheathed sword. From past experience that meant something really bad was about to happen.

Reichart, pleading and sobbing like a child, fell to his knees as the corruption slowly crawled off of little David, clawed its way along the tether of arcane energies to Reichart's hand, then up his arm, down his chest and around his head. It completely engulfed him, leaving young David cleansed and free of the taint.

Eric opened his mouth to scream, but the black taint wrapped about him disappeared into him. Then he laughed maniacally, and when Katherine looked at him he looked back at her through blood-red goat-slitted eyes.

••••

Paul knelt down beside Mrs. Garza as she caressed the specter of her grandson, hoping this didn't mean the boy was dead. And then Katherine shouted, "No."

He spun toward her, then spun to follow her gaze to Reichart, who was wholly engulfed in the black corruption. Reichart dropped to his knees, threw his head back and wailed like a wounded animal. Then, with a whoosh, the wisps of oily black smoke disappeared up his nose, down his throat, into his eyes and ears, and right up his ass.

Reichart's wails ceased, he looked at Katherine with blood-red goat-slitted eyes, then he looked at his hands and laughed maniacally. He stood, turned to the Garza boy laying in his bed, and bent over him.

Jim'Jiminie, standing next to Mrs. Garza, shouted, "I'll protect the woman."

Boo'Diddle, standing at David's bedside, shouted, "Stop Reichart."

Paul shot to his feet and charged, hit Reichart with a shoulder tackle and they both tumbled across the bed to the other side. They hit the floor in a tangled mess of arms and legs. Paul tried to struggle to his feet, but with inhuman speed and strength, Reichart stood, wrapped his hands about Paul's throat and lifted him to his feet. Then he lifted him off his feet and slammed him against the wall.

Holding Paul with his feet a good six inches off the floor, Reichart leaned in close to him and snarled, "You think you can fuck with me, mortal." Reichart's breath smelled of sewage and decay.

Over Reichart's shoulder Paul saw Katherine scramble around the bed, the sheathed sword held out. "Paul," she screamed. "Use this. I can't. I'm not the wielder."

Reichart snarled, slammed Paul's head against the wall, and squeezed down on his throat with crushing force. Strange little motes of unconsciousness danced before his eyes as Katherine slammed into Reichart's back with a shoulder block of her own. She bounced off him like she'd tried to run into a brick wall. Dazed, she stood there for a moment.

Reichart let go of Paul's throat with one hand, spun and backhanded her. She went down hard, and Reichart returned to crushing Paul's throat. The view over Reichart's shoulder grew distant and far away. Mrs. Garza and Jim'Jiminie crossed the room purposefully and helped Katherine struggle to her feet. She couldn't stand on her own and needed help from Mrs. Garza, while Jim'Jiminie supported them both. Katherine staggered like a drunk, a stream of blood dripping from her nose and down her chin, a wild, crazed look in her eyes, her hair in disarray. She lifted the sheathed sword in front of her to look at it dazedly.

Paul looked into Reichart's demon eyes, looked into their depths, saw the scared little boy that was Eric Reichart trying to hide from his own terror, saw the remnant of the demon chasing him through the corridors of his soul, actually felt sorry for the asshole. Operating purely on instinct, Paul called after the demon with an arcane shout, "Pick on someone your own size, shithead."

The demon turned its eyes back to Paul, and Paul broke eye contact with it just in time to see Katherine shake her head, trying to clear her thoughts. She looked at Paul, then at Reichart, then growled, "Fuck it."

Mrs. Garza helped her lift the sheathed sword over her right shoulder, holding it in both hands like a battering ram, the hilt aimed at the back of Reichart's head. Then the two of them charged forward with the leprechaun in their wake. At the last instant Katherine screamed, "You ass hole," and slammed the hilt into Reichart's head.

••••

When Paul activated the spell they'd worked out, old man McGowan sensed the presence enter the room. He couldn't see it, but apparently Paul and Mrs. Garza could. Mrs. Garza knelt, appeared to be caressing something.

Beside him, Colleen said, "Something's about to happen. I can feel it."

Paul walked around the bed and approached Mrs. Garza carefully. He knelt beside her, and only when Katherine screamed did McGowan realize they'd forgotten about that shit Reichart. McGowan looked Reichart's way just in time to see him activate his spell and drop it on the boy's chest. And in that instant they all disappeared: Reichart, Paul, Katherine and Mrs. Garza.

"What just happened?" Colleen demanded.

McGowan shook his head in bewilderment. "I think the shit just hit the fan."

They both advanced carefully toward the boy's bed, but they'd only taken a few steps when a blinding flash filled the room. McGowan was left with an image burned on his retina of Reichart holding Paul by his throat with his feet off the ground, Paul's face turning blue as Reichart crushed the life out of him, Katherine and Mrs. Garza behind Reichart holding something over Katherine's shoulder, something that had made contact with the back of Reichart's head, and it was from the point of that contact that the flash had emanated.

The flash had blinded them, and McGowan and Colleen could only make out gross details for several seconds. Then everyone else rushed into the room and pandemonium erupted in shouts and curses as they tried to sort things out.

••••

Paul smelled Katherine's perfume, and he realized he lay on the floor with her in his arms, his face buried in her hair. In the background he heard a lot of shouting. He whispered, "I'm getting tired of getting beat up like this."

She didn't respond, probably unconscious, so he added, "Though I guess I don't mind waking up with you in my arms."

"I heard that, Conklin, you lecher." Her voice was thick and muzzy. She moved a little, though she didn't seem in any hurry to escape his arms. "You better not have ruined more shoes."

Someone said, "Let's make sure they're not seriously hurt." It sounded like McGowan.

Paul, Katherine and Reichart were in no shape to walk on their own. They got them into the Garza's living room, sat them down on couches and chairs and checked their injuries, with everyone shouting at once, demanding to know what had happened.

"What about the boy?" Paul asked.

Raphael said, "My mother says he came to, though he's tired and scared. But she says he'll be okay. Thank you."

The room was filled with a terrible stench. Paul said, "I still smell demon stink."

McGowan curled his nose. "Ya, something stinks, but it ain't demon."

Joe Stalin squinted and looked about the room. Then he walked over to Reichart who was seated on a chair, still trembling like a frightened animal. Joe leaned down over him and sniffed. "Ain't no demon. Hot-shot here shit his pants."

••••

The voice was almost gone from his soul, almost completely silent now, and that saddened him terribly. Without the voice he didn't have the courage to go after Alice, sweet lovely Alice. But maybe he could find the courage on his own, because he needed Alice, needed to know that she loved him, only him.

Yes, one last time. He would try one last time.

••••

Anogh stood nervously in the great hall of the Unseelie Court, wearing the hereditary armor of the Summer Knight. About him the hushed whispers of a hundred conversations produced a soft roar. Like any bridegroom, his nerves were on edge as he waited for Taal'mara to make her entrance. However, his anxiety stemmed not from the usual fears of a normal newlywed, but rather from his distrust of his bride's father. Ag had been too nice about this, much too accommodating, and Anogh couldn't help but fear that the Winter King had some subterfuge in mind.

The assembled royalty of Faerie had gathered for the occasion. The Summer Court was represented by Magreth herself, along with two hundred of her courtiers. Ag had turned the Winter Court out en masse, though only those of the highest rank were allowed within the confines of the great hall. Even the non-aligned fey had sent their representatives, a boisterous clutch of leprechauns, sprites and pixies.

A sudden hush settled over the assembled throng, and all eyes turned to the far end of the hall. Ag stood on the threshold where the massive double doors of the hall had been thrown open, with Taal'mara on his arm. They stepped forward into a slow, stately walk, and as they marched the length of the hall, no one could have looked away from his bride at that moment. She wore an elaborate gown of blue silk brocade, studded with hundreds of tiny rubies and emeralds, and her hair had been piled atop her head in an intricate coif. A flock of tiny fairies hovered about her shoulders, sprinkling her with little motes of sparkling fey dust. It was an incredible sight, but it was her eyes that drew everyone's attention, for they glowed with joy and happiness.

Ag stopped in front of Anogh, and by tradition the bride's father carefully turned her to face her husband-to-be. About her neck, Taal'mara wore only a small pendent on a chain, a porcelain horseshoe with runes of inlaid silver, the traditional symbol of good-luck for the union to come. Anogh longed to take her in his arms, but he knew he must be patient.

Ag made a grand speech about the unity these vows would bring to the two Courts. Then Magreth stepped forward, and she made a speech about the joy that all would take from this union. Then silence descended.

Anogh reached into his pocket and retrieved a plain copper penny, a worthless coin. He held it out to Taal'mara with both hands, and spoke the ancient formula. "I give you this as a token of all I possess, all I was, all I am, and all I shall be."

Taal'mara reached out, took the coin, lifted it to her lips and kissed it. "And all that you shall be, is all that I shall be." She placed the coin into a little slot in the porcelain horseshoe draped about her neck, then extended her hands.

Anogh reached out, crossed his hands and took hold of hers, right to right, and left to left. Magreth stepped forward, produced a pale, blue, silken veil, then wrapped it around their hands and tied it into an elaborate knot. Anogh spoke the traditional words, "Oh woman, loved by me, mayest though give me thy heart and thy body for all time."

Taal'mara lowered her eyes, and though she spoke only a whisper, all present in that great hall heard her words. "I will."

She raised her face and looked into Anogh's eyes, and for that moment he forgot his fears. But while it was a wonderful instant, it was only that, and his fears returned.

Ag should have been less joyful, less carefree. Yes, he had required of Anogh a binding oath to forever protect Taal'mara, but the necessity of such an oath was moot, for he would protect her with his life regardless. No, he feared Ag would in some way prevent the completion of the marriage rites, interrupt it in some way. It would be so like him to dangle Anogh's most fervent desire in front of him, then withdraw it at the last instant. But when the ceremony ended without incident, with he and his love joined forever, he felt great relief. He and his bride were wed, and none could undo that.

They turned toward the assembled throng, still holding each other's hands, still bound by the silken veil, and in that moment the great hall of the Unseelie Court transformed into a vast banquet hall, and an orchestra struck up a joyful waltz. Magreth lifted the veil from their hands and wrapped it about their shoulders, tying them again together. Anogh escorted Taal'mara out onto the dance floor, took her in his arms, and his heart swelled with joy as they moved through the paces of the dance.

When the dance ended, as custom dictated Ag joined them in the middle of the floor. He wore the hereditary armor of the Winter King, a silver rapier strapped to his side, its jeweled hilt protruding from an elaborately decorated sheath. Anogh walked off the floor while Ag took Taal'mara in his arms. As they danced Taal'mara was radiant, and Ag seemed quite pleased, the happy father of the bride. When the dance ended Ag stepped back and held her at arm's length. "You are a joy to me," he said, "for today you have given me a gift I could never have hoped for."

She beamed a gorgeous smile at him. "It pleases me to give you joy, father."

Ag stepped back a pace and said, "You have no idea, my child." Then, in a single motion, he reached across, pulled the rapier and swung it in a flat arc. It sliced through her neck cleanly, and she stood there for a moment, a stunned look of surprise on her face. Then a veil of blood welled from her neck, and her head toppled from her shoulders and bounced on the floor. As her mouth screamed a wail of pain and fear, her body fell forward and hit the floor with a thud.

Anogh screamed, "Nooooo," and he lunged for Ag, but standing about him were several Unseelie warriors who were prepared for his reaction. He struggled and fought and kicked and screamed, but with the strength of numbers they wrestled him to the floor, then lifted him to his feet, his arms imprisoned behind him.

Taal'mara's head continued to shriek and scream. A great hunting hawk cried out and swooped down from the rafters of the hall, but just above Taal'mara's body it transformed into the shadowed *black-fey* assassin. Sabreatha pulled two blades of cold iron from sheaths at her waist.

"Nooooo," Anogh screamed again and redoubled his struggles, but to no avail.

Ag approached him arrogantly, stopped in front of him and said, "You have failed in your oath, Summer Knight. You are now bound to the Winter Court for all eternity."

He turned his back on Anogh, and they both watched Sabreatha crouch and stab one knife into Taal'mara's heart, and the other into an eye. Anogh struggled anew, but they beat him into unconsciousness.

. . . Anogh had relived that day a thousand times in the six hundred years since Taal'mara's passing. And he would relive it again a thousand more.

••••

It had been an exhausting week for all of them, but mostly for Paul. Katherine saw the fatigue in the lines on his face and the slump of his shoulders.

After they'd rescued the little Garza boy, they had eight confirmed demon kills to take care of, eight souls only Paul could raise, eight souls from whom only Paul could purge the essence of the demon left behind. Katherine had helped where she could, and of course, at the right moment the sword always came to her, not to Paul. So in that sense she was as essential to the process as him. But still, he took the lion's share of the burden, though knowing what to expect they had no more fiascos like those that occurred during their previous exorcisms. They'd finished the eighth exorcism two days ago, and Paul had slept ten to twelve hours a day since, but still the fatigue was visible.

The Garza's had invited them over for a big dinner. Raphael bragged openly about his mother's cooking. And it was a feast. Salisteen and Ramirez declared it some of the best Tex-Mex they'd had. They all drank a few beers and Paul got a little tipsy, though he didn't have that much to drink so it was probably another symptom of his exhaustion.

With each exorcism Paul had told them he felt the demon's presence weakening. And it appeared that whoever had helped the demon had gone to ground—if some mortal had helped the demon, a question they all agreed could not be answered definitively one way or the other. If there was someone, they'd crawled into a hole and gone completely silent. On the other hand, if there was no one, then the mere act of exorcising the remnants of the demon had removed it from the Mortal Plane.

Ramirez had checked with the families and confirmed that each of the girls had occasionally worn a pinafore. And then there was the fact that Monica Clarkson's spirit had referred to *he* and not *it*. To Katherine that stank of mortal involvement. It was not a satisfying conclusion to such a nasty business, but they couldn't just camp out in Dallas indefinitely, so it would have to do.

In any case they had a wonderful time at the Garza's, though since they were scheduled to fly back to San Francisco the next morning, they excused themselves in the early evening.

••••

One last time.

He was terrified. The voice in his soul had now grown completely silent; not a sound, not a hint of the strength and the power he'd derived from it, nothing. But he wanted to return to that glory, and he'd vowed he'd try one last time. So he would.

It was early evening with dusk quickly approaching when he turned onto the little Mexican girl's street. He spotted her house immediately, and he spotted the squad car parked out in front of it, and his heart went cold.

Of course! She was the little boy's friend, and he'd sensed the interference of some powerful practitioners. They would have made the connection. He'd hoped that one last kill might bring the voice back. But now he'd have to do it the hard way. He'd have to summon the demon again, and preparation for that would take several months.

He drove his car down the street, staying just a little above the speed limit but not so much that they'd pull him over. Cops expected people to speed a little. He turned left on the second street past her house, didn't realize he'd turned onto the little boy's street until he saw the cars and the crowd of people in front of the house.

He drove past them at his carefully chosen speed just above the speed limit. There were four older people, clearly practitioners, and a handsome young man and a beautiful young woman, also clearly practitioners, all taking their leave of the little boy's father and grandmother. He should have done his homework better, should have realized the grandmother was a witch. But now he was most interested in the six practitioners leaving the house, and for some reason he was especially drawn to the young man and woman.

He took note of the cars they'd be driving, decided to wait in the parking lot of the strip mall near the bus stop. They'd have to drive out that way.

11

The Triple Goddess

KATHERINE WAS GLAD to be back in San Francisco. After their return from Dallas she'd had a strong desire for normalcy, no wizards or witches, no spells, no demons, so for the past week she'd thrown herself into her work and purposefully avoided any contact with other practitioners, especially her father. She was a little disappointed Paul hadn't tried to reach her.

Saturday had dawned bright and clear, not a cloud in the sky, and quite warm for an early spring day. She'd spent the morning doing a little frivolous shopping downtown, purely for medicinal purposes, didn't really spend much, just enjoyed herself. Shopping cleansed her soul, especially if she bought something Eric would disapprove of. He'd rather spend her money on himself, and back when they'd been married he'd been quite happy to do so.

Around noon she took a cab to Fisherman's Wharf, actually enjoyed the crowds of tourists, and for lunch got some crab from one of those street-side stalls. Then she took a cab to the Presidio and had a thoroughly wonderful afternoon just wandering aimlessly through its streets and parks, wound up sitting on a bench in the sun in the National Cemetery as dusk approached.

••••

Anogh watched with some amusement as the little people manipulated the reality of the necromancer and the Old Wizard's daughter. Cadilus's spells, with the aid of his flunkies, did a nice job of keeping the two apart. And while the little people were not mages, could not cast spells or formulate magic, could not counter Cadilus's spells, they were masters at manipulating reality.

Anogh watched the young woman spend a leisurely day with no purpose, watched as she slowly, with no reason or intent, drifted toward the Presidio and the National Cemetery. He frequently shifted back and forth between her and the young man, and in

that way was able to watch him, through complete happenstance, end up in the Presidio, and on a whim, decide to take a shortcut through the National Cemetery.

The little people were truly masterful. The edge of the cemetery was a powerful
Boundary, and both young people were close at hand.

••••

Paul was glad to be back in San Francisco. After their return from Dallas he'd had a
strong desire for normalcy, no wizards or witches, no spells, no demons, so for the past
week he'd thrown himself into his studies and purposefully avoided any contact with
other practitioners, especially the McGowan clan. He was a little disappointed Katherine hadn't tried to reach him.

Saturday afternoon he attended a wedding at the Palace of Fine Arts, with a reception at the Exploratorium. He didn't know the bride or groom well, just casual acquaintances, so he spent only a short time at the reception, then made his excuses and
left.

He needed a cab to get back to his apartment, thought about using his cell phone
to call one, decided it might be quicker if he just tried hailing one. He'd probably have a
good chance in the Presidio, so he headed that direction. He had just begun to realize
that trying to hail a cab was a mistake, when he passed the entrance to the National
Cemetery, and on a whim decided to walk through it.

"Paul!"

He turned at the sound of Katherine's voice. She was seated on a concrete bench
just a few feet away. "Katherine, what are you doing here?"

She frowned. "Just spent the day doing a bit of this, a bit of that, ended up here.
What are you doing here?"

"Just came from a wedding at the Palace of Fine Arts. Was looking for a cab. Want
to share one?"

"Looking for a cab in a cemetery?"

"Oh, I just turned in here on a whim."

She stood. "Ok, let's go find a cab."

They turned and walked briskly toward the cemetery entrance. But then someone
shouted, "Hold up, yee daft fools."

They both stopped and turned, saw the two leprechauns running toward them. The
two little men caught up to them, both bent and put their hands on their knees, panting
for air. Between stuttered breaths Jim'Jiminie said, "And long-legged fools at that."

Paul asked, "What are you doing here?" It came out more harshly than he intended. The little fellows, while exasperating, had always tried to help him.

"We're here to save your fool ass," Boo'Diddle snapped.

Jim'Jiminie added. "He doesn't appreciate us, Boo."

"Maybe we should just leave them here."

Paul tried to apologize. "I'm sorry. I—"

Jim'Jiminie ignored him and said to Boo'Diddle, "Teach him a lesson if we did leave him here."

Boo'Diddle grimaced, "Ya, but do you want to be the one to tell Katie'O'girl we did that?"

Jim'Jiminie cringed. "Aye, she's got a sharp tongue, that one."

Boo'Diddle put his hands on his hips and looked at Paul and Katherine. "We need a boundary, so follow us."

The two leprechauns headed toward the edge of the cemetery, walking between rows of simple, white grave markers. Paul looked at Katherine. She shrugged and said, "I'm pretty sure they're our friends, so we might as well."

The two of them followed the little fellows, Paul asking, "A boundary? Why a boundary? And what kind of boundary?"

Boo'Diddle dropped back to walk beside them. "We need a boundary to get you from here to there. Without fey blood in you, the traveling is harder."

"Traveling?" Paul asked. "Where are we going?"

Boo'Diddle looked up at him and his eyes narrowed. Paul had the impression it was a look of pity. "Just follow us. We have someone who wants to meet you both."

The two little fellows stopped at the edge of the cemetery and looked it over carefully. "This'll do nicely," Jim'Jiminie said.

"Yes, indeed!" Boo'Diddle added. "Couldn't have asked for better."

Paul asked, "Why here?"

Jim'Jiminie said. "The perimeter of a cemetery, it's the boundary between life and death, which is especially appropriate for you."

A gravel strewn walking path lined the edge of the cemetery, with rows of grave markers on one side and trees lining the other. The two leprechauns walked casually along the row of trees, and as Paul and Katherine followed cautiously, he wasn't sure what to expect. They'd taken about twenty steps when Paul noticed the horizon had brightened a bit, as if the sun were about to rise, and it reminded him of the purplish sky he'd seen outside his apartment the first night the Russians had attacked him. But they were near dusk in San Francisco, not dawn, and in any case the sky appeared to have a pinkish tint to it.

The row of trees thinned out as they walked, became little more than a row of low-lying shrubs that had a rather odd look to them. He'd never seen their like so he stopped and examined one carefully. Its green leaves had a violet cast that made them appear to shimmer, with flowers so deeply purple they were near black. And as he stood there Paul felt reality slipping from his grasp along a strange spiral track, a kind of twist in reality, a sensation he'd felt several times now, and he thought he could almost understand it.

Jim'Jiminie called, "What are you dawdling for?"

Paul straightened, realizing he'd slipped into an almost trance-like reverie. Standing beside him, Katherine seemed dazed, and she stumbled as her high-heels sank into the soft earth of the path. He took her hand and they lurched forward toward the two leprechauns who stood on a hillside above a green and verdant countryside of low rolling hills. In the distance smoke curled upward lazily from the chimneys of a dozen quaint little huts as a pink sun burned off a low morning mist.

It was morning, not night, and they were certainly no longer in San Francisco. He turned abruptly and looked back the way they'd come. There was no row of trees, no gravel strewn path, no cemetery, just a dirt cart-path winding through an emerald green countryside.

Paul turned back to the leprechauns, and though he thought he already knew the answer, he demanded, "Where are we? How did we get here?"

The two little men looked at each other and shook their heads sadly.

Paul repeated, "Where are we?"

Jim'Jiminie took a deep breath and let out a long exasperated sigh. "We're no longer there, and we're now here."

"And where's here?" Paul demanded.

"He is a might thick, ain't he?" Boo'Diddle said.

Katherine put her hands on her hips and said, "You've taken us to Faerie, haven't you? Which Court?"

The little man nodded his head. "We're in the territories of the non-aligned fey. We're not taking you anywhere close to either Court."

Paul turned slowly about, turned full circle and scanned the countryside. It looked too much like pictures of a quaint Irish countryside, but color-shifted. The hillsides were green, for the most part, but the sky had a lollypop pinkish hue to it. "This is all bullshit. This isn't real."

Boo'Diddle looked pointedly at Paul, and spoke with sarcasm dripping from every word. "It's as real or not real as leprechauns, yee daft fool. And you'd better show some respect when you meet the Morrigan."

"Morrigan?" Paul asked. "Who's this Morrigan?"

Jim'Jiminie grinned. "The *triple goddess*."

Katherine leaned close to Paul and whispered, "I really don't want to meet a goddess."

A tiny female voice said, "You've really no choice in the matter, me darlin'."

A little female version of the two leprechauns now stood in the cart-path. She wore a bright green dress, with a white apron and a deep red shawl. She'd tied her grayish hair back in a bun, and her ample bosom jiggled as she unleashed her anger, "The Morrigan would've been sore displeased if you'd refused her invitation."

Paul had met her once before, on another disaster strewn romp through Faerie. To Katherine he said, "This is Katie'O'girl."

Katie'O'girl put her hands on her hips, mimicking Katherine, and looked Katherine over carefully. "Sure, she's even prettier than I'd heard."

She abruptly turned and walked toward the cluster of huts. "Come along, the two of you. The Morrigan waits, and it's never good to keep a goddess waiting."

Paul looked at Katherine and she shrugged. He let her lead and he followed.

The little huts looked like something out of a Disney movie, thatched roofs and all, though it was unlikely they'd see the inside of one since neither he nor Katherine could fit through the waist-high doors. But then, as they followed Katie'O'girl, reality shifted again and the leprechauns disappeared.

Katherine stopped abruptly and turned around. "Where are they? Where'd they go?"

Paul stopped beside her and looked about. "More importantly, where are we?"

They now stood on a game trail in a dark forest of twisted and stunted trees. And, along with the leprechauns, the little thatched huts and the verdant countryside were gone.

A crow cawed, a sharp cry that startled them both. They looked up and spotted the bird standing on a branch above them. The crow stepped off the branch and dropped toward them, but just before hitting the ground it shimmered and morphed into an old crone wearing a long, hooded cloak and hunched over a walking cane. She had a twisted nose with warts and moles all over her face, and what few teeth remained in her mouth were crooked and brown. Cataracts clouded her left eye, and her right drooped with some sort of palsy.

She cackled and laughed maniacally. "Come to see the hag, have you, children?"

She walked toward them slowly, leaning heavily on the cane, but between one step and the next she became a beautiful young maiden with long tresses of golden blond hair that hung well past her shoulders. One eye sparkled a pale blue, while the other flashed an emerald green, and she wore a shimmering, translucent gown draped over the curves of a tall goddess. The fabric of her dress left very little to Paul's imagination, though he felt no sexual attraction in any way, was not in the least titillated. She smiled at them and spoke in a lovely voice, "The wizard and the witch, I see. It's confusing, is it not?"

In the next step she turned into a naked, skeletal corpse, ribs protruding visibly, dried up old breasts withered to nothing, gobbets of rotted flesh hanging from her face, maggots filling her eyes and mouth. Her skin appeared to have the texture of old leather, with a sickly, yellowish cast that hinted at disease and pestilence.

Katherine closed her eyes and looked away, but Paul stood entranced. "Are you the *triple goddess?*"

Her appearance switched back to that of the old crone. "Maeotar," she said, her voice a barely audible hiss. "Some call me Maeotar." She shifted to the corpse. "Some call me Badb." She shifted to the maiden. "Some call me Machda."

She switched to the crone, turned to Katherine and approached her. Katherine took a step back, and the old woman screeched and cackled. The hag pointed a twisted and gnarled finger at her and said, "He cannot be victorious without you."

Katherine asked, "Victorious at what."

The crone spun away from Katherine, turned into the maiden and approached Paul. "She is your strength. Without her you are powerless."

She shifted again to the crone, then the beautiful maiden, then the corpse. The corpse said, "But are you worthy? Can you be strong? Can you be faithful? To yourself?"

She switched back to the old crone. She turned her head and looked at Katherine, then Paul. "I think . . . perhaps . . . a test for you, mortal . . ."

Somewhere, in the kaleidoscope of images that assaulted him, Paul lost consciousness.

••••

"Wake up, yee daft fool."

Paul opened his eyes to find Jim'Jiminie standing over him. He sat up, saw Boo'Diddle shaking Katherine awake. "Come on, me girl."

They were back in the green countryside with no sign of the dark forest and the crazy old—young—woman—corpse.

As Paul staggered to his feet Jim'Jiminie scrambled up a small hill carpeted in purple grass, put his hands on his hips and surveyed the countryside. They were in a copse of blue trees and purple grass, with a reddish sky. Paul helped Katherine to her feet, but her high-heels immediately sank into the soft soil and as she teetered backwards he caught her around the waist to keep her from falling. Leaning heavily on him she pulled her shoes off one-by-one and held them up to Paul. "These things cost me a fortune. I'm not giving them up."

She called up to Jim'Jiminie. "Where are we?"

He scrambled off the hillock. "We're far from the Courts here, me girl. Far in distance and time, but mostly far in dimensions your pretty little head'll never understand."

"What do we do now?" Paul asked.

"We walk, and if I'm right, we'll soon be findin' yer way back fer ya."

Paul couldn't believe what he heard. "*If you're right?* You brought us here and you're not sure you're right."

"Listen, laddie boy, if you'd be paying more attention to your surroundings instead of staring at the lass's behind all the time, you'd run into a lot less trouble. So don't begrudge me the fact we have to be playin' this tune by ear."

Katherine's eyes narrowed speculatively. "He kept checking out my ass, huh?"

"Sure, lass, he couldn't keep his eyes off it."

"Enough of this," Paul snapped. Time to change the subject. "Let's get moving. Which way do we go?"

"Just be followin' me." Jim'Jiminie scrambled back up the small hill. Katherine grinned evilly at Paul, turned, followed the little man up the hill, a little extra sashay in her hips, a little extra sway, a little extra wiggle. Paul shrugged. At least being last in line meant he had a great view.

••••

Anogh bowed before Ag. "Your Majesty, you summoned me?"

Ag was so agitated he had even abandoned fondling his favorite concubine. "He has entered Faerie. The young mage. Call out the hunt. Find him. Bring him to me. Now."

"As Your Majesty wishes." Anogh bowed deeply and backed out of the king's presence.

12

Delivery Complete

THE COUNTRYSIDE OF Faerie was the strangest thing Paul had ever seen. The sky shifted color almost hourly, sometimes reddish, sometimes bluish, sometimes greenish. The leprechaun picked an odd-looking black fruit from a tree with shiny, chartreuse leaves, and slurped on it as he walked. Grass was sometimes green, sometimes purple, sometimes brown or gray.

Jim'Jiminie told them he wanted to get them to a place where ley lines intersected, producing a simpler connection between the two Realms. He could get them back into the Mortal Plane much easier that way, but it would be a walk of a few hours. "Though I do be takin' this walk with the most uneasy of feelings. Why the Morrigan put you here I cannot fathom."

Paul said, "She said something about a test."

Jim'Jiminie stopped, looked back at him and frowned worriedly. But he said nothing, turned and continued walking.

Katherine appeared to be enjoying herself thoroughly, stopping to examine every strange plant, then running to catch up. At one point a group of pixies attached themselves to Paul, little people-shaped creatures about finger high with tiny wings. They circled his head for a few minutes, chittering and chattering in little voices that sounded more like tinkling bells.

"They're drawn to your power," Jim'Jiminie said. "And that bothers me, because if they can sense you, so can others. And Ag and Magreth have their ears tuned to all aspects of Faerie."

They walked for another hour, and in that time Jim'Jiminie grew more skittish and uncomfortable, muttering things like, "I've got a bad feelin' about this. Tis not good. Tis not good."

He finally led them into the edge of a forest of surprisingly ordinary looking trees. Their shape was odd, branches twisting toward the sky in an incredible tangle, but at least they had brown trunks and green leaves. Jim'Jiminie had them crouch down behind a thatch of brush. "There's something wrong," he said. "I know it."

"What?" Paul asked.

Far in the distance they heard the bay of a hound, an eerie, high-pitched cry that must have carried for miles. Others of its kind answered it.

"That," Jim'Jiminie said. "The Unseelie Host. They've called out the hounds. Run. We must run." The little fellow turned and sprinted deeper into the forest.

Paul and Katherine followed, but Katherine's tight skirt didn't lend itself to running so she tried to hike it up to her waist. But she was also hampered by running in her stocking feet and stumbled and fell repeatedly. Finally she stopped grabbed the bottom of her skirt with both hands and yanked, tearing it up to her waistline. "Now I can run."

They ran for several minutes, though every minute the hounds drew closer. Katherine, forced to run in her stocking feet, stumbled several times, once cursing like a stevedore. Jim'Jiminie halted suddenly, and all three of them stood there for a moment gasping for air. Paul's throat and lungs burned like the worst of bad colds.

"We're in Non-aligned Faerie here," Jim'Jiminie said, "ruled by neither Court, protected by none." He pointed ahead of them. "Not far from here is a stream. The ley lines we need are just beyond that."

They ran on, but they now heard the shouts and cries of the host following them, as well as the baying of the hounds. They left the forest behind, crossed carefully tilled and farmed open land. The burn in Paul's lungs grew even worse and he slowed down as he reached the end of his strength, saw that Katherine was doing no better. Up ahead he saw a jagged line of a depression in the countryside that must be the stream Jim'Jiminie had spoken of. They weren't running any longer, just staggering along at little better than a fast walk, unable to fill their burning lungs with the needed air.

Paul looked back as the Unseelie Host burst from the forest behind them. Tall warriors in rainbow colored armor rode steeds whose hooves appeared to never actually touch the ground, and they were led by large, black hounds with glowing red eyes. He ran on with renewed strength, caught up to Katherine, who now ran with a limp and slowed a little with each step. He grabbed her from behind and lifted her into his arms.

"Put me down," she shouted. "I can run." He ignored her because, even carrying her, he kept a better pace than she had.

He staggered up to the stream, put her down at its edge. It wasn't more than knee deep, though for Jim'Jiminie that might be a problem, so Paul picked him up and carried him as he sloshed through the water, Katherine right behind him. Paul dropped to his knees on the opposite bank, his lungs a searing fire in his chest, wheezing as he tried to pull in enough air. Katherine dropped to her hands and knees beside him. "We made it," she said, each sentence punctuated by a gasping breath.

Paul stood and looked back. The Unseelie Host had halted not a hundred paces distant, and with those amazing steeds as their mounts they could cross that in a heartbeat. Their leader, wearing some sort of colorful armor with a winged helm, reared his horse before them, as if to signal a charge. But then the cry of a hunting hawk broke the silence of the moment, and everyone looked up.

"Oh, dear mother!" Boo'Diddle said. "'Tis the *black*."

••••

Anogh really didn't want to catch the poor mortal fool, didn't want to turn him over to Ag. But with a host of Unseelie warriors behind him, he had no choice. His mount reared beneath him, and he hesitated, wondering how he could delay the inevitable. And then he heard the unique cry of the hawk, a sound no fey would fail to recognize.

He looked up to the skies, as did the warriors behind him, saw a black speck circling slowly and dropping toward them on massive wings, growing in size and proportion with each circle of its descent. This was not a visitation he could ignore.

Suddenly the hawk cried out angrily, then furled its wings and plunged toward him, its talons extended. Anogh stood his ground, knowing she dare not attack him if he gave her no cause. And as he expected, at the last instant she flared her wings, pulled up a few feet off the ground, and transformed into a tall humanoid shape obscured by shadows that fluttered about her maddeningly, a strung longbow in her left hand and a shadowy broadsword in her right.

She stood there silently, so Anogh waited, but one of the warriors behind him had far less patience and shouted, "What do you want?"

She opened her mouth, but hesitated, and when she did speak her voice hissed through Anogh's heart like the death rattle of a cold wind. "You may not interfere with my contract."

"Contract?" Anogh asked softly. "I am not aware of a contract with the *black*."

"No," that cold wind hissed, "you are not. But nevertheless your king made contract with me, and if you proceed, that contract is null and void."

Anogh considered her carefully. She could not lie about such a thing, though she could dissemble, help him to mislead himself. But she had spoken too plainly for that, so he nodded his agreement and said, "Very well. We will stand down, as we must."

The shadowy woman stared at him for a long moment, then slowly sheathed her sword and turned her back on him to look at their prey. She reached up over her shoulder to the fletching of several arrows that extended from a quiver strapped to her back. She drew an arrow with blood-red fletching and a coal-black shaft, and even Anogh looked away from that.

••••

"Oh sweet mother of me clan, no, no, no," Jim'Jiminie cried.

Katherine asked, "What's wrong?"

Boo'Diddle dropped to his knees and buried his face in his hands. "Tis the *black fey*." He looked up at Paul. "One of you is doomed, and I doubt they'd seek the death of the Old Wizard's daughter."

"Doomed," Katherine shouted. "Why doomed. We'll run, we'll fight."

Jim'Jiminie shook his head sadly. "No mortal has ever escaped *les flèche du coeur*, the heart arrow."

Paul looked toward the Unseelie Host. He'd immediately recognized the hawk and the strange giant of a woman bathed in shadows. And as he looked on she carefully nocked an arrow, then paused and looked at him, and he struggled to remember her words in the graveyard in Texas. They'd been almost identical to Jim'Jiminie's just now. But there'd been some subtle difference he couldn't recall, something about being ". . . truly mortal . . ."

The strange, shadowed woman threw her head back, looked to the heavens and shrieked out the sharp, piercing cry of a hunting hawk. Then she raised the bow, drew the string and fired.

Paul expected to see the arrow streak away from her in an arc, hoping he could watch it carefully and dodge to one side as it descended. But at the snap of the bow string the arrow shot forth only a few paces, then slowed and hovered just a few feet off the ground, moving toward them at a pace no faster than a walk.

"We're not doing this," Katherine shouted. She turned on the two leprechauns. "Get us out of here—now."

Both little men stood transfixed by the sight of the arrow. Jim'Jiminie said, "That shaft will seek its prey in any Realm, in all Realms. It has a primitive life of its own, and Sabreatha has given it the scent of his heart, so it will not stop until it has tasted his blood."

"No!" Katherine screamed. "We're not playing this game anymore."

"You've no choice, lass," Boo'Diddle shouted.

While Katherine and the little fellows had a shouting match, Paul watched the arrow carefully. It slowly drifted to within about fifty paces, then turned aside and circled them, stalking them.

Paul resolved that neither he nor Katherine would die this day without one hell of a fight. He'd come to understand it would take years to master this magic stuff. But while he didn't understand all the rules and requirements and formulas, he at least had the ability to pull a lot of power. So if he couldn't cast some carefully crafted spell, he'd try throwing a whole shit-load of power at it.

Paul pulled on all the power around him, and in Faerie there was apparently plenty to pull. It permeated everything and filled his soul. He felt little motes of it dancing up and down his arms, tickling the hairs there. He'd been warned he could burn himself out if he drew too much, go up like a roman candle, but at that moment he had nothing to lose. He sensed the ley line not too far away and he pulled on that too, and it almost overwhelmed him.

"Paul," Katherine said, her voice almost a whisper. "What are you doing?"

The arrow had circled around behind them and continued to circle. He didn't take his eyes off it as he said, "If I have to go out, it's going to be with a bang."

Jim'Jiminie said, "You're a scary one, boy-oh."

The arrow continued to circle, but closer now, and he saw the pattern. With each circle it came just a few paces closer, as if waiting for a chance to dart in without warning and punch its way through his chest. It was only about ten paces distant when he said, "Katherine, Boo'Diddle, Jim'Jiminie, get down low and hug the ground."

He didn't look away from the arrow to see if they obeyed. It was close enough to see the details of its blood-red fletching and coal-black shaft, and he thought he could distinguish something written on the shaft, some sort of runes.

It didn't dart in toward him, but turned slowly, and deliberately advanced toward his chest, slowing as it approached him, slowing to an agonizing crawl. It had advanced to within a few feet of him, coming for him an inch at a time, when he reached out and put his right hand around the shaft.

He tried to push it aside, but it wouldn't budge, and it advanced another inch. He tried to step aside and hold it to its path, but it turned with him. It was only about a hand's width from his chest when Katherine jumped to her feet and wrapped her hands around it. She screamed wildly, "No you don't, you fucking bitch."

She tried to push it to the side; they both did, she screaming maniacally while he grunted with the effort. They ended up slowly dancing in a small circle as the arrow inched toward his chest. At the last instant, just as it cut into the skin of his chest, Katherine screamed and released a flood of power. He took that as his queue and released his into the shaft of the arrow, and it nudged to one side slightly, only an inch. He turned, angled his chest to one side while Katherine angled the arrow the other way. Then the arrow pressed its way slowly into his chest, inch by agonizing inch. Sharp intense pain flooded through him. He felt it slice slowly through bone, muscle and tendon.

He screamed. Katherine screamed with him. The leprechauns screamed with them.

••••

"Paul, Paul, please don't die." That was Katherine.

Paul opened his eyes. He lay on his back on the grass in a small clearing, most of his shirt ripped away, and what remained was soaked in blood. It hurt to move, hurt even to breathe. Katherine tore away more of his shirt, working frantically and mumbling to herself. "I haven't done any internal medicine since I was an intern."

Paul asked, "Am I still alive?"

Katherine snarled at him. "Of course you're alive. You're talking to me aren't you?"

Jim'Jiminie leaned into his field of view. "You survived a heart arrow, boy-oh." There was awe in his voice.

Boo'Diddle added, "He ain't survived it yet."

Katherine growled, "Help me roll him. I need to check the exit wound."

The two leprechauns helped her roll Paul onto his side. Katherine tore away more of his shirt, probed at his back. "Owe," he hissed. "That hurts."

"Well, I'll be," Katherine said, her voice calmer. She eased him onto his back and held the black arrow up to examine it. "We got it angled enough I don't think it got any vital organs, just meat and bone. And the wounds aren't pulsing, so probably no major arteries."

Every breath sent a white hot lance of pain through Paul's chest. "You mean . . . it's not . . . bad?"

Her eyes flashed angrily. "You've got a fucking whole in your chest. Of course it's bad." She calmed a little. "But not that bad. We need to get you to a hospital right away."

She and the two leprechauns got him to his feet, helped him stagger to a level spot where the leprechauns had made a bed of leaves. He was too weak to even sit, so Katherine helped him lay down on his side, and when he started to shiver she lay down next to him to keep him warm. "Jim'Jiminie's going for help," she said. "He thinks we're close enough to the ley line he might be able to twist it and get us back."

She pressed herself tightly against him. "You're going into shock. I need to keep you warm."

"Excuses, excuses!" he said weakly. "You just want to get close to me." He had the oddest thoughts lying there with her breasts pressed tightly against him. Her blouse had been torn badly, and he had a solid view of a sexy, lacy, black bra.

She giggled. "You're looking at my boobs again, Conklin."

He looked away. "Ah, sorry."

She asked, "Was Jim'Jiminie telling the truth?"

"What?"

"That you were checking out my ass."

"I'm not telling."

She giggled again, and they just lay there. Paul drifted off into a place half way between consciousness and unconsciousness. Exhaustion weighed on him heavily, but the pain drummed at him constantly and he found breathing difficult. At some point Katherine drifted off to sleep, their arms still wrapped about each other. *What the hell*, he thought, and focused on her cleavage and the bit of black, lacy bra he could see.

Then a tall, distinguished, black man walked casually into the copse of trees, and his skin was truly black, charcoal black. The fellow wore an expensive looking business suit like one might see on the streets of any large city, which was clearly out of place in Faerie. He squatted down in front of Paul. "You don't look well, Paul."

The man's voice sounded oddly familiar. It was a struggle to speak. "Have we . . . met before? Dayandalous, right? You like to play games."

"Very good, Paul. You may be able to get out of this after all. I'll give you a hint. Think about how you got here. Think with your magical senses about how it felt."

Paul wanted to tell the fellow he didn't have the strength to think any coherent thoughts. He closed his eyes for a moment to gather the energy to tell him, but when he opened them the man had gone, though something large passed overhead and he thought he heard the hiss of massive wings slicing through the air. Definitely a hallucination!

For some reason Paul began thinking about the strange twisting of space that had brought them there, the way it had followed a kind of spiral path through reality. It was a unique feeling and he remembered it well, thought he might even repeat it if he wanted to, perhaps even reverse it. He just needed to remember it. It didn't even require the summoning or use of power, no more than recognizing which door to open and walk through. Yes, if he hadn't been half-delirious he was almost certain he could repeat it, reverse it. Almost certain . . . Almost certain . . .

••••

Walter McGowan poured a couple fingers of whiskey, sat down in his favorite chair in his office. It was an old wing-back chair, a bit worn here and there, but still infinitely comfortable. It had been a long day.

He was in mid sip when Paul and Katherine, both a muddy, bloody mess, materialized near the ceiling about five feet above his desk, crashed into it with a horrible thud and a scattering of papers and books. "Holy shit," McGowan shouted as he jumped to his feet, his heart threatening to pound its way out of his chest.

Katherine groaned, rolled over and fell to the floor in front of his desk. Paul groaned and rolled the other way, fell out of sight behind his desk and crashed into his chair with a grunt and a muffled curse.

McGowan rushed to Katherine, helped her stagger to her feet. She was a complete mess, clothes torn, blood and mud all over her. "Are you hurt?" he asked desperately.

"No, no, it's Paul's blood. He's badly hurt."

"Colleen," McGowan shouted at the top of his lungs, pushed power into the word, knew she'd hear him no matter where she was in the house

Katherine frantically pulled McGowan around the desk to Paul, who lay there only partly conscious. "We need a doctor," Katherine pleaded.

Colleen burst into the room. "Jesus, Mary and Joseph! Look at you, child."

Katherine grimaced. "I'm okay, a few scratches and bruises, but nothing serious. Paul's been shot in the chest by an arrow." She held up a black shafted arrow with red fletching. "Some sort of *black fey* thing." She looked around, her eyes wide with surprise. "Jim'Jiminie must have come back with help."

Colleen growled, "Let me at the lad." She elbowed the old man aside, pushed the toppled chair to one side and bent over Paul, examining him carefully.

He groaned, and his eyes cleared. He tried to reach something behind his back, gasped in pain and couldn't do it. Colleen demanded "What is it?" She reached behind him, tugged at something, lifted up a pair of muddy and torn high-heel shoes.

Paul looked at Katherine. "I didn't forget them."

Katherine threw her head back and laughed, and the old man wondered if she'd gone hysterical. Instead she took the shoes from Colleen, leaned down over Paul and kissed the boy, practically shoved her tongue down his throat, the kind of lip-lock fathers didn't like to see daughters doing, the little slut. And there was no doubt the kid enjoyed it too, the little shit.

13

A Bargain Fulfilled

CADILUS OPENED THE door to Magreth's private sitting room, approached her and bowed deeply, touching one knee to the floor.

"Please rise. You have news of this mortal mage?" Magreth asked.

Cadilus stood. "Yes, Your Majesty. Apparently, Sabreatha pierced his soul with *les flèche du coeur.*"

She started and the flames appeared in her eyes. "It is done then. He is dead."

"I assume so, but I have yet to confirm it."

"Of course he's dead. No one survives *les flèche du coeur.*"

"Of course, Your Majesty. No one survives that."

She frowned with uncertainty. "Get it confirmed. Immediately."

"Of course, Your Majesty."

Cadilus bowed deeply and backed out of the room.

••••

Anogh dropped to one knee before the Winter King.

"Rise," Ag said, "and tell me of your success in capturing the young, mortal mage."

"I did not capture him, Your Majesty. I was intercepted."

Frost settled on Anogh's shoulders and in his hair. "You were intercepted?"

Simuth grinned, anticipating Ag's anger, clearly hoping to see Anogh punished in Ag's typical brutal fashion.

"Sabreatha," Anogh said, and both Ag and Simuth started. "She claimed right of contract, and delivered *les flèche du coeur.*"

Ag stood stunned for a moment, then threw his head back and laughed. "Finally, someone delivers on a promise. Come, Simuth. Let us celebrate."

••••

McGowan hauled Paul off to a private clinic down the peninsula run by a friend of his. The friend apparently *practiced* more than just surgery, and he had a few special colleagues and nurses to help him. Colleen assisted, apparently used some sort of druid healing shtick to shorten his convalescence. He was weak as a kitten for several days, but Katherine had been correct: no vital organs, no serious arteries. And with Colleen treating him on a daily basis with her druid mumbo-jumbo, in one short week he felt reasonably well, though still a bit sore. He'd feel a lot worse if not for the practitioners.

Paul had returned to his apartment after only a few days in the clinic. He was there, about ready to go to bed when a knock on the door startled him. It was late, a little too late for a casual visitor.

Paul peered through the peephole before opening the door, saw three men dressed in dark business suits, but couldn't make out their faces. He took a brief inventory of his personal wards and those protecting his apartment, then opened the door carefully.

Karpov stood there in his stock attire: coat and tie, dark wool overcoat, wearing a hat that looked like it belonged in a Sam Spade private-eye movie. Behind him, and to either side, stood Boris and Joe Stalin in their horse-blanket, heavy, wool business suits. Both were large, physically imposing men; the word *thugs* always came to mind. Boris—Paul reminded himself the fellow's name was really Vladimir—had high, Slavic cheekbones pitted with acne scars, and long, stringy, greasy-blonde hair. And Paul could never put aside how much Joe—Alexei—looked like a young Joseph Stalin: bushy mustache, bristly, short hair.

"Mister Conklin." Karpov said. He pronounced *mister* more like *meester*, and he rolled his r's heavily in a thick Russian accent.

"What can I do for you, Mr. Karpov?"

Karpov spoke in a slow, fatherly way. "May ve come in, Paul? I may call you Paul, yes?"

Karpov's accent reminded Paul of Natasha, of *Boris and Natasha and Rocky and Bullwinkle* fame, actually more a mix of Natasha and Marlon Brando playing Don Corleone. Paul would much rather conduct this meeting with McGowan present, or even not at all. "It's a bit late, Mr. Karpov, and I have a long day ahead of me tomorrow."

"Ve won't keep you long."

Paul's mistake had been to hold the door wide open. If he'd only opened it slightly, then Joe Stalin would have had to push him rudely aside to get in. As it was, old Joe just kind of stepped past him, brushing Paul's arm out of the way, not really crossing the line into outright physical contact. Before Paul could say or do anything, all three of them stood in his small living room. Paul carefully avoided looking at the little end-table next to his couch where he kept the Sig in a drawer, what Devoe called his *home piece*.

"Well," Paul said. "Now that you're here, please sit down." Paul indicated the end of the couch farthest from the end-table, while he purposefully chose the other end and sat down closest to it.

"That's very kind of you, Paul," Karpov said, sitting down carefully like an old man. Paul knew darn well he was not as infirm as he pretended. Boris and Joe Stalin remained standing at either end of the couch, looming over them ominously.

Keep it polite, Paul thought. "Again, what can I do for you, Mr. Karpov?"

Karpov smiled at him in a fatherly way. "I think we have all underestimated your capabilities a bit. And Valter has certainly been . . . unforthcoming."

"I think Mr. McGowan feels kind of fatherly toward me."

"Yes," Karpov said as if swallowing some sort of bitter medicine. "Fatherly. That is a good way to put it. You are in an unusual position, Paul."

Okay, Paul thought. *Here comes the pitch*. He decided to play dumb. "I'll say. A few months ago I was a pretty ordinary guy. And now all this practitioner stuff. It's a bit overwhelming."

"Yes, Paul, it is. But that's not what I meant. You are more powerful than most apprentices. Think of it like graduate school. Professors are always looking for the genius to be one of their pupils. And when one comes along, the professors compete for him. You are like the genius, Paul."

Paul shrugged. "No one's competing over me, not that I know of. But, to continue your analogy, I only know one professor."

"No, Paul." Karpov shook his head like a patient mentor. "You know me as well."

Paul nodded and spoke carefully. "Is that an offer?"

"No, no, Paul. For me to make such an offer to you at this time would be inappropriate. But you should keep in mind there is a new order coming, and Valter may not be the best man to guide you through the coming changes."

"And you would be?"

Karpov shrugged sympathetically. "Perhaps. Valter is old, not as vital as he once was. It is sad to see him so, and you could do better."

Paul had trouble keeping it polite. "Because you're the one who's setting up this new order?"

"I and some colleagues have been—"

Paul interrupted him. "With you at the top of this new order?"

Joe Stalin, standing behind Karpov, stepped forward aggressively. Paul heard Boris, behind him, also move. Karpov raised a hand and both men froze.

"Valter is set in his ways, and it is a time of change, Paul. And those who are not flexible enough to accept change . . ." He shrugged, no longer fatherly, his meaning clear. But he said it anyway. "Well, they may not survive these changes."

"So you're setting up a new-world-order, and if we don't step in line, we're dead meat, huh?"

"Paul, please. Don't be impertinent."

"Impertinent! What happens next, Karpov? Boris and Joe Stalin here rough me up in some dark—"

Paul didn't get to finish. For a big man, Boris moved rather quickly, stepped in front of Paul and picked him up by the armpits as if holding a small child. He slammed Paul against the wall once, twice. With his head spinning Paul could barely make out Boris's words. "You vill speak to Mr. Karpov with respect, or I vill teach you respect the hard vay."

An interesting thing about wards, stationary wards, the kind one sets to protect a home or apartment, is that they're like batteries with no limit to their capacity. If you feed power into them time after time, and never have cause to discharge any of it, even the weakest of practitioners can eventually build up some strong and potent wards, wards capable of defending one from someone far stronger. And Paul was not the weakest of practitioners. Having developed a healthy sense of paranoia because of recent events, he had diligently fed his wards power every night when he came home, and each morning before he left.

As Boris snarled in his face, his nose only inches from Paul, his breath smelling of onions and garlic, Paul focused on one of his wards and triggered it. He'd never triggered a strong ward before, only minor wards for practice, wasn't prepared for the loud crack that sounded like a two-by-four snapping. And Boris wasn't prepared when it slapped him to the floor, slapped him hard.

Boris went down for the count, and the crack of the ward startled both Karpov and Joe Stalin. Paul turned quickly to the side table, slid open the drawer, grabbed the Sig and pulled the slide back, jacking a round into the chamber. He didn't aim it at anyone, held it down at his side and marshaled the rest of his wards.

Joe Stalin stood above Karpov, who hadn't moved from his seat. Old Joe had shoved his right hand into the front of his jacket where he clearly had a gun. The thug was probably faster than Paul, but they all knew Paul's wards would respond instantaneously. And since Paul hadn't actually raised the Sig and aimed it at anyone, they all accepted an uneasy and unspoken truce, though they knew Paul had the advantage.

Boris groaned and slowly rolled over painfully.

Paul nodded toward Boris and looked Karpov in the eyes. "Good old Boris there is pretty stunned, probably not thinking real clear right now. There's no need for any further violence, but if he or Joe Stalin there"—Paul nodded to Joe—"do something stupid, I cut loose with everything."

Karpov held Paul's eyes for a long moment, then said, "Alexei, help Vladimir. Make sure he doesn't . . . do something stupid." Joe Stalin didn't move immediately.

Karpov's impatience boiled to the surface. "And get your stupid hand out of your coat. I am confident Mr. Conklin won't . . . do something stupid himself."

As Joe Stalin helped Boris to his feet, with Boris emitting a series of low groans, Karpov stood and faced Paul.

"Mr. Conklin, I hope you will forgive Vladimir his . . . shall we say, enthusiasm. He is young, does not think before he acts."

As Paul recalled, between the time Boris had slapped him against the wall, and the moment he triggered the ward, Karpov had had plenty of time to call him off. Paul decided not to mention that. "I think it best, Mr. Karpov, if you leave now."

"Yes. I agree. It has been interesting, Paul."

Karpov turned his back on Paul and headed to the door. Joe Stalin, his hands full helping Boris stagger, managed to back his way to the door, keeping his eyes on Paul. Karpov held the door open, let Joe pull Boris through the door, then turned back to Paul. "Boris," he said, smiling and nodding. "And Joe Stalin." His smile turned into a broad grin, an unpleasant grin. "That's funny, Mr. Conklin. I like that. You are a funny man."

He backed into the hall and closed the door softly.

••••

"He actually assaulted you?" McGowan asked.

"Picked me up like a doll and slammed me against the wall," Paul said. They were sitting in McGowan's study. Paul had given him a complete run-down on the previous evening's meeting with Karpov and his thugs.

McGowan shook his head. "That is so like Vasily: heavy-handed to the end, about as subtle as a sailor in a whorehouse."

"What do we do about it?"

McGowan grinned, nodded, obviously pleased about something. "Actually, Vasily overplayed his hand this time. There are a few unwritten rules about the relationship between a master wizard and his apprentice, most of which are several hundred years old. For one, a wizard does not approach another wizard's apprentice without discussing it first with the apprentice's master. And it's even worse that he approached you in your own home, let himself in uninvited, then assaulted you."

McGowan's grin broadened further. "I'll make sure the story gets out. Even his supporters won't like this. The pressure will keep him off your back for a while. Especially when they hear you bested him and two of his thugs. No one likes Alexei and Vladimir. Wait a minute. What did you call them? Joe Stalin and Boris? I like that, kid."

••••

It was late when Paul got home. He and McGowan had played with some nasty stuff, and Paul had been pressed to absorb it all. Paul thought about it carefully as he fumbled for his keys. He had already learned to summon energy from ley lines and from earth magic, and also from what McGowan had called his physical magic.

"Conklin," someone said behind him as he fumbled for his keys.

He turned, saw Eric Reichart standing in the shadows of the street lights on the other side of the street. Paul waited as Mr. Nordic God crossed the street, decided to hold the high ground and stayed at the top of the steps. Reichart did nothing to hide his own strength as a wizard, was clearly stronger than Paul.

In Dallas Reichart had come across as arrogant and hostile, so Paul asked, "What can I do for you?"

Reichart stopped half way up the steps. "Are you aware I'm Katherine's husband?"

Paul corrected him, "Katherine's ex-husband."

One corner of Reichart's lips curled up in a snarl. Paul thought of two dogs, sniffing at one another, trying to establish dominance. "That's just temporary. That'll be corrected soon."

Paul hadn't discussed it with Katherine, but from what she'd said he didn't think she'd even consider reconciliation. "Not according to Katherine."

Reichart took a step forward, and did everything but growl. "Katherine is weak, doesn't know what she wants. She needs a strong man to take care of her."

"I think Katherine can decide that for herself."

Reichart came up the last few steps, forcing Paul to back-step. Paul prepared to pull power, though with an experienced wizard like Reichart he doubted he'd do well in such a contest. Reichart stopped with his nose inches from Paul's and drew power. "Stay away from her, asshole. Stay away from her or you'll regret it."

Paul stood ready, didn't draw power, knew that doing so would precipitate a fight he couldn't win. "You get one warning," Reichart snarled. "Only one." Then he spun on his heels, walked casually down the steps, put his hands in his pockets and sauntered down the street whistling some tune Paul didn't recognize.

••••

Paul got the front door of his apartment open, fumbled for the light switch in the dark, but when he flicked it on only one of the lamps lit up. The bulb in the lamp near his kitchen nook must have burned out. He headed straight for his bedroom, threw his jacket on the bed, tossed the Sig on the bed with it and pulled off the shoulder holster. The damn thing wasn't terribly comfortable. He'd have to talk to Clark Devoe about that. Maybe it needed adjustment or something.

He went to the kitchen nook, didn't bother to fumble for the light switch there, opened the small refrigerator, retrieved a beer, turned, and by the light from the refrigerator realized he wasn't alone. The silhouette of a man sat at his small breakfast table, his head and shoulders completely hidden in shadow. Paul resolved that in the future he'd carefully check his place out before dumping the Sig.

"Good evening, Paul," the man said calmly in a voice that seemed somewhat familiar. "I'm not here to hurt you. Just to talk, though I wouldn't mind one of those beers."

Paul twisted open the beer he held, carefully handed it to the man, turned only part way back to the refrigerator so he could keep an eye on the fellow, retrieved another beer.

"Sit down," the man said. Paul cautiously took the only other seat available in the small kitchen nook. "I'm sorry if I startled you, but just walking up to your front door and knocking would never have worked."

Now that he realized he wasn't going to be killed or harmed outright, Paul felt a bit belligerent. "Why not?"

The shadows hiding the man's face were too deep to be real. "Come now, Paul. You know what this is about, and you know such situations can't be handled in mundane ways."

Paul shrugged, acknowledging the fact. "What do you want?"

"To talk."

"I don't know that I know anything that can help you. I'm kind of new to all this stuff."

"I'm aware of that," the stranger said, and Paul was almost certain he'd heard that voice before. "But it doesn't really matter. I'm not here for you to talk to me. I'm here to talk to you."

"Okay . . . talk."

The man took a sip of beer, put the bottle down on the table and Paul caught a glimpse of his hand. His skin was coal black. "You're Dayandalous. I remember you."

The shadows that obscured Dayandalous's face thinned and his eyes flared red for a moment. "Yes, Paul. And you remember me because I want you to."

Paul didn't like the way that each time they met, within moments of parting he completely forgot the man. "The forty-fourth floor. That was a clever trick, really threw me for a loop. And in the Netherworld. And in Belinda's apartment. And in Faerie. You just show up at the oddest of times, and afterwards I completely forget you."

"And you'll forget me again, once we've had this conversation."

"Did you give Katherine that sword?"

"Ah, again you're quite perceptive."

"So why are you here now?"

"To impart a little information. A little lesson, as it were."

Paul got the impression Dayandalous was grinning, laughing at him quietly. "First, about the fey. The royal lines of the Sidhe Courts are immortal, nearly impossible to kill." Paul didn't miss the word *nearly*. "They don't age and die, and in Faerie they are enormously powerful, almost impossible to overcome . . . in Faerie. But they can be killed. And to do so you must separate the head from the heart. Then impale both the head and the heart on cold iron, and hold the iron fast until their struggles cease; a difficult proposition, to say the least.

"And then there is the matter of traveling between the Realms. Many of the fey do not need a boundary, or a ley line. They just need to know where they want to go, then they twist reality to make it so."

"Why are you telling me this?"

"Remember what I've said, Paul. Also remember that if you ever must fight a Sidhe royal, do not hold back. It will be a fight to the death, and you must show no hesitation, no mercy, no compassion. For they will show no hesitation, mercy, or compassion for you."

Paul had no intention of getting into any battles with Sidhe royals. "Again, why are you telling me this?"

"In time, all will become clear, Paul."

. . . Now why had he opened two bottles of beer. Just sitting there by himself in his kitchen, a half empty bottle in his hand, another on the table in front of him, as if someone had sat there sharing a beer with him. All this magic crap made his head spin, made him forgetful.

He finished his beer, poured the remnants of the other into the sink. The beer made him drowsy, so he rolled into bed, was practically asleep before his head hit the pillow.

••••

Seated on his throne, Ag screamed hysterically at Sabreatha. "We had a contract. You were to kill the necromancer."

The *black fey* stood before the Winter King casually and showed no fear at his rage. The soft hiss of her voice sent a shiver up Anogh's spine. "Yes, a contract, an agreement well-formed and properly fulfilled."

Ag stood and marched down the steps of the dais. He stopped just short of Sabreatha, and as she loomed over him, standing more than a hand-span taller than him, he seemed to doubt the wisdom of approaching her too closely. "No, you failed."

Her head turned slowly and her eyes settled on Anogh. "I delivered *les flèche du coeur*. The contract is complete."

"No," Ag screamed, "you took contract to kill the necromancer with the heart arrow."

"Nay, I took contract to deliver the heart arrow. The contract was clearly stated, and it is complete."

With a contemptuous shrug, she turned her back on Ag and strode out of the great hall.

14

An Unexpected Visitor

MCGOWAN HAD ASKED Paul to meet him at an address in a part of the Haight-Ashbury district referred to by most locals as the Upper Haight, an area filled with nineteenth century, multi-story wooden houses. While the *summer of love* had long since left the Haight behind, there were still a few retro clothing shops on Haight Street, the main drag, mixed among the tattoo parlors, restaurants and jewelry stores. It hadn't really gone upscale, though to some degree it still maintained its bohemian style. But the Haight now seemed more focused on tourists, crowds of which wandered up and down Haight Street almost any day of the week.

The address led Paul to a small shop named *Alternate Earth Books*, nestled among residential structures in the Upper Haight. When Paul opened the front door it triggered a small bell. He stepped inside and closed it behind him, stood facing row upon row of musty old books, not sure how to proceed. A sixtyish woman approached him wearing a tie-dyed dress, too much makeup, a few too many years, and a few too many pounds. She smiled at him pleasantly. "Can I help you?"

"I'm supposed to meet someone here," Paul said. He looked about. The shop was small enough that if McGowan were already there he'd spot him easily. "But it doesn't look like he's here yet."

Her eyes narrowed suspiciously. "Are you here to meet Walter?" She winked at him knowingly, gave him a conspiratorial look as if they were collaborators in some secret scheme.

"I'm here to meet Mr. McGowan. Yes."

She winked again, as if they shared some vast secret, then leaned close and whispered, "He's in the back room where I keep the old books. Follow me." She turned and spun on her heel like a schoolgirl. As Paul followed her he opened himself to his power, but couldn't sense any capability within her.

She led him to the back of the shop and into a small room where McGowan stood flipping through the pages of a large book. He looked up from the book as they entered. "Paul, glad you could make it, kid. You've met Dorothy?"

McGowan introduced him to the old hippie whom he learned was also the shop's owner, and as Paul shook her hand politely she gave him that conspiratorial look again, though at least she didn't wink this time. "I've got to watch the front of the shop," she said, beaming at McGowan, almost gushing at him like a teenager with a rock star, "so I'll leave you two to your browsing."

When he and McGowan were alone, Paul quietly asked, "What's with all the winking and nudge-nudge-poke-poke?"

McGowan turned back to the book he'd been examining, whispered, "She's a member of a coven, thinks we all share the same secrets." McGowan winked at Paul.

Skeptically, Paul said, "I couldn't sense any capability in her."

McGowan chuckled and grinned. "I made a point of meeting her sister witches, just in case one of them did have any abilities. Not an ounce of power among the lot. But they like to get together and do some chants, practice some rituals, hold a séance, call some spirits, though I'll bet the closest any of them has ever come to calling a spirit was when one of them farted after one too many tokes on the bong, and they all thought it was the smell of brimstone leaking over from the Netherworld."

McGowan handed Paul the book. "Take a look at this."

The book's title, *A Grimoire of Alternate Realities*, flowed across the cover in large, flowery script. It appeared to have been printed in the mid nineteenth century, seemed quite old, though Paul was not qualified to judge its authenticity. "A book of magic spells. Is this for real?"

"Useless drivel," McGowan said, shaking his head. He reached up, pulled another book off a shelf. "Here. Look at this one."

The instant the book touched Paul's fingers he felt a mild tingle of power from it. McGowan saw the look on his face. "When it's real, and it's been used by someone who was a real practitioner, they leave an imprint on the book. It's involuntary, like leaving your fingerprints on a glass when you drink from it. So you'll always know a real grimoire when you touch one. But that still doesn't mean the spells will be correct or accurate, or that you can trust them."

Paul picked up the first book again. "So this one's a fake?"

McGowan grimaced. "It depends on what you mean by fake. Dorothy knows her books, so if it was a fake she'd have attached a note to that effect, or a note to the effect that she hadn't been able to authenticate its pedigree. So the fact that it's here without such a note means she's done her homework and is satisfied it's real. My guess is some nineteenth century charlatan wrote it, some fellow running a scam as a fake wizard, or someone who, like Dorothy, was sincerely deluded. Séances and all sorts of mumbo-jumbo crap were quite popular about the time this was written. It may even have some antique value, but I don't collect old books for the sake of old books."

Paul flipped through a few pages of the real grimoire. "It's in Latin."

"Most of the older ones are. That's why you need to study Latin. Right now I'll make a present of this one to you, and maybe someday you'll find something useful in it. But remember this shop, and keep your eye out for others like it. Anyone collecting old books might have something valuable you can use, especially someone like Dorothy who's always picking up old grimoires. Most of them are crap, but you can spot the real ones."

••••

McGowan bought the old book for Paul then drove them both back to his Nob Hill place. Inside, he marched Paul straight to his workshop, saying, "Today, we're going to learn a bit about the Netherworld, kid. I've stayed away from it because it's really dangerous stuff, thought I'd wait until you had a chance to learn more, but recent events tell me we can't put it off any longer. You need to understand what you've faced with these demons. But I want you to promise—I want your word—that you'll stay away from demon magic and the other black arts until you've had more training. And even then, this stuff can easily leave a taint on your soul, so it's not wise to delve into it regularly or deeply."

McGowan's house was one of those early twentieth-century wooden structures built on a steep hill in such a way that the entrance let you onto the second floor, with the first floor down the hill and at the back, a total of five floors in all. McGowan's workshop occupied the entire first floor and was large enough to contain Paul's whole apartment. Like Katherine's workshop, it had a workbench, shelves, chairs, and also like Katherine's workshop all were located along the walls to leave the center of the room open and clear. However, McGowan had tiled the floor in marble, and installed a large circle of beaten silver permanently embedded in the marble. Outside the silver circle he'd also fashioned a silver pentagram, also embedded, its interior lines touching the circle as Katherine had described to him.

The first time Paul had seen it, McGowan had said proudly, "Beat that silver and installed it myself. Otherwise it wouldn't work for me, which is the reason it won't work for you."

McGowan closed the workshop door and locked it carefully. "Katherine said you're a natural with a circle. And the damping exercises we worked on yesterday took care of another prerequisite."

The previous day McGowan had taught Paul how to conceal his power from a demon, how do damp the emanations the exercise of power naturally produced, a most important prerequisite to the summoning of demons. Paul likened it to a fat man on the beach sucking in his gut so he could pretend he still had a flat stomach. If he wasn't too fat, just a little gut, it worked fairly well, but only as long as he kept those abdominal muscles clenched. And likewise, Paul's damping exercises worked reasonably well, as long as he kept his magical muscles clenched. McGowan assured him that, as he grew more experienced, it would come naturally, kind of like if the fat man went on a diet and started exercising. Eventually, he might develop nice washboard abs and the flat stomach would come without any effort.

"First I want to see you close a circle. I trust Katherine's judgment, but I still want to see it myself."

McGowan had him draw a circle of salt in the way Katherine had taught him, using the embedded silver circle as a template, then Paul sat down and began feeding power into it. And when he sensed that unmistakable moment when the circle was ready, he shouted, "Bullshit," and closed it.

"Bullshit?" McGowan asked.

Paul shrugged sheepishly. "That's my word for closing circles." And at McGowan's questioning look, he added, "Long story. Not worth telling."

McGowan shook his head, walked back to his workbench muttering, "I have to have a talk with that daughter of mine." He retrieved a walking stick that belonged more in a Victorian era movie, and walked back to Paul's circle.

McGowan slapped the walking stick against the invisible wall of the circle about waist high. It hit the wall with a muted thump but didn't penetrate. He walked around the circle tapping at it with the cane, trying several times to drag the tip of the cane through the salt to break the circle. "Good job, kid. Now break that circle and let's get down to some real work."

Paul broke the circle with a thought. He didn't have to redraw the circle, but McGowan made him draw a pentagram of salt outside it, again using the embedded silver pentagram as a template, while McGowan carefully inspected Paul's work, ensuring that the five interior sides of the pentagram touched the circle solidly without distorting it.

"Now, if we wanted to pull in a really big nasty," McGowan said, while rifling through his storage cabinet, "we'd have started fasting last night at midnight, and we'd perform the calling tonight at midnight, after twenty-four hours of fasting and some serious cleansing rituals."

McGowan lifted a small copper dish out of the storage cabinet. "We will wait until after dark, but we're only going after a minor demon so we can skip all the preliminary nonsense."

McGowan also retrieved four wax candles, each about six inches long, and a large, flat cardboard box, from which he pulled a mirror about three by two feet mounted in an ornate wooden frame. McGowan handed the mirror to Paul and he noticed it did a poor job of reflecting his image. "That's a dark mirror. Essentially a piece of glass painted black on the back side."

McGowan then handed Paul the four candles, explaining, "These candles are infused with the vaginal secretions of sexually excited, pregnant virgins."

Paul couldn't believe it, said, "That's incredible! Where do you get such candles?"

McGowan frowned at him seriously for a moment, then let out a small snort, clearly struggling to hold something in. But he finally spluttered, bent over, slapped his hands on his knees and laughed openly, loud, roaring guffaws, tears streaming down his cheeks as he gasped for breath. "Gets 'em every time," McGowan roared, struggling for air, "though the part about the virgins being pregnant is new. Made that up on the spot, special for you." He pulled out a handkerchief and wiped tears from his eyes.

All Paul said was, "You asshole."

McGowan had Paul place the four candles at four of the five points of the pentagram, saying, "The point without a candle is the principal point where you'll be seated controlling the entire event. When you light the candles you'll do so with your power, not matches or any other mundane means. You will be the fifth candle, completing the symmetry of the pentagram, and defining the principal point with your power."

McGowan then had Paul cut a few strands of his own hair and place them in the copper dish, then place the copper dish and the dark mirror in the center of the circle, arranged so that when Paul sat down at the principal point of the pentagram, he saw his own faint reflection in the mirror, with the copper dish resting just in front of the mirror. "If we were going after a primus-caste demon," McGowan said, "you'd put a couple ounces of your own blood in the dish, and sacrifice a small animal, like a chicken."

Paul grimaced. "Sounds kind of satanic."

"It is, Paul. You'll use the dark mirror to open up a pathway to the Netherworld, then use the lock of hair and a little power to draw a demon forth. In religions with a heaven and hell concept, the hell part refers to the Netherworld, and Satan and fallen angels are demons, plain and simple."

McGowan looked at his watch. "It's dusk out, so let's grab some dinner. By the time we're done it should be full dark."

McGowan ordered out for a pizza. Paul chewed a couple of slices mechanically, his mind preoccupied by what he was about to do, a tense nervousness in his gut as memories of his misadventure in the Netherworld occupied his every thought. When McGowan finally announced, "Okay. Let's do this," Paul stood and followed him down to the workshop with mixed feelings of relief and dread.

Under McGowan's tutelage, Paul lit each of the four candles with the fire spell he'd been taught, then sat down inside the circle facing the small copper dish. He pulled a small amount of power—McGowan had told him, *just a hint*—fed it into the few strands of hair in the dish. Paul then stood and stepped carefully out of the circle and pentagram, and sat down on the floor at the principal point of the pentagram facing the dark mirror. McGowan sat down behind him. Paul fed power into the circle and pentagram, found that to reach the point where it was ready to close, the combination of circle and pentagram took far more power than a simple circle. When it was ready he whispered, "Bullshit," and the circle snapped shut like the massive doors on a bank vault.

As he'd been instructed, Paul then cast a fire spell to ignite a small flame in the palm of his hand so that magical flame burned at all five points of the pentagram. Then he triggered the power he'd fed into the lock of hair and it burst into flame. He focused on the dark mirror, focused on his own faint but visible reflection there. "Darkness rules the night," he said, reciting the words McGowan had taught him. "Bring forth the night. Bring forth the darkness, and its minions."

He repeated that thirteen times, and with each repetition the mirror appeared to become more of a mirror, his reflection more visible and defined. After the last repetition the mirror reflected his image clearly, like a fine platter of silver. He focused on that image, recalled the night he'd accidentally summoned the vampires, the night McGowan had rescued him, and like that night his image slowly distorted, twisted and spiraled away from his regular features. When the moment came, when the image reformed fully, he felt that sideways slippage in reality that he'd felt going to and from the Netherworld, and an image of Katherine formed there.

She stepped out of the mirror to stand in front of it, a small replica of Katherine only about two feet tall. But then in a wink she stood her full height, though the Katherine standing in the middle of the pentagram had a chest like a porn-star queen, with an abundance of cleavage erupting from her blouse, a full, rounded figure, luscious, swollen red lips puckered into a pout. In every other way though, it was Katherine, in one of her sexy business suits, though the skirt was practically a micro-mini. "Hello, Paulieboy," she said.

"Don't ever call me that," he snarled, thinking he liked the real Katherine's small breasts much better than the obscene imitations in front of him.

As if reading his mind, the Katherine in front of him spread her hands and looked down at her chest. She pressed her hands up under her breasts, squeezing copious amounts of cleavage up from the blouse. "You don't like this, do you, mortal? Well then, let's fix that." Her breasts slowly shrank to the proper size, her figure and lips thinned and the skirt lengthened until she truly did look like Katherine, though her eyes remained blood-red and goat-slitted.

Behind him, McGowan whispered, "That's no minor demon."

Paul whispered back, "I think it's the one I met in the Netherworld."

"Be careful here, Paul. That thing is at least secundus caste, maybe even primus. Very dangerous."

The demon then took on the shape of Suzanna, a perfect Suzanna without any distorted features. It said, "You can have your love again, you know. All you need do is release me."

It took on the shape of Cloe, his beautiful little child, all brightness and happiness. "You can have anything you want, daddy. Just release me and all is yours."

Paul felt tears running down his cheeks, tasted the saltiness of his own sorrow as one touched the corner of his mouth. The demon he and Katherine had faced in the Netherworld had tried the same trick. "I'll not release you," he told the demon.

The demon shrugged, took on the image of McGowan seated in one of his wing-back chairs. "Well then, mortal, we must come to some accommodation."

"Why?" Paul asked.

The demon shrugged, still holding the form of McGowan, though a look of pure avarice washed over his features and his eyes turned to pools of black obsidian. "Because I can give you many things, mortal."

"Like what?"

The demon smiled knowingly. "To begin with, power beyond imagining."

"I don't want power beyond imagining."

"You say that now, mortal. But there will come a time. There always comes a time for your kind."

McGowan whispered in Paul's ear, "Try to determine its caste."

Paul and the demon stared at one another for some time, and the knowing smile never left its face, but the look of pure avarice in its eyes frightened Paul more than anything else. Paul said, "You promise enormous power, but how do I know you can deliver?"

The demon shifted appearance to that of Suzanna again, and spoke in her voice. "Paulie-boy, I can deliver anything."

Paul asked it, "And how will I contact you again?"

The demon's smile broadened. "I'll give you a name, mortal, not my true name, but a name I have been known to use. Call for Abrasax when next you want to speak with me."

Behind him, McGowan swore. "Shit! Get rid of that thing. Now."

Paul recalled McGowan's instructions and said, "The darkness no longer rules here, minion. Return to the darkness. Now. I command it." And he killed the flame in the palm of his hand.

Paul felt that sideways path through reality open up again, the demon disappeared and the pathway closed with a sharp snap.

McGowan stood, circled the pentagram carefully, saying, "Jesus, kid! I think that was an arch-demon, one of the princes of hell." Paul felt the old man drawing power, testing to be sure the demon was truly gone, and the pathway closed. He finally turned to Paul. "You can break the circle now, kid. And don't ever call that fucking thing again."

••••

Summoned into Ag's presence, Anogh found the Winter King sprawled upon his bed entangled with one of his concubines, both snarled in silken, white sheets. From a chair to one side Simuth looked on, watching the two cavort. Ag barely acknowledged Anogh with a shrug, continued fondling the concubine as he spoke, "The necromancer lives. So Sabreatha did not deliver the heart arrow."

Anogh was aware that Ag had already questioned several members of the host that had been present, so he knew the truth of the matter. "I saw her deliver the arrow with my own eyes. If you doubt me, then question others who were there."

"Impossible," Ag snarled. "Amazing! Unheard of!"

One of the concubine's breasts captured Ag's attention, so he leaned over and nibbled on it delicately. After several moments fondling her he looked up. "Yes. He lives. So Sabreatha violated her contract."

Anogh spoke cautiously. "Sabreatha never violates a contract."

The king turned a face to Simuth that no fey would want to see. "This is your fault."

"But I didn't—"

The king merely whispered, "Silence, fool," and frost formed on Simuth's hair, eyebrows, skin. Frost formed on everyone in the room, on the tapestries on the walls, even in the hair of Ag's concubine. "I must know more about this young wizard, this necromancer, this Lord of the Dead, and since you clearly cannot bring him to me, I want to question the Old Wizard's daughter. I am told she is quite close to him."

Simuth was smart enough to say only, "As you wish, Your Majesty."

Ag turned back to his concubine, caressed her between the legs, bit her breast viciously and she groaned with pleasure. They both became more aroused with each second. "Get her, Simuth. Bring her to me. Now go, both of you. Or stay, if you care to watch."

The Summer Knight bowed and backed carefully out of the Winter King's chambers. Simuth chose to stay and watch.

15

The Trap Is Set

PAUL NEEDED TO get out. For the past two months he hadn't gone anywhere but McGowan's place, Katherine's office and his own apartment. Well, there was the trip to Faerie, and nearly dying with a hole in his chest. But that didn't count when he thought of getting out. He needed to go someplace with normal human beings, though he was no longer that normal himself. He'd love to socialize more with Katherine, see if that went anywhere, but she apparently didn't feel likewise.

It was early evening and the sun had dropped down behind the hills of San Francisco. He wandered down the block to a bar he'd spotted that looked like a nice, little neighborhood place named *Jessie's Bar and Grill*. And he discovered to his delight it had a friendly atmosphere, no drunks and barflies hanging about trying to mooch a drink, and a fairly normal looking clientele. A couple of gay fellows had taken over two stools at the end of the bar, with three or four heterosexual couples seated at small tables eating what looked like fairly simple fare. Paul took a seat at the bar a few seats down from the gay couple.

The bartender wandered over as soon as Paul sat down. "Haven't seen you around here before."

Paul shrugged. "Just moved into the neighborhood a couple of months ago. Renting a small place a block up the street, thought I'd have a look around the neighborhood."

The bartender stuck out his hand. "I'm Jessie. Welcome to Jessie's."

Paul shook his hand. Jessie was about average height, average size, but clearly a weight lifter, which showed rather dramatically in his shoulders and arms. "Paul Conklin. I'll have a glass of red wine. And a dinner menu."

"Coming right up."

Jessie had a decent choice of red wines by the glass. The dinner menu was mostly sandwiches and hamburgers and steaks. Jessie's partner, Steven, did the cooking, and when Steven came out to take Paul's order it was clear Jessie and Steven were a couple.

Paul ordered a T-bone, leaned back and enjoyed his glass of wine while he waited for the steak.

He'd just finished the first glass of wine when Steven brought his dinner. "Jessie says you're new to the neighborhood."

"Ya. Moved in a couple of months ago. Until now I've been too busy to have a look around." Paul started in on the steak.

Steven leaned against the bar. "What do you do?"

"Architect," Paul said around a mouth full of steak. "Well, until recently. Right now I'm an unemployed architect. Hey, this is good steak."

"We do pretty good here. Need anything, just holler."

Steven turned and headed back into the kitchen. A couple of new customers came through the front door, two fellows who sat down at the bar a couple of stools down from Paul. They spoke to each other in what sounded like Russian, and after recent events, anything Russian made Paul uneasy. But they weren't bothering him, weren't even paying attention to him, so he decided to forget his paranoia, do likewise and enjoy his steak.

He had another glass of wine, which was probably one too many, but he enjoyed the food and the company, and wouldn't be doing any driving that night. In any case, on a full stomach he'd gotten only a bit lightheaded. He finished dinner, called for the check, still had half a glass of wine left, leaned back to enjoy it while he waited for the check.

When Steven brought the check, Paul paid cash, left a nice tip.

Steven stuck his hand out. "Again, welcome to the neighborhood, Paul. And what was your last name again?"

Paul shook Steven's hand and said, "Conklin." When he said it, both Russians turned and looked at him sharply, then looked away quickly. Steven's eyes narrowed and he looked from Paul to the Russians.

Paul watched the Russians out of the corner of his eye. They didn't appear to be in any rush to follow as he walked out onto the sidewalk, so he let it go. Anyway, it was one of those gorgeous San Francisco spring nights, and he'd just had a great meal, and the wine helped relax some of the tension of the past weeks. He strolled up the street, got about a hundred feet from Jessie's when something slammed into him from behind.

He hit the concrete sidewalk hard, skinning his hands and tearing his jeans. One of them pinned his arms behind him, lifted him to his feet. "Quickly. Quickly," his attacker said, and even that one word came out in a thick Russian accent. Paul drew power, but a fist slammed into his solar plexus, ending any ability to focus properly. Another fist slammed into the side of his head and his knees buckled.

The two Russian thugs lifted him up between them by his armpits, dragged him off the sidewalk into a narrow alley, spun him about so his arms were pinned behind him by one of them, the other facing him. "This is from Vladimir, motherfucker."

A fist slammed into Paul's cheek. "Vladimir wants you to learn proper respect." Paul tried to draw power, couldn't focus properly to do so as fists slammed into his ribs, his solar plexus, his cheek.

A familiar voice shouted, "What the fuck you think you're doing?"

The beating halted. One of the Russians said, "Don't interfere. This is none of your business."

"Oh, we're going to interfere, ass hole. You're fucking with one of my customers."

The thug dropped Paul and he hit the pavement. Paul managed to peel an eye open, his face sticky with blood. Jessie and Steven stood on the sidewalk, both carrying baseball bats. They advanced warily toward the two Russians. The Russians stepped over Paul, advanced on Jessie and Steven. Then both Russian's halted and reached into their coats.

Paul had to do something. Baseball bats were no defense against nine-millimeter hollow-points. He pulled power, but it was a ragged thread compared to his norm.

Jessie and Steven froze when they saw the guns. One of the Russians said, "I told you not to interfere." He raised the gun.

Paul pulled more power, couldn't do more than direct it in a broad sweep in the general direction of his two attackers. A flash of light lit up the sidewalk and a bolt of electricity slammed into the backs of both Russians. Unfortunately, Jessie and Steven stood just on the other side of them and got a small taste of it. They staggered back a step but didn't go down. The Russians had taken the brunt of it and went down hard. Jessie and Steven only took an instant to recover, caught the Russians still on their hands and knees, used the baseball bats to give them a brief taste of their own medicine. Jessie and Steven relieved them of their guns then left them lying there groaning.

They helped Paul back to the bar, sat him down at a table. The two gay fellows from the end of the bar helped them clean him up. "What the hell was that about?" Jessie asked.

Paul held an ice pack to his cheek, decided a lie would be best. "I think they were trying to mug me."

"Paul, that was no fucking mugging. And what the hell did you hit them with? Hit us with it too. Looked like lightning. Felt like we were hit by lightning."

Again Paul lied. "They must have stepped on a loose wire from one of those houses."

Steven shook his head. "Didn't look like no loose wire to me."

"What do you think happened?" Paul said, trying to sound sardonic. "Like maybe I'm like a Gandalf, and I go around throwing lightning bolts."

They all got a good laugh at that. It turned out the two Russians had raised Jessie's doubts when, as soon as Paul was out the door, they hurriedly paid their bill by throwing a couple of twenties on the bar, a big overpayment, then rushed after him. They argued a bit about calling the cops, which Paul vetoed.

They cleaned him up, and the two gay fellows—he learned their names were Chris and Sam—insisted on walking Paul back to his building. Just to be safe, Paul pulled power and held it all the way there.

••••

The next morning Paul hurt so much he could barely walk. He limped into the bathroom, looked carefully at the mess that faced him in the mirror: split and swollen lips, several cuts on his face, black and yellowish bruises everywhere, the tissue around one eye so badly swollen he had to force it open with his fingers. He stepped back, looked down, saw that his knees were scraped and cut, the palms of his hands much the same. Standing in his boxer shorts, no shirt, the bruises up and down his torso confirmed what he felt inside.

He called McGowan, told him about the Russians, though he had difficulty speaking with the left side of his mouth badly swollen. "I'm not going to make it in today. I hurt all over. I'm just going to stay in bed."

"Sit tight, kid. I'm coming over."

It would take McGowan a good half hour to get there, so Paul crawled back into bed.

The telephone by his bed woke him. He picked up the receiver. "Ya."

"It's me, kid. I'm on my cell phone, standing in the hall in front of your door. We can't get in. Did you change the wards?"

"Ya. They're my wards now."

Paul staggered out of bed, answered the door in his skivvies, experienced a brief moment of embarrassment to see Colleen standing next to McGowan. But he hurt too much to give it more than a passing thought.

"Oh dear child," Colleen said at the sight of him.

He turned away from them tiredly, staggered back toward his bedroom. Colleen and McGowan flanked him, helped him get back into bed, Colleen all the while making sympathetic, motherly sounds. Paul lay on his back and Colleen sat next to him, examining his injuries, McGowan looming behind her.

McGowan nodded, had a pleased grin on his face. "Changed the wards, eh, kid? And I can barely sense them. Good job, buddy." He looked at Colleen. "I think the kid's growing up, in a wizardly sort of way."

Colleen looked at McGowan sourly, her voice dripping with that Irish accent. "And perhaps you should stop calling him *kid*, old man."

McGowan shook his head. "Nah. It keeps him humble."

"Be gone. Be gone," she said impatiently, hustling him out of the room. "I have work to do here."

To Paul she said furiously, "You've got broken ribs, and possibly some internal damage. You should have called me right away, not waited until this morning."

Colleen spent several hours working some of her healing mumbo-jumbo, which produced a marked improvement in the aches and pains. He resolved to stop thinking of it as *mumbo-jumbo*, learn some of it himself if he could, but there were so many other things he needed to learn first.

Paul slept on and off for most of the day, finally roused sometime in mid-afternoon. He heard voices beyond his closed bedroom door, struggled out of bed and pulled on a robe.

McGowan sat on his couch, talking on the phone. Devoe and Colleen sat at his small breakfast nook, both nursing coffee. Since the nook was only large enough for two, Devoe stood, let Paul sit down, hustled up a mug and poured Paul a cup of coffee.

Paul felt much better, though still a bit weak in the knees. "Thank you," he said to Colleen. She just smiled back at him.

McGowan finished his phone call, stood and crossed the living room to stand over the two of them, with Devoe leaning against one of the kitchen counters.

Paul said, "Sorry the accommodations aren't more suited for entertaining."

That got a smile from Devoe. "He can make jokes. That's a good sign."

McGowan said, "Clark here's your bodyguard now. He'll stick close to you until we clear up this Russian mafia problem. Even our Russian friends are scared of Clark.

"Colleen tells me she was able to repair all the serious damage so you'll be okay. I've also made a few calls. We'll have to wait to see how it plays out, but everyone is really pissed they crossed the master-apprentice line again. Especially since those two idiots were ready to pop a couple of civilians right on the street in broad daylight. None of us wants that kind of attention. This'll really eat into that Russian bastard's support base."

Paul's interest focused more on the take-out wrappers in the trash: looked like hamburgers. "I could use something to eat. Where'd you get those?"

"Place called Jessie's-something-or-other down the street. Clark'll get you something."

Paul nodded. "*Jessie's*. Run by Jessie and Steven. Nice people. If they hadn't pulled the Russian's off me it would have been a lot worse. I'd hate to see it come back and bite them."

McGowan frowned angrily. "Glad you told me that. I'm tired of that Russian bastard fucking with my apprentice. And I won't let him hurt your friends, either."

Devoe left to pick up a hamburger for Paul and to check out Jessie's place more thoroughly. Once he was gone, Paul asked McGowan, "Clark as a bodyguard? I mean, he's not that strong of a wizard."

The look that passed across McGowan's face was almost one of fear. "Clark may not be a strong practitioner, but he has enough capability to delay even the most powerful wizard or witch for an instant, and in that instant he's fast enough to empty a magazine full of hollow-points in your face. Be afraid of Clark, Paul. I'm afraid of Clark. And be careful to be Clark's friend."

When Devoe returned, McGowan and Colleen left. Devoe had picked up a hamburger for Paul and the smell of the thing made Paul's stomach growl. Paul had just finished the burger when the phone rang. Devoe answered it, listened for a second, handed it to Paul. "It's McGowan."

"Guess who just called me, kid: Karpov. He wants a powwow. We'll meet in my study tomorrow at ten. Be at my place an hour before that. He even agreed to enter my home without bringing his thugs for protection, so the pressure's really on him."

••••

It had been a long day, with a couple of particularly difficult cases to contend with. As Katherine's last appointment left her office she was looking forward to a drink and a nice, hot soak in the tub.

Her phone rang, and since it was the private inside line from her receptionist, she answered it. "What is it, Judy?"

"Dr. McGowan, there's a gentlemen here to see you."

Judy's voice sounded strange, distant and preoccupied. "Does he have an appointment? I thought I was done with my last appointment."

"No. No appointment. But I really do think you should speak with him."

"It's been a long day, Judy. Why?"

Judy hesitated for several seconds. "I really think you should see him, Dr. McGowan."

Judy had been with her since she'd first started her private practice almost ten years ago, and she trusted her implicitly. Judy wouldn't ask her to break her schedule unless it was important, and if she was reluctant to discuss the details with Katherine with the *gentlemen* probably hovering nearby, she would just have to trust Judy's judgment.

"All right, Judy. Send him in."

When the door opened a tall, attractive young man stepped into her office. He was dressed conservatively in a tan suit, expensive, probably a designer label, long, blonde hair hanging down to his shoulders, broad shoulders, trim waist, blue eyes, deep blue eyes. *Attractive*, she thought. *No, not merely attractive, gorgeous.*

She stood, a courtesy she gave to any client, reached across her desk to shake his hand. As their fingers touched she felt a sudden surge between her legs, chided herself for thinking like a horny schoolgirl and allowing some fellow's good looks to get to her that way. "I'm Katherine McGowan," she said, surprised her voice was a bit shaky.

"I'm Simuth," he said, still shaking her hand. Her nipples hardened, and the sensation between her legs intensified. Not until he released her hand was she able to regain some modicum of control. And damn it, she'd gone school-girl horny, soaking-wet-between-the-legs horny.

She pointed to a comfortable chair to one side of her desk, could barely get the words out. "Sit down . . . please . . . Simuth."

He grinned at her, as if he understood fully her reaction to him, but he didn't sit down, continued to stare at her with those incredible, blue eyes.

"What can I . . . do for you?" she asked, still standing herself.

He smiled warmly, but now his eyes were green, and they sparkled like emeralds, slit vertically like cat's eyes. She didn't recall him moving, but suddenly he stood beside her behind her desk. He touched her gently on the cheek, then took her in his arms and kissed her deeply. She gasped and orgasmed just standing there in his arms.

She couldn't look away from his eyes, desperately wanted him, wanted only to please him. Her world now centered on that one thought, and only that thought. She lifted her skirt for him because she wanted him now, right then and there on her desk, but he stopped her with a touch and said, "That can wait. What you can do now is come with me."

"Yes," she said, "of course."

16

Oaths That Bind

MCGOWAN HAD DRAWN the drapes in his study, turned the lights down so the shadows were thick about the walls. He sat behind his desk, Paul and Karpov in two wingback chairs in front of it. Devoe stood in the shadows along the wall where they could all see him. They went through the polite preliminaries: McGowan offered Karpov coffee or tea; he took tea; McGowan and Paul took coffee.

They sipped at their drinks while McGowan and Karpov chatted amiably, catching up on mutual acquaintances like two old college chums. When they finally got around to the real purpose of the meeting, Karpov turned to Paul and said, "Meester Conklin, I want you to understand Vladimir acted on his own for the purposes of petty revenge. I do not condone what his friends did, and you have my apologies. My subordinates will not trouble you again."

Karpov seemed sincere, but Paul knew better than to trust him, though McGowan had told him to keep it civil and not make any hard accusations. "So Vladimir and his friends were not acting on your orders?"

Karpov looked like he'd just swallowed a glass of sour milk. "As I said, he acted on his own initiative, without consulting me first."

Paul sipped his coffee. "And you're telling me Vladimir won't act on his own initiative again."

"Yes, Meester Conklin. Especially since Vladimir suffered an unfortunate accident yesterday. It was quite painful for him, and he will take some days to recover. His friends were involved in the same unfortunate accident, and they suffered too, though not as severely. However, Vladimir and his friends know that, should they not heed my advice, they will not survive the next unfortunate accident."

Karpov looked at Devoe, then back at McGowan. "Valter, your weapon will not be necessary."

"Perhaps," McGowan said. "But I think we'll keep Mr. Devoe close at hand for a bit. He's quite fond of Paul, and very upset he was injured so. Weren't you, Mr. Devoe?"

Devoe didn't move a muscle, just quietly said, "Um hum."

Paul and McGowan both saw Karpov out the front door. On either side of the door were two, narrow, floor to ceiling windows. Paul watched Karpov walk down the steps in front of McGowan's place. Two of his thugs in cheap, horse-blanket suits awaited him on the street, one Paul didn't recognize, the other Joe Stalin.

Paul and McGowan returned to the study. "I thought you were speaking euphemistically when you said *Russian mafia*. What did he do to Vladimir?"

McGowan shrugged. "Probably had his arms broken."

"Just like that?"

McGowan nodded carefully. "Yes, Paul, just like that. Vladimir made him look bad. But don't confuse Vasily with mafia. He and his colleagues aren't involved in drugs or prostitution or any of that stuff. He'd have no support from the other powerful wizards if he were. But he and a few others believe that we practitioners are a superior race, or something like that, that we should be in charge, and he should be in charge of us. And I and some others oppose him in that.

"Be paranoid, Paul. His interactions with you have cost him greatly among his support base. And while it wasn't your fault, I don't think he's looking at it that way. You're in the clear for the time being, but eventually, we won't be able to avoid a reckoning with him."

••••

It was close to noon. Paul was at McGowan's place in the old man's study, with Colleen grilling him relentlessly on some interesting spells. He wasn't doing well, a bit preoccupied with Katherine and the way she avoided him. He'd tried to call her several times, but she hadn't returned his calls.

McGowan burst into the room, interrupting him and Colleen. "Katherine's missing."

Colleen turned to him calmly. "What do you mean she's missing?"

"Her secretary called to ask if I'd seen her. She didn't show up at her office yesterday, didn't show up again today, and her secretary's been unable to reach her by phone."

Colleen remained calm. "How can we help, Walter?"

"Judy's calling all the hospitals and the police in case she's been in an accident. I'm going to her apartment. You two go to her office, check it out, see if Judy missed anything."

••••

The first thing Paul noticed in Katherine's reception was a funny smell in the air. It was strong, not unpleasant, but clearly abnormal for such a nice office, and he couldn't identify it, kind of like one of those sweet-smelling things cabbies hung from the dash of their taxi. But this place was a Rolls Royce, not a cab.

Paul introduced Colleen to Judy. "Yes. Mr. McGowan said you'd be coming by, that I was to cooperate with you fully." She was clearly distraught. "Nothing from the police, and I've called hospitals near this office and near her house. Nothing so far. Still have a few more to call."

Colleen nodded, the personification of calm. "Keep at it. We'll find her. I'm sure she's just fine. When did you last see her?"

"Day before yesterday. It was not an untypical day, a few difficult cases, but nothing really unusual. She finished her last appointment, left just after five, and I locked up as usual."

Paul wanted to ask about the smell, but Colleen apparently knew what he was thinking and stopped him with a slight shake of her head.

"We'll be in Katherine's office," Colleen said.

"Certainly," Judy said, and turned back to her phone.

As Paul closed the door to Katherine's office he turned to Colleen and asked, "What the hell is that smell?"

"It's not a smell," she said, picking up the telephone on Katherine's desk. "Like demon stink you're confusing your senses. Close your eyes, pinch your nose, breathe through your mouth, and use the new senses I've taught you."

Paul did as instructed, then, as he'd been taught, tried to clear his mind, open his inner *sight* to his surroundings. He had a picture in his mind of Katherine's office, but as he concentrated colors overlaid the image, which was frustrating since that meant he was now just using sight instead of smell to confuse his practitioner's sense. He stopped pinching his nose and opened his eyes to tell Colleen he had failed, but she was on the phone with someone.

"Walter, the place reeks of Sidhe, clearly Unseelie Court, probably royal blood."

Paul could only hear one side of the conversation. "Um hum . . . Um hum . . . No. Nothing in her house, huh? Um hum . . . Um hum . . . I think the receptionist was beguiled, doesn't remember a thing. Paul and I will try to open up her memories."

There was a long pause while she listened to something McGowan said. "Right. We'll see you in a bit."

Colleen hung up the phone, walked to the door, opened it and called, "Judy, could you join us in here?"

Colleen had Judy sit in a comfortable chair, then said, "We think you know more than you realize. We suspect you've been hypnotized to forget certain memories. With your permission I'd like to hypnotize you and see if I can unlock those memories."

One of Judy's eyebrows lifted skeptically. "Come now, Ms. Colleen. I wasn't born yesterday, and I've been with Katherine for almost ten years. I've known for some time she and her father and their *friends* are more than meets the eye. I don't know what, exactly, and I don't care. I'll do anything I can to help Katherine, but please don't patronize me."

Colleen shrugged, and her accent came back. "Very well, darlin'. I like a plain-speekin' woman. I'm going to do some unusual things, and Paul here will assist me. We won't hurt you, and you may be able to help Katherine. May I touch your forehead?"

Judy nodded, so Colleen bent, reached out, lightly touched the tips of her fingers to a spot between Judy's eyes. Paul was happy it looked nothing like a Vulcan mind-meld. Judy leaned back in the chair, closed her eyes, her breathing slowed and she calmed noticeably.

Colleen straightened, looked at Paul. "To break a glamour induced by a member of the royal blood of the Unseelie Court, I'll have to use a powerful spell. But since I haven't been able to prepare anything I'll have to use some complex rune magic. If you remember the rune I trace, and if you remember the words I chant, please don't use them unless you practice this first with me or Walter. If the rune isn't traced perfectly, the chant not spoken properly, something very different can happen, probably something rather unpleasant."

Paul nodded. Colleen turned back to Judy, pressed her thumb to the center of Judy's forehead, reminding Paul of the priest who used his thumb to smear ashes on his forehead on Ash Wednesday's when he was a child. Her thumb traced a shape on the receptionist's forehead as she spoke, "To the mind the beguiled are un-beguiled. To the heart the beguiler is no more, and yet is ever there."

Paul couldn't discern the shape Colleen traced no matter how he tried. But she traced it again and again, repeating the chant over and over until the rune glowed with a faint blue light. But while the light was faint to Paul's mundane sense of sight, when he closed his eyes it burned like a fiery beacon to his practitioner's *sight*, a simple triangle surrounding a symbol consisting of three or four convoluted, jagged lines, probably some Celtic rune, given Colleen's background. The symbol etched itself into his mind in a way he would never forget.

Colleen then moved to Judy's right temple, but now used her left forefinger to trace the same Celtic symbol in another triangle, repeating the same chant as she traced the rune over and over. The unusual symbol was the same, but where the triangle on her forehead had been point up, this one was point down, and it glowed with a red light. When it too was almost blinding to his practitioner's *sight*, she moved to Judy's left temple.

Using her right forefinger, she repeated the chant and the symbol on Judy's left temple, a rune identical to that on her right, but glowing with an emerald green light. And after tracing it several times, repeating the chant constantly, Colleen finally stepped back and looked at Judy, who now, to Paul's *sight*, lit up the room like a rainbow on a beautiful spring morning after a night of rain.

Colleen stared at Judy for a moment, and Paul felt her gathering her power, then she stepped forward, leaned down and kissed Judy delicately in the center of the rune on her forehead, a brief, momentary kiss in which she fed the power she had gathered into the rune. Then she whispered, "The beguilement is gone."

The runes disappeared without any dramatic demonstration of sight or sound, Judy gasped, opened her eyes, blinked several times, took several deep breaths, then buried her face in her hands. Colleen held up a hand, warning Paul to be silent. Judy sat that way for several seconds, then muttered through her fingers, "I remember."

Colleen said, "Then tell us."

Judy leaned back, looked Colleen square in the face. "He came at the end of the day, day before yesterday. Had no appointment, was not one of Katherine's patients, so normally I would have told him to make an appointment and turned him away regardless. But for some reason I didn't. In fact I insisted that Katherine see him."

"Describe him."

Judy thought for a moment, then described a tall, blonde god. "He was quite charming, and I felt . . ."

Colleen nodded. "You felt sexually attracted to him in a strong way."

Judy flushed and glanced at Paul. "I'm not normally like that. I don't understand it. In any case he met Katherine in her office, and then a few minutes later they left together. I locked up as usual, went home and forgot about it, literally."

"You've helped us immensely," Colleen said.

"Is she in danger?"

"Perhaps, but with this information, we should be able to bring her back unharmed."

"I hope so. I dearly hope so."

"You mentioned earlier that we are, how did you put it, *more than meets the eye?*"

Judy nodded cautiously.

"Then please realize that the police cannot help in this, that they can only get in the way."

Judy nodded again.

Colleen spent some time reassuring the woman and they left her in a fairly calm state. The old wizard met them on the steps of the building. Colleen told him, "This stinks of Simuth. I know his scent, and I know his style."

The look on McGowan's face turned to stone-cold anger. "Let's catch a cab, go back to my place."

••••

Like any royal Sidhe, Anogh both loved and hated the Mortal Plane, so filled with passion, energy, beauty and ugliness all at the same time. It was a tapestry of sensations, whereas Faerie remained ever unchanging. But at the same time his powers were so reduced it was like suffering an illness, a slow wasting death.

The door to the building that contained the daughter's office opened, and a rather ordinary young man stepped out onto the street. Anogh would normally not have paid attention, but the young man paused, appeared to be talking to his own shadow; strange enough, unless the shadow wasn't a shadow. Then a stooped, old woman leaning heavily on a cane joined him. The old lady too conversed with the shadow, then the young man and the old woman and the shadow turned and began walking up the street. And while the old female continued hobbling on her cane, and to mortal eyes it would seem she moved slowly, to the eyes of such as Anogh she moved much too quickly for an infirm, old woman.

Anogh caught a glimpse of something behind the trio, more a shimmer in the air than something of actual substance, clearly something of Faerie, probably a Sidhe mage. The shimmer followed the three, so Anogh decided to follow the follower, and once he stood in the mage's footsteps he knew this Sidhe was an agent of the Seelie Court. It did not surprise him that Magreth had someone keeping a close eye on the young necromancer. All of Faerie had taken a keen interest in the fellow.

As he followed the Seelie mage following the three mortals, his Faerie senses told him the druid and the Old Wizard accompanied the young necromancer, all three disguised in glamours of their choosing. Here on the Mortal Plane he had been weak enough, and they had been strong enough, to fool him had he not been watching closely.

Anogh moved quickly to catch up with Magreth's agent, pulling a glamour about himself. By now he knew the mage was not of Seelie royal blood, so he could overcome him easily. The three mortals reached a major cross street with Magreth's agent close on their heels. They hailed a cab, climbed in, and as it pulled away the Seelie mage dropped his glamour, became visible and tried to hail a cab of his own. He was clearly one of the Summer Queen's young courtiers trying to curry favor by taking on an unpleasant task. It was a simple matter for Anogh to ensure that no cab stopped for the young agent.

The Seelie mage stood on the street corner and cursed as another cab passed him by. Anogh stepped up behind him and wrapped them both in his glamour so they couldn't be seen by mundane eyes. The young agent gasped, turned to face him and his eyes widened. He dropped to one knee. "My Lord, how may I serve the Summer Knight?"

Anogh nodded. "What is Magreth's concern in this?"

The young mage bowed his head and said, "She fears he will be bound to the Unseelie Court."

Anogh understood Magreth's fear. "Return to Magreth, tell her I ask her to stand down. Tell her that, on my word, she need not fear the young mage will be bound to the Winter Court."

The young Sidhe looked up, eyes wide. "But your oaths, My Lord?"

"Tell Magreth I will not betray my oaths, but they do not hinder me in this."

The young Sidhe bowed his head. "As you wish, My Lord."

"You may go."

The young man vanished.

Anogh turned, looked in the direction the cab had gone. It was time he met the young necromancer alone.

17

No Free Will

SHE SENSED THE summons as a desperate need she must answer. She took a moment to look upon the lithe body of the Sidhe man lying next to her in bed. She could only remember bits and pieces of their activities the previous night, wanted to forget every sickening second of it. And yet, she wanted more of it, even longed for it. But the summons demanded her attention, her obedience.

How she got from naked in a bed next to a naked Adonis, to walking down a corridor, she could not say. She now wore the finest of Faerie silks, though what could be seen through them would get her arrested any place on the Mortal Plane. Her hair had been wrapped and twirled elaborately atop her head, and jewels hung from her throat and wrists and ankles.

"She is beautiful, is she not?"

Now she stood before an older Sidhe, but while older, still more beautiful than all the rest. He wore a crown on his head, sat upon a throne made of precious stones of all kinds, and wore white Sidhe silks. No one need tell her she stood before Ag.

Simuth stood to one side, walked up to her, touched her cheek and she orgasmed again just standing there. She dropped to her hands and knees and lowered her head in shame.

"She is an insatiable little minx, Your Majesty."

She felt fingers lift her chin, raise her face to look into Simuth's eyes. She desperately longed for his touch. "Please," she begged. "Don't leave me . . . more . . . give me more . . ." Then something of her true self rose to the surface. "You fucking bastard," she snarled, gritting her teeth.

Simuth, still holding her chin, turned to Ag. "Do you see what I mean? She is much stronger than I thought, somehow constantly finds the strength to resist me, even if only for a moment. It makes our little adventures together even more pleasurable."

Without warning Ag stood, spun on Simuth and struck him, sent him sprawling to the floor. On his hands and knees Simuth pleaded, "What have I done wrong, Your Majesty?"

Ag's face twisted into a frightful grimace. "I told you to bring her to me so I could question her. And of course, if she were a willing partner for your proclivities, I would not begrudge you two your mutual pleasures." He shook as he spoke. "But against her will——. You idiot."

Ag kicked Simuth in the ribs, kicked him several times. And while Simuth lay there groaning, Ag turned to Katherine. "Stand, child, and let me see you."

Now she stood before him. How she got there from her hands and knees, and how she had gotten completely naked again, she had no idea.

Ag nodded. "She is quite pretty, and you say adventuresome?"

Simuth, still lying on the floor and groaning, had trouble getting the words out. "She needs a little prodding, though not much. And she is insatiable, though it never hurts to encourage her insatiability with a little spell here and there. Would you like her for this evening's pleasure, Your Majesty?"

"Been loaning her out quite a bit, have you?"

Simuth said, "Well . . . you know how it is . . ."

Ag turned, crossed the few paces to Simuth and kicked him in the face. "I did not want a war with the Old Wizard."

Ag turned back to Katherine and looked her over carefully. "Perhaps we can make some use of her. I'm told she and the necromancer share some attraction. It's possible we can use her to bring him to us."

••••

Ag dismissed Katherine with a wave of his hand, and Simuth watched her disappear.

As the king looked down on him he cringed and said, "No one has touched her."

"What do you mean by that?"

Simuth struggled slowly to his feet. "I have given her false memories, but have not actually touched her, nor allowed anyone else to do so."

Ag's eyes narrowed with distrust. "Explain."

Simuth straightened. The side of his face hurt terribly and was beginning to swell, but to heal himself in Ag's presence could reignite the king's anger. "Each morning she awakes with false memories of gladly participating in some rather lewd behavior. It's quite embarrassing for her. Within a few hours the memories dissipate, and she realizes they were false."

Ag grinned. "But the humiliation and self-loathing remain, eh?"

"Yes, Your Majesty. These mortals' psyches are so delicate they are easily mortified."

"When the false memories dissipate, are you certain she knows she hasn't been touched?"

Simuth bowed carefully. "Yes, Your Majesty. Even if she claimed to have been physically harmed, we could bring in the little people to arbitrate, and they would sense the lie in her words. And don't forget that, to all appearances, she came to us of her own free will."

"Then you are forgiven," Ag said. He waved a hand in dismissal. "Leave Us. Go heal yourself."

••••

"Unseelie," McGowan said. "That's not good." He stood and turned his back on them to stare out the window of his study.

"Yes," Colleen said. "The Seelie might play with her a bit, then discard her, perhaps even leave her with a few fond memories. The Unseelie will surely destroy her."

"I don't understand," Paul said.

Colleen stared at McGowan's back as she spoke to Paul. "Sex is the hallmark of the Unseelie Court. It is used for almost everything, to reward, punish, gratify, humiliate, to give joy or sorrow, to merely entertain. They can give Katherine more pleasure than any of us can imagine. But even though, to all outward appearances, she is a ready and willing participant, such wanton behavior is not her way, and it will torment her, perhaps destroy her mind."

Paul asked, "Can't we just demand they return her?"

McGowan shook his head and said, "It's more complicated than that."

He turned to face them, looked at Colleen and asked, "You said that Judy told you she appeared to leave with the fellow of her own free will?"

Colleen nodded.

McGowan looked at Paul. "That muddies the waters."

"That's bullshit," Paul said. "He beguiled her, and you've told me that's very powerful."

Colleen said, "But we can't prove it."

"Then how do we get her back?"

McGowan said, "First, Colleen, can you determine definitively that she's in the Unseelie Court? If that's the case, then we'll have to negotiate."

Paul asked, "What do we have to negotiate with?"

Both Colleen and McGowan looked at him sadly. Colleen's accent had suddenly gotten thick. "We suspect, me boy, that what they're lookin' to get their hands on, is you."

"But this isn't about me—"

"God damn it," McGowan shouted. "Yes it is. That's what we've been trying to get through your thick skull all this time. I'll bet you're not even carrying your piece, are you?"

"Now Walter," Colleen said. "Calm down."

"I will not calm down. It's Katherine who's in danger now, and I can't protect her, and it's his—" McGowan stopped suddenly, closed his eyes and an ugly silence descended.

Paul took a deep breath and let it out slowly. "You were about to say it's my fault."

McGowan nodded. "Yes, I was. And I would have been wrong."

"Thank you," Paul said cautiously. "And no, I'm not wearing my piece. And yes, I'll be more careful about things like that. But that doesn't answer my original question. How do we get Katherine back?"

McGowan dropped into a chair, buried his face in his hands and rubbed his forehead. "Colleen will determine exactly where Katherine is. While she's doing that I'll teach you some new kinds of magic and spells, some very nasty stuff, both offensive and defensive. And you need to learn all that in short order.

"We're also going to bring in a few friends, like Clark Devoe. When the shooting starts, you can't have anyone better at your back."

McGowan stood, paced back and forth across the room and ran his fingers through his hair. "But we can't mount a full scale assault on a Sidhe Court without starting all-out war. And in any case, Judy saw, what appeared to be, Katherine accompany Simuth willingly. We know she wasn't willing, but that appearance means the rest of Faerie would not support us if we openly assault one of the Courts. If Katherine is in either of the Sidhe Courts, and we can prove it, then they have to negotiate with us. And we won't give you up for her, trade one hostage for another. If the situation was reversed, we wouldn't give her up for you."

Paul asked, "Kind of like the government won't negotiate with terrorists."

McGowan nodded tiredly. "Something like that."

••••

"He swore? On his word?" Magreth demanded. "He swore the young wizard will not be bound to the Winter Court?"

The young Sidhe mage, on one knee before the Summer Queen, looked into her eyes and said, "His exact words were, 'Return to Magreth, tell her I ask her to stand down. Tell her that, on my word, she need not fear the young mage will be bound to the Winter Court.' I swear before you now, my Queen, those were his exact words."

Magreth turned a cold, disbelieving look upon the young mage. "But what of his oaths, Tyon?"

"I asked him that also, and again his exact words were, 'Tell Magreth I will not betray my oaths, but they do not hinder me in this.' I knew you would want to hear them as if he stood here before you himself, so I was careful to remember them exactly."

The Summer Queen nodded. "Stand, Tyon. You have done well."

She turned to her chancellor. "So, Cadilus, the Summer Knight chooses to intervene in some way. And he gives us his word, without prevarication. How un-Sidhe of him!"

He shrugged. "And I have no doubt Anogh will deliver."

"Are you saying we should stand down as he requested?"

Cadilus glanced sideways at the young warrior Tyon. Magreth nodded, took the hint and said to the young warrior. "Tyon, thank you, you have served Us well. You may go."

The young warrior bowed and backed out of the audience chamber.

Cadilus waited until he was gone, the door closed completely behind him, before speaking. "The Unseelie Court has taken the Old Wizard's daughter. Simuth is holding her hostage in Faerie."

Magreth's brows narrowed angrily. "That is disturbing, Cadilus. The Old Wizard just might choose to trade the young mage for her."

"He is a crafty, old fellow, Your Majesty, and a formidable opponent for anyone. I doubt he will turn to that recourse immediately. But it does give the Winter Court a serious edge with regard to the young mage."

"You're right, as always, my dear Cadilus. But Simuth is an animal. He could damage her."

Cadilus frowned. "Ag is no less an animal, but he knows when to control his instincts, and when to control Simuth. And since, at the time, there were no open hostilities between the Old Wizard and the Winter Court, that makes Ag the aggressor, which means he is not completely free to act as he might choose. He must move with care here, for to act imprudently might precipitate open war with the Old Wizard and his colleagues. We might then align with the old man, and even Ag is not fool enough to wage war on two fronts."

Her brows furrowed deeply. "It makes me wonder if Anogh isn't playing some game of his own."

Cadilus smiled, raised both hands palms up, as if to say, *Of course he is.* "He is Anogh. When has he ever not played a game of his own? But I wonder how he will thread the needle, not violate his oaths and deliver the young wizard to us."

She shook her head. "No, Cadilus, he did not say that. He said the young wizard will not be bound to the Winter Court. He did not say he would be bound to us. He can accomplish that in many ways, one of which is to merely kill the young fool. Perhaps it is time we play a more direct role in the events to come."

18

Memories Unlocked

KATHERINE SUSPECTED AG had intervened, though no one would admit that openly. She had a cloudy memory of standing before the Winter King while he discussed her with Simuth, though the memory did not include any details of what they had said. But the hazy veil of beguilement had lifted, the sexual exploits with Simuth and his friends had ended abruptly, and now she was frequently summoned into Ag's presence. It was a relief to think again without induced sexual desire clouding her every thought, though she could not escape the memories of the things she'd done with Simuth and his friends prior to Ag's intervention.

She still couldn't get used to walking around always dressed only in semi-transparent Sidhe silks, especially since the other women of the Court dressed as they chose, though always elegantly. It was a constant reminder she was not free to choose, that she was, for all intents and purposes, a slave. She understood the psychology of that.

"My dear," Ag said. "Your thoughts were elsewhere. Tell me."

He could easily force her. And though she and her father had never bothered with any serious instruction in Sidhe Court etiquette, she could adapt, and be as evasive as they without triggering any desire to force the truth from her. "Just a trifling thought, Your Majesty, nothing of sufficient consequence to trouble the Winter King."

They walked a pathway through a lovely garden of strange flowers and plants. She paused to admire a particularly beautiful blossom. "It's magnificent," she said.

"I'm pleased you like it," Ag said. He plucked the flower, stripped a few leaves from the stem and inserted it in her hair. He sat down on a stone bench, patted a spot beside him. "Come. Sit beside me."

She did, for she dare not disobey him.

"You are troubled, my child."

His fatherly demeanor did not fool her in the least. He had condoned Simuth's activities, even if only through his indifference. And while she had been horrified at the way she'd happily participated in Simuth's lascivious exploits, she feared most what he was doing to her mind. "I confess that I fear, Your Majesty, for myself, for my father, for my friends. I know I am merely a pawn in this game."

"Ah, but such a lovely pawn, my dear." He looked through the translucent silk at her breasts, and the smile that appeared on his face appalled her. "And you need not fear. We merely seek certain concessions regarding the young mage. He need not be fully bound to us. So with the proper assurances, you and your father and your friends can return to your mundane lives."

She couldn't believe a word he said, but she dare not confront him with that. "Thank you, Your Majesty. My heart rests easier now."

He lifted a hand and ran a finger along the side of her neck. "I'm glad of that, my dear."

In that instant she found herself standing at a window in the suite of rooms they'd given her. Beneath her stretched the countryside of the Winter Court. As she stood there the memories of her disgusting behavior prior to Ag's intervention slowly dissipated, and she understood that it was all false.

She couldn't hold back the tears.

••••

They were all sitting around McGowan's kitchen table, sucking down coffee and trying to hatch a plan to rescue Katherine, when the doorbell rang. Sarah stood and said, "I'll get it."

When Sarah returned to the kitchen she handed McGowan a business card and said, "It's the same distinguished gentleman who visited some months back. Clearly Seelie, and probably royal blood."

McGowan looked at Colleen and said, "Cadilus."

"Ah," she said, smiling knowingly. "Very interesting!"

"Holy shit!" Devoe grumbled.

"All of you wait here," McGowan instructed them. "I'll meet with him in my study." He turned and marched down the hall to the front door.

McGowan had been with Cadilus for almost an hour when Colleen closed her eyes in an odd way and leaned her head back as if listening to something. She sat that way for a few seconds, then opened her eyes and looked directly at Paul. "You and I are to join Walter in his study. Be careful to address Cadilus as *Lord Cadilus* or *Your Excellency*. I am *Lady Armaugh*, and Walter is just plain *Old Wizard*, though use that term only with the utmost respect. Do not speak your own name under any circumstances. And above all, do not let him touch you."

As usual, Cadilus had chosen to appear in his British diplomat persona. He sat in an antique wingback chair, holding a brandy snifter that contained an amber liquid. He stood immediately, put the snifter down on a small table, approached Colleen, bowed from the waist, and as she extended her hand he kissed it delicately. He straightened, spoke in a deep baritone with an upper-crust British accent, "Lady Armaugh, I am doubly blessed to see you twice in such a short period of time."

She smiled stonily. "Lord Cadilus."

He doted on her, escorted her to another chair like his, saw her seated comfortably before turning to Paul. He simply said, "Young Mage," nodded, and returned to his chair. Paul remained standing.

Colleen said, "So, what brings you among us mortals?"

McGowan answered her. "Her Majesty, the most gracious Magreth, has invited us to attend her at Court."

Colleen frowned at Cadilus. "These are trying times, Your Excellency. Any journey to Faerie could be most dangerous for us."

"Her Majesty is well aware of that," Cadilus said. "You will be granted *guest right* of the house of the Summer Queen, and escorted by a rank of Sidhe warriors chosen from among her personal guard. Your *guest right* and protection will extend from a place of your choosing in the Mortal Plane, to the Seelie Court, then back to any other place of your choosing in the Mortal Plane, be it the same place from which you began the journey, or a different one."

"A most generous offer," she said. "I shall look forward with heightened anticipation to seeing the beauty of the Summer Court again. And of course, we will bring our own protections."

There was some undercurrent here that Paul didn't understand. "Of course you may. And the beauty of the Summer Court will only be enhanced by your presence, my lady." Cadilus turned back to McGowan. "When may I tell Her Majesty to expect you, Old Wizard?"

"We can be ready at dusk tomorrow, Your Excellency. We'll leave from the garden in the back of this house. The back of my property is an old boundary between districts in the city."

Cadilus stood. "Well, then my business here is concluded. I won't impose upon you further."

McGowan stood also. "I'll see you to the door."

Cadilus was closer to the door, and in a few casual steps drew near Paul and extended his hand. "Young man, it's been a pleasure—"

Colleen did one of those moves of hers that seemed casual, didn't give an impression of quick or hurried movement, but in fact crossed the length of the room in a heartbeat, stepping between Cadilus and Paul. She shook his hand warmly. "Good friend, until we meet again."

Cadilus smiled knowingly, and Paul realized they were playing a dangerous little game. They all knew it was a game, they all knew the rules, they all knew everyone would attempt to cheat, and they all pretended it wasn't so.

McGowan escorted Cadilus out of his study. Paul started to speak, but Colleen held a finger to her lips.

They waited perhaps five minutes for McGowan to return. He paused half way through the study door, shouted down the hall. "Clark, can you join us?"

Paul asked both of them, "Was there a whole lot going on there that I couldn't read?"

McGowan grinned. "Oh yes, kid. But I got the information we really needed while I had him alone."

Devoe slipped into the room, closed the study door quietly and slipped into the shadows nearby.

"Anyone want a drink?" McGowan asked. He splashed whiskey into several glasses and passed them around.

McGowan looked at Paul. "First, you need to know that the Sidhe never lie, but are masters at getting you to deceive yourself. They are rarely direct, seem to take great pleasure in approaching everything from an obtuse angle. So realize that almost nothing I tell you was offered openly. But the picture is fairly clear."

Colleen said, "They're nervous now that the Winter Court has Katherine, aren't they? They're worried Ag can use Katherine in some way to bind Paul."

"Exactly." McGowan paced back and forth across the room. "Magreth's actions regarding Paul are more defensive than offensive. She doesn't feel any great need to have Paul bound to the Summer Court."

Paul interrupted. "What do you mean by *bound*?"

Colleen answered him. "Take oath with a Sidhe, enter into a formal agreement, and it is binding unto your life. Break such an oath and your life is forfeit. Though they might not necessarily kill you, instead they might enslave you. If they can trick you, or coerce you, into an oath, then trick you into breaking it, then you are bound in a way you cannot imagine."

"And they're good at structuring oaths with lots of hidden loop-holes in them to their advantage," McGowan added. "So be careful not to agree to anything with a Sidhe.

"The one thing Magreth does want is assurance Paul won't be bound to the Unseelie Court. She will be content if Paul is strong enough to remain a free agent. On the other hand, if he's not, and if she can't bind him to the Seelie Court, she'll want him dead."

"So she wants to look me over, see if I'm strong enough to remain unbound? That's why we got the invitation."

McGowan smiled and nodded. "You're beginning to understand the rules of the game. But it's not an invitation, though it may be couched as such, it is nevertheless a command. And she'll be looking at much more than your own capabilities as a practitioner. She'll also be looking at your support structure, your allies."

"Like you and Colleen."

"Yes, and Clark too. The Sidhe have great respect for Clark, even fear him a bit."

Colleen nodded her agreement. Paul finished his drink, let it burn its way down his throat and warm his stomach. Devoe and his mysterious abilities were a constant revelation to Paul. "So what's next?"

McGowan looked at his watch. "It's getting late. You're properly warded, and you're carrying?" Paul nodded. "Good. Go home, get a good night's sleep, return here first thing tomorrow. We'll spend the day briefing you on Sidhe court etiquette. If we pass this test, we may gain a strong ally in our efforts to get Katherine back."

••••

Paul stepped out of the cab in front of his apartment. The sun had long ago set and clouds obscured the moon so the night was dark, though streetlamps and the background light of the city lit the street well. Paul had learned to be paranoid, and looked around carefully as he paid the cabbie. He was alone on a clear and empty street.

He retrieved his key, was about to insert it into the lock on the door of his building, when a strong, male voice behind him said, "Good evening, Young Mage."

Paul jumped and turned. At the bottom of the steps a tall, handsome man dressed in jeans, loafers and a pullover sweater stood on the sidewalk. Shadows from the streetlights obscured his face. Paul reached for his gun, but the man said, "You won't need that. I'm not here to harm you, just to give you a message."

Clearly the man was Sidhe, and while Paul had become reasonably adept at recognizing which Court, this one left him with the confusing impression of both Seelie and Unseelie. Paul didn't draw the Sig from the waist holster, but kept his hand near it. He did draw power and checked his personal wards. "I'm listening."

The man at the bottom of the steps looked up and let the streetlights illuminate his face. There was something familiar about him, but Paul couldn't place it and he wondered, *Why do they all have to be so damn beautiful?* The man smiled as if he knew Paul's thoughts. "Tell the Old Wizard," he said, "Anogh's oaths bind him so he must serve at the pleasure of Ag, and he may not betray the Winter Court to the Summer. But the binding is only that, and no more."

"And from whom should I say this message came?"

"Tell the old man the Summer Knight sends his regards. But there is also a message for you, Young Mage, a private message, for you alone."

Paul knew this Sidhe from somewhere, but if so his recollection of it was locked away in some distant memory, and try as he might he could not recall it. Paul said, "I'm still listening."

The Sidhe's eyes narrowed, and now he seemed almost angry. "The love for which you grieve must be avenged. And when you learn of love's betrayal, remember this lesson . . ."

Paul waited to hear more, stood staring at the Sidhe, marveled again at how he wore beauty like a veil. Even a man could be attracted to such beauty. Paul stepped down a step, realized he was getting an erection and didn't care. He approached the Sidhe without caution, wanted to kiss him, and not merely on the cheek, fantasized about the two of them in bed together. He touched the Sidhe's cheek and his heart ached, fearing he would lose this beautiful man, that his desire for him would never be satisfied. At that moment he would have done anything for this incredible creature. He leaned forward to kiss him, but a wave of dizziness overcame him and he stumbled back a step, then sat down on the steps in front of his building.

He shook his head. What had he been thinking? The compelling attraction had disappeared, switched off like a light, and he recalled McGowan's words about their ability to beguile humans. To hear it spoken of was one thing, to experience it first hand was . . .

He looked up. The Sidhe was gone, had said something as he left, though Paul had been badly distracted at the moment, something about . . . *she could not have resisted him* . . .

••••

Paul slept poorly that night. He couldn't put the encounter out of his mind, kept replaying it again over and over, trying to make sense of the second message, the message for him. And too, he kept trying to remember where and when he'd encountered the Sidhe before, but it wouldn't come to him.

The next morning when Paul stepped into McGowan's kitchen, the old man sat at the breakfast table nursing a cup of coffee. He looked up at Paul and said, "You look like shit, kid."

"Ya. Didn't sleep well," Paul said. "Had a little visit last night before I got home. Is there any more of that coffee?"

"Sure. Help yourself. Should I get Colleen in here to hear about this visit?"

"Ya, I think you should."

Paul rummaged in the cupboards, found a mug, filled it with coffee, sat down at the table and recalled again the previous evening's encounter. He was so engrossed, staring at the steam rising from the mug, he didn't realize McGowan had returned with Colleen until they both sat down at the table across from him.

"Something's disturbing you," she said.

Paul described the encounter with the Sidhe, relayed the message for McGowan. He didn't tell them about the second part of the message, the part meant for him. And he wasn't about to tell them he'd gotten a hard-on for another man. Colleen asked, "You said Anok. Did he really say it that way, or did he say Anogh, with a guttural *gh* on the end?"

Paul nodded, "Anogh, with the guttural *gh*. Who's Anogh?"

"Oh, my boy!" Colleen said. It was the first time he'd ever seen her composure slip. "Anogh is the Summer Knight, but he is bound to the Winter Court. It is rumored that about six or seven hundred years ago he fell in love with the Princess of Winter, and she with him. I believe her name was Taal'mara. They carried on a secret love affair for about a century, very Romeo and Juliet: two lovers from houses that are mortal enemies. But apparently Ag found them out, tricked Anogh into an oath, and tricked him into violating that oath, which bound him to the Winter Court for as long as Simuth, the Winter Knight, shall live. But Simuth is royal Unseelie, so he is immortal."

McGowan added. "If you haven't figured it out by now, Ag is not a nice guy."

Paul asked, "And what did his message mean?"

"That's the interesting part," McGowan said. "I think he's telling us the oath's that bind him to the Winter Court have some loop-holes. He can't betray the Winter Court to the Summer, but since we're not Summer Court, maybe he can betray Winter to us. He could be an enormously helpful ally."

"Be careful, old man," Colleen said. "It sounds like he *can* help us. But has he? And will he? Don't forget he's Sidhe, and with them nothing is ever as it appears."

Paul still couldn't put Anogh's face out of his mind. "Can either of you help me bring back a lost memory?" He looked at Colleen. "Maybe like you did with Judy, or something?"

"What kind of memory?" McGowan asked.

Paul explained about Anogh's face, the way he'd obsessed about it all night, yet couldn't make any headway.

"I might be able to help," Colleen said. "But I need a small mirror."

McGowan stood. "I'll get one." He disappeared down the hall, came back a minute later carrying a small hand mirror.

"That'll do nicely," Colleen said. She took the mirror, stood and sat back down in a seat directly opposite Paul, held the mirror up so he saw his reflection. "This is going to be very different from what I did to Judy. I want you to look at your own image. Try to clear your thoughts, then think carefully of Anogh's face, think of each little detail."

He had no problem recalling Anogh's face; he'd obsessed about it since last night: long, dark, shoulder-length hair, strong jaw, the eyes shadowed by a dark sorrow. Colleen muttered something in the background, but it didn't distract Paul's thoughts from the beautiful Sidhe warrior. In fact, if the hair were shorter, cut more like a typical college student, the eyes a little less shadowed, less haunted, take off a few years, and remove some of the incredible beauty, he could be any handsome, young college student in the country. And then it hit him. He knew! He knew! Paul gasped out, "Summers Knight."

"You remember?" Colleen asked.

"Yes. Yes. A friend from college. His name was Summers Knight. Didn't really know him well, more a friend of other friends, ran into each other at a few parties." It all came rushing back to him. "My god," he said, burying his face in his hands. "He sort of introduced me to Suzanna. It was a party, at his place, lot of students there, some with dates, some without. I was without, and so was Suzanna. It was just a quick, casual introduction. *Paul, this is Suzanna*, that kind of thing. And she and I hit it off from there, never looked back."

"Summers Knight!" McGowan said with almost reverent awe. "The bastard's been mucking in your life for quite a while, Paul. He must have known Suzanna was a foundling."

McGowan was clearly stunned. "Anogh is playing at his own game. He may or may not be an ally, or he may be an ally now and an enemy later. But never forget he's setting something up here. And the only thing we can be certain of is that if it goes his way, it will be to his advantage. Perhaps not to our detriment, but certainly to his advantage."

McGowan and Colleen spent the rest of the afternoon grilling Paul on Sidhe Court etiquette. He listened, heard what they said, nodded politely here and there, responded a bit with a word or two when necessary, but a piece of him could not leave the issue of Anogh and Suzanna. Anogh had said, *The love for which you grieve must be avenged.*

Avenged! Why would anyone avenge an accident? You don't avenge accidents unless you're a nut case. Or unless it was not an accident.

"Paul," Colleen snapped. "Pay attention. This is important."

"Yes. Yes. Sorry."

And when you learn of love's betrayal . . . It had to mean something other than betrayal. But there were so many things he had not known about her, and back then he hadn't been dealing with Sidhe. Betrayal was in their nature, and she was half Sidhe. Betrayals, innuendo, subtle deceit, the Sidhe were not Sidhe without such. Did that mean Anogh had murdered Suzanna, for some strange reason Paul could not fathom? If so, then the only thing left for him in this life would be to avenge her death. Yes, give Anogh his due, in spades.

19

Pass-Fail Time

AS INSTRUCTED BY McGowan and Colleen, Paul dressed that morning in a dark business suit, though since gunpowder didn't work in Faerie, he left the firearms behind. But a few weeks ago, on his own initiative, he'd gone to a sporting-goods store, purchased a good-sized hunting knife made of quality steel and had a sheath made to conceal it under his arm like a gun in a shoulder holster. He also packed a small duffle with a couple changes of clothes and toiletries.

McGowan wore a hooded, floor-length robe made of heavily brocaded satin, almost oriental in appearance, though the lightning bolts embroidered on his sleeves made Paul think again of Gandalf. The image would have been complete if McGowan had sported a long beard, with hobbits scampering under foot. Slightly open at the neck with the hood thrown back, Paul saw that McGowan also wore a conservative business suit beneath his robe.

McGowan looked him over carefully, nodded his approval and handed him a large bundle of fabric. Paul shook it out. It was another wizard's robe similar to McGowan's, including the lightning bolts on the sleeves. "The traditional, formal attire of a mage when attending a Sidhe Court," McGowan said. "You armed?"

Paul opened his coat to display the knife in the underarm sheath.

McGowan nodded his approval, asking, "Cold iron?"

Paul said, "Good steel, which has plenty of iron."

McGowan grinned. "You're learning, kid."

The old man helped him put the robe on, then handed Paul a wooden staff about five feet long. It was plain and unadorned. "It's not a true staff. It'll take a few years to properly imprint one, but appearances will be important today. So carry it any time you wear the robes."

McGowan picked up his own staff, like Paul's about five feet long, but with sigils and runes and strange figures carved down its length. Paul noticed it also had some scorch marks here and there. "Do we really need the hardware?" he asked as McGowan turned toward the back of the house and Paul followed.

"Nah," McGowan said. "Not with the protections we've been granted. But as I said, appearances are important, and a show of strength, and the message that we're watching out for ourselves regardless of any promises, is part of the package."

Devoe joined them just before they emerged from the back of the house. He wore fairly casual clothing, slacks, long-sleeve shirt, lightweight, waist-length windbreaker. Paul had seen its like in Devoe's gun shop, advertised as good for concealing a weapon, or maybe two or three, if he knew Clark Devoe at all.

The Sidhe warriors were incredible, seven of them arrayed in the garden behind McGowan's house, all wearing splendid armor inlaid with silver, mother of pearl, precious stones, with proud, beautiful faces framed in open helms. Each wore a silver rapier at his side.

McGowan introduced Paul to Captain Dergindaal as the *young mage*. Dergindaal was polite, and like Paul he did not extend his hand. He looked at Devoe, said to McGowan, "I see you bring the *weapon*." There was a slight emphasis on the word weapon.

"Does that surprise you?"

Dergindaal shook his head. "You always surprise me, Old Wizard."

McGowan smiled. "Lady Armaugh should be joining us shortly. No doubt, she wants to make an entrance."

"Ah, Old Wizard, but when the Lady Armaugh makes an entrance, we all fall subject to her mercy."

When Colleen emerged from the rear of McGowan's house, gone was the dress that appeared to be a jumble of vary-colored scarves attached haphazardly to her from neck to ankles, and in its place she wore a gown of silken brocade. The hippie aspect was still there, still all earth-colors, and the gown must have had a thousand folds. Paul had the momentary impression her hair had changed color subtly. But as he looked closer he realized that, where it had been red before, it was now flaming red, literally, with little motes of fire dancing through the wild disarray of her curls. The charms plaited into her hair were still there, but she'd added dried flowers here and there, even simple bits of straw. And her face glowed with vigor and vitality. She was still past middle age, perhaps in her early sixties, but she easily rivaled younger women in their prime.

"Paul," McGowan said. "Your mouth is hanging open."

She descended the few steps carefully, one step at a time, with Jim'Jiminie and Boo'Diddle hopping and bouncing about her feet. She approached Dergindaal; he and his warriors dropped to one knee and bowed their heads. She extended a hand. Dergindaal kissed it elegantly and looked into her face. "Lady Armaugh, the Summer Court has been blighted like a winter frost in your absence."

She remained cold and aloof. "Captain Dergindaal, you are kind to an old woman." He stood, and his warriors followed suit. She indicated the leprechauns. "Jim'Jiminie and Boo'Diddle have graciously offered to escort me." The two leprechauns gripped each other in a sumo-wrestler's hug and rolled around in the grass. "I do hope you'll extend to them the courtesy of the Court."

Dergindaal nodded solemnly. "I have been instructed by Her Majesty to extend to you and the Old Wizard, and your chosen retinues, all of the protections and courtesies of the Seelie Court."

He turned away, but she caught his arm lightly. He turned back to her and she said, "It is good to see you again, Dergindaal."

He flushed. Paul thought, *I just saw a fucking captain of Sidhe warriors actually blush.*

Dergindaal merely smiled, but his eyes lit up. "I hope, My Lady, you'll have time to visit with an old friend, catch up on old times, as it were."

"I shall try, my lord"

Dergindaal's eyes lit up anew. He turned to McGowan. "Are we ready, old man?"

McGowan said, "I believe so." They then all took up positions as they had discussed previously: Dergindaal in front, McGowan and Paul behind him side-by-side, Colleen behind them with her leprechauns dancing about her skirts, Devoe last of all, around them all the six remaining Sidhe warriors. "We're ready, Captain," McGowan said.

Most fey could execute a crossing from just about any point in either Realm, but the presence of mortals made it much more difficult, and a boundary or ley line helped immensely. Without warning there came that weird spiral shift in reality, almost as if Paul saw down a strange, yet simple, path. There came no draw of power, no need to force anything, and again it felt to Paul as if one merely needed to choose the right door, then open it and walk through it, as simple as that. And there they all stood, in a large hall tiled in some sort of glistening, white stone. Stone pedestals lined the walls every few feet, and on each rested the bust of someone who was probably famous, though since they were now in the Seelie Court, it was unlikely they were famous for anything Paul had heard of.

In front of them stood two, large, wooden doors, ornately carved from some dark wood. The figures on the door to the right were of a beautiful Sidhe race, with an aura of kindness and compassion emanating from their incredible faces. The figures on the door to the left were of an equally beautiful Sidhe race, but the aura that emanated from them was one of cruelty and malice.

Paul nudged McGowan and whispered, "Let me guess: Seelie to the right, Unseelie to the left."

"Very good," McGowan whispered back. "Only a mage would see the auras beyond the shapes in the carvings. But don't forget, this is a Seelie representation of the virtues of Seelie and the depravity of Unseelie." He straightened. "Eyes forward, kid."

The two doors must have each been thirty feet high and a good ten feet wide, and yet they swung slowly inward without a sound, revealing a large room filled with a few hundred people and the buzz of an untold number of quiet conversations. The noise slowly dissipated into utter and complete silence as everyone turned to look upon the new arrivals. The crowd parted carefully, without bustle or commotion, revealing a woman in the distance seated upon a throne that rested upon a dais above them all. Recalling the time Cadilus had kidnapped him and Katherine, Paul thought of her as the mad queen. Cadilus stood at her right hand, and at the base of the dais to either side stood two Sidhe warriors in full ceremonial armor. She quietly uttered, "Enter." She hadn't raised her voice, and was at least a good hundred feet away, but Paul heard her as clearly as if she'd been standing next to him.

"You're on stage, kid," McGowan whispered. "They've all seen me and Colleen before, so it's you they're interested in today."

As they walked through the massive doors their honor guard peeled off to the sides, and Dergindaal alone led them toward the Summer Queen. Paul steeled himself to display an utterly calm demeanor he didn't feel. McGowan had warned him of this, told him he was free to glance to either side as long as he did so without any obvious excitement or emotion. "Mustn't appear to be a gawking peasant brought to Court," the old wizard had said, "and a bored glance or two to either side, nothing extreme, will only enhance your reputation." Paul tried to look uninterested as he glanced ever so slightly at the courtiers to either side of them, and he marveled at how there could be a race in which every single one of them was runway-model gorgeous.

Colleen had told Paul ordinary Court fashion could be somewhat casual, more like conservative business attire, though the style might be from any of a dozen centuries, depending upon the whim of the wearer. But now, in the full regalia of the formal Seelie Court, the women all wore floor length gowns of embroidered brocade silk in a riot of colors, most cut low with a polite but enticing bit of cleavage visible, their hair arranged carefully atop their heads, studded with precious stones and flowers and ribbons. The men tended toward pants and waistcoats with high collars in an almost nineteenth century style.

Dergindaal stopped about ten feet short of the first step on the dais, dropped to one knee, bowed and looked up to the Queen. Magreth stood above him haughtily, green eyes that sparkled like emeralds looking down upon him, flame red hair disturbed slightly by a non-existent breeze. Paul recalled that the first time he'd seen her she had stark white hair, and he wondered at the change. Strange little shadows danced about her head as she looked from Dergindaal to Colleen, to McGowan, then finally Paul. He didn't flinch, didn't look away, met her gaze squarely, and flames danced in her eyes.

"Your Majesty," Dergindaal said, his voice resonating throughout the hall.

She didn't look away from Paul as she said, "Thank you, my dear Captain, for bringing the Old Wizard safely into my presence. You are free to go about your own affairs now, though I always find it a comfort to have you near."

Dergindaal stood, bowed from the waist. "I shall remain so, Your Majesty," he said and stepped to one side.

She finally looked away from Paul and at McGowan. "Old Wizard," she said and nodded toward Devoe. "I see you brought your weapon."

McGowan smiled. "He and I have worked together for a long time. He can be of considerable aid when the situation gets interesting."

The flames in her eyes disappeared and were replaced by a glint, as if laughing at some inner joke. "Old Wizard, life is always interesting when you're involved."

McGowan bowed from the waist. "Your Majesty," he said. He had warned Paul that since they were not her subjects, they should not bend the knee. But a deep, formal bow, eyes down, was appropriate. *And to everyone else*, he'd warned Paul, *don't bow as deeply as you do to the Summer Queen.*

"Old Wizard, you attract chaos as a flower attracts bees."

"The chaos is merely as circumstance dictates, Your Majesty."

McGowan turned back to Colleen, and Paul stepped aside as she stepped between them. "You know the Lady Armaugh, I believe."

Colleen curtsied deeply, bowed her head, then rose.

Magreth's smile warmed. "It pleases me greatly that you chose to accompany the old man."

Colleen said, "I try to abate some of the chaos that, as you so correctly pointed out, seems to always accompany him."

Magreth chuckled. "We all thank you for that."

Jim'Jiminie and Boo'Diddle burst between Colleen and Paul, rushed up the dais to Magreth, shouting, "Magreth. Magreth," like little children, all sense of decorum completely forgotten. She actually smiled, something Paul hadn't thought possible. McGowan had warned him leprechauns were horrible at formality, but were tolerated just as one might accept the eccentricities of a favored child. At the top of the dais, both attempted to bow formally, doffed their hats and kissed Magreth on the hand. Boo'Diddle then tackled Jim'Jiminie, and they rolled down the steps of the dais, wrestling all the way.

Magreth turned her eyes on Paul; the smile disappeared, and the warmth in the room went with it. "And this must be the young mage I've heard so much about. The necromancer."

Colleen took a step back, a dance they'd carefully orchestrated beforehand. McGowan said, "Your Majesty, may I present my apprentice, Paul Conklin?"

McGowan had warned him they all knew his name, but it gave them no power over him unless he gave it to them himself. Paul bowed deeply, said only, "Your Majesty." He straightened, and as he'd been taught, waited for her to speak to him first.

"So, young man," Magreth said, and again the look on her face and the tone of her voice could have chilled a hot, summer day, "this is your first visit to Court. What think you?"

McGowan had told him the Sidhe loved flattery. "The beauty and majesty of the Seelie Court is incredible," Paul said, "or so I thought until I set eyes upon you, Your Majesty, and I now know that all else pales in comparison."

She smiled just a little, as if the smile had forced itself upon her, looked at Colleen. "Lady Armaugh, does the young mage speak with the tongue of the emerald lands?"

Colleen chuckled. "No, Your Majesty, he does not hale from Ireland. And no, I believe he speaks from his heart. He's much too serious a young mage to speak the blarney."

"Well that is a shame," Magreth said, and the chill in her voice warmed slightly. "Perhaps the Seelie Court can teach him to take more joy in life."

She stood, addressed the entire throng, though her eyes remained on Paul and the chill did not leave her voice. "We welcome the Old Wizard and his retinue, and they attend us under my personal protection. Now let us begin the young mage's education."

••••

Magreth descended from the dais. The aisle the assembled throng had cleared in its midst closed again, immersing Paul in a crowd of the most incredible beings and separating him from McGowan and Colleen.

Cadilus took him in hand and said, "The formal Seelie Court can be a bit overwhelming the first time, eh, Young Mage?"

Paul said, "That, it is."

"You did well with Her Majesty," Cadilus assured him.

"The Old Wizard coached me well."

Cadilus shrugged, "Perhaps in the etiquette of the Court. But it was clear to all the words were your own."

In the distance Magreth chatted amiably with Colleen. "Her presence is more overpowering than the Court."

"She is the Court, Young Mage. Never forget that."

Cadilus introduced him to a number of Sidhe, too many names and faces to remember. Paul remained cautious, ever alert should he sense the draw of power.

"Here's someone I know you'll want to meet," Cadilus said as a young goddess approached them. She appeared to be in her early twenties, and while Sidhe appearance was almost a veil they wore like a cloak, the appearance they chose became their reality. This young lady put some of the incredible creatures he'd already met to shame. Cadilus bent at the waist and kissed her hand, saying, "Your Highness."

He turned to Paul. "May I introduce the Princess of Summer, Her Royal Highness Nae'eth?"

Nae'eth held out her hand and said, "And you are?"

An old trick, that. If Paul fell into the trap, he would say, *I'm Paul Conklin, Your Highness*. But in doing so he would give up his name, and give her power over him. He bent at the waist, and as he took her hand in his, an electric thrill passed through him, though he was confident he managed to hide any reaction on his part. He kissed her hand as he'd practiced with Colleen and said, "Merely a humble apprentice mage, Your Highness."

Cadilus grinned. Nae'eth nodded approvingly. "Very good, Mr. Conklin," she said, and Paul realized it had been a little test, the first of many, he was certain. Or perhaps, only the first of which he was aware.

"I'm told you are new to your power," she said.

"Yes, my abilities only manifested recently." She was one of those beauties with a long neck, and she'd chosen a gown cut almost to her navel. The material was also slightly translucent, allowing him to see the silhouette of her areola. He imagined gently licking her nipples. *Wow*, he thought, *this is going to be a tough night*.

She smiled at him as if she knew his thoughts, and he felt a stirring in his crotch. She frowned. "You seem disturbed, Mr. Conklin. Are you ill?"

He reached deep inside to find some meaningless banter. "No, Your Highness. Not ill in the least, merely a bit overwhelmed by the beauty of the Summer Court."

She smiled, the tip of her tongue tracing a line across her lips. Paul thought of her tracing that tongue on his lips, on his neck, down his chest. "You do seem a bit preoccupied, Mr. Conklin."

He couldn't understand why he'd begun reenacting his emergence into puberty, a time when, like many young boy's, he'd been obsessed with getting laid, and in fact, at that moment he imagined getting laid by the goddess in front of him. He pulled himself together, managed to keep his face neutral. "I do have a number of things on my mind."

"I'm sure you do," she said, the corners of her mouth rising in a knowing smile. She reached up, touched his cheek lightly, and again that electric thrill shot through him, shot through his body and finished in his crotch. He was glad of the wizard's robes he wore, for without them he was certain he wouldn't have been able to hide the erection. The temptation to reach out and take her in his arms overwhelmed him, to kiss her lips, kiss her nipples, run his tongue over her entire body.

Beguilement! *She's beguiling me,* he realized, as he fantasized about pulling her to the floor and making love to her right there in front of everyone. Somehow he managed to assume a look of boredom and said, "This is all quite new to me."

Her fingers slid down his cheek to his neck, traced a line along the collar of his shirt. The fantasy became one of him pressing her against the wall and fucking her right there standing up. Barely able to control himself, he managed to smile knowingly, trying to tell her with a look he knew what she was doing. *Bring on your best, honey,* he wanted to say, though if she kept it up much longer he'd probably try to jump her bones right then and there.

Her hand left his cheek and the beguilement snapped off like a light. She laughed quietly, and he realized that the buzz of a hundred conversations had gone silent, with almost everyone looking their way.

Another test, he realized, thinking, *This is one hell of a pass-fail exam.*

••••

As Katherine and Ag strolled through the incredible Court gardens, a tall Seelie warrior approached them. She had never met him, but a Seelie here in the Unseelie Court must be non-other than the Summer Knight. He bent the knee before Ag. "Your Majesty, I have news of the Old Wizard."

Ag turned to Katherine. "Leave us, my child,"

She hesitated, fearing the consequences of even that, but also desperate to hear any news of her father. "Please, Your Majesty," she said, kneeling, kissing his hand. "If it's news of my father—she almost said, but didn't, *and Paul*—may I hear it? Please."

Ag smiled, though not a pleasant smile. "How can I refuse such a heartfelt request?" He turned to the knight. "Speak."

From one knee the knight looked up to the king. "The Old Wizard, with his *weapon,* the Lady Armaugh, two of the little people, and the young mage, has been received by Magreth. They are apparently traveling under the full protection and courtesy of the Seelie Court."

"Magreth is worried," Ag said happily.

Katherine held her breath, hoping that if she didn't draw attention to herself, Ag would forget her, allow her to continue listening. But he looked down at her. "Now, truly, leave us."

She dare not resist a second time. She stood, curtsied, turned and walked carefully away, trying to slow her pace in the hope of hearing any last words between Ag and the knight. But Ag was smarter than that, waited until she was well out of earshot.

••••

"Do you have more?" Ag asked.

Anogh rose. "The young mage has apparently acquitted himself most impressively, Your Majesty."

"Really. In what way?"

"He speaks well, Your Majesty, and doesn't gawk like a peasant his first time at Court. He's been tested a couple of times, has so far been able to resist beguilement by some of the most beautiful and powerful courtiers there."

"Interesting!" Ag turned his back on Anogh. "That may mean he is too strong for us to bind him."

"But we have the young woman, Your Majesty, and there is no doubt of their attraction for one another."

"There is that," Ag said. "Might the Summer Court ally with him and the Old Wizard?"

"That is my fear, Your Majesty. It is rumored his powers expand daily."

Ag turned back to him. "I think it time we play a more active role in the young mage's education. He is in Faerie now, where we are strongest. Send Simuth to me. It is time the young mage were bound to me . . . or dead."

20

Always a Target

THEIR PRESENTATION AT Court, the reception that followed, and the banquet that followed that, took up the entire evening. At least there had been no more tests, or none Paul had been aware of. It was late when they showed Paul to the small suite of rooms where he'd be lodged.

He pulled off the wizard's robe, tossed it on the bed, pulled off his jacket and tie, tossed them on the robe. He was bone tired, hoping for a good night's sleep, but he feared the tension that ran through every muscle would prevent that. A knock on the door interrupted his preparations.

When he opened the door a young Sidhe woman greeted him. Clearly a servant, she held a large bundle in her arms, curtsied and said, "High Chancellor Cadilus sends his compliments, Lord Mage. He thought you might wish more appropriate attire for tomorrow."

Even their servants were gorgeous. "Come in," Paul said, opening the door wider.

As she walked past him he remained alert for any signs of beguilement. She placed the bundle on the bed, unwrapped it, held up one of those nineteenth century waistcoat outfits he'd seen on all the Sidhe males. She hung it in the wardrobe, turned to him and handed him a small box that fit easily in the palm of his hand. "What's this?" he asked, opening it.

In it rested a small vial of some sort of emerald fluid. "It's a sleeping draught the High Chancellor prepared for you. It's an herbal concoction, not spell based, and it will help you sleep deeply through the night, and awake refreshed in the morning. He felt the pressures of the evening might weigh on you tonight."

Cadilus was right. "Please give the High Chancellor my thanks. When should I take it?"

"Take it now," she said. "It will take some minutes to have an effect."

Paul lifted the vial to his lips and poured it down his throat. It tasted of flowers and honey and a garden in full bloom on a bright sunny day. "How long will it take?"

She smiled provocatively and stepped close to him. "You should begin feeling it almost immediately."

He looked at her, thinking her words contradicted what she'd said a moment ago. She stood only inches away from him, the most desirable thing he could imagine, her entire posture an enticement to pleasure. She tilted her head up and smiled warmly at him, an obvious invitation. He sensed none of the confused thinking of beguilement, so he kissed her. She responded warmly, took his hand and pressed it against her breast.

Her dress slid off her shoulders with little effort. Naked from the waist up he pressed her against the wall, even though a faint voice inside him whispered that something was wrong. She lifted her skirts, put his hand between her legs. She was ready for him, beyond doubt.

He tried again, sensed no beguilement, but there was power in his gut, foreign power not his own. As she groped at his pants he realized it was a spell. No herbs to make him sleep, but a spell to drive him mad with desire and lust, pure and simple.

He had her pressed against the wall near the door to his suite, licking her breasts, nibbling on her nipples. But as she gripped his erection and tried to guide it into her, he pulled his own power, put everything he had into fighting the spell, opened the door without warning and shoved her out into the hall. He had only a moment to see the surprise on her face as he slammed the door.

He turned and staggered back to the bed, going mad with desire, passion and lust. The spell pushed at him, demanded some sort of release, tempted him to open the door and let her back in so they could finish what they'd started. But it was a test, and if he succumbed to that temptation he'd fail. To break the spell he needed a counter spell far beyond his own abilities. Or he could blunt it by completely immersing himself in saltwater. He always carried a small amount of salt, but he only had a handful with him at the moment, so he'd have to make do.

He poured a glass of water, added some salt to it, stirred it, swallowed one mouthful. He'd swallowed the spell-laced potion, so it wouldn't hurt to let a mouthful of saltwater join it in his gut. Then he stripped naked, retrieved a linen washcloth from the bathroom and tore off a small square about twelve inches on a side. He dipped the linen square into the remaining saltwater, wrung it out carefully over the glass, making certain all the drops of saltwater he squeezed out of it returned to the glass. Then he used the damp linen square to rub himself down, taking care to cover every inch of his skin. He repeated the process of wetting the linen scrap in the saltwater and rubbing himself down, managed to repeat it three times before the glass was empty. After that he continued the rubdown with the damp linen square until it finally dried. And by that time, though he sensed a slight residual remaining, he'd broken the power of the spell, at least enough so he could resist the temptation to open the door and bring her back.

"Shit. Shit. Shit," he swore. "This is fucking impossible."

••••

"Here, Young Mage."

The incredible creature standing in front of Paul held out her hand, palm down with something gripped in her fist. He extended his hand suspiciously, palm up beneath hers. She opened her fingers and a small object dropped into his hand. It appeared to be a little circle of braided hair, with the fine, silky consistency of Sidhe hair, the color of the young woman's hair.

"It's just a small charm," she said in a voice husky with promise and desire. "When you're free, without other obligations, activate it by breathing a small hint of power into it. It will guide you to my chambers." She touched his cheek. "I'll be waiting for you, ready for you."

She turned and walked away.

"No one would begrudge you a roll in the sheets with that one, kid."

He turned to face McGowan, found Colleen standing beside the old man. Like Paul, McGowan now wore one of those nineteenth century waistcoat outfits with an uncomfortably high collar.

"It's another test, isn't it?"

Both Colleen and McGowan shook their heads. McGowan said, "Since she didn't beguile you, it was an offer freely given, and one you are free to accept. You pretty much passed that test when they threw Nae'eth at you. And Nae'eth threw everything she had at you by physically touching you. Resisting that impressed everyone."

"But they tried again last night," Paul said. "Some gorgeous creature brought this outfit to my room." He told them about the spell, though he didn't go into detail on what happened when he fell for it.

"Different kind of test," McGowan said. "A spell, as opposed to their natural ability to beguile. The spell was a test of your power, and your ability to resist that of others. Completely different from beguilement."

Paul shook his head. "This ain't easy stuff, old man"

McGowan nodded with an admiring twinkle in his eyes toward the retreating figure of the Sidhe woman. "Then take her up on her offer."

Paul sighed. "No. I'll pass."

Colleen looked at him knowingly. "I think his heart is elsewhere, old man."

"Not still Suzanna," McGowan said. "You've got to put her behind you, Paul. She's long gone."

"No, old man," Colleen said. She reached out, put a finger beneath Paul's chin and looked into his eyes. "I think our Paul, here, is smitten anew."

McGowan slapped Paul on the shoulder. "You got a new girl, eh? That's great, Paul. Who is she? You have to introduce me sometime."

McGowan looked past Paul. "Ah! There's Cadilus. I need a word with him." McGowan marched purposefully away.

Colleen smiled at Paul. "For such a wise, old man, he can be such an idiot."

••••

"Lord Mage," the young servant said, curtsying elegantly. As she stood she held forth a small, silver dish upon which lay a folded piece of paper. "Lady Armaugh asked me to deliver this." There was no beguilement about the young woman, no spells.

Paul opened the note and read it: *Paul. I have something I wish you to see that I think you'll find most interesting. This young lady will guide you to me.* It was signed, *Colleen.*

Paul asked the young woman, "The note says you can lead me to Lady Armaugh?"

"Of course, my lord," she said smiling. "Those were her very instructions."

"Please, lead on," Paul said.

Every night when Paul returned to his chambers there were fresh garments laid out for him. He always had McGowan or Colleen examine them, just to ensure there was no attempt to make him look the fool, and that there were no spells he couldn't detect hidden in the clothing. Today he again wore the waistcoat outfit with the stiff, high collar. It was by no means comfortable, but he could live with it for the few days they'd be in the Seelie Court.

After the initial show of strength and the reception at Court, McGowan had told him he could leave the hardware behind since they were now under the Court's protection. But a stubborn, paranoid part of him insisted on retaining the hunting knife in the underarm sheath. He didn't mention it to McGowan or Colleen, didn't want them upset with him.

The young woman lead him down a long corridor, a turn here, a turn there, down another long corridor, then out onto the grounds surrounding the Summer Palace. Before Suzanna had gotten pregnant with Cloe, she and Paul had taken a trip to England, visited all the classic tourist sights. The Summer Palace reminded Paul of the grand eighteenth-century palaces erected by the fabulously wealthy aristocracy of the time. It boasted a front lawn large enough to encompass a dozen football fields.

The young lady led Paul about a hundred yards down a path of crushed white stones. It meandered through small gardens populated with exotic Faerie plants and marble statues of unimaginable beings and people. In the distance he saw Colleen standing with her back to them, wearing one of those elegant dresses of hers that hinted at the natural essence of her power: a little bit the hippie, but at the same time graceful and stylish.

As Paul and the young woman approached her she didn't turn to face them. The servant curtsied, said to her back, "My lady, I've brought the young mage."

The servant straightened up, stepped to the side, and Colleen turned to face Paul. But it wasn't Colleen, or any woman Paul recognized. Clearly Sidhe, Paul couldn't detect the telltale essence of either Seelie or Unseelie about her, which was most unusual. "I'm sorry," he said, "There must be some mistake." As he spoke he happened to notice that, in the distance behind her, there were two men dressed as guards, with long silver rapiers at their sides, approaching them from two corners of the garden.

She said, "No, Young Mage, no mistake." As she spoke Paul saw her eyes flick briefly to right and left, focusing on something behind him.

He glanced over his shoulder, saw two more guards approaching from the remaining two corners of the garden. When they saw him looking at them they drew their rapiers, and quickened their pace from a march to a trot. Paul sensed the woman drawing power, and only then did he recognized the essence of the Unseelie Court about her. He drew his own power, but she'd caught him off guard and she slapped him down with hers.

He must have blacked out for a moment, came to lying on his back on the crushed, white gravel, his head spinning. The woman pushed her power at him, and when he tried to draw power again, her power stood between him and his. One of the guards bent down, grabbed Paul by the lapels of his coat and lifted him to his feet like a rag doll. The woman's power kept pushing at him, confusing him. "Hurry," she said to the guard. "We must move quickly, get him out of here."

"Yes, my lady," the guard said.

Paul thought he could stand, but he decided to feign weakness, let his knees buckle. He caught the guard off balance and the man dropped him. Paul hit the ground face down, both arms underneath him, managed to get his right hand on the hilt of the knife in the underarm sheath and pulled it free.

"You hit him too hard," the man said to the woman angrily.

Paul felt the man grip him by the back of his collar and lift him again to his feet. He brought the knife up and cut the man's arm viciously.

Paul had heard what cold iron could do to a Sidhe. The man's skin smoked and hissed where the blade touched him and he cried out, released Paul and pushed him away. But he pushed him toward the woman. Paul bumped into her, caught her wrist, touched the flat of the blade to the palm of her hand. It hissed and smoked like the man's arm, and the spell she used to block his power broke. He hit her with a right cross to the jaw and she went down in a flurry of petticoats.

Paul drew all the power he could as the other three guards converged on him. He turned to face the closest one, hit him with the power he'd pulled, knocked him on his ass, turned to the next, and pulled more power preparing for the next strike, but the woman plowed into him from behind and they both tumbled to the gravel tangled in her petticoats. As he stood she kicked and spit at him, tried to draw her own power, so he slapped her hard with the power he'd pulled.

At that moment another of the armed men reached them, and still unaware Paul had the knife, he tried to wrestle Paul to the ground. Paul buried the knife to the hilt in the man's gut, then felt a sudden, sharp, searing pain lance through his chest. He looked down to see about six inches of silver rapier protruding from a point just under his left nipple. "Fucking A," he said as he fell forward on his face.

He lay there staring at the pretty, crushed, white gravel in which his cheek rested, staring at the blood pouring out of his chest painting it red. There were shouts, cries from far more voices than the women and her four cohorts could account for. He heard the ring of metal against metal. Someone shouted, "Don't let them escape."

Then Paul slipped into a cold, silent dark place of pain and agony.

••••

Paul's consciousness bubbled to the surface several times, though never for long, and each time he slipped back into that dark place, though now it no longer hurt. But finally he came to and had the strength to resist the sweet pull of oblivion. He lay flat on his back, Colleen and an older Sidhe man standing over him, both drawing power and casting spells.

"How bad?" he asked.

The older man looked at him carefully, clearly weighing him. "The sword pierced you through the left lung, Young Mage. It also nicked your aorta."

Colleen had reverted to her thick Irish accent. "You knocked on death's door a couple of times there, child."

She looked at the older man. "I think he should sleep more."

"No," Paul said. "I don't want any more sleep."

The older man ignored him and said to Colleen, "I agree completely."

As they both reached toward him, he growled, "Don't do that fucking spell shit." Then their fingertips touched his temples on both sides.

He awoke some time later. He lay in his own bed now, alone in his chambers. He managed to sit up, felt like crap, but realized he didn't feel half as bad as he should after being impaled on a Sidhe sword. He sat there, contemplating whether or not he had the strength to make it to the bathroom to piss, when the door to his chamber opened and Colleen, McGowan, Devoe and the older Sidhe man marched in. They must have had some spell set to let them know when he awoke.

Colleen and the older Sidhe immediately began poking and prodding him, mumbling back and forth between them. "Enough," Paul growled. "Leave me alone. I have to piss."

The older Sidhe looked at him disapprovingly. Colleen said to him, "I believe, Lord Sinthas, you may report to Her Majesty our patient is well enough to be grouchy and rude."

"Yes," the older man said almost regretfully. "He'll survive."

He bowed to Colleen. "If you'll excuse me, I'll go straight to Her Majesty."

Paul got Devoe to help him to the bathroom, relieved himself, pulled on a rather elaborate robe provided by his Sidhe hosts and sat down in a chair. "Was that another test?" he growled. "I'm getting tired of these tests."

McGowan shook his head. "Nope, not a test. That was an honest-to-goodness kidnapping attempt, with orders to kill you if they couldn't succeed at the abduction. But it did have the effect of one hell of a test. You took down three Unseelie warriors and a powerful Unseelie witch. Even when they took you by surprise, and they had rapiers and all you had was a knife. By the way, glad to see you were paranoid enough to carry some hardware."

Colleen added, "There won't be any more tests. Not after this."

Paul had reached the limit of his patience. "I'm getting tired of this, old man."

Colleen said, "There is a silver lining to this cloud. Magreth has been shamed that she couldn't protect a guest in her own Court, one under *guest right* and the full protection of the Court itself. She has no choice but to ally with us now against Ag. She's sent a message to the Winter Court, asking that they send an ambassador to discuss this matter. Ag would have snubbed us, might have snubbed Magreth, but now that he's violated the sovereignty of the Summer Court, he dare not."

Paul asked, "What's that mean?"

McGowan shrugged. "We'll have to wait and see, kid. Just wait and see."

••••

"And so you failed miserably," Ag said to Simuth, who knelt at his feet. Ag spoke quietly, no ranting or raving, a very bad sign.

Anogh could have told them to expect failure, if they had consulted him. The young mage had grown too strong to be taken so easily.

"You failed to abduct him," Ag continued, his voice almost a whisper, "and you failed to kill him."

"Yes, Your Majesty," Simuth said, literally trembling with fear.

"And you say he single-handedly bested one of our most powerful witches and four of our warriors."

Simuth's hands shook as he said, "He only bested three of the warriors, Your Majesty. The fourth was able to wound him gravely."

"Four warriors with rapiers and a powerful witch," Ag snarled scornfully, his anger rising with each word. "And he with naught but a short blade. Two of the warriors and the witch completely disabled, a third wounded, and all the remaining warrior could do was wound him?"

Ag flew into a rage, struck Simuth and sent him sprawling, began kicking him brutally. Anogh had suffered such punishments, actually felt a moment of pity for poor Simuth, then recalled upon whom he was lavishing compassion, and the pity died.

When Ag had sated his anger he stood over the bleeding Winter Knight. Simuth lay at his feet, whimpering, but managed an agonized whisper, "There is yet a way to bind him to us, Your Majesty?"

Ag, breathing heavily from his exertions, calmed and looked down at Simuth. "You have a plan, Sir Knight?"

"Yes, Your Majesty," Simuth said, struggling to his knees. "We must get him here, to the Winter Court, even if we must grant the protection of the Court. And then I believe we can use the young woman against him."

Ag considered that for a moment, then said, "You may yet redeem yourself."

21

Not Really Welcome

"HOW DOES IT feel?" Colleen asked.

Paul had stripped to the waist in her chambers so she could carefully examine the entrance and exit wounds the sword had made. "Like I was stabbed by a sword," he growled.

She looked at him crossly. She'd spent the day patching him up, and he had the impression she might try laying him over her knee and spanking him. He also had the impression she just might be able to do it. "All right, all right, I'm sorry. No, it feels pretty good. Some stiffness, mainly I can feel the skin pull when I lift my arm high, but no real pain." He lifted his arm to demonstrate.

She probed at both scars. "That's just the scar tissue. When I have a little more time, we can eliminate most of that too."

McGowan burst into the room and said excitedly, "An Unseelie ambassador has arrived. The Court's abuzz with the news. It's Anogh."

Colleen grimaced. "Ag has always been one to rub salt in a wound."

"Put on the wizard's robes, kid. We're going to meet with him."

••••

Magreth carefully orchestrated the meeting in a private audience chamber. McGowan, Colleen and Paul attended, meeting Anogh and two of his lieutenants, with Magreth and Cadilus present to referee. One of Anogh's lieutenants had coal black skin, which was quite unusual. Up to that point the Sidhe had all been quite uniform in skin tone, tending toward a pale shade of white; not pink-white, like Caucasians in the Mortal Plane, but white-white. Anogh introduced the black Sidhe warrior as Andalous, and Paul couldn't overcome the feeling he knew the fellow.

The scene reminded Paul a lot of their meeting with Cadilus in McGowan's study. Magreth began with introductions, then served them all the drink of their choice. Paul followed McGowan's lead, took a couple fingers of whiskey over a single cube of ice. He had expected them to square off on opposite sides of a negotiating table, but instead the first order of business was to mingle, so Paul took the opportunity to approach Anogh off to one side where they were effectively alone. Paul tried to keep his voice from trembling with anger as he asked, "When we met in the street in front of my apartment, you gave me reason to believe my wife's death was not an accident. Am I to assume you murdered her?"

Anogh looked at him carefully and smiled sadly. "You should assume nothing, Young Mage. However, believe me when I tell you that when the time comes, you will know the truth of it." He smiled again and walked away.

A bit later Paul faced Andalous, the coal black Unseelie warrior. He was polite, quite nice, in fact. That was the hallmark of Sidhe interactions: treat your enemy as nicely as your best friend, then stab them in the back at your first chance. "Forgive me for being abrupt," Paul said, "but there is something about you that seems familiar, as if we've met before, yet I know that's not the case."

Andalous laughed quietly, then leaned forward and spoke just above a whisper. "You never fail to impress me, Young Mage." He smiled, turned and walked away.

When they got down to business it was rather straightforward. They would be allowed to come to the Unseelie Court, and granted its formal protection. They would not be allowed to come armed, and they must provide their own escort. Magreth was free to provide the escort and accompany them herself, with whatever retinue she chose. Try as they might, they could not better the terms.

Later, when they adjourned to McGowan's suite, Paul asked them if they knew anything about the black Sidhe. Both McGowan and Colleen looked at him strangely, and both asked simultaneously, "What black Sidhe?"

Paul tried to remember the man's face, couldn't; tried to remember what they'd spoken of, couldn't; tried to remember anything about the man, couldn't. "I don't know," Paul said. "For some reason I keep thinking of one of them as the *black Sidhe*. But, for the life of me, I couldn't tell you why."

••••

Magreth did choose to accompany them, and brought along Dergindaal and his entire guard as escort. Dergindaal and his men rode the incredible Sidhe steeds. The animals were certainly horses, but calling a Sidhe steed a horse was like calling a Lamborghini a car. The animals each stood eight feet at the ears, two-thousand pounds of sleek, muscled tension, always ready to challenge the wind for speed and endurance. They were beasts of pure magic, elemental constructs spawned of the essence of Faerie. When they ran, their hooves touched the ground only every three or four hundred feet, and

McGowan, who had ridden a Sidhe steed, assured him it was in no way a jarring or harsh ride.

McGowan, because he was experienced, chose to ride also, even tried to get Paul to ride one of the steeds. "I'd be stupid to do that," Paul said. "I've never ridden a horse in my life. I'll fall off and break my ass."

"With these animals, if they don't want you to fall, there's no way you'll fall. And if they don't want you to ride, there's no way you'll ride."

Paul declined. "I'll ride in one of the coaches."

Jim'Jiminie and Boo'Diddle also chose to ride with the guard, sharing a steed between them. Paul had asked McGowan why they had bothered to bring the little scampering fellows along. McGowan reminded him of the hundred years of bad luck that came with killing a leprechaun in anything other than self-defense. "Remember their traditional neutrality," McGowan told him. "If those two leprechauns decide that we're the injured party, that could isolate Ag from all of Non-aligned Faerie. The Unseelie Court would then stand alone."

Magreth provided two fantastical coaches, dripping with gold gilt and silver piping, gargoyles and strange creatures carved into almost every feature. She and Colleen and Cadilus rode in the larger coach, while Paul, Devoe and Lord Sinthas, Magreth's personal physician, rode in the other, smaller coach.

It was a comfortable ride, and for the first time in a long while Paul had the opportunity to watch the countryside pass by and think. Since they'd come to Faerie he'd been obsessed with that spiral-slippage-through-reality feeling he'd sensed every time they crossed over from the Mortal Plane. He'd now felt it several times, and while supposedly Jim'Jiminie had brought him and Katherine back after the heart arrow incident, he didn't remember Jim'Jiminie returning for them. He was almost certain it had been just he and Katherine in the small copse of trees just before crossing back, almost certain. And he remembered that little, spiral twist quite vividly.

On the other hand, crossing over into the Netherworld was more a sideways slippage in reality. The two sensations were distinctly different, yet similar. And he thought if he could find time to work on it, time to experiment, he might repeat them both. But McGowan and Colleen had told him time and again that was impossible. Only the fey could indiscriminately open pathways to and from Faerie. And no one could do so to the Netherworld.

They crossed a stream, and Sinthas informed them they were now in Non-aligned Faerie, where neither Court claimed sovereignty. He explained that leprechauns, certain forms of sprite and pixie, and other forms of fey lived without fealty to either Court. Some, like the leprechauns, were welcome in the Courts at any time. And some, like the Baen'Sidhe, were shunned and never welcome under any circumstances. He said nothing about the *black fey*, and Paul thought that odd.

He thought again of Anogh's words in front of his apartment. *The love for which you grieve must be avenged. And when you learn of love's betrayal, remember this lesson* . . . He'd then shown Paul how even a normal heterosexual male could be drawn into a wild homosexual fantasy by the beguilement of a Sidhe male. . . . *she could not have resisted him* . . . he'd finished. And then only yesterday, in Magreth's sitting room, *when the time comes, you will know the truth of it.*

What game was Anogh playing at? He was Sidhe through and through, and Sidhe played games like mortals breathed air. Was he merely trying to deflect Paul's suspicions from him, confuse him, focus him elsewhere?

"Young Mage," Sinthas said, interrupting his thoughts. "We are approaching the outer boundary of the Unseelie territories. You should prepare yourself. Proper introductions will have to be made before we can proceed."

The coach slowed even as Sinthas spoke. Paul put his memories of Suzanna and Cloe away, though he swore that, if his growing suspicions were true, someday there would come a reckoning, and someone would pay.

The coach came to a complete stop. Sinthas opened the door and held it for Paul. It was awkward climbing down from the coach in the long wizard's robes, but Paul managed not to stumble and make a fool of himself.

McGowan and the leprechauns had dismounted, and gathered around Magreth along with Colleen and Cadilus. On the other side of a small stream, Dergindaal sat astride his steed facing an Unseelie warrior draped in armor of lapis lazuli, silver and mother-of-pearl. The Winter Court warrior wore a helm with a fantastic facemask of silver and peacock feathers, and scales of black flint and white opal. Dergindaal and the Unseelie warrior were in the middle of conversing as Paul approached the small group surrounding Magreth. But for an instant Paul met the Unseelie warrior's eyes, pitiless, unforgiving eyes that took Paul's measure and clearly found him wanting. The facemask ended just above his lips, and he smiled cruelly.

The Unseelie warrior looked away, but Paul couldn't take his eyes from the fellow. He nudged McGowan and asked, "Who's the shithead with the face mask?"

But it was Anogh who answered him. "That, Young Mage, is Simuth, the Winter Knight. Beware the Winter Knight. He will be your undoing, and your salvation."

Paul had had it, just plain fucking had it with the bastard's obscure, little proverbs. He drew power, drew copious and dangerous amounts of power, turned on Anogh and snarled viciously, "And I will be your undoing, Summer Knight."

Anogh backed away, and Paul got some satisfaction from seeing dread written plainly on his face. When he spoke, he spoke fearfully and barely above a whisper, "No, Young Mage, you will be my salvation."

"Paul," McGowan snarled in his ear. "You're holding enough power to blow us all to hell and back. Let it go, son. Let it go."

Paul allowed the power to dissipate, to drain away slowly, to trickle off into the trees and bushes and weeds and flowers, into the stream, into the earth itself.

Colleen took him by the arm. "You're staying with me for the rest of this journey. You've not been coached in earth magic, so until you're properly trained you should not draw such power again."

Paul said, "I'm going to have to kill him."

"You can't. Anogh's immortal."

Somehow, Paul thought he might know how to kill a Sidhe immortal, though he couldn't recall the details necessary to do so, just bits and pieces.

The Winter Knight, in his magnificent hereditary armor, crossed the stream. Introductions were made, and when Paul's turn came he met the Winter Knight's eyes again, cruel, knowing eyes.

The rest of the journey passed in a blur for Paul. Colleen insisted on riding with him, sent Sinthas to ride in the Coach with Magreth. Paul tried to think of something other than killing Anogh, but he couldn't rid his mind of that one thought.

••••

"It was nothing, Your Majesty," Simuth said smugly. "A trite display of power. He's an animal, could never rival a Sidhe mage."

Anogh held his peace. Simuth's arrogance would never allow him to see the truth. Ag looked from Simuth to Anogh. "Speak, Summer Knight. And speak the truth. I command it."

Anogh shrugged. "He drew enough power to easily rival that of a strong Sidhe mage."

Simuth's voice dripped with scorn, "You perceive him as strong only because that power was directed at you in anger. I do believe you fear him."

Anogh nodded and grinned. "It is always healthy to fear a strong opponent. It is also healthy to fear a strong ally. Your lack of fear may someday be your undoing."

Simuth scoffed at him. "I fear no mortal mage."

"Enough squabbling," Ag said angrily. He addressed Anogh, "So it is no longer possible to bind him?"

Anogh decided to remind them of his own circumstances. "Not with mere force, Your Majesty. But even the strongest of us can be fool enough to enter into an unwise oath, and be trapped into a binding from which there is no release."

Ag didn't miss Anogh's veiled reference to his own circumstances. He smiled happily. "Of course, we must be subtle."

"Might I make a suggestion?" Simuth asked hesitantly.

"Do so quickly," Ag snapped.

Simuth spoke cautiously. "We still have the woman."

Ag thought about Simuth's words for a moment, then an unpleasant grin formed slowly on his face. "Yes, we still have the woman."

••••

Katherine knew her father had come to the Winter Court. The fact of his presence couldn't be hidden from her, though whether he'd arrived as a prisoner in chains or an honored guest, she could not say. But he had come, that she knew.

She asked for an audience with Ag, was denied. In desperation, she asked for an audience with Simuth, and he granted her request. If he were true to character, he had granted her request only to torment her. She didn't care. Her father had come, and she would risk any indignity to gain even the tiniest spark of information. But then another realization touched her, something she would never have guessed would penetrate the cloud of uncertainty cast upon her by the Unseelie Court. She sensed that Paul too had come, and for some reason that gave her even more hope than the presence of her father.

When they finally admitted her to Simuth's presence, he sat upon his little throne. He had created it in his own private apartments, where Ag would never condescend to come, for should he ever see Simuth's throne, the punishment would be beyond imagining.

Katherine dropped to both knees before Simuth, bowed so deeply she touched her forehead to the floor. "Your Highness."

"And what would you have of me, mortal animal?"

She kept her forehead pressed to the floor. Simuth was such a transparent idiot that anyone could manipulate him. "Now that the Old Wizard and the young mage have come to the Unseelie Court, I thought you might wish to consult me."

A chill passed over the room. "How do you know they're here?" he growled.

She lifted her forehead off the marble floor and met his eyes. "I didn't," she lied. "Not until you spoke."

She awoke the next morning with vivid memories of how happily she'd participated in his sexual antics.

••••

Ag did not receive them officially at the Winter Court, certainly not in the grand style Magreth had chosen. When presented to him, it was with him seated upon his throne in the grand throne room of the Unseelie Court, with only a few dozen courtiers present. It reminded Paul of the massive wooden doors to the Seelie throne room, and how the carved figures of the Seelie emitted an aura of kindness and compassion, while those of the Unseelie radiated cruelty and malice. He met the eyes of at least a dozen Unseelie courtiers, and they all shown with what seemed almost obsessive malevolence, overlaid by lascivious desire. Colleen had warned him that in Faerie he would be sensitive to the aura of Sidhe desires, and only now did he understand what she'd meant.

The throne room was not unlike that of the Seelie Court: large and spacious, the throne resting upon a dais at the end of the room, situated so that to face the king, one must cross the entire span of the hall. Magreth led the small group as they faced Ag, surrounded by Dergindaal and a dozen of his warriors.

When Magreth stopped about thirty feet from the dais, Paul realized that by keeping her distance, she minimized the effect of the dais, minimized Ag's ability to loom over them in the position of power. She did not curtsy, merely bowed her head, one sovereign to another. "My dear Ag, it has been long since we last met."

The cruelty and brutality that shown from the Winter King's eyes made that of the Winter Knight pale in comparison. "Magreth," Ag said, and Paul felt a chill in the air. "My dear, as always your beauty outshines my most gracious courtier. But I must confess I am disappointed in the company you keep." Ag looked at the mortals behind her, let his eyes rest for a moment on each, allowed them to see the open contempt in his face.

Magreth smiled. "These are my dear friends, Your Majesty, and during their sojourn here in Faerie, they journey under the sovereign protection of the Seelie Court, and now, by the word of your representative, also under that of the Unseelie Court. Surely, the hospitality of the Unseelie Court is not so meager as to deny them your courtesy."

Ag smiled a cold and cruel smile. "Of course, Magreth. It shames me, that I must have you remind me of my responsibilities. They will be granted every courtesy of this Court. But first, please introduce them."

Everyone but Paul was introduced with something like, . . . *and of course, you know so-and-so . . .* She saved Paul for last. "And here, Your Majesty," she said, indicating that Paul should step forward, "is a young mage new to Faerie and the Courts. May I present Paul Conklin?"

Paul bowed at the waist as he'd been taught, waited for Ag to speak first. "Mr. Conklin, a pleasure to meet you at last."

"The pleasure is all mine, Your Majesty." Paul met Ag's eyes, and neither of them tried to hide the true displeasure they felt.

"I'm told, Young Mage, you recently suffered a grave injury at the hands of some rogue Sidhe warriors."

So that was how they'd play this, rogues of which Ag would deny all knowledge. Paul decided to take a chance. "It was nothing, Your Majesty. They were easily dispatched." Paul didn't say it, but all present knew he meant, *because they were mere Unseelie.*

Paul had struck home. Ag's eyes flashed with anger, and frost formed in Paul's hair and on his shoulders. Paul pulled some power, warmed himself and the frost dissipated. Colleen, standing to one side, gave him a look that said, *Don't push it, boy-oh.*

Paul decided to withdraw politely. "But, Your Majesty, I stand in awe of the magnificence and power of the Unseelie Court." Colleen smiled.

"Well then, Young Mage," Ag said magnanimously. "Let us adjourn. We shall dine together tonight, all of us, and you can sample the pleasures of the Unseelie Court."

22

The Truth of the Beast

THE BANQUET SEEMED almost medieval in character and style. Where Magreth had preferred small, informal gatherings, Ag had turned out the entire circus. The floor of the banquet room had three levels. The highest tier held only one table, at which Ag, Magreth, McGowan, Colleen, Jim'Jiminie and Boo'Diddle sat, along with one of Ag's concubines, all seated on one side of the table and facing the two lower tiers. Jim'Jiminie and Boo'Diddle couldn't remain seated or still for more than a few minutes at a time.

Anogh escorted Paul to a table on the second tier, and they were the first to arrive there. On the lowest tier long banquet tables ran down either side of the room, leaving a large open space in the center of the floor.

Alone with Anogh at their table, waiting for the festivities to begin, Paul said, "So, Summers, it's been a long time. Summers Knight, wasn't it?"

One of Anogh's eyebrows lifted. "You remember. I'm surprised you were able to lift the veil of my glamour."

"I had some help. What were you doing in my life back then?"

Anogh shook his head. "The two of us meeting, becoming casual acquaintances, merely coincidence. It was a lark, to live as a mortal briefly."

Paul didn't believe a word he said, but before he could press the issue further, Simuth arrived with a beautiful woman on his arm. She reminded Paul a bit of Suzanna, but where Suzanna had disdained opulence for simple good looks, this woman wore rich silks and velvet brocade, long hair piled elaborately on her head. Paul and Anogh stood.

Simuth looked to the woman on his arm. "Nezmodie, I'd like you to meet the young mage, of which I'm sure you've heard." He looked at Paul. "My sister, Nezmodie."

Paul bowed carefully. She extended her hand and he kissed it. "I'm honored," he said.

Simuth turned to Anogh. "I think you were right, Sir Knight." He turned to Nezmodie. "It was our dear Anogh, here, who suggested I bring you tonight so you might meet the young mage. And I now see what an excellent idea that was."

Nezmodie and Simuth sat on one side of the table, facing Paul and Anogh on the other.

The banquet was a bawdy affair. They didn't serve individual plates of food. Instead, servants placed large platters of steaming dishes in the center of the table from which they all helped themselves. The cleared space in the center of the third tier filled with entertainers, jugglers, mimes, singers, dancers, with a small string orchestra playing soft music in the background.

Paul ate sparingly, didn't have the appetite for more. He also learned he needed to pace himself with the wine, since after every sip or two, a servant stepped forward to top off his glass.

Simuth was actually a bit charming, though always arrogant. Nezmodie kept sneaking glances at Paul, and each time her eyes narrowed in careful thought. He finally asked her, "Lady Nezmodie, is there something I can do for you?"

She blushed. "I'm sorry, Young Mage. You must think me rude. It's just that . . . there is . . . something familiar about you."

"I'm sure we've never met before," Paul said. "Believe me; I would not forget you so easily."

She smiled at him warmly. "You are kind, Young Mage, and I agree, we have never met. But there is something vaguely familiar in your aura, something I can't place."

They continued eating and drinking and chatting politely. It drove Paul nuts. He wanted to immediately dive into the subject of Katherine's captivity, to negotiate her release, to do something. But Colleen and McGowan had warned him certain protocols must be followed, so he'd have to be patient.

After Paul finished eating he listened to Simuth expounding on some feat. Simuth waved his hand expansively, and as he did so Paul noticed a glint from one of the rings on his fingers. When Simuth put his hand on the table and held it still for a moment, Paul got a good look at the ring. A wave of nausea washed over him, and he swallowed several times to keep from vomiting his dinner right onto the table. He knew that ring.

"Young Mage, are you ill?" Nezmodie's voice brought Paul back to the moment.

"No," he lied. "Perhaps a bit too much wine. That's all." He carefully focused his attention on Simuth. "Sir Knight, that's an interesting ring you wear."

There couldn't be two like it in the universe, a small, antique silver ring, with four little diamond studs alternating with four small ruby studs, all arrayed in a circle, and set in a baroque setting that made it truly unique. That ring, or one like it, had been the only possession Suzanna had ever had from her unknown family, and because of that she had valued it greatly. She hadn't been wearing it at the time of her death, and afterwards Paul had searched every inch of their apartment to find it, in vain it turned out.

"Oh this little bauble," Simuth said, holding up the ring and wiggling his finger. Paul noticed Nezmodie stiffen angrily. "It's a family heirloom, not worth much, but it's been in the family for centuries." He looked at Nezmodie, and all color drained from her face. "Though it did have a brief sojourn outside the family recently, but I corrected that."

Nezmodie literally shook with anger. "You murdered her," she whispered.

"Murder?" Simuth asked, and any sense he could be charming disappeared, replaced by the cruel and brutal Winter Knight. "When is it murder to exterminate an abomination?"

Simuth turned to Paul. "My sister chose to bed an animal, and from her womb she bore a half-animal abomination."

Nezmodie snarled at him. "He was no animal. He was a mortal man, kind and loving, and you murdered him too."

Simuth shrugged at her coldly. "Mortal, animal, what's the difference."

Paul's hands trembled more at each word, so he put them in his lap to hide them. Simuth turned back to him, clearly warming up to his story. "She tried to hide her spawn in the Mortal Plane. Took me years to find the little beast."

Nezmodie snarled, "She was no beast. She was my child."

Paul felt rage climbing up from his gut, but he managed to control his voice as he asked, "And what did you do then?"

Simuth laughed. "I made the little beast pleasure me for a few days. Then I helped her commit suicide."

"She didn't commit suicide, you animal," Nezmodie shouted. "You as much as murdered her with your beguilement."

Paul wanted to climb up over the table, wrap his hands around Simuth's throat and wipe that smug smile from his face. Anogh, sitting next to him, clamped a hand on his wrist, whispered in his ear, "Not now, Young Mage."

Then Anogh turned to Simuth and spoke casually. "Nezmodie's child bore a child of her own, did she not?"

Simuth laughed. "Yes, the spawn of the spawn. Didn't know it at the time, went back later and took care of the little whelp myself."

Paul's world narrowed to one thought. Everyone's attention had focused on Nezmodie shouting at Simuth. Paul had brought the knife in the underarm sheath, though that broke the terms of their parole in the Unseelie Court. He could pull it, lunge across the table, possibly bury it in Simuth's eye before they stopped him.

Paul didn't know Colleen was standing behind him until she put her hands on his shoulders. "Paul," she whispered in his ear. "You mustn't do anything rash."

"She's right, Young Mage," Anogh whispered in the other ear. "Now is not the time for a reckoning."

Colleen spoke up so others could hear her. "I believe the young mage is ill."

"Yes," Anogh said, standing, pulling Paul to his feet. "Possibly a bit too much wine."

Colleen lied, "I believe it's more his recent injuries we must be concerned with. Will you help me get him back to his chambers without incident, Sir Knight?"

"Of course, Lady Armaugh."

Anogh held Paul's arm in a vice-like grip as they escorted him back to his chambers. Paul didn't resist, let them lead him back to his room, recalling all the way Anogh's words: . . . *you will know the truth of it.*

At the door to his chambers he stopped and met Anogh's eyes. "You knew all along. Why didn't you tell me?"

Anogh shrugged. "Would you have believed me?"

"No. Probably not."

"But now you've heard the truth from the lips of the beast himself."

. . . *you will know the truth of it.* "Thank you," Paul said.

••••

Until that day Paul had never, in fact, understood the words *blind rage*, not in his gut, not the way he understood it now as a white-hot fury burning from within. He had only one desire in life, to hunt Simuth down and kill him. He ranted and raved in his room, shouted at McGowan, Colleen, Devoe and the leprechauns, all of whom ganged up on him, wouldn't let him leave.

"You can't kill Simuth," Colleen shouted at him. "He's immortal."

"I can hurt him," Paul shouted back.

"And he'll kill you, you young fool."

Jim'Jiminie said, "He is entitled to vendetta in this. Though I see no way he can gain true satisfaction."

They argued for quite some time. At one point Paul started for the door, but Devoe intercepted him, twisted his right arm behind his back, pushed him against a wall and said, "Face it, kid, you ain't gettin' out of here."

It was McGowan who finally got to him. "If you attack him, regardless of the circumstances, we'll never get Katherine out of here."

Devoe, who stood against the door blocking the exit, said, "You put it away now, kid, until after we get Katherine back. And then I'll help you go after the bastard. My word on that."

McGowan added, "And I too will help you, after Katherine has been safely rescued."

"And I," Colleen said.

"Vendetta it is," Boo'Diddle said, looking to Jim'Jiminie. "We will bear witness the vendetta is just." Jim'Jiminie nodded his agreement.

Paul capitulated, not just outwardly, but honestly so. Going after Simuth right now would only get in the way of any attempt to rescue Katherine. And in any case, he didn't know how he could hurt Simuth, let alone kill him. He finally realized the best thing to do would be to become the most powerful wizard he could manage, to work at it with all his energy. Then someday come back and do it right.

Colleen stayed with him while he sat and brooded, and thought a great deal about Suzanna and Cloe. At some point, sitting in a chair, he drifted off into a restless sleep, awoke to the sound of a knock at his door. Colleen had left and he was alone, so he stood and opened the door. Nezmodie stood there, her eyes red-rimmed, her cheeks glistening with tears.

"You were her lover, weren't you," she said breathlessly, "and the father of my grandchild. I see it now. I see her in your aura. You loved her deeply, didn't you?"

"Yes." He couldn't add anything to that.

"Come with me." She turned away.

"Wait. Where are we going?"

She turned back to him. "To see the Old Wizard's daughter."

Paul followed Nezmodie without question. It could be a trap, and if it was, he'd be prepared. But Nezmodie's anger at Simuth was obviously genuine, and he paid particular attention to the route she followed, hoping he could find it again. She led him to a set of double doors, paused outside them, closed her eyes and he sensed a small flow of power. She opened her eyes. "She's alone." She passed her hand over the doors and they opened. She walked in and Paul followed her into a sitting room. Nezmodie crossed to a doorway in the opposite wall, waved at Paul to follow her.

Paul found Katherine asleep on her bed, the covers tangled around her hips, wearing a diaphanous gown that showed more than it hid. Nezmodie slipped out of the room to allow them privacy, and Paul sat down next to Katherine.

She opened her eyes, and as they widened with recognition she sat up and threw her arms around his neck. "Paul, is it really you?"

"Of course it's me." He held her at arm's length. "Why wouldn't it be me?"

She shook her head dazedly. "For me, here, half the time I don't know what's real. I live in a world of spells and illusion." She suddenly realized what she wore, blushed, pulled the blankets up to cover her breasts.

He grinned. "Darn, I was rather enjoying that."

She returned his grin. "You're still incorrigible."

"Come with me," he said. "Now. We'll get you back to your father and Colleen."

"I can't," she said, shaking her head. "The threshold of this suite is spell locked. If I cross it without being summoned, they'll know immediately, and then none of us will get out of here."

"There's got to be a way," he pleaded.

"Go back to my father. Now that you know where I am, how to find me, he'll know what to do, maybe cast some spell that'll cover my escape."

They argued for a bit, but Paul knew all along Katherine was right, though before he left, she planted a kiss on him that left him breathless. He let Nezmodie lead him back to his own suite, concentrating again on the path they took.

••••

Anogh waited with Ag in the King's private meeting chamber. Neither of them spoke as they waited for Simuth. Then there came a polite knock on the door and Simuth entered.

He bent the knee. "It worked, Your Majesty. Nezmodie was so furious she led him to her."

"Excellent," Ag crowed. "The young fool isn't subtle enough to spot the trap we set. Rise, Simuth. Rise."

Simuth stood. "He will try something foolish now, Your Majesty. I am certain of it."

"Perhaps," Ag said. "But do not underestimate the Old Wizard. His influence may yet hold the young man in check. So we need time for his impatience to grow unbearable. We must encourage the Old Wizard to bide his time, to think we are capitulating, and that with patience he will have his daughter back unharmed. That's when the young man will lose all patience and make a move, and then he'll be mine."

Anogh was pleased to see that neither Ag nor Simuth had realized the true connection between Paul Conklin and Nezmodie's daughter. Ag had been too far away during the banquet, and Simuth too preoccupied with taunting Nezmodie, to see the depth of the young mage's reaction.

23

Many Paths to Betrayal

THEY ARGUED HEATEDLY about a plan to rescue Katherine, especially now that Paul knew where her apartments were located.

"But you don't," Colleen insisted. "This is Faerie, the Unseelie Court. Those corridors and halls out there are as much illusion as they are substance; they constantly change and shift. They're never the same from one moment to the next. Even these rooms with toilets and showers and beds are a concession to us. They've conjured them for us. The Sidhe don't live like this. I don't know how they do live, but it's not like this. Haven't you noticed you're always escorted to your destination? The act of walking along a path is a mere courtesy, since we would find it disconcerting to step to our destination in an instant. Only the Sidhe can find their way through these halls because they don't travel a path from one place to another. Do you remember the sensation you felt when we crossed-over into Faerie?"

Paul nodded. "Ya, it felt strange. I can only describe it as a kind of spiral slippage, though I'm not even sure what I mean by that."

"We all perceive it differently," she said. "Here in the Courts, not out in the countryside of Faerie, the Sidhe's powers are consolidated and they're able to repeat that sensation spontaneously."

Paul sat down. "Then what do we do?"

"Nothing for the moment," McGowan said. "You have to understand, we've made a lot of progress. It's been clearly established to everyone's satisfaction you won't be bound, so at this juncture, holding Katherine is almost a moot point. All we need do is take a few more steps in that direction, especially if we can get the leprechauns to speak in our favor. When that happens, we make a few concessions, and Katherine is home free."

Paul couldn't find a way to be happy with that, but he had to trust that McGowan knew what he was doing. Eventually, they left him alone in his suite with no concrete resolution to Katherine's situation. But it haunted him that she had gained some hope from his nocturnal visit, and had expected her father and him to rescue her somehow.

He tried to sleep, only managed to drift off into a light doze, came fully awake with a start. His suite consisted of a sitting room, bedroom and bathroom. He sat up in bed wondering what had awakened him, noticed light leaking into the bedroom from the sitting room, recalled having carefully turned out the lights.

He climbed out of bed, peered cautiously into the sitting room, saw the man with coal black skin sitting in a chair. Paul ignored the fact that he wore only his shorts and marched right up to him. "Dayandalous, I'm tired of this crap."

Dayandalous didn't react overtly, merely pointed to a nearby chair and spoke softly, "Sit down, Paul. Let's talk."

Paul sat down, saying, "You're Andalous too, aren't you? The black Sidhe."

At that, the dark man did grin. "I am most pleased you can see through my guises. That tells me I may be right about you."

"What? What are you right about? You're worse than Anogh, with his obscure little bits of information. Every time you show up I end up in some sort of deep shit. And then after you're gone, I can't even remember you exist. You leave me to pick up all the pieces."

Dayandalous frowned, obviously chagrined. "Paul, have I ever harmed you?"

"Not directly. But I've been dragged into the Netherworld, nearly lost my soul to a demon, been shot with an arrow and stabbed with a sword. I'm tired of being toyed with."

Dayandalous grimaced. "But that was all necessary."

"Necessary! It wasn't necessary, it was insane."

"Calm down, Paul," Dayandalous said quietly, but forcibly, like a parent to a child.

Dayandalous's vertically slit pupils dilated and flashed red for a moment, then returned to thin, black slits, and Paul felt calmer. He didn't raise his voice when he said, "You did that to me, just now, didn't you? Some sort of spell thing."

"I need you to remain calm, Paul. Because you can't learn anything if you're agitated. Do you remember how you got back from the Netherworld? You looked not into the demon's eye, but through it, and then you came back on your own, didn't you?"

"But what if I hadn't figured it out?"

"That would have been a shame." Dayandalous stood, walked to the door and said, "Let's take a walk."

Paul stood. "Where are we going?"

"To show you a little bit of the real Unseelie Court, without illusion or glamour."

That, Paul couldn't resist. "Let me put on some—" Paul had been about to say *clothes*, but where a moment ago he'd worn nothing more than his shorts, now he stood fully attired in one of those waistcoat outfits. He sighed deeply.

Dayandalous opened the door of Paul's suite, and Paul followed him out into the hall. Magreth had arranged for them to be housed together in a large block of suites.

The hall just outside of Paul's door led to a large sitting room, which, at this time of night, was deserted. And from there a set of double doors led into the palace proper. But when Dayandalous opened those, instead of a corridor into the Palace, they opened onto a pathway in a small garden. Paul frowned, and Dayandalous said, "I said without illusion or glamour. Let's go to the south garden. It's lovely at night. And pay close attention to the path we take."

Dayandalous began walking. Paul followed and felt that spiral slippage through reality, but it was so faint he almost missed it, would have missed it had he not been alerted to watch for something, realized that every time he'd walked to some destination in the palace, either Seelie or Unseelie, that slippage had been there ever so faintly, as a distant and almost imperceptible background. He found himself standing on a path of crushed, yellow stone in a formal garden lit by a full moon.

Dayandalous took him by the arm, walked down the path slowly, talking as they went. "Colleen had the right of it, or at least close to it. Here in Faerie, in either of the grand palaces, the Sidhe influence is so strong they do not think of a route between places, they merely think of the place they wish to be, and they are there. Beyond the palace proper, but still in Faerie, they can do the same, but to a lesser degree. And it becomes harder the farther they travel from the palace, until eventually, in Non-aligned Faerie, they can only travel by more mundane means."

Paul had a thought that made him laugh quietly. "I certainly wouldn't consider a Sidhe steed mundane."

"How true," Dayandalous said. "But between the Realms it's a different story. The Realms leak back and forth into one another. And the Sidhe are masters at traveling between them. They think of the place they want to be, and they are there."

He stopped walking, released Paul's arm and faced him squarely. "It's time we returned. But I'll let you find you own way back."

••••

Paul stood in the middle of his bedroom in his shorts, had had a vivid dream of walking in a beautiful garden in the moonlight, a dream so realistic it left him a bit disoriented, left him wondering why he'd gotten up. Ah, yes, he had to go to the bathroom.

He stepped into the bathroom, relieved himself, then returned to bed. And as he lay down, for some reason he couldn't shake the dream from his mind.

••••

As Paul and McGowan walked down the corridor, escorted by an Unseelie servant, he sensed something faintly in the background, not a sight or sound, but something similar to that spiral slippage he'd felt when crossing over into Faerie. He tried to shake it from his mind, to think of something else, and his thoughts turned to Colleen's words about the hallways in the Unseelie palace, . . . *as much illusion as they are substance.* It made him uncomfortable to think they so easily manipulated reality, and his thoughts returned to that faint background he sensed.

McGowan had asked to meet with Katherine, for reassurance that she remained unharmed. Simuth had agreed to receive them in his chambers where they would meet her. He was alone when they arrived.

"Please. Sit. Relax." The bastard could be charming, but never charming enough for Paul to forget he'd murdered Suzanna and Cloe.

They sat. Simuth served them wine, Faerie wine that tasted like good Mortal wine, and yet it also had the taste of sunshine on a clear day after a cleansing rainstorm. Paul could not have described such a taste, but without a doubt it was there.

McGowan was good at this game. Paul knew he was anxious to see Katherine, to see that she was well, and yet they chatted for a good half hour about useless crap, and the entire time the old man showed not the faintest hint of concern.

Simuth looked at Paul, grinned knowingly. "I sense the young mage's unease, so let's bring on this lovely reunion, eh?"

Simuth waved a hand and Katherine walked into the room as if she'd been standing just beyond the doorway the entire time. She walked as if in a daze, wearing that diaphanous, revealing gown she'd worn in her bedroom. Simuth waved a hand again, and she came out of the daze with a start. Her eyes widened at the sight of McGowan. "Father," she said. He stood and she rushed into his arms.

She shed no tears, showed real strength in that. They held the embrace for several seconds until she looked Paul's way. "And Paul," she said. She let go of McGowan as Paul stood, and she hugged him as tightly. "Thank you for coming," she said as they parted. Then she looked down at her dress, blushed, and only then did he see a trickle of a tear in her eyes.

"Ah," Simuth said. "The gown embarrasses you. My apologies, dear girl." He waved a hand, and with no transition whatsoever she now wore one of the elaborate brocade gowns of an Unseelie courtier. Paul couldn't help but be impressed with such power. "Is that better?"

She turned to Simuth. "Thank you, Sir Knight," she said in a frigid voice that brought a chill even to Paul.

They sat down again, and as Simuth personally served Katherine a glass of wine, he said to McGowan, "Your daughter has been a most . . . entertaining addition to Court life. A refreshing breath of mortal air, as it were."

Paul wanted to smack the son-of-a-bitch. McGowan gave him a look that said, *I want to smack him too, but now's not the time to do so.* Simuth was so focused on gloating he didn't see the look Katherine sent his way, a look so cold and intense Paul was amazed it didn't kill the bastard right then and there.

While they bantered back and forth, Paul kept his mouth shut for the most part. Clearly, they'd not physically harmed her, not in any way visible to the naked eye, but, beneath her cold exterior Paul sensed a seething hatred for Simuth.

As McGowan and Paul returned to their chambers, again escorted by an Unseelie servant, Paul realized he'd become even more conscious of that faint background of spiral slippage.

••••

"Your Majesty," Simuth said. "I believe he is now ready to do something foolish."

Anogh stood patiently by and held his own counsel.

"How so?" Ag asked cautiously.

Whenever Simuth felt he had been particularly clever, he strutted like a cock in the hen-yard. "When the Old Wizard and he met with the woman, he was a seething cauldron of anger." Simuth's arrogance fueled his confidence and he spoke expansively. "And she played right into my hands, made no attempt to hide her hatred of me. Every look of scorn she threw my way only brought him closer to the boiling point. He is ripe for the plucking. He will do something stupid, and soon."

Ag looked to Anogh. "And you, my Summer Knight. What think you?"

Anogh considered his own words carefully. "The young mage is perhaps angry enough to . . . do something foolish. But I think the Old Wizard will keep a tight rein on him—"

"You fear to act," Simuth said, interrupting him. "As always—"

"Silence," Ag shouted, and Simuth wisely held his tongue. To Anogh he said, "You were saying?"

Anogh shrugged. "The Old Wizard and the druid will keep a close eye on him. But in any case, until he leaves this Court he is under the protections you have granted him. Anything short of a criminal act—say an assault upon your person—can be met with nothing harsher than expulsion. Non-aligned Faerie is watching the situation closely, even leaning a bit toward the Old Wizard's camp. And were you to violate those protections, they might throw their support wholly behind him."

Simuth rolled his eyes, but once commanded to silence, he dare not speak until invited to.

Ag asked, "So what do you suggest, Sir Knight?"

Again Anogh shrugged. "You must get him back here without any protections guaranteed by the Unseelie Court. Simuth is right in that the young mage is primed for action. Send them away, end your protections, then we're free to act. We can now easily locate him in the Mortal Plane, bring him back here at our leisure, on our terms. And if the young mage does something foolish, it will only be to our advantage."

Simuth clearly had something to add but Ag ignored him. "I will think on this for a time. Now leave me."

••••

After Simuth and Anogh departed, Ag spoke as if conversing with the air itself. "Come, my friend. Enter."

In the middle of the wall, to one side, a panel swung open on hidden hinges and Vasily Karpov stepped into the room. Ag poured Sidhe wine into two crystal goblets, handed one to Karpov and said, "An interesting series of developments, eh my friend?"

Karpov sipped the wine, then spoke in his thick Russian accent. "The Summer Knight is correct on both counts: Valter will not allow the young man to do anything foolish, and you can do nothing beyond expulsion."

Ag sat down in a comfortable chair and sipped at his wine. "Surely, Mr. Karpov, we can find some common interest."

Karpov remained standing and smiled. "I suppose I could be of some assistance back on the Mortal Plane, perhaps help you get your hands on the young man without any guaranteed protections."

Ag looked at the wine in his goblet as he spoke. "And if you were to help me bind the young mage, what would you require in return?"

Karpov's smile broadened into a wide grin. "Once he is bound, you can send him back to the Mortal Plane and dictate his actions, can you not?"

Ag nodded slowly.

"Exactly," Karpov continued. "And I would find it of some advantage if he returned and volunteered to apprentice with me."

Ag's face widened into a smile that mirrored Karpov's. "Yes, it appears we do have some common ground. But I am informed you have had some recent setbacks, that you dare not act openly against the Old Wizard or his apprentice."

Karpov's smile remained undiminished. "There is a man who can assist me. We have had some discussion on the matter. He is strong, confident, and has a personal grudge against the young mage. I can claim his intervention was a personal matter between two hot-blooded, young men. So while there might be suspicion, the Old Wizard will not be able to make a solid enough connection to act against me."

Ag's eyes narrowed suspiciously. "How will you induce him to assist you?"

"He is the young woman's former husband. She won't have anything to do with him, and that hurts his pride. And she appears to be attracted to Valter's apprentice, and that angers him further. He is easily manipulated through his own anger and hatred, and will think he is acting in his own interest."

Ag stood and faced Karpov. "Then we have an agreement, Mr. Karpov."

"Not yet, Your Majesty." Karpov's smile disappeared. "Such a contract must be carefully structured. But, with a little further discussion, I am confident we can come to mutually agreeable terms."

••••

Early the next day Ag summoned McGowan, Colleen, Magreth and Paul into his presence, and this time there were no niceties. With no preliminaries he revoked the protection of the Unseelie Court and expelled them immediately. They had until sundown to be out of the Unseelie territories. Magreth argued with him heatedly, to no avail.

As the short and unpleasant audience came to an end, and as they filed out of Ag's audience chamber, Anogh took Paul by the arm. "A private word with you, Young Mage."

Paul had nothing to lose. He looked at McGowan. "I'll catch up with you."

Anogh led him out to the stables at the side of the palace. The stable yard consisted of packed earth and gravel, surrounded by the palace on one side, stables and a barn and a large gate on the other three sides, all under an open, purple sky. Pages and stable hands hustled about, but they all gave the Summer Knight a wide berth as he stopped in the middle of the stable yard, turned and faced Paul squarely. "Can you walk the halls of Sidhe, Young Mage?"

Paul made no attempt to hide his confusion. "I don't know what you mean."

"I mean, can you to walk the halls of Sidhe as we Sidhe do?"

Paul grimaced with frustration. "I have no idea what you're talking about."

Anogh continued as if he hadn't spoken. "Because, when I walk beside you, I sense that you see the true halls of Sidhe. Do you truly sense nothing more than stone walls and floor and ceiling?"

Paul had sensed something, decided to be honest. "I don't know. I do sense something, but I'm not sure I know what it is. It's the same sensation I get when we pass between Faerie and the Mortal Plane."

"Yes," Anogh said, nodding his head thoughtfully. "And can you induce that sensation?"

"I doubt it. It's just there."

Anogh turned away, stepped a few paces away from him, rubbing his chin with his hand and thinking intensely. He walked back to Paul and looked him directly in the eyes. It surprised Paul to see doubt and fear in the Sidhe's eyes. "All you need do to walk the halls of Sidhe is induce that sensation, picture the place you wish to be, and step there. Above all, do not picture a path to that place, just the place itself. Can you do that?"

Paul trusted Anogh only so far. The Summer Knight had messed in his life as far back as the day he met Suzanna. "I seriously doubt it. Why are you telling me this?"

"I think it will benefit us both if you know this."

With regard to Anogh there was always the question of trust. "Why would you help us? Doesn't that violate your oaths?"

Anogh's expression hardened. "My oaths bind me to the Winter Court, and by those oaths I may not betray the Winter Court to the Summer Court."

Paul's aggravation boiled to the surface. "Ya, ya, I've heard all that before. But what exactly does that mean?"

Anogh refused to say more, was clearly frustrated by Paul's ignorance as he escorted Paul back to his chambers.

••••

When they assembled in the stable yard the coaches were ready, with steeds in harness and coachmen attending. Dergindaal's men each stood by his mount, many checking their saddles and harness. To Paul it appeared to be a confused tangle of whinnying horses, stable hands running about shouting orders, the coachmen desperately trying to calm the animals in harness.

Paul had decided against wizard's robes and nineteenth century waistcoats in favor of jeans, a shirt and a lightweight windbreaker. At this point, with them leaving Katherine behind and no resolution to the situation, he didn't care who he impressed.

McGowan seemed okay with the whole thing, and refused to discuss the situation openly while they were in either Court.

Paul climbed into the coach he would share with Devoe and Sinthas, took a seat where he could see Magreth's coach through the window next to him. One never kept a queen waiting, so everyone made sure they were ready before her. McGowan, Colleen and Cadilus waited near their coach, and as Paul had guessed, Magreth was the last to emerge from the palace proper with Dergindaal at her side. Dergindaal assisted her into the coach, then Colleen, then the two men. There was a moment while they adjusted themselves for comfort, then the coach lurched forward and they left the Unseelie Court in a cloud of dust.

24

Reality Redefined

"WHY AREN'T WE doing something?" Paul demanded, pacing back and forth in the old man's study, his voice close to a shout.

Colleen spoke softly. "Calm down, Paul."

Devoe, leaning against the wall, said, "Can't blame him for being a bit impatient."

McGowan said, "I wasn't able to tell you this while I was there, but I met privately with Ag. We're going to cut a deal."

Paul stopped pacing and dropped into one of the chairs. "What kind of deal."

"I don't know yet, but Ag's trying to save face. He says Simuth acted without his knowledge, but he can't publicly admonish the Winter Knight."

Paul asked, "And you believe him?"

The old man shrugged. "Not a word, but it doesn't matter. Maybe Simuth acted on his own, or maybe Ag just wants to use him as a scapegoat. In any case Ag's backed into a corner. The Seelie Court is aligned against him, and the non-aligned fey are close to it. So he just wants out. We might have to toss him a bone or two, but we'll get Katherine back. And Magreth, because they attacked you in her court, is helping us with the negotiations."

Paul stood again. "So we just sit and do nothing?"

McGowan pointed a finger at him. "You sit and do nothing. Colleen and I are working behind the scenes."

••••

Paul decided to grab a hamburger at *Jessie's*, the pub down the street from his apartment building. Alone. At this point he was completely out of the loop regarding Katherine's rescue.

Paul was most of the way through his hamburger when Eric Reichart sat down at the bar next to him. But as Paul eyed him warily, Reichart raised both hands and said, "Truce, Paul. I'm not here to pick a fight."

Paul took a pull on his beer and said, "The last time we met I got the impression we're not going to be bosom buddies."

Reichart nodded reluctantly and shrugged. "Look, I admit I don't like you seeing Katherine, and I want to get her back. And I know I haven't been very pleasant about it. But ... this kidnapping thing, her being a prisoner in the Unseelie Court, I've thought about it and I realize I should put our differences aside until we've rescued her. After that you and I can snarl at each other, and not be friends and all that stuff."

He sounded quite reasonable, not at all like the Eric Reichart Paul knew. "So why are you here? Why me?"

Reichart sighed with frustration. "Old man McGowan won't let me help, won't let me be involved in any way. I figured if I talked to you first, maybe you'd tell him I want to help, that I'll cooperate, do whatever is needed."

Reichart was a powerful wizard, had been more powerful than Paul, but Paul suddenly realized they were now on a par. The only possible explanation was that Paul had grown. In any case, Reichart seemed quite sincere, and they needed all the allies they could get.

Paul finished the last of his burger, paid his bill and he and Reichart walked out to the street together. It was a dark, moonless night. "My car's just down the street here," Reichart said, pointing in the same direction as Paul's apartment.

They turned that way and walked side-by-side down the sidewalk. When they got to Reichart's car Paul said, "I'll talk to McGowan tomorrow morning, tell him you want to help."

As Reichart fumbled for his keys he said, "Thanks. I really appreciate it."

He found his keys, unlocked his car, turned back to Paul and stuck out his hand. It would be rude to refuse to shake it, and maybe he really wasn't a bad sort, just a little screwed up because of a failed marriage. Paul could understand that, so he extended his hand.

The instant their hands touched he realized his mistake. He felt that surge of power that comes only from a previously prepared spell. The ground swayed and his muscles went weak. Paul's knees hit the grass next to the sidewalk with Reichart still holding his hand. Reichart said, "You stupid, fucking sucker."

As four dark shapes stepped out of the shadows of a nearby building, Paul put all his effort into drawing power, was completely blocked from earth and ley line magic. He turned to his physical magic, managed to pull quite a bit and slammed it into Reichart's hand, knocking him across the hood of his car out into the street.

Two Unseelie warriors grabbed Paul's arms, pulled them painfully behind his back. He struggled, but Reichart's spell had weakened him badly and they bound his hands with some sort of rope. They held him as a Sidhe mage in wizards robes approached him and lifted his hand toward Paul's face. Paul pulled more power, tried to picture the mage's arm broken. It snapped with a loud crack, bent half way down the length of the forearm at a sharp angle. The mage cried out, staggered back, holding his arm and screaming in agony. One of the two warriors slammed a gauntleted fist into the side or Paul's head, knocking him to the ground. Badly dazed, hovering on the edge of consciousness, Paul could still pull power, but a boot slammed into his face and he lost consciousness.

••••

"Your Majesty." Simuth bent the knee before Ag.

"Well," Ag demanded impatiently.

"It took a mortal mage, two Sidhe mages and two Sidhe warriors to subdue him, but he's ours."

"Excellent," Ag crowed. "Excellent. He's as powerful as we thought. Once he's broken he'll be a valuable asset. Keep at least seven mages on him at all times. He mustn't escape under any circumstances."

Simuth asked eagerly, "And shall I begin his education?"

Ag leaned back on his throne and sighed happily. "Oh yes, dear Simuth. We will teach this young mage a bit about reality here in Faerie."

••••

Paul dreamed he and one of those beautiful Sidhe creatures were clutched together in a tangle of naked arms and legs and silken sheets. They'd made love for several hours now. She groaned as he nibbled on her ear, and a piece of him noted it was pointed. He put a line of gentle kisses down her throat, took a nipple in his mouth and bit it softly. She groaned even louder, rolled on top of him, guided him into her, cried out as he thrust into her with every bit of strength and power he had. She responded by grinding her hips desperately against him, and they thrashed back and forth for several minutes until she arched her back and growled like an animal as pleasure washed through her. But try as he might he could not find relief, had not yet found release through all his dreaming hours of lovemaking.

"Enough, darling," she said, panting breathlessly.

She rolled off him, and he realized it wasn't a dream. Simuth leaned against the wall just inside the door and began applauding. "Excellent show," he said.

She swung her legs off the bed, stood, not in the least shy or embarrassed by her nakedness. To Simuth she said, "Glad you enjoyed it, dear. Perhaps you'd like to join us sometime. The more, the merrier."

She turned back to Paul, stood there looking at him, sweat and Paul's saliva glistening on her breasts. "I do thank you most sincerely, Young Mage, for a very pleasurable evening." She picked up her gown, didn't even bother to put it on as she walked out of the room. Simuth turned and followed her.

Paul sat up and buried his face in his hands. The last thing he remembered was the confrontation in the street with Reichart and his Unseelie friends. He didn't recall the end of it, but he'd clearly not come out on the winning side. He did remember slapping Reichart with some power, and hoped he'd given the jerk a thing or two to think about.

He untangled his legs from the sheets, stood and found his clothes in a heap on the floor. He had a vague recollection of meeting the young woman in a bar and going back to her place, but bars and one-night-stands weren't his style. It had to be some sort of false memory.

He pulled on his jeans, sat down on the edge of the bed and tried to draw power, but nothing happened. He tried again, but just when he thought he could wrap his mental hands around that maelstrom, it slipped through his fingers and drifted away. Something seemed to be blocking his abilities.

The door to the room was open, so he decided to simply leave. He stood again, pulled on the rest of his clothes, turned and headed for the exit. But when he reached the doorway he slammed into an invisible barrier there, mashed his face against it and bounced off it, staggering back into the center of the room. "Shit," he said, rubbing at his cheek. He was going to end up with a nice welt just beneath his left eye.

He returned to the doorway and carefully reached out, pressed his fingers against the invisible barrier of a containment circle. They had him isolated from his power, and locked up nicely inside a circle.

He explored the room, which turned out to be the equivalent of a simple hotel room: bedroom and bathroom. For a moment he considered the bathtub drain, recalled how the leprechauns had flushed him and themselves down a similar hole when escaping from the Seelie Court. But even if he had access to his powers, he didn't know the first thing about pulling that trick.

He sat down on the edge of the bed to think. He could scream and holler for someone to come and pay attention to him, but that would just give Simuth some satisfaction at seeing him helpless. He was stuck, a prisoner, his only hope that McGowan might be able to bargain for his release.

••••

"We can't find any trace of him," McGowan said. "I've searched quite thoroughly on the Mortal Plane."

Clark Devoe slipped through the door into McGowan's study where all but Paul had gathered. He immediately said, "Eric Reichart's in the hospital. SFPD found him three days ago, his right hand nearly crushed, and suffering from severe hypothermia."

"Hypothermia?" Colleen said. "That would be Paul's doing. And three days ago, that would be when Paul disappeared."

Devoe smiled, though there was nothing pleasant about the look on his face. "Guess where they found Reichart: lying in the middle of the street less than a hundred feet from Paul's apartment building. And there were nearby traces of Unseelie magic."

McGowan said, "That little shit. He's got some questions to answer. What hospital?"

"I've already been there," Devoe said. "Had a little talk with my good buddy Eric. He stinks of Unseelie too, and it's clear he had something to do with Paul's disappearance. But the asshole won't admit to anything, and I was . . . persuasive."

Colleen said, "More like scary."

Devoe looked at her, his expression flat and almost inhuman. "But he was more scared of somebody else, wouldn't talk." Devoe turned to McGowan. "You thinking what I'm thinking?"

McGowan closed his eyes and nodded slowly, tiredly. "That son-of-a-bitch Karpov. Reichart doesn't have the wherewithal to cut a deal with the Unseelie Court. It's got to be Karpov. But unless we can prove it, I can't take any action against him. On the other hand, if I can confirm Ag is holding Paul against his will. If I can do that, that means he's taken both my daughter and my apprentice, and I'll have the support of every practitioner on the Mortal Plane. But first I need solid confirmation of the situation."

Colleen sighed heavily. "Can you get it before they break Paul?"

••••

It had been a long week, but it was Friday and they'd just closed that new account with one of Paul's designs. He and old man Strath had just seen the client off after signing the contracts, a big job that would keep them in the black for months. Paul sat down behind his desk and leaned back just as Strath walked into his office.

"Paul, that was great work. Why don't you take the afternoon off, on me, spend the time with that beautiful wife of yours."

"You mean that?" Paul asked.

"Of course I do. Get out of here, now, before I change my mind. And say high to Suzanna for me."

Paul grabbed his coat, threw it over his shoulder, glanced at his briefcase, decided that for once, no working on the weekend. So he left the briefcase there and headed for the door.

He was waiting at the elevator when Strath stuck his head out of the entrance to their office suite. "By the way, there's going to be a nice bonus in this for you."

On the way down in the elevator he thought, *A bonus*. Maybe he could get something nice for Suzanna, or maybe now they could afford a little vacation, take Cloe to Disneyland. He thought about that all the way home, was looking forward to a glass of wine with Suzanna, and sitting in the kitchen watching her make dinner. They might even have a chance to make love before Cloe got home from school.

He opened the door to their apartment, didn't see Suzanna in the kitchen or living room, figured she must have stepped out for a bit, probably on some errand. He headed straight for the bedroom, pulling off his tie as he walked, hoping she'd get back soon so they could take advantage of their time alone. But when he stepped into the bedroom he was confronted with the most pornographic view of a man screwing the hell out of some woman, his buttocks pumping up and down, his erect penis pumping in and out of her. Paul's first thought was that somehow he'd walked into the wrong apartment, and he was going to be horribly embarrassed when the couple on the bed realized they had an intruder in the room. He started to turn, to sneak out, hoping he'd get away clean and they'd never know, but then the woman groaned and cried out in Suzanna's voice, "Oh god that's good. I've missed you . . . so much . . . darling."

Paul froze, and stood for a moment staring numbly at the scene on the bed. "Suzanna?" he asked.

The man stopped pumping in and out of her, turned to look over his shoulder at Paul, his eyes wide with surprise. It was their next-door neighbor, a single guy named Healey, who was always telling Paul what a lucky guy he was. Suzanna's head rose and also peered over the man's shoulder. "Oh my god!" she cried, struggling to push the man off her. "Paul!"

Paul turned and headed for the door, heard Suzanna crying out behind him. "Paul, wait. No. Let me explain."

••••

Paul had a window in his small room that looked out over the fantastic Faerie countryside. He stood at it, staring out it but seeing nothing, tears running down his cheeks.

Sometimes that dream ended with Suzanna begging for forgiveness. Sometimes she scorned him, told him he was a rotten lover, that he should be glad she chose to take another lover to satisfy her physical needs instead of leaving him. So far he'd experienced it a dozen different ways, with a dozen different men as her lover, and a dozen different endings to each one, none the same. And the most difficult part of it all was that the dreams didn't have a dreamlike quality, were instead vivid and real and painful. And while intellectually he knew they were just dreams, illusions cooked up by Simuth, each time he awoke his sense of betrayal was new and raw.

"Young Mage."

Paul recognized Anogh's voice, turned to face him. If there wasn't that circle blocking his power he'd summon all he could, go for Anogh's throat and damn the consequences. But without his power he couldn't even touch the bastard. "What do you want?"

"I thought I'd come see how you're doing."

"How do you think I'm doing?" Paul demanded angrily as he turned away from Anogh, turned back to the window.

Anogh crossed the room, stopped close behind him and spoke softly, "I think Simuth must use three strong mages to dampen your power and control you, and seven to maintain this circle. I think Ag expected you to be broken by now, is frustrated you're not, is growing increasingly unhappy with Simuth. I think Simuth is growing desperate. And I think you may be strong enough to withstand the fool."

"What do you care?"

"I care a great deal, mortal. You just don't understand how and why. Remember this, if Simuth stumbles, you can walk the halls of Sidhe all the way back to the Mortal Plane."

It took a moment for Anogh's words to sink in, and when they did Paul turned to confront him. But there was no one there. Paul stood alone in the room, wondering if it had been just another illusion, all part of the game they played on the landscape of his mind.

••••

Ag demanded angrily, "When will it be done?"

"Any day now," Simuth answered, on his knees before Ag's throne and trembling visibly. Clearly, Ag's patience had reached its limits.

Ag stared at him for a long moment, and when he spoke his words were soft, sibilant, almost like the hiss of a snake. "Any day now, my dear Simuth. You've said that for several days now. And the Old Wizard is using the time to muster his support."

The temperature in the room dropped suddenly and frost formed in Anogh's hair. Ag stood, took each step down the dais slowly, one at a time, stopped at the bottom next to the kneeling Simuth. He leaned down and put his lips close to Simuth's ear, and while he spoke in a faint whisper, all there heard his words clearly. "If he is not broken and bound soon, then I will have to release him, and the woman. Do you understand what such a failure will mean for you?"

Simuth's trembling increased. He whispered. "I do, Your Majesty."

Ag smiled. "Then see to it that it is finished tonight."

"Yes, Your Majesty. Tonight. It will be so."

25

A Choice of Desires

PAUL WALKED KATHERINE up the steps at the front of her house. They'd had a wonderful evening: dinner, then an opening at an art studio run by a friend of Katherine's. At the art studio they'd laughed quietly at the art; they both agreed it was atrocious crap.

Their relationship had turned a little serious, though no sex yet, just a few kisses at odd little moments here and there. Nice kisses!

At the top of the steps she turned and faced him, leaned into him, let him wrap his arms around her. "You seem a little preoccupied tonight," she said, an odd look passing over her face.

He shrugged. "Had a bad dream last night. Really strange, some parts bad, some parts good. You were in it, and your father. I was a wizard, of all things, and you were a witch, and we were involved with fairies and leprechauns and demons and all sorts of weird stuff. Can't tell you how glad I was to wake up this morning and find out it was just a nightmare."

She gave him a little evil grin. "Well one part of it was real. Trust me, I can be a real witch, when the mood strikes me."

He laughed. "I don't doubt that."

She pulled out of his arms. "Come on in, have a cup of coffee. It's been too nice of an evening to end it now." She turned to the door, dug her keys out of her purse and opened it. He followed her into her living room, through the living room and into the kitchen where she threw her purse on the counter, then turned and faced him squarely. She looked into his eyes, so he put his arms around her and kissed her. She responded warmly, her body tight against his. The kiss started out slow, soft and delicate, but quickly turned hot and passionate. He could tell she was as reluctant as him to end it.

Her house was a lot nicer than his dump. He helped her out of her coat. She wore slacks that emphasized her long legs and nice figure, a pale, blue blouse with a ruffled collar, open at the neck and cut just a bit low, exposing a hint of some sort of red lacy thing. She caught him checking out her ass as she stepped out of the coat, grinned imp-ishly. "Here," she said, took the coat from him and hung it in a closet near the front door.

She took his hand, led him into the living room, laughing and commenting about the ridiculous art they'd seen earlier. In the living room she stopped, turned and pulled him against her. They kissed again, their tongues dancing back and forth. When the kiss ended, he couldn't think of anything better to say than, "I like my coffee black."

She didn't pull out of his arms to go make the coffee, looked into his eyes and said, "I think the coffee can wait a bit."

They kissed again, and he became conscious of her body molded tightly against his, her breasts pressing against his chest, but he wasn't sure how far she wanted to go. When they came up for air she had a twinkle in her eye as she hesitantly said, "I'm hav-ing trouble developing any interest whatsoever in coffee."

A wave of intense, passionate desire washed through him as he stumbled over the words, "Ya. To hell with . . . the coffee."

As they kissed again, she pressed herself against him. He pressed back and kissed her on the neck, and she let out a low pleasurable growl.

At that point they both lost control, idiotically tried to maintain the kiss and as much body contact as possible while struggling toward her bedroom and attempting to pull Paul's jacket and tie off at the same time. She stumbled backwards and he stum-bled with her, ended up pressing her against the wall, his arms tangled behind him in his coat. He kissed her on the throat trying to fumble with his jacket, kissed the swell of her breasts exposed just above the red, lacy thing.

She pushed him away. He stumbled backward thinking he'd gone too far, but when the back of his legs hit the edge of her bed, he fell back onto it, his hands still pinned behind his back in the tangle of his coat, the bulge in his pants embarrassingly obvious. She made a point of looking at it, grinned evilly, laid down on top of him with his hands still tangled behind him.

"I've got you trapped right where I want you," she said, then she kissed him on the chin, ran her lips lightly down the side of his neck, leaned back for a moment, pulled off his tie and tossed it aside, then planted several kisses on his chest. He'd never felt such intense desire, and sensed that they both felt the same desperate need for each other. Their kisses grew more heated, and he finally got his hands free, cupped one of her breasts, pinched the nipple lightly through her blouse. She groaned with pleasure, whispered, "It's almost unnatural the way I want you at this moment."

Their kissing grew desperate, frantic. He tried to unbutton her blouse, accidentally tore the red lacy thing, exposed her breasts and began kissing them, bit one ever so gently. She groaned, cried out, kissed him on the ear, bit him on his neck. "I can't . . ." she said breathlessly. "I've never . . . felt such . . . overwhelming need. God I need you!"

She tore at his belt, got his pants open, put her hand inside them and stroked him desperately. It drove him insane, and he bit her breast almost viciously, tasted a trickle of blood, was amazed he would do such a thing, because he just wasn't like that, not rough and harsh and cruel. But she groaned with pleasure at the bite, and that wasn't like her either. Then he got his hand in her pants, caressed her between her legs, and her cry of pleasure was almost a full-throated scream. "There's something wrong here," she cried, "but I don't care. I don't care."

They pulled desperately at each other's pants, both stupidly trying to undress the other one-handed, refusing to remove the other hand from the pleasure they so urgently needed. She arched her back and growled like an animal as waves of pleasure washed through her. "There's something wrong here," she screamed, thrusting her hips against his. He'd gotten her pants open, but only that, didn't recall tearing them badly in the process. His were open, and like hers still up around his waist. For an instant they abandoned the desperate struggle to undress, pressed frantically against each other, his shorts and her bikinis and their half-open pants the only things that separated them. "I know it," she screamed, "I know it, I know it. It's a glamour, a beguilement."

Then she completely lost control, rolled them both over so he was on top of her, ground against him, her bikinis and his shorts still in the way. And while he had no less control, there was a piece of him that heard her. As they continued their mad, frantic struggles, she tearing at his pants, he tugging at hers, that piece of him that she'd awakened to the absurdity of their struggles managed to pull power, to feed it into his personal wards. Their passion had them both desperately trapped, unable to control anything they did, but the walls of Katherine's bedroom shimmered and wavered as if they were just barriers of smoke slowly dissipating on a gentle breeze.

They rolled over again and now she was on top. He bit at her breasts, licked them, and a piece of him realized they were writhing on the floor in the middle of a large banquet hall, the main entertainment for the Unseelie Court's dining pleasure, trapped in a magic circle of protection powered by Sidhe mages, performing for the entertainment of all, especially Simuth, who grinned at him knowingly and nodded.

"Spell," Katherine said breathlessly as they writhed together on the floor. "Amplify . . . our own . . . desires . . . thousand fold."

Paul tried to draw power, managed only a trickle. Understanding was one thing, resisting another. As she tugged at his pants all he could do was fumble clumsily at her hands, delaying the inevitable spectacle. His own power only fed the spell more, and he realized he couldn't fight it, that there must be several Sidhe mages feeding their power into it, fighting against him. If he couldn't fight it, he and Katherine would tear their clothes apart and screw their brains out on the floor of the banquet hall, an ugly pornographic show for the Unseelie Court.

Simuth was truly enjoying himself, fondling the breasts of the woman lying beside him, both of them enjoying the floor show. Their eyes met, and in Simuth's Paul saw victory, contempt, cruelty. He focused his thoughts on Suzanna and Cloe, realizing now there was no way he could fight such a powerful spell-crafting. But if he couldn't fight it, could he turn it against them? If it amplified his desires a thousand fold, then need it only amplify his desire for Katherine? Looking into Simuth's cold, cruel, triumphant eyes, perhaps it would amplify other desires. Yes, he desired Katherine. She was beautiful and intelligent and sexy, and a little bit vulnerable. But he had many desires, like his desire for vengeance on the man who'd murdered his wife and child, his desire for Simuth's death, his desire to break the circle, his desire for revenge on the entire Unseelie Court. *Desire that*, he thought. *Focus on that desire,* he told himself, *and only that desire, and let them amplify that.*

It was so incredibly difficult to put Katherine aside, especially with her writhing in his arms, a willing partner. But she wasn't really willing, for they were both just Simuth's toys. And with that thought, no other desire existed for him but his wish for revenge. He focused on that, focused on the power the Sidhe mages fed into the spell, and he gave them that desire to amplify. His own passion waned, and he saw his new desire grow into an ugly, angry cloud of hatred. He drew even more power, drew it without regard to McGowan's warnings, without regard for himself, and fed it into the Sidhe spell.

A deafening explosion rocked the hall, and the mad, uncontrollable desire they both felt disappeared. He lay there for a moment on top of her, savoring the freedom of the now broken spell, stunned by the explosion and bleeding from several cuts, some rather serious.

He pulled himself off her and she curled up into a fetal ball, trying to cover herself with her torn clothing. She too bled from cuts and scrapes and bites. He wanted to help Katherine, to console her, to help them both pretend they'd never gone through what had just happened. But he had to act now, while he had an advantage, if he had an advantage. He struggled to his feet, she clutching at her torn clothing, he clutching at his. "I'm sorry," he said, turned and staggered toward Simuth.

The explosion had blown outward from the circle and had stunned everyone, left a few unconscious. Paul half crawled, half walked toward Simuth, who was slowly climbing to his feet. But just as Paul reached him he stood upright, turned, faced Paul, laughed insanely and growled, "Fool mortal. You think you can best me in combat?" He backhanded Paul.

Paul hit the floor hard skidding on his back, had no idea how far he'd been thrown by the blow, lay there with his head spinning, little motes of unconsciousness sparkling in front of his eyes, hoping his jaw wasn't broken. Simuth marched across the room, picked Paul up by the front of his shirt and threw him like a broken toy doll. Paul slammed into a wall, crumpled to the floor. His left shoulder sent fiery waves of agony through him, and he was certain he had several cracked ribs. He tried to struggle to his feet but his right knee gave out in a lance of agony. The banquet was in chaos, but Simuth stood over Paul and announced to them all as if he was the ringleader of a circus, "My guests, ladies and gentlemen. It's time to end this foolish game."

Paul's head spun sickeningly, and he was too stunned to do anything but watch the Sidhe kill him.

"You pathetic animal," Simuth said, but as he bent to reach for Paul, Katherine, screaming maniacally, hit him like a linebacker. They tumbled past Paul in a tangle of arms and legs.

Paul scrambled to his feet, kept most of his weight on his left leg, staggered toward them like a drunkard. Katherine groaned and rolled over, but Simuth recovered immediately, stood, looked down at her and kicked her in the ribs. As he drew his foot back to kick her again Paul charged, but with lances of pain spearing through his knee he only managed to produce a clumsy shuffle. Simuth heard him, turned and slapped him to the floor. He turned back to Katherine, kicked her one last time, turned back to Paul and reached down, grabbed him by the throat with one hand and lifted him to his feet, lifted him off his feet, held him dangling in front of him like a small child, choking and gasping for air. "It's time to end this, mortal."

Hefting Paul by the throat with one hand, his feet dangling a few inches off the floor, Simuth used his other hand to pull his shiny, silver rapier. He drew the rapier back, preparing for a long sweeping stroke. He clearly intended to hit Paul in mid-torso, and from what he'd heard of the power of a Sidhe silver rapier, in Faerie it would cut him in two, easily severing his body. Simuth didn't want him to have a quick or easy death.

Paul had no defenses left. Here in Faerie Simuth was just too powerful. But Anogh's words echoed in his mind, . . . *walk the halls of Sidhe all the way back to the Mortal Plane.*

Paul didn't know if he could do it, had no confidence in his ability and no trust for Anogh's words. But he had nothing to lose, so just as Simuth started the stroke that would cut him in two, he lifted one hand, placed it on the hand Simuth had wrapped about his throat, thought carefully of that spiral shift in reality between their two worlds, pictured his own small living room and mentally stepped into it.

••••

Katherine rolled over, was certain Simuth had broken a couple of ribs. She rolled over just in time to see him swing his blade, knew there was no hope for Paul, none for her either. And then Simuth and Paul disappeared, just blinked out of existence.

The explosion had filled the hall with chaos, wounded Sidhe slowly staggering to their feet and taking stock of the situation. Katherine somehow managed to get to her feet, though she wasn't sure she could remain standing for long, especially holding the weight of the heavy long-sword.

Sword!

She looked at her hands, both curled about the sheathed blade, its long hilt protruding from one end.

••••

Paul was getting better at it because they were only about five feet off the floor when they materialized, but horizontal, with Paul on top of Simuth. They hit the floor with a heavy thud; Paul's weight slammed into Simuth, reminding him painfully of his cracked ribs, but giving Simuth an even better lesson in the physics of gravity. And while Paul had been prepared for the transition, it caught Simuth completely off guard. He groaned and gasped for breath as Paul rolled off him.

Nursing broken ribs Paul scrambled to his feet and staggered toward the kitchen, limping painfully on his damaged knee. Behind him he heard Simuth struggling to his feet. Paul had two thoughts in mind: they were no longer in Faerie so Simuth was no longer all-powerful, and cold iron. He needed cold iron.

He made it to the kitchen barely an instant ahead of Simuth, knew he didn't have time to go for the drawer with the knives, spotted a dirty cast-iron skillet in the sink, grabbed it and turned to face the Sidhe. Simuth looked at the skillet in Paul's hand and laughed, then swung his rapier.

An iron skillet against a three-foot rapier, ordinarily there would have been no chance. But Paul remembered, and Simuth forgot, that his rapier was pure silver, harder than the hardest steel in Faerie, but soft and compliant in the Mortal Plane.

The rapier caught Paul in a slashing blow across the ribs, and had they been in Faerie it would have sliced him in two, cutting through bone and flesh and organs. But here, while it cut him, it didn't have the hardness to slice through bone and it bent into a misshaped arc around his ribs. Simuth hesitated, lifted the bent rapier and frowned at it stupidly. Paul swung the skillet, put everything he had behind a two-handed blow and hit Simuth in the side of the head. The skillet made a surprisingly pleasant clang as it crashed into his skull, and the Winter Knight went down like a sack of potatoes. He groaned, didn't attempt to rise, the side of his head smoking where the iron had slapped him.

Paul staggered, leaned against the kitchen counter, nausea threatening to empty his stomach as a wave of agony from his shoulder lanced through him. But he gritted his teeth and waved the skillet at Simuth like a sword. "Touché, you sack of shit."

Blood oozed from the slash across his ribs, and ran down his face from more than one cut on his forehead, but he didn't have time to worry about that if he hoped to get Katherine back before the chaos in the Unseelie Court cleared. He pulled open a drawer in which he kept a mix of all sorts of knives. The smaller ones like paring knives and steak knives weren't terribly sharp, but he didn't need sharp so he stuffed three of them into his pocket. There was a small box of two-inch nails, and on a whim he stuffed a couple of handfuls into the other pocket. Behind him Simuth groaned, attempted to get to his feet. Paul turned back to him, gave him a two-handed swing with the skillet to the side of his head and the asshole went down a second time.

There was one big butcher knife he kept sharp, good steel that held a good edge, and another one that didn't have a sharp edge, but did have a good, sharp point. In some unknown memory he recalled someone saying, *. . . decapitate them, separate the head from the heart. Then impale both the head and the heart on cold iron, and hold the iron fast until their struggles cease.* He staggered back to Simuth. *. . . you must show no hesitation, no mercy, no compassion . . .*

Simuth struggled to his feet in the middle of the living room, stood there for a moment dazed and unsteady. Paul approached him from behind and grabbed his hair, kicked the back of his legs and he dropped to his knees . . . *show no hesitation, no mercy, no compassion . . .* Standing behind Simuth, Paul raised the butcher knife with the sharp point and said, "This is for Suzanna, you shithead," then plunged the knife into Simuth's chest.

The Sidhe screamed; the skin around the knife hissing and spitting and smoldering. Simuth screamed again, tried to grab it, but as his fingers touched the hilt they too burned and sizzled and sputtered. He threw his hands out away from the knife in his chest, looked at it and wailed frantically. "No, no, no, no, no!"

"All right, asshole," Paul said, "let's go back and teach everyone a lesson." He clutched the other butcher knife in his right hand, grabbed the hair on the back of Simuth's head in his left, concentrated on that spiral twist of reality and the Unseelie banquet hall, and he and Simuth appeared amidst the chaos he'd left only a few moments earlier.

They were back in Faerie, Katherine standing a few feet away holding that god-awful, giant, sheathed sword, a stunned look of awe on her face. She saw Paul, and extended the hilt toward him.

Simuth flinched, clearly realizing he'd be more powerful now. But before he could react, Paul said, "This is for Cloe," and without hesitating he cut Simuth's throat with a broad slash, then pressed the blade of the big butcher knife in the open wound. As Simuth's throat sizzled and spit a greasy smoke, filling the air with the smell of burning flesh, he screamed a long wailing cry of dread and fear. Paul held the knife steady, put a knee in the small of Simuth's back, pulled on his hair, arching his neck upward, then stabbed the knife into one of Simuth's eyes. Simuth wailed like a strange beast

. . . show no hesitation, no mercy, no compassion . . .

"Paul, look out."

Paul looked up at the sound of Katherine's voice. Two Sidhe warriors were running toward him. Paul reached into his pocket, pulled out two of the small knives, pulled all the power he could hold, tossed the knives in the air and fed the power into them. They took the two Sidhe by surprise, dropped them both to the floor screaming at the cold iron in their chests. He reached over and past Simuth to the sheathed sword Katherine had extended toward him, gripped the hilt in his right hand and pulled it free. The blade glowed with a strange hoary light.

With his left hand he reached into his other pocket and pulled out a hand-full of nails. Katherine stood there unsteadily clutching at her torn clothing and holding the sheath. Paul shouted, "Katherine, down." Her eyes widened and she dropped to the floor without hesitation. He pulled power again, threw the nails in the air, dumped the power into them and they streaked in all directions, buried themselves in random Sidhe targets like shrapnel on a battlefield.

Simuth still knelt with his back toward Paul shrieking like a wounded cat, one knife protruding from an eye, the other from his chest, both crackling and spitting a greasy black smoke. Paul gripped the hilt of the great sword in both hands. It had the weight of a heavy baseball bat, so he pulled it back, screamed, "And this if for Katherine," then swung it like a Louisville slugger in a long flat arc.

It chopped into Simuth's neck, and his head literally popped up a few inches before it tumbled down, bounced off his now headless shoulders and dropped to the floor. Simuth's body knelt there for a moment, his head still shrieking, the two knives still sputtering and crackling. Then his torso toppled forward and collapsed onto the knife buried in his chest.

Simuth's severed head screamed again, a long wailing cry of despair. Paul saw more Sidhe coming toward him purposefully. He grabbed the last of the nails, shouted, "Stay down, Katherine," trusted she would, pulled dangerous amounts of power, tossed the nails in the air and fed the power into them. They pinged and zinged as they ricocheted off stone, popped and hissed as they punched holes in Sidhe flesh, brought on more chaos and pain.

Paul turned back to the screaming severed head and the thrashing body. He rolled Simuth over and put a knee in his chest, and with one hand on the butcher knife in Simuth's eye, the other on the knife in his chest, Paul poured power into them both. Simuth's head screamed louder, and his body thrashed powerfully beneath Paul, but he held on, refused to let go, continued channeling power into the two blades. Slowly, bit by bit, Simuth's cries died away and his body stilled. Paul held on, pulled more and more power, watched as the two pieces of the Summer Knight smoldered and sizzled, finally dissipating into a pile of gray ash. Into the silence Paul whispered, "And that was for me, shithead."

The Unseelie Court roiled with absolute chaos. Paul's nasty little nails had done the job, and quite a number of Sidhe screamed in pain. All that remained of the Winter Knight were bits and pieces of clothing and jewelry amid the ashes. Paul sifted through it quickly, found Suzanna's ring and shoved it into a pocket. He struggled to his feet, staggered to Katherine, almost fell over because of his knee, helped her to her feet and turned to Ag. There was no sign of the sword.

The Winter King sat on his throne gasping in pain, a fist-sized hole burned into his side, and Paul realized he'd gotten him with one of the nails. Ag just stared at him, wincing at the pain.

Katherine whispered, "They fear you. You broke a circle, killed several of their mages doing so. No one breaks a circle." Her voice was filled with awe. "No one."

Paul didn't tell her he hadn't broken it, he'd just turned their own power back on them, turned the twisted spell that fed on their desires against them. But if that made them fear him, then they didn't need to know the truth.

Ag snarled, "You brought cold iron into the Unseelie Court. The penalty for that is death."

Paul shrugged. "Self-defense, asshole." Then he pointed a finger at Ag. "You or any of yours come for me or any of mine again, and I'll make this look like a walk in the park."

Ag snarled, "I'm going to kill you where you stand."

Jim'Jiminie materialized between them in a sparkling of pixie dust. "And you'll have to be killing me first."

Ag screamed, "He violated Unseelie Court law. He murdered the Winter Knight."

Jim'Jiminie shook his head. "You were the aggressor here, Ag. And vendetta was justified. It's settled. All Faerie stands against you in this."

Jim'Jiminie turned back to Paul. "Leave now, Young Mage, while you can."

Paul wrapped his arms around Katherine, thought carefully of that spiral twist in reality, and thought of McGowan's kitchen.

••••

He was getting better at it each time. They still came back four or five feet off the floor, but he'd managed to make sure Katherine was on top so he didn't crush her with his weight, and they came out over McGowan's kitchen table so they only had a few feet to fall.

                    J. L. Doty

They hit the table with a thud and crash of scattering dishes. Katherine's weight on top of him reminded him painfully of his broken ribs.

"Oh my god," Sarah cried, standing in the kitchen.

Katherine rolled off Paul, groaned painfully. Paul rolled the other direction, rolled off the table, bounced off a couple of chairs before hitting the floor in a tangled mess of chair legs.

"Mr. McGowan," Sarah screamed. "Colleen, they're back. And hurt."

Paul didn't try to disentangle his legs from the chairs. He no longer had the strength, and every breath brought a sharp stabbing pain in his chest.

As McGowan and Colleen rushed into the room, Katherine staggered to her feet. Colleen tried to help her stand but she pushed the older woman away, and gave Paul an odd, wary look. Her voice came out in a hiss. "He broke a Sidhe circle backed by thirteen Sidhe mages, killed several of them. Killed Simuth, butchered him there in front of the entire Unseelie Court." She collapsed in a faint, and McGowan caught her just in time to ease her to the floor.

Paul didn't have the strength to hold onto consciousness, found a place without pain, a place where he could forget the look he'd seen in Katherine's eyes.

Epilogue:

Doubts and Fears

WHEN THE DOORBELL rang Paul limped across the living room of his small apartment and looked through the peephole. McGowan stood on the other side of the door, so he opened it.

"How you doing, kid?" the old man asked as Paul stepped aside.

McGowan had called in his surgeon friend. They'd stitched Paul up and covered him in bandages. He'd had two days to recuperate, which meant the soreness from the cuts and sprains and bruises was at its worst. He'd spent most of the day half-stoned on painkillers.

"I'll be all right," Paul said. "How's Katherine?"

McGowan walked past him into the room and tossed his coat onto the couch. "About the same as you. Got any coffee?"

"Just made a pot," Paul said as he closed the door.

He walked into the kitchen, retrieved a couple of mugs from a cupboard and filled them with coffee. He handed one to McGowan and sat down at the little breakfast nook.

"She refuses to see me," Paul said, "won't even talk to me on the phone."

McGowan grimaced. "I know. She's having a hard time with it. Simuth filled both your heads with unpleasant memories over a period of several days, which left the two of you doubting your own sanity, probably left you doubting your own morals, as well. She just needs some time, time to come to terms with her own feelings. She's having a little trouble with the brutality of the situation. I confess I didn't know you had it in you."

It saddened Paul that what, at the time, had seemed the only way to save them both, had frightened Katherine so. Paul didn't know how much he could tell McGowan, didn't understand much of it himself. "I was scared shitless, backed into a corner. No way out but take him down, knew that once I started, I couldn't stop, dare not stop, until it was done."

McGowan sat down at the only other seat in the small nook. "You broke a circle from the inside, a circle backed by thirteen Sidhe mages. You killed four of them, by the way, left nothing but four piles of incinerated ash. How did you do that?" McGowan's eyebrows narrowed in a look of unmistakable distrust.

Paul had yet to confess the truth of that to anyone. He could always fess up later, but right now their misconception that he'd actually broken a circle had everyone he didn't like steering well clear of him, which was a good thing. He trusted McGowan, but still decided to keep his own counsel. "If I ever figure it out, I'll let you know. But I don't think I really broke it." There, not a complete lie.

"Could have fooled me," the old man said. "And all of Faerie too, which, by the way, is abuzz with such amazing news. And where did you find out how to kill a Sidhe immortal?"

"That too I don't know." Not a lie, this time. Every time he tried to think about that, he had the vaguest impression of vast, dark wings obscuring the moon overhead, but he couldn't put the thoughts together into a coherent chain.

"Well, you scared the hell out of a lot of Sidhe. Hasn't been anything like this come along in centuries. By the way, you've graduated to the third tier of wizardry."

Paul frowned, winced, had yet to find a muscle that didn't complain when used, including minor facial muscles involved in simple expressions like a frown. "How do you mean?"

"I can no longer sense how powerful you are."

That came as a surprise to Paul, though now that he thought about it, on a subconscious level he'd gotten in the habit of continually clenching those magic muscles that damped other's sense of his capabilities. Apparently it now worked on other practitioners as well, not just demons. Next, if he could figure out a way to conceal the fact that he was a wizard from other practitioners, he could disappear for a while; have some time to think through this wizard stuff.

"And Karpov is making noises that you're dangerous, out of control. That you murdered a Sidhe royal, alienated a valuable ally. But don't worry about it. The leprechauns are making sure the real story is getting around, that you were the injured party, acted only in self-defense."

Paul dearly hoped to find a way he and Karpov wouldn't have to butt heads. Karpov didn't like those who didn't see things his way, needed to have them change their outlook to one more compatible with his, meaning Karpov as the head honcho, the rest of them toeing his line. Paul wanted to keep a low profile, let more experienced practitioners like McGowan and Colleen deal with Karpov.

"You scared the be-Jesus out of Magreth. No Sidhe royal likes to see a mortal kill an immortal. Makes them uncomfortable. I still don't understand how you bested him in Faerie. They're just too powerful in Faerie. Katherine says you disappeared with Simuth there for a moment, just before reappearing and beheading him."

It was a question, a big question. Paul decided on the truth. "I dragged him to my kitchen, here, where he was weaker." The cast iron skillet still sat in the sink. Paul gave McGowan a blow-by-blow description of his fight with Simuth here in his apartment.

McGowan shook his head. It was the first time Paul had ever seen him at a loss for words. "You shouldn't be able to do that, kid, not just pop between the Realms like that to any location you choose. Must take an enormous amount of power."

"It's more complicated than that." Paul tried to explain the spiral twist in reality between the Mortal Plane and Faerie, and how it didn't require any power, was more like understanding the right door to open. The look on McGowan's face told him the old wizard didn't understand a word. A knock at the door interrupted him.

McGowan stood and said, "I'll get it." He took two steps toward the door, but stopped short and turned back to Paul. "It's probably best if you don't mention this spiral slippage thing to anyone. And in any case, everyone thinks you bested a Sidhe Royal in mortal combat in Faerie. That makes you one powerful honcho, which you can use to your advantage. No need to enlighten them as to how you did it, is there?"

McGowan turned back toward the door and opened it. The door, only partly open, hid whoever stood on the other side while McGowan spoke briefly with them. McGowan then opened the door completely to reveal Jim'Jiminie standing there.

Jim'Jiminie doffed his hat and bowed deeply, like the finest of Sidhe courtiers. "Young Lord Mage, I come bearing a message. If you'll grant me the grace of your abode, I'll guarantee the parole of me inclinations for the duration."

Paul frowned at McGowan, and the old man answered his unasked question. "He can't cross the threshold of your home without your permission, and guarantees his good conduct while here."

"Sure," Paul nodded and waved his hand, the motion again reminding him of his bruises. "Come on in."

Jim'Jiminie sauntered up to Paul as McGowan closed the door behind him. He stood with his chest out and spoke officiously. "Young Lord Mage, I come to act as the intermediary between yourself and an ambassador of Her Most Gracious Majesty, Magreth, Queen of the Summer Court and ruler of all that is Seelie. Because of your previous relations with her chosen ambassador, His Royal Highness, Prince Anogh, august Knight of the Summer Court, she fears you will not readily accept his parole so that he may discuss the business of the Court with your noble self, so she asks you to accept her personal parole, and that of the Crown of the Seelie Court, allowing his presence in your magnificent domicile."

Paul had to think the words through carefully. "Magreth thinks I don't trust Anogh, so she's vouching for him so I'll allow him here to deliver some message."

The leprechaun grinned. "Exactly."

Paul looked to McGowan questioningly. The old wizard said, "You can't have a better guarantee than that."

"Okay," Paul said to Jim'Jiminie. "Bring him on."

The instant Paul finished speaking there came a knock on the door. McGowan answered it and Anogh stepped into the room. Jim'Jiminie bowed, stepped aside. Anogh bowed deeply, again the bow of a Seelie courtier. "Lord Mage," he said. He turned to McGowan, bowed again, "Old Wizard."

McGowan remained leaning against the wall casually, didn't move a muscle.

Anogh turned back to Paul. "I am indebted to you, for you freed me from the oaths that bound me to the Unseelie Court. And Her Majesty wishes you to know that the Seelie Crown is indebted to you for restoring me to my rightful place at the Summer Court. To show her gratitude, she offers you a boon. What boon would you have, Lord Mage?"

Paul couldn't imagine what he might ask for; decided having them indebted to him might be the best boon he could wish for. "Tell Her Majesty . . . I'll think about it."

Anogh smiled. The sly bastard knew exactly what Paul was doing. "As you wish," he said, bowing as if he were about to leave.

Paul spoke up before he could do so. "I am thankful you gave me the hint I could walk the halls of Sidhe back to the Mortal Plane. But I am mindful it was convenient for you that I met Suzanna and fell in love, convenient that her murder and that of my child led me to kill Simuth, and convenient that that freed you from your oaths. Very convenient, wasn't it?"

Anogh's smile disappeared.

Paul continued, "If I ever find that you took any overt action that lead to their deaths, such as helping Simuth find them, the boon I ask of Magreth will be your death at my hands."

Anogh bowed and said, "You will never have cause to doubt me." Then he disappeared.

••••

"One moment, Mr. Conklin, I'll see if she's available."

The sound in the phone changed to canned music as Katherine's receptionist put Paul on hold. He'd tried to call her twice before, with the same result.

It didn't take Judy long to get back to him. "I'm sorry, Mr. Conklin," she said quite loudly, as if she wanted Katherine to hear her tell him to go away. "Dr. McGowan is unavailable at the moment. I recommend you call back later."

The same message as before. Paul was about to put down the phone when Judy said in a hurried whisper, "She does want to see you, she just doesn't know it. Be here at three o'clock sharp. Wait in the hall outside the office. I'll make it happen."

Paul had hours to kill until three, tried to think of something to occupy his mind, and couldn't think of anything but Katherine. He couldn't put her out of his mind and moped around the apartment. When the time came, he removed all bandages that weren't absolutely necessary, which left some nasty scrapes and bruises visible, but he no longer looked like the walking wounded. He threw on a pair of khaki slacks, a nice sports shirt and a coat.

He arrived a few minutes early, waited in the hall, and true to her word Judy stepped out of the door at exactly three o'clock. She closed the door, looked at him, appraised his bruises for a moment and frowned. "I don't know what you two went through, but you've got even more bruises than her."

Paul simply said, "It wasn't good."

"Well whatever it was, I know it wasn't you. And I know she wants to see you, though she's in denial about that." She chuckled quietly. "Look at me. I'm a better shrink than she is."

She leaned close to him conspiratorially. "I told her I had to go to the ladies room, so I forwarded the phone lines into her office, and she's got a half-hour gap before the next patient. Just walk right in."

Judy disappeared down the hall as Paul carefully opened the door to the reception area. No one there so he crossed to Katherine's office door and opened it slowly.

Katherine sat behind her desk, her eyes on some papers, her hair pulled back in a ponytail very unlike her. Without looking up, she said, "That was fast. I need the records for—" She looked up and spotted Paul, her mouth frozen in an open, unspoken word. She'd managed to hide the bruises on her face beneath makeup, though since Paul knew what to look for, he could still see faint traces here and there.

All he could say was, "Hi." He closed the door behind him.

"Hi," she said and smiled, but it was one of those artificial smiles of the lips only, with nothing but sadness in her eyes.

As he crossed the room to stand in front of her desk she frowned. "This is a Judy conspiracy, isn't it?"

Paul smiled at her. "Well, more a Judy and Paul conspiracy."

Her eyes glistened with moisture. She looked down at her desk, shuffled some papers, "Paul, I'm busy. I have another patient in—"

He interrupted her, "In half an hour."

She shook her head and said, "Damn her!" but she smiled, and this time it was a genuine smile.

Paul stepped around the desk, but she stood, stopped him with the palm of her hand in the middle of his chest. "No. Don't."

She wore one of those suits he found so attractive, navy blue coat and skirt, white blouse with a frilly collar. He said, "I'm sorry."

She turned away from him, walked around the desk as if it gave her comfort to put it between them. "Don't apologize. It's not you. It wasn't you. You did what you had to do. I know that. It's just . . . you don't know what it was like to think I would happily do the things he put in my mind."

"But I do."

She turned back to him sharply, frowned, and met his eyes carefully for several seconds. "Yes, I suppose you do. But . . . I can't forget it."

He didn't know how to address that, so he went by instinct. "You said it was a spell to amplify our own desires. So there must have been some desire there to begin with, otherwise there would have been nothing to amplify."

She shook her head no, nodded yes, somehow managed to do both. "Yes. That's true. But it's just . . . it's just . . ."

If he could just touch her, hold her, comfort her, he could break down any barriers between them. But to do that he'd have to literally chase her around the desk and force her to let him hold her, and that wouldn't work at all. So he waited, just waited.

She shed a few tears that rolled down her cheeks, didn't sob or cry. Then without warning anger boiled up and clouded her features. "I wanted him dead too. I wanted to kill him with my own hands, and I cheered when you did."

She gasped, shook her head at him, and turned away from him again. "I don't understand how I could be that way."

He said, "He deserved it."

With her back to him she shook her head again, and he saw the finality of her decision in the set of her shoulders. He turned and quietly left her office.

••••

When he got home Dayandalous was sitting at the breakfast nook in his apartment, sipping on a cup of coffee, a long narrow bundle of cloth resting on the table in front of him. "Hello, Paul," he said as Paul stepped into his apartment.

Of course, with Dayandalous there, Paul remembered all their previous interactions, and knew that as soon as Dayandalous left, he would forget everything. He sat down at the table next to him, resigned to the inevitable. "What do you want this time?"

"Actually," Dayandalous said, smiling pleasantly. "I want nothing. In fact I've come to give you something." He waved a hand at the bundle in the middle of the table.

Paul reached out carefully, not sure what to expect, pulled aside a flap of the cloth bundle, ready for almost anything to happen. He unwrapped the cloth, which smelled of something like gun oil, and uncovered the sheathed sword he'd come to recognize.

He'd never had a chance to look at it carefully. It had ornate scrollwork running the length of the sheath. The hilt was long enough for a two-handed grip, with a simple cross brace. On the end of the hilt sat a cast, metal dragon, with two tiny rubies for eyes that shown an unnatural red, and the dragon's tail coiled about the hilt in an endless spiral. Paul gripped the sheath in his left hand, the hilt in his right, felt power in the blade, mortal power, not Sidhe power. He drew about six inches of the blade, saw a patchwork of runes running its length. It appeared to be a mortal, steel sword, not an enchanted Sidhe blade. He snapped the blade back into the sheath. "What is this?"

Dayandalous smiled that irritating, knowing smile of his. "You will know what it is, when you have the strength to know what it is." His expression made it clear Paul would get no more out of him.

••••

Paul awoke with a start on the couch where he'd been napping. He had a vague impression of dreaming something about a sword with runes etched into the blade and the sheath, wanted to recall the dream, but couldn't bring to mind any more than that.

He sat up, swung his legs off the couch and planted his feet on the floor. He closed his eyes and tried to get his thoughts in order, needed to absorb everything that had happened to him, make some sense out of it. It was then that he heard the sharp cry of a hunting hawk. He opened his eyes and looked around his small living room. It had sounded so near, as if it was there in the room with him. Perhaps he'd left the window open and it was just outside.

He stood, crossed the room to the only window and eased the cheap curtains slightly to one side, but it was tightly shut. The cry sounded again behind him, and he spun about. He was alone, no strange black fey, no hunting hawks from Faerie come to haunt him on the Mortal Plane.

It sounded again, right in front of him, sharp, distinct, somewhere close. Instinctively, he dropped into a crouch, and edged his way across the room to the little end-table where he kept the Sig in a drawer. He opened the drawer, grabbed the gun, pulled the slide back and jacked a round into the chamber. He'd be damned if he'd let that crazy bitch put an arrow in him again without a fight.

The cry sounded again and he started. There was no doubt it had come from within the room, but there was nothing in the room but the couch, two end-tables, a cheap coffee table, two chairs . . . and the mirror on the wall. He'd warded the mirror against demon entry, had never thought to ward it against the fey, wouldn't know how to do that if he had.

Remaining crouched, he side-stepped his way across the room, staying as far from the mirror as possible. Then he edged his way toward it, keeping low, thought he saw something moving within it. Huddled beneath the mirror at the other side of the room, he rose up very slowly and peered over its lower lip. He saw the San Francisco skyline, with the hawk flapping its wings and flying straight at him only a few feet away. He stumbled backward, lost his balance, fell on his butt and dropped the gun. It bounced across the floor and thankfully didn't go off.

The hawk erupted from the surface of the mirror, spread wings that almost filled his entire living room, and shifted into the shape of the seven-foot-tall crazy woman with dreadlocks and haunted eyes. She wore tight gray leathers, had that enormous broadsword strapped to her side, and held a longbow in her left hand.

Paul glanced aside to his gun lying on the floor, too far away for him to reach before she cut him in two with that sword. She turned her head slowly and followed his gaze.

She didn't really walk over to it. One heartbeat she stood over him, and the next she stood over the gun. She reached down, picked it up, and in a third heartbeat stood over him again. She gripped the gun by its barrel, reversed it and held it out to him, still cocked, hammer back.

Paul reached up and gently took it from her—a peace offering he supposed. He decocked the hammer and put the gun on the floor beside him.

She squatted down on her haunches and looked at him. Her eyes shifted color constantly, blue, brown, hazel, amber, black, every color imaginable, and her dreadlocks fluttered slightly in a breeze that wasn't there.

Paul asked, "What do you want?"

She opened her mouth, and her voice sounded like a whisper on the wind. "Les flèche du coeur."

"The arrow?"

She didn't say anything, just stood there crouching on her haunches, waiting.

Paul had kept the arrow with the blood-red fletching and coal-black shaft. He didn't want to trigger any sort of reaction from her so he moved slowly, though as he rose to his feet she rose with him. Without making any sudden moves, he turned to the bedroom, and was surprised that she didn't follow. He retrieved the arrow from a drawer in his bedroom where he'd hidden it under some clothes, and as he walked back into the living room her eyes never strayed from it. He held it out and she took it, lifted it up in front of her and stared at it for a moment. Then she put it to her lips and kissed it, once on the point, once on the shaft, and once on the fletching. She handed it back to him, and stood there staring at him.

She licked her lips and said, "It tastes of your blood."

He didn't know what kind of answer she expected of him, but before he could think of something she suddenly spun about, the giant hunting hawk unfurled its wings, flapped them once, pulled them in to its sides and disappeared into the mirror. Paul stood there for a moment, then crossed the room and looked into it. It was now just a mirror.

He turned around, picked the Sig up off the floor and returned it to the drawer in the little side table. He glanced into the kitchen, and spotted an old rag lying on the floor there. When he picked it up he noticed it smelled of something like gun oil, but it was just an old rag so he tossed it in the trash.

••••

As he drove across the Bay Bridge into the city, he didn't think he'd like San Francisco very much. Dallas was much better, because that was where he could find more Alices.

Don't worry, the voice said. *We can find them here as well, though we'll have to be careful.*

"Why can't we just go back to Texas?" he asked. "I hate California."

We have unfinished business. He's here, and she's here, and we'll have no peace while they live.

Acknowledgements

I'D LIKE TO thank Durelle Kurlinski for fixing all my dotted t's and crossed i's, Karen for both supporting my dream and being my most valuable critic, and Steve Himes, and the whole team at Telemachus, for getting a quality product out the door.

Books by J. L. Doty

Series: The Treasons Cycle
Of Treasons Born
A Choice of Treasons

Stand Alone Novel
The Thirteenth Man

Series: The Gods Within
Child of the Sword
The SteelMaster of Indwallin
The Heart of the Sands
The Name of the Sword

Series: The Dead Among Us
When Dead Ain't Dead Enough
Still Not Dead Enough
Never Dead Enough

Series: The Blacksword Regiment
A Hymn for the Dying
A Dirge for the Damned
A Prayer for the Fallen
A Requiem for the Forsaken

About the Author

JIM IS A full-time SF&F writer, scientist and laser geek (Ph.D. Electrical Engineering, specialty laser physics), and former running-dog-lackey for the bourgeois capitalist establishment. He's been writing for over 30 years, with 15 published books. His first success came through self-publishing when his books went word-of-mouth viral, and sold enough that he was able to quit his day-job, start working for himself and write full time—his new boss is a real jerk. That led to contracts with traditional publishers like Open Road Media and Harper Collins Voyager, and his books are now a mix of traditional and self-published.

The four novels in his new hard science fiction series, *The Blacksword Regiment*, were released in July 2020. Right now he's fleshing out ideas for the next book in *The Dead Among Us*, he's writing another episode in *The Treasons Cycle*, and he's working on a new fantasy series *The Deck of Chaos*.

Jim was born in Seattle, but he's lived most of his life in California, though he did live on the east coast and in Europe for a while. He now resides in Arizona with his wife Karen and three little beings who claim to be cats: Tilda, Julia and Natasha. But Jim is certain they're really extra-terrestrial aliens in disguise.

Visit the author's website at http://www.jldoty.com

Contact the author at jld@jldoty.com